THE SHADOWS WE HIDE

ALLEN ESKENS

MULHOLLAND
BOOKS

Little, Brown and Company
New York Boston London

Copyright © 2018 by Allen Eskens

Mulholland Books / Little, Brown and Company
Hachette Book Group
1290 Avenue of the Americas, New York, NY 10104
mulhollandbooks.com

First Edition: November 2018

Mulholland Books is an imprint of Little, Brown and Company, a division of Hachette Book Group, Inc. The Mulholland Books name and logo are trademarks of Hachette Book Group, Inc.

[permissions or interior art credits]

ISBN 978-0-316-50978-7
LCCN [tk]

10 9 8 7 6 5 4 3 2 1

LSC-C

To Ben

Part I

CHAPTER 1

I'm lying on the hood of my car, my back reclined against my windshield, knees bent, fingers laced together on my stomach, my breathing relaxed to ease the throb of pain. I'd like to say that having the tar beat out of me was the low point of my day, but that would be a lie. The beating that thug laid on me can't compare to the hurt I inflicted upon myself. The night around me is large and weightless, the kind of a night that demands honest contemplation, and I'm doing my level best to oblige.

I feel like I'm in exile, a nomad of sorts, sharing my night with the stars and the trees and the occasional thistle seed that floats by on the summer breeze. I try to ponder the wrong turns that brought me here, but I can't seem to get past my pathetic excuses about why this shouldn't be my fault. I want to be like Adam and point my finger at the one who handed me the apple or, better yet, find a way to blame the serpent, but my conscience won't let me do that. I want to believe that I am a better man than I am, but I know that I am not. This one is on me, nobody else.

I don't know when it happened, but at some point I got cocky. I stopped counting my faults and became charmed by the image I put forth for the rest of the world—a side of me that allows people to find their own kindness in my plight. You see, I've been taking care of my autistic brother, Jeremy, going on six years now, and I have a girlfriend who I helped put through law school. People see those things and think, *What a good guy that Joe Talbert is.* They have become so blinded by the gleam of my armor that they haven't notice that it's only tinfoil. I always expected the world to someday figure out that I didn't belong here, that I had risen far above my ditch-digging station, so I shouldn't have been surprised when it all started falling apart.

Years ago, when I ran away from home to go to college, half-cocked and broke, I had no real expectation that I'd ever earn a living with my head instead of my hands. Working my way through school as a bouncer, I often found myself harboring equal measures of contempt and envy for those guys who lived in that higher strata of life, men who wore pants wrinkled at the hip from sitting all day, their soft hands holding drinks poured with high-end vodka—no steel-toed shoes needed where they worked. If I could just be one of them, I thought, I'd be happy.

I still remember getting my first paycheck from the Associated Press, how I held it in my hands and stared at it for hours before taking it to the bank. Someone had actually paid me to think— to use my brain. No scraped knuckles. No sore back. A far cry from when I first ventured into the workforce back when I was sixteen—the summer that I worked for my mother's landlord remodeling apartments. His name was Terry Bremer, and I learned a lot from him, but boy that job sucked.

Once, on a scorching August day, half-blinded by the stinging sweat in my eyes, I crawled into a dusty attic dragging thick batts of fiberglass insulation to its farthest corners. The itch from that experience stuck with me for a week. Another time, I wore out a pair of leather gloves digging a truly foul-smelling trench to replace a collapsed sewer line. Who'd have thought that I could screw up a desk job so badly that I'd look back at shoveling sewage with a fond nostalgia? Yet I had managed it.

When it comes to bad days, it's hard to beat one that starts with a short, bald man serving you with a summons and complaint. I was absorbed by an article that I was writing that day and didn't even hear the man knock—you need a punch code to get into the AP office. I had no idea that he was in the room until I heard him say my name. Another reporter pointed me out, and the man walked up to my desk with a smile on his face.

"Joe Talbert?" he asked.

"Yeah."

He held out an envelope, which I instinctively took. Then he said, "You've been served."

I didn't understand at first because he performed this act with the cheer of someone hoping to receive a tip. "Served?" I asked.

His smile grew bigger. "You're being sued for defamation of character. Have a nice day." Then he turned and left the office.

I stood there with the envelope in my hand, not sure what to think. Then I looked around the room at the faces of my fellow reporters, hoping to see the smile of a prankster, someone holding back a laugh or biting a lip, but all I saw was a mixture of fear and pity in the eyes of my colleagues, people who were figuring this thing out one step faster than I was. I opened the envelope, pulled out the documents, and recognized the name of the man listed as the plaintiff. State Senator Todd Dobbins. I knew then that this was no prank.

This wasn't supposed to happen to me. I had done everything right. I had written the article over a month ago and it had everything: sex, scandal, political power—everything, that is, except a second source, a fact that made my editor, Allison Cress, more than a little nervous at the time. But I had given Allison the bona fides of my one source as well as the corroborating evidence to back up the story. I had convinced Allison that the source was solid. In the end, Allison ran the story as much on the strength of my word as anything else.

I walked to Allison's office to show her the document naming me and the Associated Press as co-defendants in a lawsuit, hoping to hear words of comfort, something like: this happens all the time, or don't worry, it's just a stunt by a corrupt politician. But what she said chilled me to the point that I nearly threw up. Her face went pale as she read the documents; then she told me to close the door and have a seat.

"This is bad, Joe," she said. "Really bad."

"But the story's true," I said. "Truth is a defense to defamation."

"The story's only true if we can prove that it's true. That's the problem with stories where you only have one source—an anonymous one at that."

"But I *have* a source. That's the important thing," I said, hoping that Allison would agree.

"The last I heard, your source doesn't want to be identified. That's a problem. If we can't produce a witness—especially given the circumstances of this story—it's going to look like we made it up. It'll be your word versus his word."

"Their word," I said meekly. Allison looked confused. "Mrs. Dobbins wrote out an affidavit backing up her husband's story."

Allison had large, chocolate eyes that undermined any chance of her holding a poker face. I could tell she was trying to look calm as we spoke, but I could see fear settling in. "What are the odds that the source would agree to come forward?"

Come forward? My source had let go of her rope and now dangled in my grip, trusting that I would not let her fall. Unmasking her identity not only would break a promise that I had made, but would cost her everything. Some lines can't be crossed. "But reporters use anonymous sources all the time," I said.

"Yes. And those reporters run the risk of something like this happening." Allison shook her head slowly as she continued to read the complaint. I eased back into my chair and waited. When she came to the end, to the part where Dobbins was making his demands, she looked up. "He wants a retraction, and he wants you fired," she said.

"He also wants a buttload of money. Did you read that?"

"Yeah, but I don't think this is about the money. Your story killed his political career. He's finished at the Capitol. The only way to get that life back is to get some kind of declaration that the story was false. To do that, he needs the retraction. I think having you fired is just icing on his cake."

"They wouldn't fire me, would they?"

Allison looked at me with a sad expression that all but said, *Oh, you poor, naive little boy.* Then she told me about a reporter who got fired last year for making a single mistake. He had a perfect record—not one error in twenty-eight years; but then he misidentified a set of initials on a document, attributing the initials to the wrong politician. That was all it took.

I stared out through the windows of Allison's corner office, a view I'd taken in many times before, the last time being a week ago when Allison and I discussed whether my article would be submitted for Pulitzer consideration. Now we were talking about the end of my career. She balled her hands together and leaned onto her desk, the legal papers at her elbows, her knuckles pressed against her lips. "There'll be an investigation," she said without looking up. "I'm on the hook with you. I approved the story. If they fire you, they'll fire me too."

And I didn't think I could feel any worse than I already did.

"The AP will give you an attorney. I went through this once when I was a reporter. It sucked. You'll have to waive any conflict of interest, or you can hire your own lawyer."

"Lila's about to take the bar exam." I'm not sure why I said that; I guess I was thinking out loud.

"You'll need someone who specializes in journalism law. I'm sure Lila's very smart, but don't take this lightly. If you get fired, no legitimate news outlet will ever hire you again. You'll be blackballed. Just sign the waiver and let the AP lawyers handle it."

"Yeah, I guess that's the smarter way to go."

I waited for Allison to say something to lift my spirits, but that didn't happen. By the time I left her office my head hurt and my chest squeezed in around my lungs making it hard to breathe. I spent the rest of the day staring at my computer screen; I didn't trust myself to type a single word. I kept seeing the accusations from the complaint, words and sentences floating across my field of vision. This could be the end of my career. Then what? Go back to digging ditches? Pull up a barstool and man the door at Molly's Pub again? Every time I let those thoughts loose, they nearly choked me.

When I couldn't take it anymore, I went home to tell Lila the bad news. The twenty-minute trip took me from the crystalline towers of downtown Minneapolis to the working-class neighborhood of St. Paul's Midway, an old part of the city where small houses elbowed each other for space and boxy apartments wore the same dingy yellow brick as the outdated storefronts.

The apartment that Lila and I shared, a two-bedroom inside of an eight-unit complex, was the kind of place that most people would drive past and never think back on. It had no balcony, no lawn, no view other than that of the apartment building across the street, and because of a weird guy in that building who liked to stare into our windows, we kept our blinds closed, adding to the prison-block feel of our place. It was cheap, however, and close to Lila's law school, and that's what we needed for now.

Lila Nash was still just my girlfriend, and when I say *just*, I mean that I hadn't done the one-knee thing yet. I'd thought about it often, but it never seemed to be the right time, with college and then law school. I didn't want to propose to her when she had *this* final or *that* memorandum of law to work on. I was pretty sure that she would say yes if I asked, but then she would have put the ring aside and gone back to her books. I wanted to wait until we could enjoy the moment, give it the gravitas and attention it deserved. I had hoped that the right moment might come after she graduated from law school—but then came the bar exam.

We were only eight days away from that soul-sucking ordeal, and Lila was riding the bull with white knuckles and gritted teeth. She had a job offer with the Hennepin County Attorney's Office, an offer that would disappear if she failed the bar. So for the past two months she'd been studying for that test to the exclusion of everything—everything except for Jeremy, that is. In the middle of all the chaos, Lila somehow found time for my brother.

From the start, it was Lila who took the lead in caring for Jeremy. She was the one who trudged through the bureaucratic maze to get Jeremy his first job, sorting items at a recycling center. Lila educated herself on autism, reading a dozen books on the subject after Jeremy came to live with us. She found time for this even as she trimmed back her time with me, because law school was "kicking her ass." She and I used to play gin or cribbage almost every night. I can't remember the last time we did that.

Her latest project had been reading books with Jeremy. My brother learned to read when he was in school, but our mother never valued that skill, so at home he watched movies. Lila started him on children's books, classics like *Snow-White,* and *Beauty and the Beast*. And though Jeremy didn't like reading books at first,

9

Lila persisted, working with him every day when he came home from his job, going over the words and the pictures, comparing the story on the page to the story on the DVD. After a few months, those books became part of his routine.

That's where I found them when I came home that day, sitting on the couch together, going over the words of a new book—*Dumbo*. They both looked up when I came in, Jeremy for only a second before turning his attention back to the page. He had no idea that I was home three hours early. Lila, on the other hand, looked at me, then at the clock, and back at me again, lines of confusion tracing across her forehead.

"You're early," she said. Neither a question nor an accusation, more of a note that she was jotting down in her thoughts.

I walked to the couch, sat next to Lila, and handed her the summons and complaint. Then I leaned back and waited for her to read it.

"Oh my God," she whispered. "This is . . ." She looked at me, her confused expression melding into concern. "You're being sued?"

I nodded.

"What did you do?"

"I didn't do anything," I said, sounding more defensive than I had intended.

"I'm sorry, that's not what I meant." She turned on the couch to face me, as if she wanted to look in my eyes as she asked me her next question. "They're saying that you made up a story. You didn't do that, did you?"

"Of course not. I would never make up a story."

"Todd Dobbins . . . he's that state senator you wrote about . . . the one who beat up his wife." Lila turned her attention back to the complaint.

"Yes, he beat up his wife."

"But . . ." Lila read some more, and I could see that she was reading the affidavit, where Mrs. Dobbins was now swearing that her trip to the emergency room happened because she fell down some stairs. She was swearing, under the penalty of perjury, not only that her husband did not hit her, but that he had saved her life by taking her to the hospital.

Lila looked up from the document. "If he says that she fell down the stairs . . . and she says that she fell down the stairs . . . then . . ."

"I have a source."

"Who?"

"I can't divulge that—not even to you. I gave my word."

"Joe, this is serious."

"Don't you think I know that?" I heard my voice rise, and I immediately felt bad. Lila wasn't the enemy. I took a deep breath to calm down.

"If you don't give up your source, how can you prove your case? Libel law . . . *Times v. Sullivan* . . ." Lila began speaking as though she were reading from a flash card—her preferred method of study. "There's a different standard if Dobbins is a public figure, and as a state senator, he's got to be a public figure. They'd have to prove that you wrote the article with actual malice—that you knew it was false and wrote it anyway."

"My story wasn't false."

"But your witness is someone you won't disclose. You have nothing to contradict their version of events. You see how this looks, don't you? You've put yourself into a box."

"I can't give up my source," I repeated. "I won't." But even as the words left my lips, I knew that Lila was right. I was screwed. My mind flashed back to my conversation with Allison and the prospect that I would get fired over this, and I was once again on the verge of throwing up. I leaned forward on the couch and cupped my face in my hand. Slow breath in. Slow breath out. Lila brushed her hand up and down my back, which didn't help but was a nice gesture.

And then Jeremy spoke. I had forgotten that he was sitting on the couch with us. "Joe," he said. "Maybe it will be all right."

I sat up and looked at my brother, his hands on his lap, the book lying beside him, the expression on his face one of uncertainty, probably questioning whether his response was appropriate in that situation. I have no doubt that he didn't understand what a lawsuit was, but he understood my reaction to it. He understood that the papers in Lila's hands had hurt me somehow. That was all he needed to know. And the thing he thought to say was the one thing that I wanted to hear—that everything would be okay.

I smiled. "Of course it'll be okay."

"That's right," Lila said, tossing the papers to the floor.

And with that, Lila and I came to an understanding that, at least around Jeremy, nothing bad had happened that day. We dropped the subject and pretended that it was a normal Tuesday. She went back to her studies, and I went to the kitchen where I could sit on the floor, out of Jeremy's sight, and let the world around me spin out of control. Yet, as bad as that day had been, the day that followed would prove that things can always get worse.

CHAPTER 2

I considered taking that next day off, calling in sick to tend to my wounds. I didn't want to wade past the downturned eyes of my colleagues or hear the low hiss of whispers escaping from the breakroom as they discussed my failings. But I needed to face this thing. I hadn't done anything wrong, and staying home would have made me appear guilty. Besides, staring at my apartment walls would only let the worms of my self-pity burrow deeper into my brain. Working on another story might help keep my mind off the lawsuit. Who knows, I might even get my appetite back.

The AP office was housed in the Grain Exchange Building, a nine-story structure that probably constituted a skyscraper back in 1902 when they built it—the sky being so much lower back then. It stood hunched and heavy on the northern edge of downtown, the thick-fingered uncle of the Minneapolis skyline. Over the past four years, I had come to see that office as my second home. Now, as I walked to the elevator, an image popped into my head of my being escorted back out with a box of my personal effects in my arms. Do they really do that when they fire someone?

On the fifth floor, I punched the code into the key pad and entered the office of the Associated Press, a smaller space than most people might expect, especially if their concept of a newsroom comes from movies like *All the President's Men,* where a small army of reporters fills an entire floor. The AP office, which covered news in a four-state area, was just big enough to house six reporters, a breakroom, a conference room, and a separate office for Allison Cress.

We wrote the news while sitting at workstations, a modern form of cubicle with shorter walls so that you had the confinement of a cubicle, but not the privacy. The setup had the appearance of a big raft made up of six inner tubes tied together. I was fine with having no walls, though, because I worked on the windowless side of the raft. In slow times, I could look out through the windows— my view bouncing off the top of Gus MacFarlane's head— and let my daydreams catch the breeze. Those musings usually transported me to the glass towers of Manhattan, or the granite enclaves of Washington, DC, places where I had once hoped my career might take me. Now, my highest aspiration was to make it to quitting time and still have a job.

I had just plopped down into my nest, when Gus leaned toward my workstation and whispered, "Hey, Joe, Allison said she wanted to see you when you got in."

The bottom fell out of my stomach. "How'd she look?"

Gus pondered that for a second before answering, "Serious."

I started to get up, but then I changed my mind and sat back down, taking a minute to clean up my browser history. It's not that I had anything scandalous to hide, but I didn't want my replacement to know how frequently I used my thesaurus, and that I still struggled with the proper use of *lie, lay, laid,* and *lain.* I looked in my drawers to get an idea of how big of a box I would need for my stuff, and the answer depressed me. The entire accumulation of my personal items would likely fit into a shoe box. Maybe, subconsciously, I'd been preparing for this day all along.

A gurgle churned in my stomach as I made my way to Allison's office. She had always been a good boss. Smart. Levelheaded. I was going to miss her, and it killed me to know that I had pulled her into my mess. I paused at the door to gather myself, then knocked.

"Come in," Allison said.

When she saw me, her neutral expression took on weight.

"Hi, Joe. Have a seat." She waved me to a chair. I closed the door and sat down, my hands already sweaty against the tan vinyl of the armrests.

"Am I fired?" I asked.

"What?"

"If you're going to fire me, do it quickly." I kept my eyes open, but I held my breath.

"No, Joe. That's not why I wanted to see you."

I slowly exhaled.

Allison gave me a half-smile. "If that were the case," she said. "I'd probably be heading out the door with you."

I wanted to say that I was sorry, but I was pretty sure she knew that already.

"Joe, do you have any relatives in Caspen County?"

"Caspen County? No. Not that I know of. Why?"

"Not that you know of?"

"My family tree is more of a patch of scrub. I can never be sure what's out there. I have a brother, Jeremy, but you know about him already."

"What about the rest of your family?"

I hesitated, but then answered. "I have a mother in Austin, but I haven't spoken to her in years."

15

"What about your father?"

"My father? He took off when I was born. Left me with nothing but his name."

"You have the same name as your father?"

"Yeah, but I never..." I sat back in my chair, seeing now that Allison was drawing me to a specific target. "What's going on?" I asked.

She picked up a piece of paper. "Do you have any idea where your father might live now?"

"None whatsoever," I said with a hint of pride. I had managed to live my entire life without ever seeing the face of the man whose name I carried. I convinced myself that other than donating his spermatozoa to my cause, my father could just as well have been a myth, a fairy tale that fed my childhood imagination, something I had discarded long ago, tossed aside like an outgrown pair of sneakers.

"What's this about?" I asked.

She slid a piece of paper across her desk to me, and I read it. It was a press release about a man named Joseph Talbert who had been found dead in a horse barn by sheriff's deputies in rural Caspen County, Minnesota. The press release stated that foul play was suspected.

"Do you think that might be your father?" she asked.

There had to be a lot of Joe Talberts walking around this planet at any given moment, but this one died in Minnesota, and it involved foul play; those two factors had to increase the odds that this man might be my father.

"I don't know," I said. "Other than a few stories that my mom told me, I don't know anything about him."

"You think your mom might know if he lived in Buckley?"

"Like I said, I don't talk to my mother."

"I'm sorry. I'm not trying to pry. I just thought you should know. I mean if it were my father—even if I'd never met him, I'd want to know."

"I appreciate that," I said. My tone had turned cold; that wasn't my intention.

"Are you okay?"

"Honestly, Allison, I'm not sure."

"There's one thing more," Allison said, pulling a second piece of paper out of her drawer. "I asked the Sheriff's Office in Caspen County to send me a picture of the man they found dead. Would you like to see it?"

I stared at the paper in her hand, unable to answer. This man meant nothing to me—less than nothing. I should have walked out of Allison's office and left it that way, but I didn't. I held out my hand, and she handed me an old mug shot. And just like that, the myth that was my father began to grow flesh and bones.

CHAPTER 3

When I was in fourth grade, a kid named Keith Rabbinau called me a bastard. I wasn't sure exactly what the word meant, though I'd heard my mother use it often enough, a blunt-tipped arrow shot at the many men who'd screwed her over. Back then, the word *bastard* fell into a basket of swear words that I could use with some dexterity. That day in fourth grade, however, I learned that bastard had a special meaning, making it a glove that fit some of us better than others.

Rabbinau's attack came out of the blue. We weren't in an argument—not that he and I were ever all that far from a fight at any given moment. Keith was one of the few kids in my class who knew about my mom. What I had pieced together was that our mothers had been friends at one time, back when they were both young and new to the bar scene in Austin. My mom's version of the fall of their friendship was that Libby Rabbinau, the tramp, stole a piece-of-shit named Willard away from her. I used to wonder why my mother cared that Willard had been stolen away from her if he was such a piece of shit. That mystery got cleared up as I came to know my mother better.

When Keith called me a bastard, I quickly returned the insult, calling him a bastard, to which he replied, "I'm not a bastard, I have a father." His response threw me because I didn't understand how fathers figured into our little clash. Before I could think of a comeback, Keith read my face and started heaping it on.

"You don't even know what a bastard is, do you?"

"Yeah, I do," I said. "Just look in the mirror and you'll see a bastard."

"A bastard is a kid that doesn't got a dad," he said. "You don't got a dad, so you're a bastard."

"I got a dad," I yelled back.

"No you don't." Keith smirked. "My mom says that your mom's a drunk, and a bitch, and no man's gonna stay with her no matter what. That makes you a bastard. Joey the Bastard. That should be your name. Joey the Bastard."

Some of the other boys on the playground sensed the tension and started forming a small circle around us. A couple of them repeated, "Joey the Bastard" in taunting fashion. How Keith didn't see this next part coming is beyond me.

Anger clogged my ears, turning Keith's words into a thick, watery hum. I charged in and shoved my hands into his chest, sending him stumbling backward to the ground. He looked up at me with wide eyes, as if my assault had been the last thing he expected. I watched his mask of shock give way to rage—and it was on.

Keith scrambled to his feet and came at me with his head down, throwing a shoulder into my chest and clasping his hands around my torso. Landing on my butt with his weight on top of me, I twisted to my right, then to my left, trying to roll him off. He lost his balance enough that I was able to get beside him, my arm now around his neck. With him pinched in a headlock, I fought to steady my hold.

By now, a throng of kids had amassed around us, some

cheering me on, and some shouting Keith's name, exactly what I'd been hoping for. With our skirmish raising that kind of ruckus, it was only a matter of time before a teacher would break up the fight. It would be a draw.

I took my eyes off Keith for a second to look beyond the mob. No teacher yet. And that's when Keith dropped a shoulder and rolled into some kind of jujitsu move that sent me flipping over his back. I closed my eyes as my head hit the ground. When I opened them again, Keith was climbing onto my chest, his arm cocking back. I raised my head, hoping to take the force of his first punch in the top of my skull instead of the face, a move I saw on TV once. It didn't work.

He hit me square in my left cheek, and everything went black and sparkly. I was expecting another punch, and frankly I had no plan on how I might avoid it, but it never came. I felt Keith being pulled off my chest as the chants of the mob died in the breeze. When I opened my eyes, one of the teachers was holding Keith away from me and yelling for me to get up and follow him.

When Vice Principal Adkins asked me what caused the fight, I didn't answer. The teacher who broke up the scuffle told Mr. Adkins that they found Keith on top, so they assumed that he had been the instigator. Keith, however, said that I started it, that I'd gone crazy and attacked him for no good reason. In the end, Adkins leveled the same punishment against us both. We were to go to the library, open a dictionary to a particular page, and write out every word and definition from that page. He could have assigned a hundred pages to rewrite that day; it wouldn't have mattered to me. The punishment wasn't the thing that left the mark.

As soon as Keith left the office, he ran to find the smallest dictionary in the library, calling dibs on it, and leaving me with the huge *Merriam-Webster*. Keith had apparently done this punishment before. I opened my dictionary and started to turn to the page chosen by Adkins, but then paused and flipped back until I found the word *bastard*.

Bastard:
    1) a person born of unmarried parents; an illegitimate child;
    2) something irregular, inferior, spurious or unusual.

There were expansions on those two definitions, but I didn't read any further. I began writing the punishment, my world now colored by the understanding that I was illegitimate and inferior. I was a bastard.

The tongue-lashing I got at school was nothing compared to what awaited me at home. The school had called my mother and told her that I'd been in a fight. That would have been bad enough, but it was the fact that I had been bested by the son of Libby Rabbinau that truly got my mom's teakettle to whistle. When I walked in, she was waiting with a beer in her hand and a scowl on her face. "What the hell's gotten into you, Joey?" were the first words out of her mouth.

I didn't expect to see her home, because back then she had a job serving cones at the Dairy Queen, one of the few times in my life that I can remember her holding employment for more than a few weeks. When I walked into the apartment, the heat of her anger was already thick in the air, so I didn't respond to her question.

"I had to miss work today. That's fifty bucks out of my pay-check because of you."

I wanted to ask how getting my ass kicked caused her to miss work. They didn't bring her down to the school for a confer-ence. They knew better. My mother was a grenade just looking for someone to pull the pin.

"How do you think it feels to have to call in sick because your son can't stop and think for once in his life? And Keith Rabbinau? You had to pick a fight with Keith Rabbinau of all people? You let that little prick get the better of you? I bet he ain't got no shiner on *his* face."

My head sank under the weight of my shame.

"Of course not," she said. "I can just hear that bitch Libby laughing because her son beat you up. What was this fight about anyway?"

I looked up to see if her question might be rhetorical, just another ripple in the skipping stone of her tirade, but she stared at me with her hand on her hip awaiting my response.

"He...called me a bastard," I said. I didn't tell her about how Keith called her a drunk and a bitch. Even at ten, I knew that such a revelation had no upside.

"Well, you are a bastard, goddamn it. That no-good piece-of-shit father of yours didn't want nothing to do with you. You got into a fight about him? You may as well...just..." She waved her beer hand around in the air as if the gesture filled in the words that escaped her. Then she took a drink. "Face it, he screwed us both. You have a problem with being a bastard? Take it up with your father. And good luck finding him."

This next part came out of my mouth before I could stop it. I said, "If he was such a no-good piece of shit, why did you go out with him? Why would you name me after him?"

Those words hit my mother hard, twisting every muscle in her face and causing red blotches to bloom on her neck. She slammed her beer can down on the table and took a step toward me, her arm shooting out to the side, her finger pointing at the door to my bedroom. "GO—TO—YOUR—ROOM!" she screamed.

She didn't have to say it twice. I ran to my bedroom, closed the door behind me, and sat with my back pressed against the door, my ten-year-old body ready to block any attempt she might make to come inside. I didn't want to hear another word from her, but more than that, I didn't want to lose my grip on the venomous thoughts that lay coiled in my brain. Some things were better left unspoken. I was a bastard. She was a drunk and a bitch. Those were the monuments we built to each other—the ones that would survive the eventual fall of our relationship.

As my anger thinned, I spotted Jeremy rocking forward and back on the bottom bunk of our bed, the tendons in his jaw flexing as he gnashed his teeth together, his right thumb rubbing the knuckle of his left hand, his skin red from the effort. I slid away from the door, scooting across the floor until I was in his line of sight.

"Jeremy, don't do that," I said, putting my hand on his thumb. "You're going to get a sore. It's okay, Jeremy."

Jeremy didn't stop, so I started singing *You Got a Friend in Me*, a song from *Toy Story*, his favorite movie at the time. I eased into it, my faulty notes seeping into his consciousness, slowing the velocity of his downward spiral. I was well into the second verse before the pull of the song overcame the turmoil in his head. He joined in, his three-note range nowhere close to being in tune; but that didn't matter. He knew every word without fail, and singing them—out of tune as he was—brought Jeremy peace.

After I got Jeremy calmed down, I climbed to my top bunk and stared at the plaster swirls on the ceiling above my head, my thoughts drifting not to my mother, not to Jeremy, not even to Keith Rabbinau, but to my father, a man who wanted nothing to do with me. I had always known it, but before that day, I never understood how his cowardice branded me a bastard. I was illegitimate. I was inferior. He had done this to me.

My life came to a divide that day. Before my fight with Keith

Rabbinau, I would sometimes dream of my father and imagine that he had been torn away from me, held at bay by forces beyond his means, a quiet hero who might someday fight his way back to rescue me from my mother. But after that day, I understood—my father chose to leave. His action made me what I was. He was the reason that I had gotten into the fight with Keith Rabbinau. He was the reason my mother yelled at me. My father wasn't a hero, he was a villain, and I cursed him under my breath as the first tears of that day spilled down my cheeks. I vowed to myself that I would never give my father another thought. I would never seek him out. It was over. I would cram the shadow of this man into a box and bury him so deep in my memory that it would never again see the light of day.

As I grew older, and came to understand the power of Internet search engines, I held true to my vow. I never once searched the Internet for his name, which meant that I could never do a search for my own name. Like a recovering addict staring at a syringe full of heroin, I would sometimes find myself in front of a computer with my fingers on the keys itching to type in the words *Joe Talbert*, just to see where it might take me. But every time that urge arose, I beat it back. I had never once looked for my father.

Seventeen years after I made that vow, I found myself sitting at my station in the Associated Press office, a press release in my hand announcing the death of a man with my name. I took in a deep breath, and for the first time in my life, I typed my name into the Internet search box and hit Enter.

CHAPTER 4

My first Internet search for Joe Talbert Sr. gave me over four hundred thousand hits. I spent half an hour culling through those links, looking for something relevant, before giving up.

On my second attempt, I did an image search, looking for people named Joe Talbert and using the mug shot as a guide. In no time, I found another picture of the man, also a mug shot, but a slightly younger version. I clicked on the image, and it took me to a page where I read about Joe Talbert stealing corn from a grain silo. The picture was a grinning image of a man who looked like he had just shared a joke with the officer taking the picture, the kind of familiarity that comes with being arrested a lot, I suspect.

His face had a tougher veneer than mine did, but with a little imagination, I could see parts of myself in that old mug shot, especially around the eyes. He had an intensity that I'd seen in my own reflection on occasion. As I stared at this man's face, it dawned on me that I now had mug shots of both my parents to add to the family photo album.

After hours of digging, using the Internet as well as a handful of databases I could access through the AP, I managed to compile a pretty good list of offenses for Mr. Talbert. In addition to the grain-silo fiasco, I found nine criminal convictions, including criminal damage to property, disorderly conduct, restraining-order violations, assault, two threats of violence, and three DUIs. I was a little surprised, though, to find that Joe Talbert, Senior, had not been arrested in the past seventeen years, not since his last DUI arrest in Caspen County. That suggested that he either became a better criminal or had cleaned up his act.

As I wrote down the basic information from the Minnesota Court Information System database, I noticed that one of the older cases, an assault, happened in my hometown of Austin at a time when my mother would have been three months pregnant with me. That connection made my fingers twitch with energy as I tapped and clicked my way deeper into this man's past.

MNCIS had no information about the specific facts of that case beyond the one-line descriptions of various court proceedings. I put a call into the Mower County Court Administrator's Office and learned that the physical file would have been purged from the system after ten years. My call to the County Attorney's Office yielded the same response. My last hope was that the Incident Complaint Report might still be retained by law enforcement. I crossed my fingers and called the Austin Police Department.

"I'm looking for an ICR for a case that occurred twenty-seven years ago," I said. "Would that still be in your system?"

"Oh, heavens no," she said with the politeness of a pastor's wife. "Our records don't go back that far. I'm not even sure we were on the ICR system that long ago."

My shoulders sagged. There had to be some way to uncover the facts behind that assault. My mother would know, but if that was my only option—forget it.

"If you're looking for something that old," the lady continued. "I'd have to go to the archives and find it on microfiche."

It took a second for me to catch up. "Wait. You have old police reports on microfiche?"

"Yes, we do."

I wanted to tell her that she should have led with that. Instead, I said, "I'd really appreciate it if I could get reports from an incident that happened on . . ." I squinted into my computer screen to find the exact date.

"I'll need a request in writing," she interrupted. "I can't give out stuff like that over the phone."

I popped a page of Associated Press letterhead onto my computer screen and typed as we spoke. "What do you need in the letter?"

"Let's see. I'll need the name of the party and the date of the incident if you have it. If you don't have a date—"

"I have a date," I said, looking at the MNCIS report. "I also have a court file number if that helps."

"No, just a name and date of the incident. I can't give you anything if the case is still pending, but a case that old . . ."

"He was convicted, so it's closed."

She gave me an email address and told me that if there weren't too many pages to the report, she might be able to send it to me within a few minutes. I thanked her and hung up the phone.

I grabbed a couple granola bars from a box I kept in my drawer, ate them in place of lunch, and was about to go back to my search when I noticed that I had an email waiting in my inbox. Too soon to be Mower County, I thought. I looked and saw that it came from the Legal Department of the Associated Press.

I froze, and again my stomach went queasy on me. I didn't open it right away. Would the AP fire me through an email? I had no idea. I'd never been fired before. I looked at Allison's office.

Her door stood open, and I could see her at her desk. She didn't seem upset—like she'd been fired. And if they hadn't fired her yet, this email might not be bad news.

Finally, I clicked on the email and read it.

Hello Mr. Talbert. My name is Joette Breck. I have been assigned to look into the lawsuit recently served upon you and the Associated Press. I have reviewed the article you wrote and the Complaint of Mr. Todd Dobbins and have come to the conclusion that your interests and the interests of the Associated Press are joined. As a preliminary matter, I do not see a conflict of interest. As such, we would offer our services to you should you want them. I have attached a Waiver of Conflict of Interest form to this email. Please read the three-page explanation carefully. If you understand and agree, sign the form and send it back. After I receive that form, I'll be in touch. Respectfully, J. Breck

I read the attachment she referenced, and most of it was blah, blah, blah. But there was this one line that stuck out. They informed me that representing me in the lawsuit did not preclude them from firing me. In fact, they could use any information gathered in their representation of me, other than privileged communication, to justify my dismissal. I had second thoughts about signing the waiver after reading that line, but I brushed those doubts away. I was getting a free attorney, and I wouldn't be looking that gift horse in the mouth.

After signing, scanning, and sending the waiver back to Ms. Breck, I returned to my project, typing *Joe Talbert* into a search engine and adding Buckley, Minnesota, to the query. That search eventually led me to a news article. A photo attached to the article showed Joe Talbert with touches of gray now invading his crown and lines under his eyes that put his appearance closer to fifty. He stood at a podium with his mouth open, his face crinkled in anger, and his index finger pointing up as if he were about to fling it at someone. The story had appeared two years ago in the *Caspen County Courier*, and it chronicled a city council meeting where Joe "Toke" Talbert fought against the city's decision to have his property declared a public nuisance due to the number of inoperable cars parked on his lawn.

"Toke?" I said out loud. His nickname was Toke—and he collected junked cars. Somehow that seemed fitting.

I read the rest of the article, but it gave no further details. Then I checked my email and saw that the Austin Police Department had responded to my document request. I clicked it open and read about a fight in a McDonald's parking lot.

A man identified as Joe Talbert—this must have been before he came up with the slick nickname—had been seen yelling at a woman and shoving his finger into her face. A McDonald's employee reported the disturbance, watching from inside the restaurant as the argument escalated. The employee could not hear the argument itself, but stated that he saw the man push the woman and then punch her in the stomach, causing her to drop to her knees. The report identified the woman as Kathy Nelson—my mother.

He hit my mother when I was in her womb.

The investigating officer questioned my mother, who confirmed that her boyfriend had gotten mad and punched her. When asked what caused Talbert to become upset, my mother told the officer that she was pregnant and refused to get an abortion.

He wanted to abort me. That son of a bitch! My cheeks grew hot, and for a moment the lawsuit and everything else shitty in my life melted away, leaving this piece of human waste alone in my spotlight. I didn't know that I could detest Joe Talbert Sr. more than I already did, but now the notion that this man was found dead in a barn filled me with an odd sense of contentment. I don't think Hallmark makes cards for families like mine.

I went back to my search, clicking on the next hit for Toke Talbert, and found an obituary for Jeannie Talbert, a forty-two-year-old woman who had died six months ago on her farm in rural Caspen County. The obituary read that Jeannie had been born Jeannie Hix and graduated from Buckley High School. She attended college at Mankato State University, where she received a degree in paralegal studies. After that, she returned to Buckley and went to work for a local attorney.

At the bottom of the article I read that Jeannie was survived by her husband, Joseph "Toke" Talbert, and a daughter, Angel Talbert. I stopped reading, my mind slowly wrapping around those last words: survived by a daughter, Angel Talbert.

I had a sister.

CHAPTER 5

By the time I got home, Jeremy had already finished his reading assignment and was sitting in front of the TV watching his new favorite movie, *Guardians of the Galaxy*, which Lila let him watch as a reward for making it through the day. There was a time when his reward was tied to Jeremy finishing his reading assignment, but he had grown to like reading his books. Now the greatest challenge for Jeremy was his new job, having moved from sorting bottles at the recycling center to cleaning classrooms at a nearby high school. This advancement came with a tangle of new stressors, and we were still in the process of getting Jeremy acclimated to his new routine.

For someone like Jeremy, consistency could be as important as food. He preferred dark clothing over light colors, green above all else. He ate his meals in order of meats first, then potatoes, then vegetables. If we served soup or chili, the biggest chunks went first. Cereal—cinnamon Life, nothing else. What would be a banal routine for most people was for Jeremy a dance, choreography that could move him from the beginning of the day to the end as smoothly as possible. With the disruption brought on by the new job, we had been giving Jeremy a little extra time with his movies.

When I came through the door, I said my usual, "Hey, buddy. How's it going?"

He looked at me, a hesitant smile cracking across his face, and said, "I am Groot."

I forced myself to laugh, and he briefly joined in before going back to his movie. He'd been greeting me that way a lot lately, mimicking the tree character from *Guardians of the Galaxy* who communicated a wide range of topics using only those three words. At first, I thought it was funny, even encouraging that Jeremy understood the concept, but lately, it had begun to wear on me.

I went to talk to Lila, finding her in her usual spot, sitting in the middle of our bed, books spread out around her, a tablet of notes resting against her knee and headphones on her head to keep the sound of Jeremy's movie out of her ears. When she saw me she smiled, slipped the headphones off, and rubbed exhaustion from her eyes.

"How goes the battle?" I asked.

"I hate property," she said. "If they ask an essay question on property, I'm screwed."

I hovered over her, trying to figure out the best way to launch into the crazy left turn that my life had taken. I wanted to draw my presentation out, maybe make it a guessing game that she could never win. But when I saw how tired she looked, and knowing how the stress of studying could sometimes shorten her patience, I decided to abandon my game and simply hand her Toke Talbert's mug shot.

"Who's this?" she asked, only half interested.

"That's Joe Talbert, Senior."

She sat up straighter. "As in . . . your dad?" She looked at the picture, then at me, doing the same comparison that I had done a few hours earlier. "I don't understand. All these years...I mean why would you...?"

"He died last night."

Lila went quiet.

"I don't know much about it, but the press release said they suspect foul play."

"They think your dad was murdered?"

I took a seat on the bed beside her. "The press release didn't give any details other than that he's been living in Buckley, Minnesota."

"Where's Buckley?"

"About an hour north of the Iowa border, out in the middle of nowhere."

She leaned toward me and put her hand on my forearm. "I'm sorry...I think...I'm not sure what to say here."

"There's more," I said. "I have a sister—well, half-sister. Her name is Angel. I found an obituary from when her mom died. The mom's name was Jeannie Talbert, and she died six months ago."

"So if her mom died six months ago, and her dad died last night..."

"That would mean that my sister's an orphan," I said.

"How old is she?"

"I don't know."

Lila picked up her laptop and typed Angel's name into a search. It took a little sifting to find the correct Angel Talbert, but we found her on a social media site, her profile light on both content and followers. She had a picture posted, a mousy image of a girl with hair the color of old hay that hung down in tangled strands, hiding much of her face. Her profile gave her age as fourteen.

I reached down and enlarged the picture, searching for a

resemblance behind the fallen hair, and finding none. Instead, I found a set of deeply shadowed, furtive eyes. My sister, the orphan. Her brother, the bastard.

The most recent activity on her page was a post made that morning. It came from a girl named Amber, and it read: *Get well, Angel. We're praying for you.* Below that were some replies. Lila clicked on them.

Brandon:

Get well? Praying? What happened?

Amber:

They found her unconscious at her house last night.

Jayce:

I heard she died.

Amber:

Her dad died. She's still alive, I think.

Brandon:

Does anyone know what happened?

Tyler:

OMG! First her mom then her dad. Does she have anyone left?

Amber:

Any relatives? I don't think so.

Rob:

My mom's an EMT. I heard her telling Dad that Angel tried to kill herself.

Jordan:

That sounds like Angel. She can't do anything right. She even f'd up her own suicide. What a loser.

Tyler:

Stop being a troll Jordan. Have some respect.

Jordan:

You all need to stop being so fake. Stop pretending that you were friends. If she didn't try to kill herself, none of you would give a crap about Angel Talbert. That's the truth and you know it. I'm just being honest.

Tyler:
This is Angel's timeline, you dickweed. You want to be a jerk, DON'T DO IT HERE!

That was the last entry.

"Poor girl," Lila whispered. "How could they be so mean to her?"

"No one down there knows that I exist," I said. "No one knows that Angel might have a brother."

"To blast her like that and call her a loser for a failed a suicide attempt. How could anyone . . . ?"

"I need to go to Buckley," I said.

"Go to Buckley?" My statement seemed to catch Lila off guard. "What are you talking about? You can't go to Buckley right now."

"Angel might be my sister. She's an orphan. I could be her only relative, and no one knows it."

"Yeah, but . . ." Lila looked at me as though her point was so obvious that she shouldn't have to finish the sentence, but then she did. "The bar exam is next week. I'm not ready. If I don't pass the bar, I'm out of a job."

"What if this Toke Talbert guy is . . . or was, my father? I can't just stay here and ignore that."

"If you really want to know about your father, maybe you should start by talking to your mother."

I stiffened and pulled back like a dog getting jolted by a shock collar. The look on my face was enough to drop Lila's gaze. "My mother is dead," I said.

"She's not dead. And quit saying that. What if Jeremy hears you?" Lila nodded toward the open door. I walked over and closed it.

"She may as well be dead. You know that."

"No, I don't," Lila said in a soft voice, her thoughts seeming to turn inward.

I stared at Lila, not really sure of what I was hearing.

"It's been five years, Joe," Lila said, quietly. "People change."

Where was this coming from? Had she forgotten the hell that my mother put us through? People change? What did she mean by that? I hardened my gaze but kept my voice level and said, "No."

"All I'm saying is—"

"No," I said again, although not as level this time.

Lila stared at me like a cat about to hiss.

"I'm sorry, Lila," I said, hoping to smooth down the rough edge of our conversation. "You know why I can't open that door again. What she did to Jeremy? What she said about me at that guardianship hearing? We can't go back there—ever."

Lila didn't respond.

I wanted to move to a different topic, get us away from my mother, so I brought up my trip to Buckley again. "If Angel's in a hospital, do you think they'd they let me visit her?"

"What?"

"Angel...my sister. Will the hospital let me in to see her?"

"You're going to visit her? You don't even know for sure that she is your sister. Don't you think you should wait?"

I didn't really have a plan to visit Angel. I just wanted to ease back into the conversation about my trip with something neutral, maybe knock a few stones off the wall building up between us. "I suppose you're right," I said.

"You're still planning on going to Buckley?"

"I won't be gone long, an overnight at best."

"Who's going to take care of Jeremy while you're gone?"

"Jeremy's fine. He's——"

"Jeremy's not fine." Lila found her footing again. "He hates his new job. It takes me half an hour of working with him before he stops rubbing his knuckles when he comes home. And you're not here in the mornings when I'm getting him ready for work. It breaks my heart to put him on that bus. He hates his job."

"He'll get used to it. He did the same thing when he started at the recycling center."

"But that's the point; he's not used to it. This is the week before the bar. I don't need this, Joe. Not right now."

"Angel's all alone. She's just a kid."

I was hitting below the belt by aiming at Lila's soft spot for the helpless and weak. Behind her narrowed eyes, I could see her thoughts whirling: my mother, the bar exam, Jeremy—colors that refused to blend together. I could tell that she had a lot more to say on each of those subjects, but she held her tongue. Instead, she closed her eyes and softly shook her head. Then she slipped her headphones back on.

Our conversation wasn't over, but she had put her headphones on, so it was over *for now*. It would resume after supper, and again as I packed my bag for the trip to Buckley—neither conversation advancing the banner one way or the other. By bedtime, the matter still had not been resolved.

After I got Jeremy settled in for the night, I rolled out some blankets to sleep on the couch—a sleep that would refuse to come, of course. Instead, I lay there staring at a shadow cast against the wall by the light from the oven clock. As fatigue settled in, that shadow blurred, and I saw the mug-shot face of Toke Talbert staring at me. I closed my eyes, and the words of the press release invaded my thoughts: *Joseph Talbert found dead in a barn*—my dad, dead.

All of my life I had been pretending that I didn't care if my father existed, but now that he might be dead, he became real to me. Learning about the death of this man had ripped open the rotted planks that I had used to hide him. In the quiet of that night, as my thoughts found their way past years of anger and resentment, one sad truth remained: I *wanted* to know my father.

Around midnight, as I lay staring at that shadow, I heard the creak of our bedroom door, and then the padding of feet approaching the couch. Lila came and sat on the edge of the cushion beside me.

"I can't sleep," she said.

"Me neither." I leaned up on my elbow to make room for her. "I'm sorry about all this," I said. "I can't really explain why, but I just need to go to Buckley."

"I know," she said. "I'm sorry I freaked out." I rubbed my hand down the soft skin of her arm as she spoke. "I'm really stressed about this exam. I know you have to go. I just wish the timing weren't so . . ."

I reached my arms around her waist and pulled her closer to me. "I won't be gone long."

I felt her stiffen at those words. Then she relaxed, and she kissed the top of my head. "Come to bed," she said.

CHAPTER 6

I woke with the sun the next morning and carefully slipped out of bed so as not to disturb Lila's sleep or the delicate truce we had reached the night before. I'm not sure that Lila actually came around to my way of thinking so much as she took the steps that she needed to take to get some sleep. There was still much that went unsaid, details that could upset a true meeting of the minds, but I went ahead and filled in all of those blanks, in my favor. She agreed that I should go to Buckley—at least those were the words that I heard, so I was going.

I brewed a pot of coffee for the road and slid a few snacks into my bag. Buckley was two and a half hours away—closer to three with the city's morning traffic. A couple stale doughnuts would tide me over. I also put a call into Allison's voice mail to let her know that I was taking a personal day, maybe two. I couldn't imagine her having a problem with that, given the cloud that had been following me around lately.

I poured my coffee into a travel mug and snuck back into the bedroom to give Lila a kiss goodbye. I expected to find her asleep, but instead, she was sitting on the edge of the bed holding what, in the dim light of morning, looked like an envelope. I ignored the incongruity of the scene and leaned in to give her a kiss. She did not look up to receive me, so I kissed the top of her head.

"You okay?" I asked.

"No," she whispered.

I sat on the bed beside her, expecting that we were about to have another go-around about my leaving, but her attention remained focused on the envelope in her hand.

"Joe, there's something we need to talk about." She didn't look at me when she spoke, and the seriousness in her tone chilled me. "Last night, when I told you that . . . you should talk to your mother about your dad, I . . ."

Lila fiddled with the envelope, kneading it the way Jeremy rubs the back of his knuckles when he's upset. I could see cursive writing on its face, but I could not make out any name on it.

"What's that?" I said, nodding at the envelope.

"I know you told me that you never wanted to hear from your mom again . . ."

"And you know why," I said.

"Joe, she's your mother. She—"

"What's in your hand?" I knew what it was, even before she answered.

"It's from Kathy."

"Throw it away." I stood up. "No mail. No phone calls. No communication. That's the rule, remember? She's out of our lives, and it's got to stay that way."

"Just read it." Lila held the letter out to me.

"You . . . did you read it?"

"Yes, and you should too."

I backed away from her, as though the paper she held might come to life and claw me. "When did you get that?"

Lila paused and looked at the floor.

"Lila, how long have you had that letter?"

40

"It came just before Christmas."

"Jesus Christ! Seven months? You've had that for…" I couldn't finish my sentence. Lila and I have had disagreements over the years—but this? Stunned, I backed out of the room.

At first Lila didn't follow after me. I paused as I picked up my bag, fighting against my urge to be somewhere away from her, waiting for her to utter an apology. When none came, I picked up my bag and made for the door, forgetting all about my coffee sitting on the kitchen counter. I had reached the door to our apartment before I heard the words I was hoping to hear.

"Joe, wait."

I paused in the opened doorway, my back to her, my ears listening to the familiar sound of her bare feet on the carpet. When she caught up to me, she took hold of my arm, and I turned to face her, expecting to see remorse in her eyes—not the anger that met me. Before I could say a word, she shoved the letter into my hand and took a step back.

"You can read it, or you can throw it away," she said.

This was not the act of contrition I had been expecting. "Who are you?" I said. "How could you…" A clutter of harsh words tumbled through my head, jostling to get past my lips, but I held them back, knowing that nothing good could come from speaking. I looked at Lila and said, "I gotta go." Then I turned and walked away.

Once in my car, I wadded up the letter and threw it to the floor, adding it to the mess of empty water bottles and crumpled-up fast-food bags on the passenger side of my car. The morning traffic on Snelling crawled at a pace that would normally have had me cursing the vehicles around me, but I barely noticed the gridlock as thoughts of Lila shoving Kathy's letter into my hands stabbed at me. It was the same gesture used by that short, turd-of-a-man who served me with the lawsuit. I couldn't hold anything against the bald man, though; he was only doing his job. But Lila's gesture came with a layer of betrayal that blindsided me. She had been holding on to Kathy's letter for seven months. She had read it. She broke the only rule I asked of her.

I fumed and sputtered as I worked my way south, the curtain of my anger never really parting until I passed through the first tier of suburbs on my way out of the Twin Cities. Only then did I pause to question whether I could have been at fault for what happened. But try as I might, I couldn't see that I'd done anything wrong. Lila can't hold it against me that I got upset. She knew the destruction that my mother caused. She also knew what my mother was still capable of doing if we let her back in. Lila had been there from the beginning. She was there the day that we rescued Jeremy from that woman. Hell, Lila drove the getaway car.

As I left Shakopee, Highway 169 thinned out enough that I set my cruise control and hit the scan on my radio, hoping to find some music to block out the thoughts of my mother, and the letter, and my fight with Lila. I inhaled a few deep breaths, halted my radio scan on something classical, and relaxed my grip on the steering wheel. I had two hours more to go.

Chapter 7

My trip took me south along the Minnesota River Valley for an hour or so and then west into farm country, a fairly treeless part of the state painted green with crops of corn and soy beans. I traveled on a two-lane highway where each mile looked exactly like the last mile, my travel hindered occasionally by a small town, some not even big enough to support their own gas station. The world had turned so flat that I could see Buckley— or at least the water tower—from a good eight miles away. I expected the town to grow bigger as I drew closer, but it never really did.

As a county seat, Buckley had been laid out around the courthouse, with small stores lining the four bordering streets. The highway that I'd been traveling turned into Main Street and ran along the front of the courthouse. I drove around the square, curious to see what Buckley might have to offer a ne'er-do-well like Toke Talbert. What drew him here—and, more important, what kept him here? I made a mental note of the stores and shops: antiques, hardware, a café, a bar, used clothing—the normal fare.

It never occurred to me that Buckley might not have a motel until I'd completed my loop and found none. I noticed the

Sheriff's Office across the street from the courthouse and parked in front of it. I hadn't planned to make that my first stop, but if nothing else, I might get directions to some type of lodging.

The door to the Sheriff's Office opened into a small lobby where, at the other end, a lady sat at a desk behind bulletproof glass. To my left, a thick, metal door marked *Visitor* told me that the jail was also part of the building. To my right, a wooden door led, I assumed, to the interior of the Sheriff's Office. I approached the receptionist, a woman in her forties, who glanced up at me for a second before turning her attention back to something more important on her computer screen. She made me wait a full thirty seconds before she asked, "Can I help you?"

"I'm looking for a motel or hotel...or some place that I can stay here in Buckley."

"Did you try the Caspen Inn?"

"I didn't try anything," I said. "Where's the Caspen Inn?"

"It's two blocks that way." She pointed over her shoulder.

"Do you know the address?"

She looked at me as though I'd just asked her how to tie my own shoe, and said, "It's on Maple, this street right here." She held her left arm out and made a sweeping motion with her finger.

I was about to leave, but a thought came to me and I said, "While I'm here, could you tell me who the lead investigator is in the Toke Talbert case?"

Now I had her attention. She shifted in her chair to face me and said, "And you are?"

"I'm...a reporter with the Associated Press." That was a true statement, but Allison would chew me out if she knew that I was using my AP credentials to get the skinny on my dad's death.

The receptionist picked up the phone and whispered into the receiver.

"No," I said, waving my hands to stop her. "I don't want to meet them now. I just want a name."

She ignored me and kept whispering. Then she hung up the phone and pointed to a row of chairs next to the entrance. "Have a seat and someone will be with you."

I didn't want to go into this interview cold. I had hoped to get some background on Toke before sitting down with the investigator. I wanted to steer the conversation, not be led through it. I opened my mouth to beg out of the meeting, but stopped when a deputy entered the receptionist's office and spoke to the woman in quiet tones, both of them studying me as they talked.

The deputy, a big guy with a serious face and a buzz cut, disappeared from the reception office and a moment later popped through the door beside me, his thumbs tucked into his belt. "Can I help you?" he asked.

I stood up. "I'm a reporter with the Associated Press in Minneapolis. I'm here about the death of a man named—I think he went by Toke Talbert. I was hoping to speak to the lead investigator. Would that be you, Deputy"—I looked at the name clipped to his shirt—"Calder?"

"Associated Press? Why does the Associated Press care about a guy like Toke Talbert?"

If I had been truthful, I would have said that the Associated Press didn't give a hoot about a guy like Toke Talbert, and that my editor would have my hide if she knew what I was doing. I briefly pictured Allison with the lawsuit papers in her hand and a what-were-you-thinking expression on her face, reprimanding me for poking my nose into a story that I had no business covering. I shook off that thought by remembering that I had no intention of writing a story. Of course, Deputy Calder didn't have to know that. I answered the deputy by saying, "There's no such thing as an unimportant murder."

Calder crossed his thick arms over his chest and looked dismissive. "Murder? I don't recall any information being released about this being a murder."

"The press release mentioned foul play. I figure that to be a murder. Are you saying that this wasn't a murder?"

"I'm not saying anything. You have identification?"

Crap. I reached into my back pocket, pulled out my AP card, and handed it to Deputy Calder. He read the card, his eyebrows lifting about the time he read my name. He looked at me and then at the card, then back and forth one more time before his eyes finally settled hard on my face.

"Your name is Joe Talbert?"

I nodded.

"You related to Toke?"

I didn't answer.

"Christ, we got friggen' Talberts crawling out of the woodwork today." Calder leaned his chin into the mike attached to his shoulder and said, "Sheriff, could you meet me in the conference room? I have something here you might want to see."

The answer came back, "Ten-four."

"Mr. Talbert, would you mind coming with me?"

"Why?"

"We'd like to ask you a few questions." Then with feigned politeness he added, "Please."

He waved me through the door and into an open space that held three metal desks running in a row along the cinder-block wall. Straight ahead was an office with a sign beside its door that read J. T. KIMBALL—SHERIFF. To my right, behind a large windowed wall, was a conference room, which I assumed doubled as an interrogation room given the cameras mounted to the ceiling.

Calder offered me a chair in the conference room, one facing the cameras, then stepped out, closing the door behind him.

Through the glass wall I watched another deputy enter the frame. He and Deputy Calder appeared to be about the same age, late forties, but where Calder had the body of a power lifter, the second deputy had the sleek build of a triathlete.

They chatted and pointed at me for a minute before a rotund man wearing a white shirt joined them. That had to be Sheriff Kimball. Calder again mouthed words that I couldn't read, showing the sheriff my AP credentials. The three of them exchanged a few more words and then came in.

"Mr. Talbert, I'm Sheriff Kimball," said the man in the white shirt. "This is Deputy Nathan Calder." He pointed at the big guy. "And this is Deputy Jeb Lewis." They all three sat down, with Kimball directly across the table from me. "You wouldn't happen to have a driver's license on you?"

"I would," I said.

Kimball waited for me to pull out my wallet, but I remained still.

"Could I take a look at it?" he said finally.

"Am I free to leave?"

Kimball looked at Calder, who gave a slight shrug. Then Kimball said, "Of course you can leave. You're not under arrest. We're just a little curious about something. I have a card here that gives your name as Joseph Talbert. I would like to confirm that you are who this card says you are. Is that okay?"

I reached into my pocket and pulled out my driver's license, handing it to Sheriff Kimball. He looked at it, compared the picture to my face, then handed my license and AP card to Deputy Lewis, who stood up and left the room with them.

Kimball said to me, "You told Nathan here that you're looking into the murder of Toke Talbert. You know his real name don't you?"

"I do," I said.

Through the glass I could see Deputy Jeb sitting at one of the desks, probably running my driver's license information.

"You have the same name as him," Kimball continued. "Is that a coincidence or are you possibly related?"

I looked at Calder, then back at Kimball and said, "I have reason to believe that Toke Talbert is my father."

"Reason to believe?"

"I never met the man," I said. "He got my mom pregnant, and when she refused to abort me, he punched her in the stomach and left town—at least that's what I've been able to piece together from the police reports."

"And yet your mother seemed to think enough of Joe Talbert Senior to give you the man's name."

"My mom has a strange sense of humor," I said. "So tell me, Sheriff, was my father murdered?"

"Where were you the night before last, say around midnight or so?"

I cocked my head back, caught off guard by the question. "What are you talking about?"

"Just need to button a couple things up. You understand."

"No, I don't understand. You think that I—"

"We don't think anything," Kimball said. "But you have to admit, it's a little strange. Toke turns up dead and then, boom, all these relatives start showing up."

"Relatives—plural?" I asked.

Deputy Jeb reentered the conference room, handed my driver's license to me, and then handed some papers to Kimball. Jeb took the seat farthest away, his eyes studying me with quiet curiosity. Nathan Calder, on the other hand, stared at me like I was an overdue lunch.

"I would also like to know how Angel is doing. I'm her brother and—"

48

"Hold on a second," Sheriff Kimball said. "We don't know that you're related to anyone here."

"If I'm Toke's son, then..."

"If—if you're Toke's kid. We need to know that you are an actual relative before we can pass out anything as private as medical information. We wouldn't be doing our jobs if we gave information like that to a reporter just because he claims to be related. If it turns out that you're her brother, then you can get in line with any other relatives and we can go from there."

"What other relatives are you talking about?"

"While you're here, can you give me your whereabouts two nights ago?"

"You can't think that I killed Toke? I didn't even know that the guy was alive until I saw the press release yesterday."

"He ran out on your mother, didn't he? Something like that might cause resentment."

"Everybody runs out on my mother—even me," I said. "I can't hold that against him."

"And he punched your mother in the gut when she was pregnant with you. Sounds like he tried to abort you. What about that?"

"And don't forget about the inheritance," Calder added.

Kimball gave the deputy a look that caused Calder to slump back into his chair.

"What inheritance?" I asked.

"Look, son," Kimball leaned in, "I don't think you're involved here. But I've got a job to do, and I aim to do it. You understand. I just need to know if you were in the area two nights ago. That's not asking too much is it?"

The word *inheritance* threw me off my game. I wanted to ask Calder what he was talking about, but the scolding glance Kimball had thrown him told me that I'd get nothing, so I answered Kimball's question.

"Two nights ago, I was in my apartment, asleep. My girlfriend can verify that."

Kimball slid a piece of paper and a pen to me. "Can you give us her contact information?"

I wrote Lila's name and phone number on the paper and slid it back to the sheriff. "Now tell me, was Toke murdered?"

Kimball leaned back in his chair and rubbed the loose skin on his neck with the back of his hand. "We're going to do an updated press release this afternoon. That release will confirm that Toke Talbert was the subject of a homicide."

"How was he killed?"

"Can't tell you."

"Is there a suspect—besides me, of course?"

"Can't say."

"Is his daughter a suspect?"

Kimball looked at his deputies. Then he stood and hitched his pants up. "You know I can't answer any of those questions, Mr. Talbert."

"I'd appreciate it if you called me Joe."

"Okay, Joe. And I would appreciate it if you'd be so kind as to voluntarily give us a sample of your DNA."

"My DNA? Why?"

"Whether or not you have Toke's blood running through you may be of interest to the investigation. Just buttoning things up. You understand."

My first reaction was to object to Kimball's request. I knew that they couldn't take my DNA without a search warrant. But it occurred to me that Toke might not be my father. I mean, I only had my mother's word on the matter. This might be my only chance to settle that question for good. In the end, the curiosity of it all won out, and I agreed to give a DNA sample.

Kimball assigned the task to Jeb, the quiet deputy. All three left the room together, and Jeb returned with a swab kit. He leaned against the side of the table as he opened the package.

I said, "That other deputy, Nathan, said something about Talberts coming out of the woodwork. What'd he mean by that?"

"Just that you're the second Talbert to drop by today."

"Who's the other one?" I asked.

Jeb stuck the long-stemmed cotton swab into my mouth and swirled the tip against my cheek. "Charlie. Toke's brother. He dropped by this morning wanting to know what happened to Toke."

I waited for Jeb to finish scraping my cheek, then said, "Did you question him about where *he* was two nights ago?"

"You ask a lot of questions."

"I'm a reporter."

"We've got it under control."

"So, you know who killed Toke?"

"I think everyone in town knows who killed Toke."

"Who?"

He smiled. "I'm one of the few people who can't say. We have a suspect, but that's about all I can tell you." His eyes lifted to the camera mounted on the ceiling in the corner of the room. "Buckley's a small town, Joe. Most folks have a pretty good idea of what happened to Toke."

"So, why take my DNA if you have this wrapped up?"

"Because if you are Toke's son, that could change the math." He slid the stick with my cheek cells in it into a sleeve and sealed it. "Who knows," he said with a sly grin. "We might be looking at this all wrong."

CHAPTER 8

I had no trouble finding the Caspen Inn. It was, as the receptionist had said, a couple of blocks down the street she waved at. I didn't expect too much in the way of accommodations, and those expectations were barely met: one level, ten rooms on each side, back-to-back, with an exterior painted bright yellow to distract from the overall decrepitude of the place. Room number eight, my room, had water stains in the ceiling and chips of grout missing from the bathroom tile. The one window to the outside—to the extent you could see around the air conditioner—gave a grand view of the gravel parking lot and looked as though it hadn't been washed since the Ford administration. But the room had two comfortable beds, and that was more than I needed.

I laid on one of the beds, and my thoughts immediately walked back to the Sheriff's Office, to Deputy Calder and a word he used—*inheritance,* a word that seemed out of place in any discussion of my family. Nothing I'd come across so far suggested that Toke Talbert would die with more than a month's rent in his pocket. And then there was his brother Charlie, who I'd never even heard of. If Toke was my father, it meant that I had an uncle wandering around town. Maybe he'd be able to fill me in on what kind of man my dad had been.

The Caspen Inn didn't have Wi-Fi, so I turned on my phone, with the intention of looking up what I could about Charlie Talbert, and saw that I had missed a call from Lila.

I contemplated whether to call her back, a hesitation I'd never had before. I didn't know if I was ready to open that discussion again. How could she have read that letter from my mother? I had drawn a single line in the sand: no contact with Kathy Nelson. A simple rule, easy to follow. We don't give her our phone numbers. We don't open her letters. We give her no chance to worm her way back into our lives. Did Lila forget the extortion? The meth-induced ravings? Did she forget how Kathy let her shit-eating boyfriend hit Jeremy? I didn't forget the bruises, and I sure as hell didn't forget Larry.

The first time I saw a bruise, it was a thin line on Jeremy's back. I gave Larry a stern warning to never touch my brother again; and with me being a bouncer back then, it seemed fitting that my warning came with an abrasion to Larry's nose. But to be fair, things would not have become physical had Larry not gotten in my face. He actually poked at me for addressing him in my chosen tone. The way I saw it, I had no choice but to take him to the ground and pressed his face into the grit of the sidewalk.

That should have been the end of it, but apparently Larry was a slow learner. The night that I took Jeremy away—kidnapped him, as my mom told the judge at the guardianship hearing—Larry had punched Jeremy in the face, causing a bruise that nearly swelled my brother's eye shut. That night, as Lila and I drove to Austin, we never actually discussed what we would do. I think we both just knew.

I stormed into my mother's apartment without saying a word to her, or to Larry. Once in Jeremy's room, I threw some of his clothing into a pillow case and was leading him out of the house when Larry stepped in front of me. I saw what was happening, so I sent Jeremy outside, where Lila was waiting for him.

My mother made a show of her token resistance, screaming at me and crying that Larry didn't mean to hurt Jeremy. I ignored her ranting and focused on Larry. We both knew that this had nothing to do with him wanting to keep Jeremy around and everything to do with having a second go at me, repayment for the raspberry I gave him. Larry raised his fists, arms jutting out, knuckles pointing up. I probably had other options, but I didn't wait for those thoughts to find a footing. Instead, I gave Larry a quick kick to the side of his knee, sending him to the floor howling through the pain of a torn ACL.

We've had Jeremy ever since then, and there hasn't been a day when he wasn't protected and cared for. He was safe because Kathy was out of our lives. She could never touch him unless we slipped up and let that trouble find us again. That's why we had the rule. Lila, who doted on my brother like he was her own, should have known that better than anyone. She had let her guard down, that's all. We could fix that.

I picked up my phone and returned the call.

"Hi, Joe." Lila spoke in a soft, hesitant voice.

"Hi."

I waited for her to talk, giving her the opportunity to offer up an explanation or maybe even an apology. Instead, I got a long, silent pause. Then she said, "That was a shitty thing you did today."

"What I did?" I couldn't stop my tone from turning hot. "What do you mean, 'what I did'?"

"You walked away. You turned your back on me and walked away. You didn't even give me a chance to explain."

"What's to explain? You lied to me."

"I didn't lie."

"You opened a letter from my mother. We had an agreement."

"No, we had a rule—a rule that you made without asking me. There was no agreement."

"She's my mother. I'm the one she screwed over. You don't get a vote on that."

"Is that how it is? You make the rules, and I shut up and do as I'm told? Is that how you see me?"

"No, Lila. That's not how I see you. You know better than that."

"When it comes to your mother, I'm not sure I do."

"You're playing right into her hands. Give one inch, and before you know it, she'll be calling me to bail her out again, or she'll find some way to extort money. My mother's a lost cause."

"There's no such thing as a lost cause."

"Yes, there is. My mother is one."

"People can change, Joe."

"Not Kathy. I've known her all my life. The only changing she did was to get worse. People like her don't change. She's a drunk—an addict. She's mentally unstable. A combination like that doesn't change. They may hide it for a while, but the monster always comes back. That's just a fact."

The phone went silent, and I waited for Lila to speak. The silence went on long enough that I glanced at the face of my phone to see that we were still connected. Then she said, "Is that what you think of me?"

"You? No, that's not—"

"Did you forget that I'm a drunk? I'm mentally unstable. Remember? I have the scars to prove it. Did you forget that I used to cut myself?"

I had seen her scars on our first date, tiny striations descending off her shoulder in neat rows. In time, I would learn about

her high school days, how she fell into drinking and party-
ing and how that led to promiscuity and blackouts and cutting
her arms to deal with the pain. But there was another de-
mon, one that had opened the gate for all the rest, one that
she kept hidden from everyone except me. I understood why
she had once sought to numb her pain with alcohol, how the
sting of a razor blade against her skin could feel like a salve. I
understood the hurt that twisted its tendrils around every bad
decision she'd ever made.

But I also understood that Lila faced her demons and beat
them. My mother was not Lila. Where Lila had built a wall to
keep out the beast, my mother laid down a welcome mat. But
what I said just now could have applied to Lila as easily as it did
to my mother. Christ, I was an idiot.

"You're not my mother," I said. "You were a kid—a teenager.
You pulled yourself out of it. You haven't touched a drop of
alcohol in what . . . eight years now?"

"But it's a part of who I am, Joe."

"You wanted to change. My mother has never wanted to
change, and she never will."

"I am the same person, you understand that, don't you? You
act like there's some kind of baptismal font that we drunks can
walk through to change who we are—wretched on one side, but
saved on the other. That's not how it works."

"You're not a drunk, Lila. You're not—"

"Why is it so hard for you to think that maybe your mother
can change?"

"I know my mother."

"You haven't spoken to her in years. How do you know?"

"What makes *you* think she is capable of change?" I said. "One
letter?"

"No, not just one letter."

Now it was my turn to pause as I tried to decipher what that meant. Then I asked, "Are there more . . . letters?"

"No."

"What then?"

"I talked to her . . . on the phone."

"She called you? How did she get your number?"

"I called her after I read her letter."

"You . . . called her?"

"I did."

I let my phone drop away from my ear. For seven months, Lila had been living with me as though nothing had changed: eating with me, laughing with me, sleeping with me, all the while hiding this secret. I felt like I had no idea who my girlfriend was anymore.

I looked down to find my phone resting in my lap, and I pressed the red dot to end the call.

CHAPTER 9

Lila spoke to my mother. I should have asked how many times, but why would that matter? The damage was done; Kathy had discovered a crack in our wall, and she would work it open with that same slow force that weeds use to split stones. She would sink her roots deeper and deeper into our lives until the tiny cracks became fissures and then chasms too wide to cross. She would find angles and traps. She would create havoc and start fights, while always painting herself as the victim. My mother never missed a trick.

In truth, I never actually intended to seek guardianship of Jeremy after we rescued him. I guess I thought that Kathy might leave us alone if we took Jeremy but not his social security money. I mean, what more could she want? I took the burden and left behind all the benefits. She should have been happy. She should have left us alone. But that was asking too much, I guess.

When I kicked Larry in the knee that night, I thought I broke it. I didn't care at the time, but I should have known that Kathy would use it against me. I found out that it was an ACL tear when I received a letter from my mother telling me how lucky I was that they didn't bring in the cops. But in exchange for her and Larry's silence, she wanted me to pay cash for what I did to him. She framed it in terms of reimbursement for his medical expenses, but she did little to hide the extortion: pay her money whenever she demanded, and this matter won't go to the police.

In her letter, she didn't bother to ask how Jeremy's eye was doing. That would step on her narrative. She kept the fact that Larry punched Jeremy in the face out of the letters, as though by not putting it in she could deny that the punch even happened. I don't think I ever felt more rage in my life. She didn't care about Jeremy. She didn't give a rat's ass about anything except getting money from me—as if Jeremy's disability checks weren't enough.

I refused her demands, of course. I took pictures of Jeremy's eye, and both Lila and I wrote detailed accounts of what happened that night, in case we would ever need to recount the events in court. Kathy could threaten to call the cops all she wanted to, but I knew that Larry had a criminal record, and they would never risk the tables getting turned on them by bringing in the authorities.

Kathy's threats, veiled or otherwise, fell on deaf ears until the day came that she threatened to take Jeremy back—legally—if we didn't pay her some money. That's when Lila and I took our first hard look at fighting for guardianship of Jeremy. Even with my mother's many problems, getting guardianship of him seemed an uphill battle—that is, until she got arrested for possessing meth.

On a particularly hot July night, Kathy's neighbors called the police because she and Larry were screaming at each other again, the caller telling 911 that it sounded like someone was getting murdered. I know this because I read the reports and attached them to my guardianship petition. When the cops entered the house to break up the fight, they found thirty grams of methamphetamine on a coffee table.

Of all the adjectives I have conjured up over the years to describe my mother, meth-head had never crossed my mind. Kathy had always been volatile, but in those years with Larry, she had vanished inside the husk of someone that I didn't recognize. It was as if she wore her demons on her skin, the crazy no longer content to swing on vines in her head. On those few occasions when I saw her, she looked like she hadn't slept for days, and she would pace around, picking at her arms and face. Looking back now, I should have known that she was using meth; but who would think that of their mother?

Even after that arrest, I held off filing for guardianship, waiting to see if things might finally change. They didn't. The court released her from jail into a treatment facility. She wrote me a letter from there, demanding that I return Jeremy to her once she finished treatment. She didn't make this request because she loved her son, but because "no one would send the mother of an autistic boy to prison." I couldn't believe that she would actually admit her scheme in writing. Instead of responding to that letter, I called my lawyer and told her to proceed with the guardianship petition.

When they served the papers on Kathy, she went nuts, absconding from the treatment center and showing up at our apartment. Lila was the one to answer the door that day and was so stunned when she saw my mother that she lost the presence of mind to shut the door in Kathy's face. My mother tried to push past Lila, which caused Lila to scream my name.

Kathy was tiny and frail by this point, and I had little difficulty pushing her into the hallway, sending her stumbling to the floor as I closed and locked the door. Lila took Jeremy to his bedroom and sang to him while I called the police. As we waited for the cops, Kathy remained outside our door screaming at me, accusing me of assaulting her, and demanding that I hand over Jeremy.

I didn't know this at the time, but leaving treatment, when you've been furloughed there from jail, is considered an escape, another felony to add to her list. The officers who came to haul her away had been in touch with the courthouse in Austin and knew her status. They dragged Kathy out of the building, her insults echoing off the walls.

That was the last time I would see her until the hearing, but I did receive one more letter from my mother, this one sent with the return address of the Mower County Jail. I didn't have to read it to know what it would say. My mother made her hatred of me perfectly clear as the police officers dragged her away in handcuffs. That would be the first letter I would throw into the garbage unopened.

Looking back now, I was naive to think that storming into my mother's apartment and pulling Jeremy out would have been the end of it. Even having her arrested and dragged away from my door did little to get her attention. Those were but the first salvos in a battle that would scorch the earth between us, our fight devolving from shots fired across a desolate no-man's-land to a hand-to-hand slog. In the end, I would be the one to deliver the blow that would destroy what little remained of our relationship.

CHAPTER 10

I did my best to brush the bad memories of my mother aside and refocus my attention on the life and death of Toke Talbert. Deputy Jeb said that everyone knew who killed Toke. If that was true, then I knew where to look for that answer. Having spent much of my life around bars, either working in them or hauling my mother home from them, I knew that the best place to learn local scuttlebutt would be the town's watering hole. The bar I saw when doing my short tour around the town square wasn't far from my motel, so I left my car at the motel and walked.

The bar, the Snipe's Nest, had very few windows along its century-old exterior. Dark, huddled on the street corner like a stubborn vagrant—I knew that place. I could have sketched the floor plan on a napkin before I walked through the door: a bar running half of its length, stools bolted to the floor, and a brass foot rail. There'd be booths running down the long wall and high-tops in front, a black tin ceiling and sticky floors. It was the kind of place where town gossip would float through the air like dust motes.

It was just before the lunch hour, so the place stood mostly empty. One man in his late forties, wearing a suit jacket and khakis, sat at the end of the bar typing on a laptop. On the other end, two old-timers complained loudly about some chicken operation that was bringing "all those damned Mexicans" to town.

The bartender was an attractive woman, my age, maybe a little younger, with long cinnamon hair and deep eyes that held steady on me as I walked up. She wore a black T-shirt, its short sleeves revealing toned arms, a small tattoo of a candle decorating her left biceps. Beneath the candle I could see some cursive writing, but I couldn't make out what it said.

"What can I get you, stranger?" she asked.

"Just a Coke," I said.

She poured my drink and turned to go talk to the old-timers.

"Excuse me," I said. "I was wondering if you could help me out a bit."

She returned her attention to me. "Whatcha need?"

"I'm in town doing some research on that death that happened two nights ago."

The guy in the khakis sat up and made no bones about turning his attention to my conversation. The old men to my left also stopped jabbering and listened in.

I said, "His name was Toke Talbert. Did you know him?"

She looked at the old-timers and then back to me. "Everyone around here knew Toke."

"What can you tell me about him?" I asked.

"Who's asking?"

"My name is Joe. I work for the Associated Press."

"Associated Press, huh?" She held out a hand to shake. "How do you do, Joe? I'm Vicky Pyke—shortstop for the Minnesota Twins."

I shook her hand and accepted her jab. Then I pulled out my wallet, and for the second time that day, crossed a small ethical line by showing my AP credentials. This time I covered my last name with my finger. "So what's it like playing for the Twins?" I asked.

"You really are a reporter."

I returned my card to my wallet. "Is your name really Vicky Pyke?"

She smiled. "Yes, it is."

"Well, Vicky, I'm looking for a little background."

"Shouldn't you be at the Sheriff's Office asking those kinds of questions?"

"I find that I can get better information by talking to people without badges, people like you. I bet you know everything that goes on in this town."

"Ain't much to know, but I hear stuff," Vicky said.

"Tell me what you know about Toke Talbert."

"Toke Talbert was an asshole," she said, dropping her smile. "He's dead and it ain't a bad thing."

I don't know what I was expecting, but her candor surprised me. I found myself wanting to defend the man who had once punched my mother in the gut, but I resisted. "Did you know him well?"

"You didn't have to know Toke Talbert well to know that he was an asshole." Vicky turned toward the old-timers. "Bill, what did you think of Toke Talbert?"

"He was an asshole," one of the men said. The other guy nodded in agreement.

"See?" Vicky said. "I'm not speaking ill of the dead, I'm just giving you the facts."

"Why?"

"Because you asked."

"No, why was he an asshole?"

"Born that way would be my bet."

I paused to put together a more coherent question. "What I mean is: what kinds of things did he do to make people believe he was an asshole?"

The guy that Vicky referred to as Bill spoke up. "He cut down two of Connie Alber's walnut trees five years back. Just cut 'em down in broad daylight. Didn't like the nuts falling on his property. Told the sheriff some cock-and-bull story that he thought those trees were on his side of the property line. Never got charged with nothin'."

The second guy leaned into the bar so that he could talk past Bill and said, "Yeah, and last year he shot Karen Halverson's cat. Saw it crossing the street toward his property. Shot it with a twenty-two."

"Kill it?" Bill asked.

"He shot it with a twenty-two."

Bill said, "That don't mean nothing. I shot a cat with a twenty-two once. Still see it running out my barn every now and again."

"That's because you can't shoot worth shit," the other man said with a laugh.

They then began a debate on their respective shooting skills, and Vicky turned to me with a smug expression, her opinion vindicated. "I don't think there's a person in this town that he hasn't pissed off at one time or another."

"How about you?" I asked. "What did he do to piss you off?"

Vicky looked at me as though I'd crossed some line. "What business would that be of yours?"

"None, I guess."

"What kind of story are you writing anyway? Why would a reporter care about a dead man out here in Timbuktu?"

I gave her question some thought before pulling out my AP card again, this time showing it to her with my last name uncovered. She looked at the card and then at me.

"Talbert? Are you related to Toke?"

"I'm pretty sure that I'm his son."

The man in the khakis coughed and then closed his laptop. I could feel his stare without having to turn to look. The two old-timers stopped their bickering and fixed their eyes on me as well. Vicky laid my card on the bar. "I didn't know Toke had a son," she said, her tone not as harsh as it had been a few seconds earlier. "He never mentioned you." Then as an afterthought, she added, "I'm sorry for calling him an asshole."

"Don't be. I'm not sure that I disagree with you. He kind of disowned my mother and me."

"Is that why you're here? Looking for your father?"

"Honestly, I'm not a hundred percent sure why I'm here. I guess I'm just curious. You have any idea who might have killed him?"

She glanced at Bill and his friend as if looking for permission to share a secret. Then she said, "They think Moody Lynch killed Toke. They've been looking all over the county for him."

"Who's Moody Lynch?"

"That's . . . wait, you know about Angel, right?"

"Toke's daughter. Yeah."

"Moody is Angel's boyfriend. He's got a bad reputation with the cops. They think he's trash, so they pull him over every chance they get, always looking for drugs in his car or something."

"They ever find any?"

"No. Moody's too smart. He may be the son of white trash, but he's no dummy. Just the opposite. I heard that he was a decent student in high school before he dropped out. Never saw the need for a diploma if all he wants to do is hunt and fish."

"Why do the cops think Moody killed Toke?"

"Bad blood between them two."

"How come?"

"Moody was dating Angel. I guess that was reason enough for Toke."

"How is Angel? I heard something happened to her the same night Toke died."

Vicky looked at me as if she were about to tell me that my dog got run over. "You don't know, do you?"

"Know what?"

"I live across the road from Toke. He and Jeannie and Angel moved into the farmhouse after Jeannie's old man died. That's where Toke was killed—in the barn. Someone bashed his skull in. I was across the road watching when they carried Angel out of the house. She was on one of them gurneys."

"Did someone attack her too?"

"Word around town is that she tried to commit suicide. That might be true or it might not. You hear a lot of stuff. But I can tell you that they took her off in an ambulance because I saw that with my own eyes."

Bill said, "My daughter's one of the EMTs that took her up to Mankato. Said that girl was in pretty bad shape. Died a couple times on the trip up there."

"Do you have a library in town?" I asked.

"It ain't much, but we got one. Go down to Oliva's Antiques," she said, pointing south. "Take a right and you're there."

I stood and tossed a five on the bar. "This cover it?"

"Yeah," Vicky said. "Stop by any time."

I walked to the front door, and as I passed the man in the khakis, he stood up and followed me.

CHAPTER 11

I stepped into the midday sun, paused to get my bearings and let my eyes adjust. I had seen Oliva's Antiques earlier and thought it to be to my right. I was about to head that way when the man in khakis came out of the bar behind me.

"Excuse me," he said. "You got a second?"

I turned and squinted at him. He was about my height, five foot ten, but heavy and thick like a tree trunk. I would put him around twice my age, with a touch of gray in his tight curly hair. His white teeth and tanned skin suggested that he worked hard on his appearance, though he had a crooked nose and a flat face that looked like he'd been hit hard with a shovel.

"Sure," I said.

"I didn't mean to eavesdrop in there, but did you say that your name is Joe Talbert?"

"That's correct."

He began eyeing me up and down as if studying me for a test. We stood on the sidewalk in an awkward silence, him with his arms folded across his chest, me with my hands shoved in my pockets, enough room between us that anyone looking at us from a distance could see the discomfort that filled that space.

"I don't think so," he said finally.

"You don't think so, what?"

"I don't think you're a Talbert—at least you're no relation to the Joe Talbert who died here two nights ago."

"Is that a fact?" I said.

He pursed his lips and nodded his head as if satisfied with his answer. "Yep," he said. "I can see right through you."

"And who are you again?" I asked.

"I'm Joe Talbert's brother."

"Uncle Charlie?" I said.

"I'm not your uncle anything and you aren't Joe's son. My brother didn't have a son. He only had one kid. I don't know what your angle is here, but your con won't work. They have ways of testing those things nowadays. You ever heard of DNA?"

"You ever heard of Kathy Nelson?" I said.

The expression on his face flipped from smug to confused, and he eyed me up and down again, this time probably looking for traces of my mother in me. Then, as if some slot machine in his head finally stopped spinning, he took half a step back, and said, "Bullshit."

"So you know her."

"Yeah, I know her," he said. "I knew her real well back in high school—all the boys did. If Kathy Nelson's your mother, then there's no telling who your father might be." He laughed, and I found myself in the bizarre position of wanting to defend my mother's honor, a task for which I was wholly unqualified. "If you think you're Joe's kid because Kathy Nelson says so, boy, have you been duped."

"Look asshole, I hold no illusions that my mother—"

"Hold on there, boy." His smile fell away, and he stepped toward me with stones for eyes. "I don't take kindly to being called names. I don't care who you think you are, and I don't care what kind of game you're playing, but if you go to insulting me like that, we're going to have a problem."

His attack caught me off guard, and I lost my voice.

"I didn't say anything about your mother that wasn't the truth. Now you may think that her lies give you some kind of standing to stake a claim, but her words don't mean shit. I'm here to take care of this family—my family. I got this under control, so you may as well go back to whatever hole you crawled out of because there's nothing for you here in Buckley."

"I didn't come here to stake any claim." My words sounded overly apologetic, so I summoned a touch of anger into my chest. "I'm just trying to figure out who my father was. You got a problem with that?"

"Your father wasn't Joe Talbert." He took another step closer and pointed his finger at my face. "Get that through your head."

I hadn't noticed the squad car that rolled to a stop across the street until I heard the door close. I turned to see Deputy Jeb Lewis making his way toward us. Charlie saw it too, and in a flash, he had slapped a salesman's smile onto his face.

"What's going on, boys?" Jeb said.

"Nothing, Deputy," Charlie said. "We were just having a friendly chat."

Jeb said, "It didn't look like a friendly chat."

"That's just the heat," Charlie said. "Makes my face flush red for no good reason."

Jeb stopped walking when he reached Charlie. "Well, maybe you might want to head inside where there's air-conditioning," he said, pointing at the Snipe's Nest.

Charlie broadened his smile and held his hand out for Jeb to shake. "That sounds like an excellent idea." Jeb shook the man's hand.

Then Charlie turned his smile to me and reached out to shake my hand. I hesitated at first, but then raised my hand up, and he gripped it hard and gave it a short shake. "Good to meet you, Joe."

I didn't know what to think as Charlie backtracked his way into the Snipe's Nest. Jeb waited until Charlie was inside before turning to me and saying, "Let's have a talk."

Chapter 12

Jeb and I walked across the street to his squad car, where he leaned against the front fender and pushed his sunglasses up the bridge of his nose. "What was that all about?" he asked.

"Family squabble," I said. "You know Charlie?"

"I've heard of him but never met him until he stopped by this morning."

"If you don't mind me asking, what did you hear about him?"

Jeb chewed on my question before he answered. "I was friends with Jeannie, Toke's wife. I remember her telling me some years back that Joe had a brother, and from what I understood, Joe and Charlie hadn't been on good terms since they were kids."

"Did you ask Charlie where he was two nights ago?"

"We asked."

"And?"

"We're looking into it."

"The same way you're looking into me."

"We wouldn't be doing our jobs if we didn't ask those kinds of questions. No stone unturned, as they say."

"But you guys are thinking that Moody Lynch is your man?"

Jeb smiled. "It didn't take you long to come up with that one."

"I'm a reporter. It's what I do. Besides, that's probably the worst kept secret in town."

"You understand that I can't confirm anything—even if I wanted to."

Another squad car pulled out of the parking lot of the Sheriff's Office, heading our way at a slow roll. Deputy Calder gave a nod to Jeb as he passed, but for me he had nothing.

"Are you sure it's okay for you to be seen talking to me?" I said.

"Why wouldn't it be okay?"

I leaned up against the squad car next to Jeb. "I get the feeling that Deputy Calder isn't a fan of mine."

Jeb spoke in a slow rhythm that made me wonder if the man had ever been in a hurry in his life. His words seemed softened by the heat of the day, like butter left on the table. "Nathan's all right. I've known him since grade school. He could stand to work on his people skills a bit, but trust me, there's no better man to have on your side when things get hairy."

"So when he accuses me of murdering my father—that's just bad people skills?"

"It's his first homicide. He'll settle down."

"You've never handled a murder before?"

"I have. Nathan and the sheriff... well, there isn't much need for killing in this part of the country."

"But you've handled homicides?"

"I did eight years in the army, the last two in the Criminal Investigation Command."

"Maybe you should be in charge of this investigation then."

"If I have input, the sheriff is more than happy to listen, but this is his show."

"Well, tell the sheriff that I think you should give a hard look at Charlie. There's something wrong with that guy."

"What were you and Charlie squabbling about?"

I didn't want to tell him the truth—that we were arguing about my mother's bad reputation—so I focused on something else Charlie had said. "He accused me of wanting to stake a claim in something. He acted like I should know what he was talking about, but I don't have the foggiest." I said, "I get the feeling I'm missing something."

Jeb folded his arms across his chest and turned his eyes to the pavement, his head slowly drifting back and forth as he gathered his thoughts. Then he said, "This morning, Charlie told us that he plans to seek guardianship of Angel. I think most people see that as a fine idea. Hell, he's already met with social services to get the background investigation started—and he hasn't even filed the petition yet."

"I take it you don't see it as such a good thing?"

"Jeannie didn't like Charlie. She never told me why, but she didn't trust him. If I recall, I think she once called him a soulless human being. Now I never met the man before today, but if Jeannie had that opinion of him, it makes it all the more likely that he's only here to get his hands on the money."

"What money?"

"The inheritance—the Hix estate."

"Deputy Calder said something about an inheritance when you guys were interrogating me this morning. What's that all about?"

"You call that an interrogation? Hell, that was nothing."

"Deputy, you're dodging my question. What's going on?"

"Call me Jeb."

"Okay, Jeb. Why does Deputy Calder think that I killed Toke Talbert for an inheritance?"

"You really don't know, do you?"

"No, I don't. What's he talking about?"

"Where do I start?" Jeb bit his lip as he pondered this answer, letting the seconds tick away to the point that I wanted to nudge the man. Then he said, "In a way, it's all Nathan Calder's fault—at least that's how I see it."

"Come again?"

"Keep in mind, this was back when I was still in the service, but the story I heard is that Nathan pulled this car over for a DUI, and the driver turned out to be Toke Talbert. He was just passing through town, had no reason to be here, but he ended up going to jail."

I thought back to the mug shot Allison had given to me. That would have been his arrest for DUI here in Buckley—his last arrest.

"Because it was his third offense, we took his car through a forfeiture action. Toke was living out of that car. After he got out of jail, he had no way to leave town. Looking back now, I think everyone wishes that we'd just given him his car back and told him to keep driving."

"People say that Toke was an asshole," I said.

Jeb gave me a sideways glance and a grin. "You got that right."

"So how does a drifter like that come to have money?"

"The way they all do; he married into it. He got a job as a body man down at Dub's Repair." Jeb gave a nod down the street as if I should be familiar with the establishment. "Toke may have been a jerk, but he could do wonders with body filler and paint. That's how he met Jeannie Hix. She'd hit a fence post with her car and brought it into Dub's to get it fixed. Things kind of went from there."

"But if Toke was such a jerk, why would any woman . . ."

"Jeannie was a rebel back then. She probably got swept up in that bad-boy thing. Personally, I think she started dating Toke just to piss off her old man. But it got out of hand, and they ended up getting married. Toke could be a charmer if he wanted to be."

"And Jeannie had money?" I asked.

"Arvin Hix, her dad, had the money. The Hix family owned some of the best river-bottom farmland in the state." Jeb pointed west. "Head down the highway about eight miles and you'll find their farm."

"He *had* money?" I said.

"Hix passed on about a year ago. You see, Arvin Hix hated Toke. He told Jeannie that she wouldn't get a penny of inheritance unless she divorced him. But then Arvin died without a will. I suspect he couldn't bring himself to put his anger into writing. When he died, the law gave the whole kit-and-caboodle to Jeannie."

"I read about Jeannie's death when I was researching," I said. "She died six months ago, right?"

Jeb nodded, his eyes again fixed on the pavement at his feet. I waited for him to say something more, but he didn't. So I asked, "How'd she die?"

He tightened his lips as if fighting to hold back something deep. Then he said, "She committed suicide. Angel found her hanging in their horse barn." Jeb stumbled a little on his words as he spoke, and I could sense the history between them.

"Angel found her?"

"Yeah. Really did a number on that girl."

"Why would Jeannie...I mean, did she leave a note or anything?"

"Jeannie was always an anxious girl, and after she had that falling out with her father, well I guess the anxiety just got worse. She left a note, talking about how Arvin's death put her into a depression that she couldn't climb out of. After she and Toke moved out to the farm, we got at least three calls from Jeannie because of her panic attacks. EMTs would show up, and she would be curled up in a ball trying to breath."

"You knew Jeannie pretty well, didn't you?"

"Yeah...I did."

Given the melancholy that showed on his face, I left it at that. We stood there in silence until it became too awkward for me to handle, and I said, "When Jeannie died, I take it she left every-thing to Toke?"

"Jeannie didn't have a will either," he said. "Toke got the farm by law. And now that Toke's dead..." Jeb looked at me as if it was my turn to say something, but I just blinked at him. "If you really are his son..."

Then it hit me. "Holy crap," I whispered.

"You and Angel."

"I had no idea. I swear, I didn't..."

"So you see why Nathan thinks that you might be a suspect."

"I would never...I know you don't know me from Adam, but I would never..."

"It's a lot of money."

"How much are we talking about?"

"I don't know the exact figure. The guy you need to talk to is Bob Mullen. He's the attorney handling the estate. Jeannie worked for him as a paralegal before she...."

"And what about Angel?" I asked. "I've heard rumors that she's in a bad way."

"You know, Joe, I did some checking on you this morning. I found that police report you mentioned—the one where Toke hit your mother. Everything seems to match up with what you said happened. As far as I can tell, you just might be Toke's son."

"I think that's a pretty good bet," I said.

Jeb turned his head to look at me, pausing again before saying what he had on his mind. "I'm going to tell you something, Joe...I'm probably crossing a line here, so I'd appreciate it if you don't hang me out to dry on this."

I nodded my agreement.

"The way I see it, if you are Angel's half-brother, you have a right to know—Angel's in a coma, up in Mankato."

"A coma? What happened?"

"I was the first one out to the farm the night Toke died. I found Angel in her bedroom—nonresponsive. She was barely breathing, and there was an empty prescription bottle on a table near the bed. clonazepam. It was Jeannie's prescription. Toke should have thrown it away. He had no business keeping meds like that around the house."

"Will she be okay?"

Jeb didn't answer.

"So that's why you think Charlie's in town."

Jeb nodded. "I doubt if Charlie could pick Angel out of a lineup if he had to. Toke dies, leaving all that money to Angel, but Angel's only fourteen. She can't legally do anything with the farm. Whoever becomes her guardian will control her share of the estate. I think that's why Charlie crawled out of the woodwork."

Then Jeb turned to face me, planting one arm on the top of his car. He lowered his sunglasses to lock his eyes onto mine and he said, "I'm telling you all this because I think Angel deserves better than what she's getting. If I find out that you are just here for her money, I'll..." He didn't finish his thought. He didn't have to.

I said, "If I went up to visit Angel, do you think they'd let me see her?"

Jeb smiled at that. He struck me as a thoughtful man, the kind of guy who had seen enough in his lifetime to walk with

deliberate steps. I could see him thinking on my question, waiting for the heavy stones of right and wrong to balance out. Then
he said, "I was planning on heading up there tomorrow. You can
ride along with me if you want. I'm willing to bet that we can
get you in to see her."

Chapter 13

The library in Buckley was smaller than my apartment, and empty of people except for a mother reading children's books to her three docile kids. I sat down at one of the two computer carrels and fired up the Internet. My first search—Charlie Talbert.

Charlie lived large on the Internet, the kind of guy who found celebrity in having his name appear in as many places as possible, self-promoting tripe that blared his accomplishments like a row of heralding trumpets. Uncle Charlie wanted the world to see him as a successful businessman, and he seemed to excel at getting his picture taken with famous people: politicians, movie stars, even a former governor of Minnesota. At first glance, he appeared to live on the opposite end of the spectrum from his brother, Joe.

But I was an AP reporter; research was my stock in trade. I knew the false fronts that people could present when they had something to hide, so I took my time, clicking past what Charlie wanted me to see to find what he wanted to hide.

Nearly two hours had passed before I found my first bread crumb, a news report about a fire at a warehouse in St. Paul

three years ago. The building housed the offices and manufac-
turing floor of a company developing a new form of prosthetic
limb, and a man named Casey Levin died in the fire. The article
reported that the origins of the fire were under investigation.
Charlie's name came up only once, when the article identified
him as a minority partner in the company and the beneficiary of
a million-dollar personal insurance policy on the dead man.

I clicked around looking for a follow-up story or anything
that might give me more information on the fire, but came up
with bubkes. So I decided to research two other subjects that I
had on my mind: comas and clonazepam. On comas, I found
a great deal of information but very little that helped, as it all
seemed intentionally vague. Yes, comas were bad, and yes, if it
was bad enough, you'd die. They could last hours or they could
last months. They could result in total brain damage or no brain
damage at all. After an hour of searching, I felt like I had found
nothing concrete on any of the sites.

On the other hand, I found a ton of good information on
clonazepam, an anti-panic medication that had recently become
a go-to date-rape drug. It could disorient a person, take away
their inhibitions, knock them out, and hide the crime with a nice
blanket of amnesia. Too much of the drug could put you in a
coma or kill you.

As I read about clonazepam, my mind drifted to thoughts
of Lila; she had been raped in high school, waking up in the
backseat of her own car, naked and unable to remember what
happened. She always suspected that she had been drugged, and
after reading about clonazepam, I wondered if that had been the
pill they used.

I had been lost in my research for hours and didn't realize
how much time had passed until I felt the sting of fatigue in my
eyes and the pang of hunger in my stomach. I had worked right

through the lunch hour, and dinnertime was fast approaching. I needed food, so I headed to the Snipe's Nest. The bar was about half full of people, one of whom was my Uncle Charlie, sitting at a high-top in the corner eating fries from a red basket and watching the Twins on the TV on the wall. He gave me a cold look as I passed. Vicky was still working the bar, shuffling food orders from the kitchen and mixing drinks. She smiled at me as she passed with a big plate of chicken wings.

I took a seat on the same stool I'd sat on earlier. Beside me, a couple of women, one in her midfifties and the other a decade younger, leaned against the bar in a stance that suggested they were awaiting food orders. The older one, the one closest to me, said, "That's him down there."

I glanced at her in the mirror above the bar and saw that she was pointing at Uncle Charlie.

"He knows Clint Eastwood *and* Governor Pawlenty. I saw the pictures online."

"That's Toke's brother?" the younger woman said, twisting her neck to get a better look.

"Yeah," the older one said. "He's wants guardianship of that poor girl, God bless him. He's exactly what she needs after what she's been through. I met him when he stopped by the office yesterday, asking if I can speed up the background study, and I told him that I can't do anything until a petition is filed. And today— voila—he files a petition."

"That couldn't have worked out any better," the younger one said.

"I think the judge is anxious to get him appointed. Someone has to look out for Angel. This might be the fastest background study I've ever done."

"Who'd have thought that Toke Talbert could have a brother who knows Clint Eastwood?"

"Well, Cain had Abel, didn't he?"

Vicky stepped back behind the bar, gave a couple of sandwich baskets to the ladies, and they retreated with their food to a nearby booth.

"Drink?" she asked me.

"A beer," I said. "Something local."

"Coming right up." She poured a beer and placed it on a coaster in front of me. "Here you go, Little Toke."

"Oh, no. Don't even start. I'm Joe. Just plain Joe."

I heard someone in the booth behind me say *Toke*. I glanced over my shoulder at three guys drinking beer, construction workers given the paint on their jeans and the worn shine on the tips of their steel-toed boots. One of them, a guy wearing a Pink Floyd T-shirt, looked at me like I was a crossword he couldn't figure out. Then to Vicky he said, "How about another round over here?"

"You might want to pace yourself, Harley," Vicky said as she reached under the bar for three bottles of Budweiser. "This ain't a race." She set the bottles on the bar and opened them.

"Bring 'em here."

"You want beer, get off your ass and come and get it."

The man in the Pink Floyd shirt, the one Vicky called Harley, stood up and walked the three paces to the bar. I could feel his eyes on me as he picked up the bottles of beer. Then he returned to his booth.

"Any update on who killed your old man?"

It struck me as odd that she asked that question with the same nonchalance that she had when she asked me if I wanted a beer. "They're not telling me much, but I believe you were right when you said that they have their sights set on Moody Lynch."

"Nathan Calder would blame Moody for the Kennedy assassination if he could," she said.

"Why's that?"

"Them two have a history." Vicky leaned on the bar and spoke in a voice just above a whisper. "And it's a juicy one."

"Do tell."

"A couple of years ago, Nathan busted Moody for some minor possession. I think it was just pot. After that, Nathan started pulling Moody over every chance he got: window tint, loud muffler, that kind of crap. And every time, Nathan would search for drugs. Well that started to piss Moody off, so Moody took up watching Nathan. Spying on him. And Moody Lynch ain't gonna be seen if he don't want to be. He can disappear into the leaves like one of them lizards that change colors."

"Chameleon?"

"Yeah, a chameleon. So Moody's watching Nathan every day, and pretty soon he figures out that Nathan's been sneaking off in his squad car with Janice Meyer from the Court Administrator's Office. He followed them out to the river and found where they liked to get it on. Well, the next time they decided to sneak off, Moody was waiting with one of them infrared trail cameras. Caught Nathan and Janice in the act. The next thing you know, a copy of that footage shows up in the mail, addressed to Nathan's wife and Janice's husband. It was a huge scandal. Nathan got divorced over it—almost lost his job. I think if he had the chance, he'd put a bullet through Moody's head."

Again, from the booth behind me, Harley yelled, "For Christ's sake, Vick, will you stop flirting with that douchebag and do your job?"

"What the hell you squawking about?" Vicky said.

"I want another beer. The service here sucks."

"I just gave you a beer."

Harley stood up and walked to the bar, slamming his empty beer bottle down. "As you can see, it's empty."

He slid the bottle toward Vicky, and it fell behind the bar, landing on a rubber mat without breaking. Again, I could feel his eyes on me. Instead of getting Harley a beer, Vicky went to the opening between the bar and the kitchen and got the attention of the cook. As they spoke, Vicky kept glancing over her shoulder at Harley. But Harley didn't notice; he kept his eyes locked on me.

"Are you really Toke's kid?" he said, his words slurred and dripping with contempt.

I didn't answer.

"I said, are you Toke's kid? Are you Little Toke?"

"Who I am is none of your business." I said it as calmly as I could.

"The hell it ain't. If you're Toke's kid, you owe me some money."

I pinched my lips and slowly shook my head and said, "I don't owe you shit."

"Harley, go sit down," Vicky said.

"Not until Little Toke here agrees to pay me my money."

I could tell that Harley had been drinking for a while: one hand on the bar to steady himself, eyes as glassy as frog's eggs.

"Your old man screwed me out of fifteen grand. You're gonna get some of that Hix money, so the way I see it, you can pay off his debt." He gave a shove to my shoulder that nearly pushed me off my stool.

"Damn it, Harley!" Vicky yelled. "Leave him alone." She reached across the bar, grabbing Harley by his shirt. He swatted her hand away.

Now I stood up and faced him. "I don't know you," I said. "And I don't owe you any money. Go sit down."

Harley looked at his buddies, who, I suspected, were ready to jump into the fight if Harley needed them. Then he turned back to me. "Are you calling me a liar?"

"No. You've made a mistake, that's all. Just go back to your friends."

"Are you a cheat like your old man?" Harley took a step into me—although I think it was more a matter of losing his balance than anything else. I stepped back to keep an arm's length between us.

"You're drunk, Harley," Vicky said. "Go sit down."

"You stay out of this, Vick. This is between me and Little Toke here."

He reached out to poke me on the chest, and I swatted his hand away. "Don't go there," I said.

With that he perked up like I'd just slapped his face. "Oh, you want to have a go, do ya?" He took another step into me, this time on purpose. I again stepped back.

"Don't do it, Harley," I said. "I don't want to fight you."

"I bet you don't." He stepped at me a third time, and before I could step back, he reached out for my shirt.

I grabbed his hand with both of mine and twisted his arm upside down so that the knot of his elbow pointed at the ceiling. I pulled his upturned elbow under my armpit, lifted my legs, and let gravity take us to the floor. He landed harder than I had intended, and the sickening crack of his face hitting the wood worried me a bit.

One of Harley's friends, the smallest of the three, began to slide out of the booth, so I yelled, "Don't move, or I'll break his arm."

The kid stood up, unsure of what to do next. I raised my foot to kick the kid if he came any closer and cranked Harley's arm some more. "Tell your friend to stay put!"

"Ow! Son of a bitch!" Harley hollered.

The kid moved a step closer, his eyes darting around, looking for a way to come at me.

"Tell him to sit the fuck down!" I leaned into Harley's twisted arm, taking his wrist and elbow to the edge of breaking.

"Sit down! Fuck!" Harley screamed.

The guy moved back to the booth. I eased up on Harley a bit to stop his screaming.

"Now here's what we're going to do," I said. "You boys can either leave peacefully out that back door, or I can keep Harley here in pain until the law arrives. It's your choice."

"Fuck you!" Harley said.

"Law it is."

"No, man," said the kid. "I'm on probation, and hell, so are you. Let's just go."

The third guy, the one who sat quietly while the fight went down, dropped a ten-dollar bill on the table, got up, and walked out without saying a word. The guy on probation hesitated for a couple beats but relented and followed his friend out the door.

With Harley alone, I felt pretty good about my situation. I loosened his arm a bit. "Harley, I got nothing against you. I'm going to let you up. You can walk out of here or you can stay and fight, but you should know that Vicky has already called the cops."

Vicky picked up her phone and held it as if that were true. With his face against the floor, Harley didn't know the difference.

"You can walk out of here and let it be, or we can go another round. It's your choice."

I let go of his wrist and scrambled up. Harley climbed to his feet, his face almost purple with rage, his eyes watering. He held his right wrist, working his fist in a small circle, probably gauging its strength. Then he looked at Vicky, who still held her phone halfway up to her ear. He spat at the floor near my feet and walked away.

Most of the patrons looked at me with a mix of fear and

surprise. The lady doing Charlie's background study seemed particularly shocked by what I'd done, her eyes popping, mouth hanging open. Charlie remained at his table in the corner, a strange smile on his face like he'd just bested me somehow.

I sat back down on my bar stool, my fingers shaky from the adrenaline rush. Vicky stood across the bar from me, leaning in close enough so that I could smell her perfume and catch a glimpse of the black lace of her bra behind the V-neck of her T-shirt. "Where'd you learn to handle drunks like that?"

"I used to be a bouncer," I said, averting my eyes away from Vicky's cleavage. I looked at the tattoo on her arm, the candle with the cursive writing below it. From this close I could read the words under the candle: *my mother, my light.*

"You were a bouncer? And here I thought you were just some desk-jockey reporter. Damn."

"Don't be too impressed. I mostly just checked IDs."

"The way you handled Harley Redding just now—you may not be burly, but you got some moves."

I took what she said as a compliment, even though I didn't like being reminded that I was a bit undersized. "I've had my ass handed to me plenty of times," I said. "My luck was bound to run out sooner or later, so I went to college. You don't need survival skills when you sit behind a desk."

"What I wouldn't give to go to college and get the hell out of this hole. You have no idea."

"You should do it," I said, sounding like the jackass that I often was. "When I was at the U, I knew people who went to school by day and bartended at night."

"If only it were that easy," she said.

"If I can do it, anyone can."

"No," she said, looking at me through wistful eyes. "Not anyone. For some of us it's just not in the cards."

The heaviness in her words told me to let it go, and I suspected that the ground we were covering had become hard-packed long before I arrived in Buckley. She moved down the bar to serve drinks to some of the other patrons, and by the time she returned, I had prepared a question for her that had nothing to do with college, or bartending, or being stuck in a small town.

"Do you have any idea what that guy, Harley, was so mad about? What'd Toke owe him money for?"

Vicky's playful side came back. "I don't know, but I bet I could find out. A small town like this, someone's bound to know."

"And how'd he know about me being in line for Toke's money?"

"Toke's murder is a big deal around here. It's all people are talking about. And if you're Toke's son, then you and Angel get the Hix farm, right? At least that's the gossip."

"Gossip? I just got here."

"Oh, honey, this place is nothing but dry grass and tinder waiting for a spark of gossip to set it on fire. Nothing stays a secret in Buckley."

"If it works out that I get a dime, I'll be surprised," I said.

"Have you seen the farm—the Hix place?"

"No."

"I'm off after the dinner shift. Stick around and I'll take you out there."

"I wouldn't want to put you out."

"It's no big deal," she said. "That's my neck of the woods. I could show you around."

I thought about her offer. What could it hurt? If nothing else, I'd have an idea of what Uncle Charlie had at the center of all his scheming. If it turned out that I was, in fact, Toke Talbert's son, it might be nice to have some perspective on the tides moving around me. If not, all I would have wasted was a couple hours of my time. "Okay," I said. "Let's do that. But I'm going to take my supper back to the motel and eat it there. I don't want Harley rethinking his decision and coming back here for me. I'm staying at the Caspen Inn."

"I know, room eight."

"How'd you...?"

"I told you, nothing stays a secret in Buckley."

CHAPTER 14

In July, the evening sun can linger in the sky until after nine o'clock, so when Vicky showed up at my motel at eight, I figured that an hour would be more than enough time to drive out to the Hix farm and back before dark. When the knock came, I answered the door to find Vicky in a black leather jacket, black gloves, and her hair tied back in a ponytail.

"You got a jacket?" she asked.

"A sweatshirt," I said, giving a quick glance to the cloudless sky.

"You may want to put it on." She nodded toward a motorcycle parked across the lot. It was a mean-looking thing, black and sleek, arched like a running back ready to shoot the A-gap. It reminded me of something from a *Transformers* movie, an evil robot just waiting to stand up and spit lasers. I grabbed my hoody and a pair of sunglasses, and followed her across the parking lot.

"Quite the bike," I said, sounding a little more nervous than I'd intended.

"That's my baby." She rubbed her hand down the seat as though it were a pet. "It's a Triumph Tiger—as good in the dirt as it is on the road."

She jumped on and nodded to me to mount up behind her.

When she fired the engine, I could feel the power surge against my thighs and groin. I wrapped my arms around Vicky's waist, the strength of her stomach muscles apparent even through the leather jacket. As if she sensed my apprehension, she turned her head, her lips curled up in a sly smile, and said, "Don't worry, I got my first dirt bike in fourth grade. I'll take care of you."

We headed out of Buckley on a two-lane highway that cut through a vast plain of green fields. When we came to a long straightaway, Vicky opened the throttle, and I tightened my hold on her waist, pressing myself into her as she leaned forward. Over her shoulder, I could see the speedometer climb to a hundred and ten before she let off. Despite wearing sunglasses, tears streamed across my cheeks as we settled back down to the speed limit. I have to admit that her acceleration scared the hell out of me. A single pothole or startled pheasant would have been enough to kill us both—Minnesota being a no-helmet state. But at the same time, the rush of adrenalin caused my skin to tingle and my breath to stay high in my chest. It was like one of those carnival rides, the kind with rust on the bolts and grease trailing across peeling paint, whose hinges groan and pop for want of repair. Eventually something is bound to go wrong; yet having survived it once, I wanted to do it again.

About fifteen minutes outside of town, the fields gave way to thick woods, where we dropped into a river valley, crossed a bridge, and climbed back up the opposite valley wall. At the top, she let off of the gas, and we coasted.

Up ahead, two farms emerged, one on either side of the road. On the right stood a farmhouse painted a handsome blue with bright white trim. A row of dormer windows jutted out from the roof, and a porch ran along its entire front, the kind of porch that beckoned company to come and sit. The house stood amid a cluster of barns and a grain silo, all painted bright red.

On the left was a smaller house, a one-level rambler squat-ting in front of a silo and barn, both in need of a fresh coat of paint. A faded metal shed, white with a gray sliding door, stood next to the house, completing the hodgepodge of mismatched structures. Weeds had invaded much of the prop-erty, and a patch of scrub in front of the faded, red barn grew unchallenged. The contrast between the two farms told a story of boom and bust, separated by a single stretch of blacktop.

I couldn't take my eyes off the rich colors of the farm on the right, even as Vicky turned into the farmstead on the left, following the gravel driveway around the side of the house and parking in the metal shed.

"Come on," she said, waving me to follow her.

As we walked toward the front of the house, I heard the sound of a door creaking open. We turned the corner to find a man in his late fifties, unshaven, his shirt pitted from days of wear. He held a cup in his hand, and although I was still fifteen feet away, I swear I could smell alcohol seeping from his body.

"Hi, Pop," Vicky said.

"Who's your friend?" he asked, pointing his whiskey mug at me.

"This..." Vicky looked at me with a strange expression of betrayal on her face. "This is Joe Talbert, Toke's son. Joe, this is my father, Ray."

I started to take a step toward Ray, my hand reaching out in greeting, but the old man pulled back and glared at me.

"Get off my property," he said.

"Dad, he's not Toke. He didn't even know Toke."

"He's a Talbert, ain't he? I'll have no Talbert on my land. Never! Get him out of here."

For a second, I thought Ray might throw his mug at me. His hands trembled as he snorted air in and out of his bulbous nose.

"Calm down, Dad. I'm showing him the Hix farm." Vicky's tone remained tranquil, dismissive, replying to her father as though she were telling him how her day went. "I'll be back in a little bit."

"Don't you go over there," he said. "You got no business on that farm."

"Just go watch some TV. I'll be in to fix your supper later."

"Don't you be bringing that Talbert back here—you hear me?"

"Go inside, Dad."

Vicky walked down her driveway with me in tow. I looked over my shoulder and saw that Ray remained on the porch watching us. He pointed at me, I suppose to let me know that he'd be keeping an eye on me. I could tell that he had been a big guy at one time, but his build, like his silo and barn, had succumbed to the ravages of time. His big hands were knotted and bent, his back curved.

"Don't worry about him," she said. "He wasn't a fan of Toke's."

"I could tell."

As we were about to cross the highway, a car came from our right, a red Lexus. I had seen that car parked at the Caspen Inn a couple doors down from my room. We waited for the car to pass, and as it neared us it slowed. Uncle Charlie sat behind the wheel, looking at us—at me—like my mere presence on Earth irritated the hell out of him. After he passed, he kicked the accelerator and sped away.

"That was creepy," Vicky said.

"You know who that was?"

"No, but he's been at the bar all day."

"That's Toke's brother, Charlie," I said.

She looked at the car as it shrank into the distance "Should have guessed that was Toke's brother. He kept staring at my ass every time I walked past him." We started across the highway, but Vicky stopped, and again she looked in the direction of the disappearing car. "You know, now that I think about it, I've seen him before. Yeah, he was at the bar a few weeks ago with Toke, arguing about something or other."

"Does the sheriff know that?"

"I only call in the law when things get really out of hand. They were arguing, but it wasn't a fight."

"Do you know what the argument was about?"

"I didn't catch it all, but it was mostly name-calling. Toke was yelling something about him having no obligation. And that guy, Charlie, was calling Toke a selfish son of a bitch. It didn't last too long before Toke got up and left."

"Was Charlie around the night Toke died?"

"I didn't see him again until this morning."

"You sure?"

"He's got a face you don't easily forget." Vicky gave a light chuckle. "Who'd have thought that Toke was the good-looking one in the family?"

The Hix property didn't have what you might call a driveway. Rather, it had a large gravel turnaround that narrowed to one lane where it met the road. The house lay straight ahead, and a long, red barn stood to my right. Both buildings had yellow police tape crossing their doors. The place smelled of hay and dirt and manure, but seemed to glimmer in the evening sun. She led us around the side of the house and down a gravel trail that took us past a grain silo and a second red barn, our path becoming dotted with hoof prints.

"Toke had livestock?" I asked.

"Not for very long," she said. "Hix raised cattle. He also raised a few horses back when Jeannie was a kid. My dad always thought that the horses were Hix's way of spoiling his daughter."

"Where are the cows now?"

"Toke sold them off as soon as he and Jeannie took over the place. Cattle are work, and Toke wasn't much for farming, which is too bad because he inherited one hell of a chunk of land."

Vicky took me to the edge of a knoll, beyond which the land sloped gently into a broad river valley, green crops stretching out to the horizon. She pointed and swept her arm from left to right. "This is your farm," she said.

"Holy crap," I whispered, looking out at a sea of green, where leaves of the corn rippled lightly in the breeze. On my drive to Buckley, I had passed mile upon mile of farm fields, a view that I thought might cause me to fall asleep behind the wheel, but now the sway of the crops nearly took my breath away.

"Ain't it beautiful?"

"Gorgeous," I said. "But I thought you said Toke wasn't much of a farmer."

"Oh, God, no. This ain't Toke's doing. He rented out the land before Hix was cold in his grave. As soon as the lawyer said the farm was going to Jeannie, Toke was on the phone getting bids. The only part of the property that ain't under lease is the house and the horse barn."

"How did Hix die?"

"Heart attack."

"So, no chance that Toke might have...you know."

"Killed Hix? It crossed our minds. Don't get me wrong, I think Toke had it in him, but no; it was a heart attack."

"How many acres are we talking about here?"

"Dad once told me that Hix owned about seven hundred fifty acres."

"Seven...hundred..."

"And fifty. Yeah. But don't quote me on that."

I didn't even know what an acre of land looked like, my life having been defined by city blocks, but that much land might be the kind of thing that could persuade a man like Toke to forsake his nomadic bachelorhood and start a family. I also had a better understanding of Charlie's effort to gain guardianship of Angel. I pictured Angel in her hospital bed, clinging to life, and I suddenly felt like a jerk. Here I stood calculating angles and motivations for a land grab while this girl, who was probably my sister, lay in a coma. All around me lurked the remnants of her fallen life, the barn where both her mother and father died, the house where she tried to kill herself; I felt ashamed at how easily she had become just another chess piece in my mind.

"Did you know Angel?" I asked.

"I was ten years old when Angel was born—that age when all a girl wants to do is hang around babies. I remember Jeannie bringing her out here to the farm a couple of times. I ran across the road, and Jeannie let me hold Angel. Thinking back now, though, I don't think Toke knew about those visits."

"Why do you say that?"

"At the time, I didn't think nothing of it, but when I was older, after I got the job at the Snipe's Nest and got to know Toke a little better, I got the feeling that he controlled Jeannie, told her where she could go, who she could be friends with. And he used to say terrible things about Angel, calling her retarded and referring to her as his idiot daughter."

"Was she . . . ?"

"Retarded? No, just fragile. I would see her in town every once in a while—Toke and them only lived a block and a half from the bar back then. She would keep to herself, and she never answered with more than a word or two before she excused herself from the conversation and left. She reminded me of one of those scared dogs, afraid of its own shadow. Don't get me wrong, she was sweet, but . . . well, fragile."

"Where was Toke killed?"

"In the horse barn. Come on." Vicky turned and headed back down the trail, cutting across a dirt path that led to the back door of the barn. Crime-scene tape had been stapled in two big Xs across the doorway. She pulled it free and we stepped inside.

It took a moment for my eyes to adjust to the dim light of the barn. It was long and narrow, with empty horse stalls down one side. The walls were filled with nails holding horse tack, gears, mower blades, and tools. The barn had a row of high, west-facing windows through which the waning sun glowed, speckled with dust.

Vicky pointed up at a thick crossbeam about three feet above our heads. "Jeannie hung herself from this beam."

"You saw her?"

"I had just gotten home and was sitting on my porch watching the stars, when I saw Angel come out of her house. She called for Jeannie and looked around the courtyard."

"Where was Toke?"

"He wasn't home, so Angel wandered down to the barn and opened the front door. Next thing I knew, Angel was screaming her head off. I came over here as fast as I could. When I got here, Angel was holding Jeannie up by her legs—you know, trying to get her loose from the rope. There was a bale of hay on its side, like Jeannie had stood on the bale and kicked it over to hang herself."

Vicky looked up at the beam as she paused in her story; then she shook her head and said, "She was dead already. There was nothing we could do."

The barn turned quiet as I stared at that beam and pictured a woman hanging from it. My trance was broken when Vicky said, "They found Toke over here."

She led me toward the front door, where she flipped on a light.

"He was over there." She pointed to a dark spot on the bottom of the wall about ten feet inside the barn. "He was lying on his stomach with his head pressed against the wall."

I bent down to look at a dark stain on the lower boards of the barn wall.

"That's blood from his head," she said. "I heard they beat him with some kind of gear or something."

I touched the stain of my father's blood. This wasn't a mug shot on a computer screen; it wasn't the bitter stories told by my drunken mother. This was real. This was the blood from his head, and it occurred to me that if Toke Talbert turned out to be my father, this would be the closest I would ever come to touching the man who made me. I remained squatting and stared at the spot of blood.

"Are you okay?" Vicky asked.

I shrugged. "It's just strange, I guess, knowing that this is where someone killed my father. That's Talbert blood there, and I'm a Talbert. It's just . . . I don't know."

"You may be a Talbert, but you ain't nothing like the Talbert who died here."

"Your dad doesn't seem to agree with you," I said. "I think he wanted to punch me when you introduced us back there."

"Sorry about that. My father has . . . issues." She didn't need to say the word *alcoholic*. His appearance and actions back at her house said the word for her. She dropped her eyes as though embarrassed.

"My mother has issues like that," I said, trying to be sympathetic. "In fact, that's a good part of why I left home to go to college. I guess you could say that I ran away from home to go to school."

"I could never do that," she said. "He needs someone to take care of him, and I'm all he's got."

Vicky went quiet, and in that silence I remembered something that she had said back at the bar. She told me that going to college wasn't in the cards for her. I stupidly assumed that she didn't have the grades for it, but that wasn't it at all.

"Is that why you didn't go to college?" I asked. "Because of your father?"

"It sounds dumb, I know, but I can't leave him alone. It's more than just the alcohol. Something happened that messed him up—emotionally. It's gotten so bad that he can hardly function anymore."

"Does it have something to do with Toke?" I asked. "Is that why he wanted to rip my head off when you told him my name?"

Vicky nodded her head slowly and said, "It has everything to do with Toke. Your father is the reason that my mom is dead, and why my dad can't get out of bed in the morning."

My bewilderment must have been plain on my face because she followed with, "Come with me. There's something I want to show you."

CHAPTER 15

The sun was already beginning to set when I once again got on the back of Vicky's Tiger. Her father either didn't hear us walk past his house or decided that he had made his point and didn't need to come out again. Vicky drove us back in the direction of town, but when we crossed the river, she pulled the bike over to the side of the highway and parked at the top of a boat access.

We dismounted, and she walked me to the bridge to a spot where a three-foot-tall concrete wall rose up from the bridge deck. She pointed at the leading edge of the wall, where a chunk about the size of a watermelon wedge had been busted off.

"This is where my mom died."

Vicky brushed her fingers along the damage and then stepped around the side of the bridge and started down the embankment. "Mom was coming home from work when it happened... would have been ten years ago now. Her car rolled down here and landed upside down in the river."

At the bottom of the hill, she walked to a fallen cottonwood tree and sat on its trunk, leaving space beside her for me to join. I did. "Toke came out to the farm that night. Back then he drove this piece-of-shit Ford, the kind you see in movies from the seventies, bright red, like fire-engine red. He came out around sunset. I remember because I had plans that night, and I was waiting for the sun to go down."

"Plans?"

Vicky smiled to herself. "I was a teenager, and in love. The boy lived on this side of town and..." Vicky pointed across the river. "See that gap in the trees over there?"

I squinted in the dying light to see it, and could just make out an opening cut to the left of the blacktop. "Yeah," I said.

"Remember how I told you that I've had a bike since fourth grade? Well, I have trails all over back there." She waved her hand at the woods across the river. "That gap in the trees is where one of my trails comes out. I could ride all the way to my boyfriend's place and only touch the road a couple times."

"This was ten years ago?"

"Yep."

"Why would Toke be going out to see Hix? From what I've put together, Hix and Toke hated each other by then."

"Toke was raising all kinds of hell that night. Me and Dad went to the porch to watch it all. Toke parked in the courtyard and was banging his fist on the door of the house, screaming for Hix to come out and face him. About then, Hix came out of the horse barn carrying some kind of pipe. He told Toke to get off his property. He said that if Toke didn't leave, he'd bash his head in. That didn't seem to scare Toke in the slightest. He jumped off the porch and squared up with Hix, making sure to stay beyond Hix's reach."

"What were they fighting about?"

"Jeannie—as always. That was around the time that Hix told Jeannie he was going to cut her out of his will. Jeannie must have told Toke about that because he was calling Hix a monster, and evil, and just about everything under the sun. He wanted to know what kind of a man would forsake his own daughter and granddaughter."

"You heard all this?"

"Yeah. We had a front-row seat. Dad was ready to call the cops if things got out of control, but it never came to blows. Toke finished his tirade and told Hix that if he wanted to put his daughter and granddaughter in the poorhouse, well he could go to hell. Then Toke jumped into his truck and lit out of here like a crazy man."

Vicky didn't move as she spoke, her gaze locked on the murky water beyond us.

"After Toke left, I thought it was dark enough for me to sneak over to my boyfriend's place. I rolled my minibike down through the hayfield behind my house, push starting it as I went. When I crossed the bridge, I saw the scattered parts of my mom's car. I didn't know what it was at first, just a bunch of busted plastic in the road. I stopped to look around and saw her taillights glowing just under the surface of the water. I ran down to see if I could help. That's when I recognized her car."

Vicky sniffed and folded her fingers together.

"I pulled my mother from the car and dragged her to the bank. That river may seem calm, but I promise you, there's a powerful current out there. I almost lost my grip. After I got her on the shore, I tried mouth-to-mouth. I hit her in the chest. I did every-thing I could think of to get her to breathe again. No cars came by. No help. So I got on my bike and raced home to get my dad. He called the ambulance, and we came back down here."

Vicky pointed to a small clearing near the bottom of the boat launch where the ground was fairly level. "That's where she was lying." Vicky wiped silent tears from her eyes. "There was nothing we could do."

As she spoke, Vicky became small and vulnerable, no longer the hellcat who taunted death on a motorcycle, but a woman holding in her hands the broken heart of her fourteen-year-old self. I wanted to put my arm around Vicky, but there were so many reasons why that was a bad idea. Instead, I let her face the memory alone while I sat by, a voyeur to her pain.

When she seemed to come back to the present, I asked, "Toke?"

She nodded. "When they pulled Mom's car from the river the next day, they found red paint on the side. The skid marks showed that she caught the shoulder and was trying to regain control when she ran into the bridge wall."

"Couldn't they match the paint to Toke's truck?"

Vicky looked at me with a wry smile and said, "By some freakish coincidence, Toke's truck was stolen that very night. He reported it gone before the ambulance carrying my mother even made it back to town. It's never been found. My bet is that it's at the bottom of the river somewhere between here and Buckley."

"So they could never prove Toke hit your mom's car?"

"The county attorney said that without matching the paint to Toke's truck, all he had was speculation."

"So that's why your dad hates me."

"He doesn't need a trial to tell him what's what. And you being Toke's boy, well, that's a little too much for him to take, I guess."

"I'm sorry about your mom," I said. "I'm sorry that my dad was such a..."

Vicky put her hand on my forearm. "Joe, I'm not like Harley—or my dad for that matter. I don't think you carry the sins of your old man with you. You didn't even know him."

"But somehow, I feel guilty for being his son. I know I shouldn't."

"This is all on Toke. Not you. You have no responsibility for your father."

"Like you have for yours?"

She slid her hand off of my arm and returned her gaze to the water, now black against the closing dusk. "My dad used to be something," she said. "When I was a kid, he was my hero. I would watch him chop wood or string up a fence and think how lucky I was to have a dad like that. That all went away when Mom died. After the funeral, he took to his bed and didn't get up for days. He was never one to shy away from a drink or two, but after she died, he went at it with a passion. He gave up on just about everything. The farm went to pot. We sold off a good chunk of the land."

"And you've been taking care of him ever since?"

"I'm his daughter. What choice did I have?"

"He's your father," I said quietly. "He has no right to ask that of you."

No sooner had those words rolled off my tongue, then I regretted saying them. Over the years, to assuage my guilt, I had convinced myself that Kathy's downfall wasn't my fault. I was merely an eyewitness to her undoing. I didn't force her into addiction. I didn't twist her thoughts and emotions into knots. She made those choices, and she had no right to use those bad choices to mess with my life. At least, that's how I saw it.

Vicky, apparently, saw it differently.

"I'm sorry," I said. "It's none of my business."

She didn't respond one way or the other; she just stared calmly into the night.

It had gotten dark enough that we could no longer see the river in front of us, although the lapping of its current filled the night air. At some point our shoulders had touched, and I could feel her leaning into me. The hairs on the back of my neck found a chill in the breeze, or maybe it was something else. Either way, I knew that the time had come to leave.

"It's getting late," I said

"Yeah, I should probably get you back to town."

We rode slowly back to Buckley, the Tiger tamed as we cruised down the smooth black highway. We cut through town on the way to my motel, and as we passed the Snipe's Nest, I spied Harley Redding standing outside of the bar talking to the same two guys he'd been sitting with earlier. Vicky had to have noticed him, although she didn't show it. But Harley noticed us. He nudged one of the guys and pointed. As we passed by he yelled out something. I couldn't make it out with the wind whistling past my ears.

CHAPTER 16

As I waited for Jeb to pick me up for our trip to Mankato, I sent a text to Lila—a text because I wasn't ready for the conversation that awaited us. I told her that I was *on my way to see Angel*, thus fulfilling the reason for my trip to Buckley. I ended the text by wishing her good luck on her studying, my way of letting her know that there was no need to respond. Cowardly, I know.

Jeb pulled into the lot just after eight a.m., driving a black Ford Explorer, his personal vehicle. We would have a little over an hour of driving, and I had made it my goal to use that time to impress Jeb. For one thing, other than Vicky Pyke, Jeb was the only other person in Buckley who seemed to want to talk to me. For another, I had an idea on how to draw Moody Lynch out of the woods, and I needed Jeb's help.

"Got you some coffee," he said as I climbed in.

I'd already downed a cup of coffee, but as far as I was concerned there was always room for more. I waited for the Explorer to bounce out of the rough motel parking lot before venturing my first sip.

"I made some calls yesterday," he said. "I thought you should know that I don't think you had any part in what happened to Toke."

"I appreciate that," I said. "I honestly didn't know the man was alive until I saw your press release—at which point he was dead."

"That's what your editor said."

"You called Allison?"

"I called a few people. I can't speak for the sheriff, but I crossed you off my list."

"Is Charlie Talbert still on your list?"

Jeb paused as if considering what to say before he answered. "This is Sheriff Kimball's show, not mine."

"But you think Charlie's a possible suspect?"

"Not as far as the sheriff is concerned."

"You're dancing," I said.

"Investigations are confidential, Joe. I'm not at liberty to discuss it."

"It's the fire, isn't it? The one that killed Charlie's business partner."

"How'd you know…" Jeb caught himself and pulled back. "Joe, there's stuff I can talk about and stuff I can't. You get my drift? People say that you're a guy to be trusted, but I can't go where you want me to go."

"People say I can be trusted?"

"Like I said, I checked you out." He looked at me sideways as if waiting for me to guess. Finally, he said, "I called the Minneapolis PD. They told me about what happened when you were in college."

"I thought those records were confidential."

"They're non-public—that's not the same. Besides, I'm a cop. I can get my hands on all kinds of secret stuff. That's quite the adventure you had. Hell, you're a hero."

"It sounds cooler than it was," I said.

"You brought down a serial killer."

"I almost got myself killed—my girlfriend too."

"But you solved a crime that was three decades old. That's impressive."

"I was an idiot. I was impulsive and lucky, that's all. My girl-friend, Lila, she should get the credit. She was the brains. My only contribution was to stumble through it without getting killed."

"And I hear that you got some reward money for...not get-ting killed?"

"Yeah. A hundred grand. I thought I was rich, but you'd be amazed how fast money drains away when you have college and law school tuitions to deal with. After all was said and done, we had to take out a loan to pay for Lila's third year."

"Well, the folks up in the Cities speak highly of you. I also hear that you're a pretty fair reporter."

"Fair? I'd say I'm better than fair."

"No, I mean *fair* in that you don't have an agenda. You keep confidences."

I thought about the lawsuit and my source, Penny. I was on the verge of losing my job because I was being "fair." I was keeping my word, and it had landed me in the middle of a defamation suit that made my stomach churn every time I thought about it. All I had to do was give her up and I'd be out of that jam. But I don't give up sources, and because of that, people—even cops—thought that I was a fair reporter.

"Yeah, I can keep a secret," I said. "So is the sheriff still looking at Moody to be Toke's killer?"

"Again—confidential."

"What if someone were able to get Moody to come out of hiding? Maybe get his statement? Would that help?"

"Someone like...you?"

"Exactly," I said.

"Yeah, that's not going to happen."

"Hear me out. I could help."

"You're a reporter."

"A fair-minded reporter. Don't forget that part."

"You're Toke's son."

"Maybe. That's not for sure until that DNA test comes back."

"Doesn't matter; it's a bad idea all around."

"Maybe, but I really think I can help."

"How?"

"Like you said, I'm a reporter—for the Associated Press. That carries some weight."

Jeb gave me a questioning glance. "What do you mean?"

"You want to find Moody Lynch, right?"

"Yeah."

"And from what I've heard, if Moody doesn't want to be found, you won't find him. Would you agree?"

"He knows how to hide, I'll give him that."

"He's hiding because he doesn't trust cops. He probably thinks Nathan Calder will set him up. I heard those two have issues."

"Issues?"

I could see that Jeb was testing me to see what I knew about Nathan's entanglement. So I obliged. "Moody caught Nathan Calder having sex with some woman from the Court Administrator's Office. Moody videotaped their tryst and sent a copy to Nathan's wife. How am I doing so far?"

"Not bad."

"And you expect Moody to just come waltzing into the Sheriff's Office and turn himself in to Calder? That'll never happen."

"We'll find him, one way or another—"

"Jeb, people sometimes call reporters because they want their stories in print as protection against bad cops. It's the old saying:

sunlight is the best disinfectant. They understand that if their story is out there for the public to read, there's less chance they'll be railroaded."

"We don't railroad people."

"But suppose there was a reporter in town, someone who could write Moody's story, someone with the clout of a major news organization behind him. Moody might be willing to talk to that reporter."

"You think Moody will talk to you?"

"Why not. What's he got to lose?"

"And if he contacts you? What then?"

"I get his version...and maybe I can convince him to turn himself in—to you, not Nathan."

"Just like that?"

"I said maybe. But if nothing else, I get him to talk, tell me what happened that night."

"You'll let us record it?"

"No. I won't set a trap. He has to know that I'm independent of you guys, or else he won't trust me—and I won't lie to him."

"You'll share what he tells you?"

"I'll make sure he knows it's on the record."

"So why are you telling me all this? If you're so independent, you don't need my permission."

"I need information. I need to get some of the detail of what happened that night, so that I can challenge him. I don't want Moody bullshitting me."

"You want me to share investigation details with you?"

"It's a simple bargain. I'll share if you share."

"Or I could just throw you in jail for interfering with an investigation."

"I know the law, Jeb. I have no obligation to say a word to you, and my silence won't be a crime. You have no grounds to arrest me as long as I'm not physically getting in your way. All I'm asking for are a few details so that *if* I have contact with Moody Lynch, I can ask the right questions—just a few basic facts to get the ball rolling."

"If he contacts you, you'll let me know?"

"If you share—I'll share. Just give me a thumbnail sketch of what went down."

Jeb paused to consider what I was leading him toward. Lines would need to be crossed, but they were insignificant compared to the possibility of bringing in a man wanted for murder—at least that's how I saw it.

After a minute or two of silent contemplation, Jeb looked me in the eye and said, "This goes no further than this car, okay?"

"I promise."

He fixed his gaze back on the highway and said, "We got a nine-one-one call that night. It came from the Hix place, but there was no one on the line. It was a cell phone, but we have the technology to track down cell phones now, especially the newer GPS kind. I was off duty when I heard the call on my scanner. I don't live all that far from the Hix place, so I was the first to arrive at the scene."

"You were driving this car?"

"Yeah."

"No dash camera?"

"Nathan was in his squad car, so he has footage."

"Can I see it?"

"I thought you just wanted some background?"

"Fine. What happened next?"

"There was a light on in the barn and also in the house. Because there was no voice on the other end of the nine-one-one call, I assumed a medical emergency of some kind, and I went to the house. I knocked, and when I got no answer, I went inside and searched until I found Angel in her bedroom. I tried to wake her, but she was unconscious."

"No one else around when you got there? Did you hear anything?"

"Not a thing. But I wasn't expecting to find a murder scene. I thought . . . I don't know what I thought, but I didn't think that."

"Did you go to the barn?"

"No. Angel's pulse was so light. She stopped breathing once, and I gave her mouth-to-mouth. It was like she was becoming too weak to live. Nathan arrived a few minutes after me. He went to the barn. He's the one who found Toke."

"How was Toke killed?"

Jeb agonized over that one a bit before answering. "I can't tell you everything, but if you get a chance to talk to Moody, it might be helpful to know that Toke was hit in the head. That's as much as I can say right now. If Moody killed Toke, he'll know that already."

I wanted to tell Jeb that his secret was out. Vicky had already told me most of what Jeb was now taking great pains to reveal. I guess she was right when she said that nothing stays a secret in Buckley. But I needed more from Jeb.

"Why is Moody on the top of your list?" I asked. "I know that he and Toke didn't get along, but if that's the only thing you got, then Moody's just one of many. As I hear it, just about everyone in the county hated Toke."

"Don't sell Toke short—it's not just Caspen County that hated him."

"That's my point, there has to be more than just bad blood."

"We have Angel's phone. She and Moody were texting that night. Angel told Moody that she was freaking out. She said that she needed him to come out to the farm. Moody agreed. They were going to meet in what Angel called 'their usual spot' at midnight. We think the usual spot was the horse barn, and the autopsy suggests that Toke was killed around midnight."

I thought about that scenario, but something didn't fit. "If Angel and Moody are meeting in the barn at midnight...why was she in bed with pills in her stomach?"

"We're not sure. Our working theory is that Toke saw the text messages and forbade Angel from going out to the barn. If Toke went out there to confront Moody, that might be how it all started. We won't know exactly what happened until we hear from Moody."

"Or until Angel wakes up."

"Maybe, but clonazepam tends to cause amnesia. When she wakes up, it's likely she won't remember much of anything. So you see why it's important that we talk to Moody. Maybe there's an explanation as to why this all happened."

"And that's where I come in."

"Joe, if Moody calls you, let us know. This isn't a joke."

"You'll be the first to know," I said.

CHAPTER 17

Jeb led me down the corridors of Immanuel–St.t Joseph's
Hospital, straight to the Intensive Care Unit, and when
we arrived at the nurse's station, Jeb said, "Hi, Jen," to a nurse
who wasn't wearing a name tag, which made me wonder how
many times he'd been there to visit Angel. Jeb told the nurse
that I was Angel's brother. She gave me a polite smile, and I
nodded my hello, and that was all it took to get me into Angel's
room. I probably could have managed that on my own.

The room smelled of bodily fluids and alcohol swabs, thinly
masked by disinfectant. Angel had a tube in her mouth, another
in her nostrils, and an IV in her arm. She had wires clipped to
her fingers and more disappearing under the collar of her gown.
A thin strip of tape held her eyelids closed, and her hair was
splayed out on the pillow in oily ribbons. She seemed too small
to be fourteen.

"Joe, meet Angel," Jeb said in a hushed tone.

I moved to the side of the bed. "Can she hear us?" I asked.

"Her ears work, so what we say is making it inside her head.
Whether her mind understands those sounds, they can't say."

I wanted to whisper something to Angel, but she was a stranger to me, as much my flesh and blood as Jeremy was—if my mother had it right—but a stranger nonetheless. She looked helpless and alone, her tiny figure tangled in the wires and tubes that kept her alive. I wanted to tell her that she had a brother, let her know that I was there for her. But I held my tongue and pondered how it was that blood carried such weight?

I turned and whispered to Jeb, "Is she...you know...brain dead?"

"No. She has activity in her brain. She can even open her eyes and move her arms sometimes. The doctors are hopeful that she'll pull out of it. But, Joe...if she does wake up, there's a good chance that she'll have problems."

"Problems?"

"Neurological and maybe physical. She'll need therapy. They can't say for sure right now, but that's usually the case."

A picture in a silver frame stood on a small table beside her bed. I recognized Jeannie in the photo, remembering her picture from the obituary. She stood between a child and an older man. The child was a girl of maybe four or five, whom I assumed was Angel—which meant that the older man was probably Jeannie's father, Arvin Hix. Curious as to when the picture was taken, I opened the back of the frame and looked. I didn't find a date, but someone had written an inscription on the back of the picture. I read it out loud, "My Bapu, my baby, and me."

"What?" Jeb asked.

"This picture." I showed it to Jeb. "My Bapu, my baby, and me. Is this Jeannie?" I pointed to the woman in the photo.

"Yes, that's her."

"She called her dad Bapu?"

"Yeah, but I'm not sure where that came from."

"Gandhi," I said.

"Gandhi?"

"Well, that's where I first heard it. You ever see the movie—the one with Ben Kingsley? Gandhi's followers sometimes referred to him as Bapu. I think it's a sign of fatherly respect."

"I suppose that makes sense."

"But I thought Jeannie didn't get along with her father?"

"Relationships can be complicated, Joe. Jeannie loved her dad, but he was a strict man. Maybe *strict* isn't the right word. He had a temper, and when it came to Jeannie, he seemed almost . . . well, I guess greedy, like he needed to control every aspect of her life. Back when Jeannie and I were dating, I—"

"Wait. You and Jeannie dated?"

"Yeah. I guess you could say that she was my high-school sweetheart. It ended when I left for basic training. Back then, her old man was quite the ballbuster. Did his best to keep her in line, but all it did was make her more rebellious. I suppose that's about the time things started falling apart for them."

"But she still called him Bapu."

"He was her father, always would be. She wrote about it when . . ." Jeb looked at Angel and held back what he was about to say. He nodded toward the door. "Let's go grab some coffee."

Once we were in the corridor and walking, he said, "Jeannie wrote about her father in her suicide note. Hix died of a heart attack last year. In the end, he and Jeannie weren't talking to each other. They hadn't spoken in quite a while. That was mostly on Hix though. He hated Toke Talbert with a passion like nothing I'd ever seen before. He did everything he could to get Jeannie out of that marriage. When she stood her ground, they just stopped talking."

"You think she stood her ground because she really loved Toke?"

"Honestly? I think if Hix had stayed out of it, Jeannie would have eventually found the courage to leave Toke. Jeannie had traded one controlling man for another. Toke was as big of an ass as they come, Joe, but he had that bad-boy quality about him. I think Jeannie thought that if she could scrub hard enough, she'd find what she was looking for somewhere deep down."

We came to a sitting area with no coffee, where we took seats across from each other, separated by a small table with children's coloring books and magazines spread across it.

"So what did she write in her suicide note?" I asked.

"She said she couldn't live with the guilt of how things ended with her father. Hix always said that she was cut out of his will, but when he died, it turned out that he never made a will. It was all a bluff. Her note said that when she realized that Hix loved her that whole time, she lost it."

"She killed herself out of guilt?"

"Doesn't make sense does it?"

"Where'd you find the note?"

"It was on her computer."

"On her computer?" I didn't even try to hide my incredulity.

"I know what you're thinking, and I thought the same thing. No handwritten note. No signature. She kills herself just a few months after inheriting millions, which, by the way, also made Toke a millionaire. It all sounds fishy."

"You investigated?"

"We did. Toke had an alibi."

"A good one?"

"Video footage. After Jeannie inherited the farm, Toke quit his job at Dub's Repair. But then he bought himself a car, an old nineteen seventy GTO. On the evening that Jeannie died, he was at the shop working on that car. The shop has two surveillance cameras. We had exterior footage of him walking into Dub's. And then they had an interior camera aimed at the office door, where they keep vehicle keys and cash. You can't see Toke on that footage because he was working in a bay on the other side of the shop, but you can see shadows and movement cast off by the light where he's working."

I leaned back in my chair to study Jeb's face. His words sounded sincere, or at least matter-of-fact, but I could see the doubt behind his eyes. "You think Toke killed Jeannie, don't you?"

"I think Toke Talbert was a dog," he said. "I think he looked at Jeannie and saw nothing but money, a big payday if he could keep the marriage together long enough. And...I think that if Toke did anything to Jeannie, we'll never know."

"And what about Angel?"

"What about her?"

"Why would she take those clonazepam? What happened that night?"

Jeb dropped his eyes to the table and twisted his wedding band around on his finger. "That's my fault," he said.

"How do you figure?"

"The day Toke died, Angel came by the office. I was there and we had a little chat. She wanted a copy of Jeannie's suicide note. We had a copy of it in a file that we opened up after Jeannie's death. I didn't think it was a good idea to give it to her. You're not a dad, are you, Joe?"

"I'm not," I said, though I couldn't help thinking of Jeremy.

"I got two girls. That's what came to my mind when Angel wanted to have a copy of her mother's note. I didn't know what to do. I mean, Angel had the right to see what her mother left behind. I had no lawful reason to keep it from her, but I asked myself: if I were her father, would this be the right thing to do? Would I want my daughters to read their mother's last words? In the end, I thought she had a right to have it, so I gave it to her. I wish I hadn't."

"You think her reading that note led her to attempt suicide?" I said.

"That picture—the one beside her bed—I found that under her pillow when I was trying to keep her alive that night. I also found Jeannie's suicide note under that same pillow. So, yeah, I think that note pushed her over the edge. That's my best guess. Otherwise, why would she have them tucked away together?"

Chapter 18

We got back to Buckley before noon, the town seemingly down for a nap. When Jeb dropped me off in the motel parking lot, I noticed Charlie's Lexus parked two spots down from my door. As Jeb pulled away, I scanned the windows and saw a curtain jiggle shut in the room next to mine. Uncle Charlie and I were neighbors.

I had turned my phone off before we left for Mankato to visit Angel, so as I walked into my room, I turned my phone on to check for messages. I had one missed call from a number and area code that I didn't recognize. That person left a message, and I played it.

Hi. This is Joette Breck. I have some questions about the story you wrote on Senator Dobbins. Could you call me back please?

And there it was again, that bubble of nausea that roiled my gut every time that goddamned lawsuit came to mind. I knew that my entanglement continued to live and breathe regardless of whether I gave it a thought—a monster lurking just beyond the corners of my concentration—but like a child with his hands over his eyes, a part of me wanted to believe that it would disappear if I could only keep it from the front of my mind. If nothing else,

I might not feel sick all the time. I looked at the number that Ms. Breck left, took a couple breaths to calm my stomach, and returned her call.

"Ms. Breck?"

"Yes."

"This is Joe Talbert."

"Hello, Joe. Thanks for calling back. I have a few questions about the story you ran on the senator. First of all, you should know that as your attorney, anything you tell me remains confidential. You understand?"

"I do."

I could hear Ms. Breck flipping through some pages, probably finding a good starting point for our discussion. After a few seconds, she continued. "Joe, according to the complaint, Senator Dobbins asserts that you made up all of the facts in your story. I guess we should start there. Did you make up any facts?"

"No. I didn't. Everything in that article came from a reliable source."

"And who is that source?"

"I can't tell you that. The source has to remain anonymous. That's the deal."

"I understand," she said. "But remember, anything you say will be confidential."

"Why do you need her name? I gave everything to Allison Cress, my editor. She knows who the source is. She approved the story."

"Allison's not your attorney, Joe. I need to know all the facts in order to help you—the good and the bad."

"I don't feel comfortable about this. I gave my word. I told my source that no one other than Allison and me would know her identity."

I thought of my source and the night I met with her, how she cried as she told me her story. We sat in my car on the top floor of the Mall of America parking ramp. It was a slow shopping day, so we had the floor mostly to ourselves, and a light rain further hid us from prying eyes. Her name was Penny, and we knew each other from our days in journalism school at the University of Minnesota. I didn't know her all that well, but well enough to know that she was bright and funny and married.

She told me that after college she had gotten a job with a public relations firm and parlayed that into a position as a communications director for a state senator by the name of Todd Dobbins. And then, through a torrent of tears, she said, "I messed up, Joe. I messed up bad."

I handed her a tissue from my console and turned in my seat to face her. She kept her eyes forward, fixed on the rain dotting my windshield. I wanted to say something comforting, but I had no idea what she had done. Besides, people opened up best when you gave them a silence to fill, so I waited.

"I had an affair, Joe. I don't know why. I love my husband— you remember Mike, don't you?"

I didn't, although I was certain we had been introduced at some point. I nodded and said, "Yeah."

"I love Mike. He's a great guy. But there was something about Todd that . . . I don't know."

"Todd Dobbins? The senator you work for?"

"I quit this morning."

I could see where this was going, so I asked, "What happened that made you quit?"

"We were . . . we've been having an affair for about six months now, and last night . . . " Penny started to lose it again but closed her eyes and took in some deep breaths to calm down. "Last night we were at his house. His wife was supposed to be gone. She told Todd that she was going to South Dakota to see her mother. And...well...I went to Todd's house. He made a candlelit dinner."

Penny looked away from me, her forehead resting against the passenger window, the glass laced with rivulets of rain. "I don't know why I did it, Joe. I swear I don't know why. I love Mike. We have a beautiful son. I don't want this to ruin my marriage. You have to promise me that my name is never used. Promise me."

"I promise. I won't run any story unless I can do it without using your name."

"I'm trusting you on this, Joe. I have to tell someone what happened. He can't get away with what he did."

"What did he do, Penny?"

"Todd's wife came home. She walked in on us...you know. Joe, it was ugly. Todd started screaming at his wife like this was somehow all her fault. I gathered my stuff, but I couldn't get out of the room. They were in my way. I was scared. She was yelling at him and she was yelling at me."

"Did she try to hurt you?"

"No. That's the thing. She was yelling, but she was heartbroken, not angry. And Todd kept getting in her face. I just wanted to leave. And that's when things got out of control."

"What happened?"

Penny turned in her seat to face me, her eyes red and puffy from crying, but the tears were gone. "Todd called her some terrible names, and she spit on him. And then—it happened so fast it was like a blur—he punched her, hit her in the face as hard as he could. She dropped to the floor, and I thought he might have killed her. I'd never seen a man with that much rage. It was like he forgot that I was even there. I ran past them and left."

I shook away the memory of my meeting with Penny and turned back to my conversation with Ms. Breck, weighing the promise I made to Penny against the juggernaut of problems heading my way. I didn't want to break my word, but Ms. Breck needed to know about Penny. She needed to know that the story was true. "If I tell you who my source is and what she said, that will stay between us?"

Ms. Breck paused and then said, "I won't give out that information without your permission."

"I have your word on that?"

"Yes, Joe. You have my word."

With that assurance, I told Joette Breck about the night when State Senator Todd Dobbins hit his wife in the face hard enough to send her to the hospital.

"I have copies of the text messages between Dobbins and Penny showing that he invited her to his house that night. I have the nine-one-one tape where Dobbins called for an ambulance. I have the police reports confirming the injury. These back up what Penny told me happened."

"Except, in the nine-one-one call and the police reports say that Dobbins' wife fell down the stairs."

"Of course he's going to say that to the police. Dobbins isn't going to admit that he smashed his wife's face in. The facts line up. They prove that Penny was there that night."

The phone went silent, and I assumed that Ms. Breck was letting the pieces fall into place. The story I wrote was true.

"He's rolling the dice," she said.

"Excuse me?"

"This defamation suit—it's all a huge gamble. Dobbins' career is already shot. Your story killed him, politically. If he has any aspirations of climbing back up that ladder, he needs to reverse this story, turn it around. If he can make this about media lies and fake news, he can rally around it. But that strategy relies on you not being able to prove the truth of your story. It relies on you not revealing the identity of your source. He's gambling that Penny won't come out of the shadows. If she doesn't, he may well get his retraction."

"I won't give up my source," I said.

"I understand, Joe, but that paints us into a corner. It's your word against his word—and his wife's word. Remember, she's backing up his version. As far as the rest of the world is concerned, those two were the only two people in the room. Without Penny, we have nothing."

I didn't answer. I wasn't going to give up Penny, that was all there was to it. I thought back to that night in the rain, how she stared out at some thought, far away, and said, "Mrs. Dobbins didn't deserve what Todd did to her. No one deserves that. I can't let him get away with what he did."

Then, as if Penny saw hypocrisy in her words—seeing the harm Todd had inflicted upon his wife without seeing the harm that she had caused, Penny added, "I know that what I did was wrong. I'm doing my best now to right it. That's why I'm talking to you. But I don't want to lose my family over this. I can't lose them over this."

It was Ms. Breck who spoke next. "Allison Cress mentioned that you've taken a couple days off."

"Yeah, I ... had a death in the family."

"Joe, you should know that there's a raging debate about what to do with you—and with Allison. They haven't decided yet. You might want to think about taking a leave of absence for a while."

"Why?"

"Look at this from their point of view. If you're out of the office and not writing stories ... well ..."

"If I'm not in the office to mess things up, they might not need to fire me?"

"I wouldn't put it in those terms, but, yeah, it might cool the situation down a bit."

I'd been pacing around my room as I talked to Ms. Breck, but her suggestion that I was on the bubble over losing my job turned the bones in my knees to jelly, and I had to sit down. "How long are we talking?"

"I don't know," she said.

I felt queasy again. "I'll talk to Allison."

After I ended my call with Ms. Breck, I flopped backward onto the bed. A leave of absence; there goes my paycheck. And for how long? After the bar exam, Lila would go back to work, but could we get by on what little she made? What if she didn't pass the bar, and what if my leave turned permanent? I didn't want to call Allison, but Ms. Breck seemed to think it might help me save my job in the long run. Who knows, maybe Allison would put the kibosh on the whole idea. I sent her a text:

I'm thinking about taking a leave of absence. Your thoughts?

I spent the next ten minutes staring at my phone, waiting for a reply. Then it came:

That might be for the best.

CHAPTER 19

How was I going to explain to Lila that I no longer had a job? I wasn't fired, but I also wasn't going to bring home a paycheck for a while. Should I even tell her? She was under enough pressure to pass the bar exam. This was bad.

I lay on my bed in that crappy motel, thoughts of my professional demise floating around my head, when a new thought suddenly emerged, an image of Vicky Pyke gesturing out to a sea of green and saying, "This is your farm." Was that possible? Could it be that I was wallowing in that darkest hour that came before the proverbial dawn?

Jeb had mentioned an attorney in town—Mullen—who could tell me about the Hix estate. The time had come to pay Mr. Mullen a visit to see what lay behind door number two. Whatever it might be, it had to be better than the shitstorm swirling behind door number one. I looked up Mullen's address on my phone—only a few blocks from the motel. It seemed like everything in Buckley was only a few blocks from everything else.

Mullen's office, a small box made of yellow brick, had tiny windows that lay hidden behind a row of overgrown shrubs. It was the kind of place that would go unnoticed unless you were looking for it. I walked past it on my first trip down the street and had to look twice before I saw the small sign on the door that read LAW OFFICE. The structure did not instill confidence.

I checked the doorknob and found it locked. I knocked and waited. I was about to knock again when I saw a Post-it that had fallen to the ground. It read: *If you need me, call me.* Below that it gave a number.

I called.

"Hello?" a deep voice answered.

"Hello. I'm trying to reach Bob Mullen, the attorney."

"You reached him. What can I do for you?"

"I was hoping to make an appointment or talk to you. My name is Joe Talbert."

There was silence on the other end.

"Hello?" I said.

"Joe Talbert? As in . . ."

"As in the son of Toke Talbert. I was told to come see you. I'm at your office."

"I'll be right there." He hung up without saying goodbye.

A noise from across the street drew my attention to an old Victorian house that stood on a large corner lot, its siding painted the blueish-green color of oxidized copper. I hadn't taken stock of all the houses in Buckley, but from what I had seen, that house was probably the nicest in town. I heard the noise again—the creak of a door—and I saw a man exiting the house. He was older, maybe seventy or so, with a bald head and a full beard. He carried a sandwich in one hand and a bottle of water in the other.

He made his way down his front walk, his eyes on me, his gait slow and careful, as if he had bad knees or a rusted hip. He transferred his sandwich to his hand with the water bottle so that he could avail himself of the handrail as he descended the steps to the street level. At the bottom of the steps, he paused to catch his breath. Then he crossed the street, heading to his law office.

"Mr. Mullen?" I asked.

"None other." He pulled out a key and unlocked the door. "Come in."

The inside of his office was no nicer than the outside: paneled walls filled with faded pictures, brown carpeting worn thin by foot traffic, and dingy ceiling tiles that sagged with age. The office had a small, unmanned reception area where a metal desk, something he probably purchased at a school auction, sat barren except for a computer monitor. Beyond the reception area, another office opened up, a larger office with a handsome wooden desk, stacked full of papers, and four metal cabinets lining one of the walls.

I waited in the reception area as Mr. Mullen cleared files off the top of his desk. As I waited, I walked to one of the pictures on the wall, an old photo of Anwar Sadat, the former president of Egypt shaking hands with President Jimmy Carter. The two men were talking casually, while a cadre of other men smiled and chatted in the background. I wondered why this photo rated a place on the wall of this small-town lawyer—then I saw it. One of the men in the background bore a striking resemblance to Mr. Mullen. I looked at the attorney and back at the picture.

"Is this you?" I said, pointing.

"Huh? Oh, yeah, that's me." Mullen looked over his shoulder as he slid papers into one of the file cabinets.

I went to another picture and saw him in the background of a handshake between India's prime minister, Indira Gandhi, and a man whom I believed was Cyrus Vance, the former secretary of state. I walked around the reception area looking at picture after picture spanning the late seventies to the early nineties, dignitaries and heads of state posing for photos, and there, in the background of each, was Bob Mullen.

He put the last of his files away and invited me into his office.

"Those are some great pictures, Mr. Mullen."

"My wife put those up. And please call me Bob." He pointed to a chair and we both sat down.

"Were you in the State Department?"

"Up until the second Clinton term, when I retired."

"That's amazing," I said.

"It sounds more impressive than it was." He moved off the subject. "So tell me again— your name is Joe Talbert?"

I settled in and told Bob the story of my birth, at least what little I knew. Bob was a patient listener, keeping his eyes on me for most of the story, glancing away only when he seemed in need of a mental picture—like when I told him about Toke punching my mom.

"You never met Toke?" he said after I had finished.

"Never."

"And you never met Jeannie?"

"No."

He pointed behind me to a picture on the wall of his office; I recognized Jeannie. Bob stood next to her, and on the other side of Jeannie, a woman, older with silver hair and a genuine smile, had her arm around Jeannie.

"That's her with me and my wife. Jeannie worked for me as my . . . well, she was my right arm, for lack of a better term. It broke my heart what happened to her."

"I'm sorry," I said.

"You know about Angel?"

"I went to visit her this morning," I said.

"Any improvement?"

"I don't think so."

Bob let out a heavy sigh. "It's a goddamned shame what hap-pened to that family. A tragedy. And here you come to add more drama to the mix."

"I didn't come here to add drama," I said. "A man who might be my father was killed, and I wanted to look into the matter. I had no idea about Jeannie or Angel. I never expected to find any-thing beyond some loser holed up in a run-down trailer, living off odd jobs. It wasn't my idea to come see you, but Jeb Lewis thought you should know about me. That's the only reason I'm here."

Bob stroked his beard and nodded. "I suppose that's the case. I'm sorry for...well, being the old curmudgeon that I am. Jeannie and Angel were like family."

"And not Toke?"

"No. Not Toke. No offense, but Toke was a jerk."

"I've been hearing that, and I keep asking why Jeannie stayed with him if he was such a jerk."

"That's a good question. Personally, I think it started out as a screw-you to her father. Jeannie was a strong-willed girl, but she also had some deep insecurities. Then, after Angel was born and the whole custody battle—"

"Custody battle?"

"Yes. Hix brought an action to have Jeannie declared an unfit mother—because she stayed married to Toke, who was unques-tionably an unfit father. Hix wanted to convince a judge that the mere fact of Jeannie living with Toke put Angel's life in danger. Probably true, but try convincing a judge to take a little girl away from her mother. I tried to talk Hix out of it, but he felt he had no choice. He was desperate to get Toke out of Jeannie's life."

"Were you her attorney?"

"No, I stayed out of that one. Hix hired some big name firm up in the Twin Cities. Jeannie managed to afford a local gal from over in Jackson. It got real ugly. When Hix lost that fight, well, that was the end of his relationship with Jeannie. I don't think they ever spoke again."

"Kind of sounds like Hix got what he deserved."

"What do you mean?"

"Hix tried to take Angel away from her mother. On top of that, I heard that Hix told Jeannie that he was cutting her out of his will, hoping that might break up her marriage. Hix comes across looking like a bit of a jerk too."

Several seconds passed as Bob thought this over, as if I had just presented Hix to him in a new light. Then he said, "But he didn't though."

"He didn't what?"

"He didn't cut her out of the will. He may have threatened it, but he couldn't do that to his daughter."

"True, but...how could someone even threaten that with their own daughter?"

"What Hix did, he did with the best of intentions. Deep down, he was a good man. Let me tell you a story about Arvin Hix. After the last recession, one of Hix's neighbors, a guy named Ray Pyke, was going through a bad time. The man needed money, and Hix came up with a way to help Ray out without hurting the man's pride. Hix offered to buy an option on Ray's land. Do you know what an option contract is, Joe?"

"Vaguely," I said.

"Well, Hix paid Ray twenty grand to option nearly one hundred acres. By giving Ray that money, he locked in a price on the land, and Hix had ten years to execute the contract. But the thing is, Hix never intended to execute. He was always going to let the contract expire. That way, he could give a gift of money to Ray Pyke without Ray ever knowing that it was an act of charity."

"I shouldn't have said that about Hix," I said. "It's none of my business."

Mullen shrugged. "It might be more your business than you think. After Jeannie died, and the property passed to Toke, he sent Ray Pyke a notice of his intent to execute that option. That's the first step in the process. Now that you may be in line to inherit that estate, Ray's land could become yours—as if that farm wasn't big enough already."

"How big is it?"

"Before you add on the Pyke section, it's just over seven hundred fifty acres. Prime farmland. Do you know how much good farmland is worth?"

"I don't have a clue."

"It fluctuates, but a conservative number would be around seventy-five hundred dollars per acre."

The digits tangled in my head as I tried to do the math. I gave up when the number grew too large. Bob did the math for me. "Just the land alone will be north of five million, probably closer to six. Add to that the house and some barns and equipment."

I couldn't speak.

"Of course, if you are Toke's son, you'd be splitting that with Angel."

"Of course," I said, trying to sound calm and disinterested. He started explaining the probate process, and his words fell behind a wall of numbers and noise in my head. Six million dollars. Half of six is three. Three million dollars. Three million friggin' dollars! Holy crap, I'm a millionaire—a multimillionaire! And Bob said he was being conservative. I tried to imagine that much money.

"...and when we get that proof, the next step is to—"

"I'm sorry," I said, as the word *proof* pulled my attention back to the conversation. "What do you mean by proof?"

"Well, Joe, I'm sure you understand—I'll need more than just your story to declare you an heir. It's just a formality, but there will need to be a DNA test."

"Already did one," I said.

"You did?"

"Yeah, Sheriff Kimball took a sample of my DNA when I first got here. They thought I might be a suspect in Toke's death. If I'm his son, that gives me motive and all."

Bob leaned back in his seat, his forehead wrinkling up. "I can see the sheriff's point," Bob said. "And you should know that Minnesota has a law—the slayer statute—that says that if you had any part in killing someone, you cannot inherit from them."

"For Pete's sake, I didn't kill Toke."

"I'm not saying you did. I'm just saying that there may be issues in probating the estate. Those questions have to be resolved. If there's any question, nothing can be done. I've seen cases like this stay open for years waiting to see if the crime gets solved. Let's hope that doesn't happen here."

"Have you met Toke's brother, Charlie, yet?"

"Charlie." Bob nearly spat the name to the floor. "He came here wanting me to file a petition for guardianship of Angel. I told him to get the hell out of my office."

"You don't like Charlie?" I asked.

"Jeannie didn't like Charlie. She said that he wouldn't have anything to do with her and Toke. Never came to visit. Never met Angel. But when Hix died, suddenly Charlie was at their door, all smiles and bullshit, wanting to borrow money against Jeannie's estate. When that didn't work, he tried to get Toke to go into business with him. Jeannie didn't tell me all the details, but it sounded shady. She convinced Toke to say no. It wasn't long after that that she . . . well, passed on."

"Did you ever look into Charlie?"

"Nothing more than a cursory search. Why?"

"There's something wrong about him. I'm not sure, but I think it has to do with a fire some years back. Charlie's business burned down, along with his business partner."

"You think it might have been arson?"

"I don't have anything concrete, but when I was talking to Deputy Lewis yesterday, I got the feeling that there was something there."

Mullen looked up at one of the photos on his wall. "You know, I still have some contacts in the FBI. I could see if they can dig up anything. I got to tell you, Joe, the thought of Charlie getting Angel breaks my heart. That's the last person Jeannie would have wanted looking after her little girl. The man just wants her money; I'm sure of it. He'll be able to syphon quite a bit of her inheritance away before she turns eighteen."

"What about social services or a foster home?"

"The courts tend to place children with relatives. Charlie has the pole position in that race." As Bob looked at me, the sadness behind his eyes lifted away. "But if there were another relative . . . like—say—a brother."

"No," I said quickly. "I have an autistic brother, and I'm his guardian already. I couldn't possibly take on another sibling." My phone jingled, and I apologized to Bob as I pulled it from my pocket. It was Lila. I let it go to voice mail. I'd call her back when I finished with Attorney Mullen.

"Really? You've been through a guardianship process?"

"Yes, and it was not pretty. My mother and I haven't spoken since."

"You have a job?"

"I'm a reporter for the Associated Press."

"Married?"

"Girlfriend."

"You'd have a good shot at knocking Charlie out of the running."

"I'm sorry, Bob. I can't do it. I don't even know Angel."

"Just think about it. That's all I ask."

My phone buzzed again, indicating a text message. "Excuse me," I said. "I need to check this." I looked at the message. It was from Lila. I clicked on it.

Jeremy's been hurt. I need you to come home right away.

I looked up at Bob. "I'm sorry, but I have to go."

CHAPTER 20

I left St. Paul yesterday morning pushed by a tailwind—a tempest—that hurled me south and west and into the heart of farm country. I felt pulled there by thoughts of my father and at the same time driven there by the hope that a change of scenery would undo some of the problems at my back. But since arriving in Buckley, I had managed to make things worse. I had hung up on Lila and took a leave of absence from my job. These developments weighed on me now as I headed back to St. Paul.

Yet, despite the tempest, I couldn't help singing along to almost every song that played on the radio. I smiled and tapped my thumbs on the steering wheel, unable to get my conversation with Bob Mullen out of my head. I might be in line to collect three million dollars, and that, I thought, would go a long way to smoothing down all those rough patches.

I walked into the apartment to find Jeremy sitting on the couch, alone, the door to our bedroom shut, where I assumed I would find Lila sitting in the middle of her books. Jeremy had an ace bandage wrapped around his left wrist, and he held that arm tightly against his stomach. He was reading a book that lay open on his lap, using the fingers on his right hand to press the pages down.

"Hey, buddy," I said quietly, not wanting to summon Lila from the bedroom just yet. I sat down beside Jeremy and looked at his arm. "Does it hurt?"

"I think it does," he said. "Maybe I sprained it."

"How'd that happen?"

Jeremy turned his eyes back to his book, *Dumbo*, and didn't answer my question. I didn't push it, knowing that I would hear the full story from Lila.

"What's your book about?" I asked.

"Maybe they locked Mrs. Jumbo up in the prison wagon," he said.

I looked at the book and saw the picture of the mother elephant and baby Dumbo reaching out to touch their trunks together through a barred window, a big tear sliding down the cheek of the little elephant. I looked at Jeremy's expressionless eyes and wondered how much of the story remained after he turned each page. He rarely spoke of the past, and when he did, those memories seemed blissfully void of any emotion. He talked about the night of the big fight—the night that I kicked Larry in the knee, but he never hinted that he felt one way or another about leaving our mother's apartment— his home. And, I guess, I never asked.

"Is Lila in the bedroom?"

"Maybe she is in your room," he said.

"I'll be back in a bit." I stood and walked to the bedroom, knocking lightly before I entered.

Lila floated in a sea of papers and books, a lone survivor battered by the debris of a sinking ship. "How goes the study-ing?" I asked, ignoring all of the harsh words that had passed between us.

Lila also seemed willing to overlook our recent trouble and said, "I can't think straight. I read words and try to pound them into my head, and an hour later I can't remember a thing." She put her book down.

"You worry too much. Try to relax. You'll do fine."

"Telling me to relax does not help me relax." There was a sharpness in her tone that told me to move on.

"What happened to Jeremy's arm?" I asked.

"He fell," she said. "According to Bruce, he was mopping the floor, and he slipped down some stairs."

"Bruce," I said half under my breath. Jeremy's coach was supposed to prevent things like this from happening, shepherd him through processes, and watch over him. "Where was Bruce when Jeremy fell?" I asked.

"I don't know. He called at about ten this morning and said that he found Jeremy at the bottom of some stairs. I had to go to the school and take Jeremy to the hospital. It's only a sprain, but Joe, we spent three hours in Urgent Care. I feel like I've been gone all day." She pointed at her books. "The bar exam's in four days. I need every minute I can spare on this. I don't have time . . ."

"I know," I said absently. "It'll be okay."

"No, Joe. It won't be okay. Jeremy can't go to work until his arm heals. Are you going to stay here with him? I need to study. I'm freaking out. I can't screw up this test. I can't."

I leaned toward Lila and put my hand on her knee. "You don't have to stress out," I said, with a stupid grin on my face. "We are going to be millionaires."

"I'm being serious here, Joe."

"So am I," I said. "My father was rich—sort of."

I moved some books out of the way so that I could face her as I told her the story of Toke and Jeannie and the tangled thread of

how seven hundred and fifty acres of farmland was about to become mine—or at least half mine. I ended with a flourish sure to
wow her. "The attorney told me that my share is worth...three
million dollars."

Lila looked stunned and a bit confused. Swept up in the
excitement of the moment, I foolishly continued. "All that pressure you've been putting on yourself—to pass the bar—you don't
have to worry about that now."

She looked at me as if she couldn't believe the words that had
just come out of my mouth. "You understand that my taking the
bar—becoming an attorney—has never been about the money."

"I know," I said. "I'm just saying that you don't have to have
all that pressure."

"And you don't have any of this money yet. God knows when
you'll see it, or if you'll see it at all." Lila paused to take a breath.
"Joe, I'm happy, I really am. If this money exists, it'll be great.
But it's not your money yet. Too many things can go wrong."

"As I see it, the only thing that can go wrong is that my
mother got pregnant by someone else and blamed Toke Talbert."

"And is it all that far-fetched?"

"All my life she's been telling me that I'm the bastard son of a
no-good son of a bitch named Joe Talbert. Why would she make
that up?"

"I'm not saying that she made it up. I'm saying that until everything is signed, sealed, and delivered, that money is a bird in the
bush."

"Three million birds," I said, again with the grin.

That made her smile. "I'm glad you're home," she said, laying
her hand on mine. "I really need help with Jeremy. I didn't get
any studying done today."

"Yeah, about that..."

"What?" She let go of my hand.

"I need to go back to Buckley."

"Jeremy has to stay home until his wrist heals," she said. "You need to stay here and take care of him."

"I can take him with me." The words shot out of my mouth as if that had been my plan all along. I hadn't thought it through, but ran with it anyway. "I can take him to Buckley for a couple days and—"

"A couple days? What about your job. What's Allison going to say?"

"Yeah, that's another thing; I'm kind of unemployed right now."

Lila's eyes went wide. "They fired you?"

"No, but they strongly encouraged me to take some time off— a leave of absence. My attorney said that they were on the fence about firing me, and this might take some of the heat off."

"Oh, Joe." Lila looked stunned.

"It's just until this thing with Senator Dobbins gets resolved."

"That could take months."

"But I don't need that job—not if I'm Toke's son. Don't you see?"

"And what do we live on in the meantime? We're barely scraping by."

"That's why I need to go back to Buckley. I can help with the investigation. The sooner Toke's murder gets solved, the sooner they can probate the estate."

"Don't they have professionals who investigate crimes down there? How can you help?"

"The sheriff is convinced that this kid named Moody Lynch killed Toke. I think I can get Moody to turn himself in, or at least give me a statement. I'm a reporter. People love talking to reporters. If I can flush this kid out of hiding, the case might get solved faster."

"Jeremy won't do well in a motel room. You know that. Don't take him down there. It's a bad idea."

"No, it's a great idea. You'll have a couple days to study in peace. I'll get to hang out with my brother, and Jeremy won't have to go to work. It's a win–win–win."

"Just think about it before you take him down there. Sleep on it, and if you still want to take your brother to Buckley, I won't stop you."

"I'll sleep on it," I said. "But it'll be okay, I swear."

Lila simply shook her head.

Chapter 21

That night I made spaghetti, and it brought me back to the first meal that the three of us ever shared, back when I was turning cartwheels to get Lila to notice me. She was my neighbor back then, and the source of most of my distracted thoughts. I'd done my best to open a door into her world, but my efforts went largely ignored. It wasn't until Jeremy came to stay with me for a few days that I was able to persuade Lila to join us for a spaghetti dinner. I've never told her this, but sometimes I made spaghetti for dinner just to relive a small piece of that night. Back then, I wanted nothing more than to have Lila in my life—if only for a meal. Over the years, that memory had grown distant and small, but I still made spaghetti; I still longed to go back to that place.

Lila remained in our bedroom, studying, as I made supper. When she came out, we ate in near silence, Lila going through flash cards and mumbling her mnemonics, Jeremy focusing on eating the spaghetti without dripping sauce on his shirt, and me watching the two of them, wondering whether we'd make it through the summer. Money had always been tight, but now I had no job and the line between success and failure for our little family seemed as thin as piano wire. To calm my blood pressure, I thought about the money just beyond my reach. That would be our saving grace, I was sure of it. That's why I had to go to Buckley.

After dinner, I packed clothing and toiletries for Jeremy, being careful not to make a big deal out of it. I didn't want to reopen the issue with Lila, and Jeremy didn't need to know about the upheaval coming in the morning. I made sure to pack movies that I could play on my computer, something to keep him preoccupied so I could get some work done. I also had him choose a couple books to read on the drive. He chose his two favorites, *Dumbo* and *Bambi*.

About the time the sun set, I guided Jeremy through his bedtime routine and saw him to bed. I peeked in on Lila, who was deep in her own head, memorizing terms and cases, so I went to the couch to watch television. I normally watched news programs, but that night, I turned to the Travel Channel. I had never watched the Travel Channel before because—well, why would I? It would be like a starving refugee flipping through pictures in a cookbook.

As I sat there watching a show about Norwegian fjords, it dawned on me that in the six years that Lila and I had been together, we had never gone on a trip, at least nothing that required booking an overnight stay. We didn't think that Jeremy would do well in a hotel. Jeremy was my brother and a big part of my life, but there were times when he seemed to block out the sun. For his sake, our vacations, if you want to call them that, consisted of going to local parks and attractions.

I remember our first such trip together was to Minnehaha Falls, back when Lila and I still lived apart. Jeremy had never seen a waterfall before; for that matter, neither had I. I think I found it more impressive than he did, because he looked at the falls like it was just another picture in a book.

For my part though, I wandered down to a cave behind the waterfall, leaving Jeremy with Lila while I moved in close enough to feel the power of the falls—the concussion of air hitting my chest, the spray of water in my eyes, the smell of mud and moss filling my nostrils. All I could hear was the violence of the water slamming into the pool below, pounding it so hard that no other sound could get through.

When I came back to the path where Lila and Jeremy waited for me, Lila had a black-eyed-Susan in her hand. "Look what your brother gave me," she said.

"Are you trying to steal my girl?" I joked.

"No," Jeremy said, utterly serious. "Maybe Lila said she loves *you*."

It was an innocent comment, Jeremy's way of disproving that he was trying to steal my girlfriend, but at the same time, his words were huge. Lila had never told me that she loved me before.

"Jeremy?" Lila said, her voice lifting with embarrassment. "That was supposed to be our secret."

"Oh," Jeremy said.

I had told Lila that I loved her, maybe four or five times by that point in our relationship, without ever getting those words in reply. Lila and I became a couple when I persuaded her to help me with an English assignment, an interview with a dying man that brushed the dirt off of a cold-case murder and nearly got us both killed. Because our relationship had been forged in that crucible, we never really discussed the merits of our love story. We came together, we fit, and we didn't question it. I always believed that she loved me, but I had just about given up on hearing those words.

"You love me?" I asked.

Lila handed me the black-eyed Susan and said, "Of course I do."

That was how Lila Nash told me that she loved me for the first time. She had always been very guarded that way, protective of the deep wounds left behind by a tragic childhood. She kept much of that past to herself, but every now and again, she would let a thought slip, a hint of what had happened to her, and I began to see figures and shadows but never the full details of her nightmare—until one night when she told me what happened.

We were in bed, watching a movie about a girl who had been molested. I was barely paying attention, but at one point, I looked at Lila and saw a tear etching its way down her cheek. I asked her what was wrong. At first she stayed silent, and I thought this would be like all the times before, when we would reach the edge of the summit only to turn around and walk back down the mountain. But this time she talked.

She told me about an uncle and his horses. She loved his horses, especially a mare named Elle, and Uncle Gary would let her ride Elle all on her own, despite her mother having forbidden it. That would be the first secret they would share. Kissing would be the second. She had been seven when it started and ten when it ended. Lila didn't look at me as she told me her story. This strong, amazing woman trembled in my arms as she opened up to me, her breath faltering at the darkest parts of the story. But she kept going.

She finished by telling me how her Uncle Gary warned her that no one would believe her if she told on him. And he was right—at least at first. Her mother went so far as to ground her for telling lies. That's when her Aunt Paulette, the youngest of her mother's siblings, came forward to say that Gary had molested her when they were children.

Lila said, "It wasn't until Paulette said what Gary did to her that they finally believed me. If it weren't for her, I'm pretty sure I would have killed myself."

She said that statement with the resolve of someone who had given the calculation a great deal of thought. After that, I had a better sense of why her path had turned so dark: the thin scars on her shoulder left by a razor blade, the drinking and promiscuity that stained her teen years. Knowing the hole that she climbed out of, the hell she had overcome to get to where she was, made me love her more.

My show about Norwegian fjords was rolling its credits when I stepped out of my reverie of Lila and her past. I shut the TV off and went to the bedroom, expecting to find Lila still hard at work studying. Instead I found her asleep, her flash cards lying loose where they had fallen from her hand. I lifted the covers from my side of the bed and pulled them over her. She looked so peaceful. I wanted to kiss her and hold her. I wanted to crawl into bed beside her and fold myself around her the way I'd done a thousand times before, but that would wake her.

I sat on the edge of the bed and tried to remember the last time I told her that I loved her, or when she had last said those words to me. Two months? Four? I couldn't remember. It had gotten so hard lately. It would get better after the bar exam. It had to. And then when Toke's money comes.... We just had to hold on for a little longer.

I shut the light off and went to go sleep on the couch.

CHAPTER 22

Jeremy didn't question why we left the apartment carrying suitcases that next morning. I told him that he didn't have to go to work, and that was good enough for him. It wasn't until we were leaving the city, heading south, that he raised a question.

"Where are we going?" he asked, in his slow, measured way.

"We're going on a little adventure," I said.

"Maybe we're going to Mom's house?"

That caught me off guard. The last time he was in the same house as Kathy had been the night of the big fight, yet her name seemed to come to him without a second's hesitation, as if time and events had not passed in his world.

"Jeremy, why would you think we're going to Mom's?"

He looked at the book on his lap, *Bambi*, and didn't answer.

"Jeremy, buddy, what's wrong?"

He kept his head down, his eyes on his book. I waited, hoping he might say something, and he did. "Maybe Mom is not there," he said.

"Maybe Mom's not where?"

Jeremy stared at the opened pages of his book and didn't answer.

"Buddy, talk to me. What's the matter?"

"Maybe when Bambi ran to the thicket his mother wasn't there."

I looked at Jeremy's book and realized where he was in his story. I'd heard Jeremy read that page aloud many times. Bambi's mother hears the hunters and tells Bambi to run to the thicket. Bambi runs, and when he gets there, he says, "We made it, Mother!" But Bambi's mother didn't make it. She had been shot by the hunter. She *wasn't there*. "You think Mom is . . ." I stopped myself before I said the word *dead*. If I was wrong about what he was trying to say, I didn't want to put that thought into his head. But that had to be what he was thinking.

Jeremy didn't look up, but I could see his eyes drop and his lips tighten, the way he sometimes did when I've guessed his thoughts.

"No, buddy. No. Mom's not—. She's just . . . she's very sick. It's a kind of sick that never goes away, and she can't take care of you." My lie was weak, I saw that. I had made it up on the fly, and I had my doubts that it would work. But how do you tell someone like Jeremy that their mother is poison? What I did—ripping him away from that woman, keeping him away from her—it was for his own good. But he might never understand that.

I waited for Jeremy to respond, but he remained quiet and went back to reading his book. What he said made me wonder if somewhere, deep down, he was trying to tell me something by bringing Dumbo and Bambi on this trip: one book about a child ripped away from his mother when she was imprisoned, the other book about a child left motherless in the aftermath of a hunter's bullet. What old memories curled through my brother's mind? What feelings hid behind those expressionless eyes? I had been so wrapped up in my emotions at the time that I never stopped to think about how Jeremy might feel. Had I done the right thing by taking my brother away?

I shook off that thought. Of course I did the right thing. I brought the guardianship action to save Jeremy. To my mother, he was little more than a meal ticket, and given her spate of legal troubles, I honestly didn't expect her to show up for the hearing. But show up she did, and when she walked in, she looked . . . well . . . respectable. She still had a few small scabs on her face—residue from the meth use—and her cheeks were thinner than I remembered. But she walked with a straight back, wore clothing appropriate for court, and didn't hiss at me when she walked past to take her seat at the counsel table. *This was going to be quite the performance,* I thought to myself. Still, I remained confident, because I knew the chaos that lay just behind that thin veneer.

Lila and I scraped up enough money to hire a lawyer named Sherri Knuth, a very nice person and, as far as I could tell, smart as a whip. Kathy, of course, didn't have two nickels to rub together, so she had to go it alone. My attorney told me that the assault I committed on Larry might be a problem; Kathy would use it to paint me as volatile and dangerous. The way I saw it, I was acting in self-defense, and Larry got what was coming to him.

Sherri and I presented our case to the judge first. I thought it would be easy to testify against my mother, but sitting on that witness stand, I had to look her in the eye as I told the judge about the monster that lurked behind the makeup, and despite my best effort to remain focused on my mother's faults, I couldn't avoid the torrent of what-ifs that came flooding in.

At first, Kathy sat quietly in her chair, her face made of plastic, lest she give away her true self. But the more I talked, the more I could see crumbling around the edges, where the dried clay of her facade was too thin to hold up. When I told the judge about the time that I had to use my dwindling college money to bail her out of jail for a DUI, Kathy's lip curled up into a snarl. I was getting to her.

"And that's when she took up with Larry Hogermiller," I said.

She had to know what was coming, yet she twisted her face into an expression of bewilderment as I explained how she and her new boyfriend left Jeremy alone for a weekend so they could go gamble. Jeremy nearly set the apartment on fire when he tried to heat up a piece of pizza in the toaster. Then the crack in my mother's false respectability opened wide, and she let loose her first interjection. "Why don't you tell him how you beat Larry up that day?"

"Ms. Nelson," the judge snapped. "You'll have a turn to ask questions later. If you have an objection, state it succinctly, but there'll be no outbursts while Mr. Talbert is testifying."

"I object," she said. "He's not telling you everything that happened."

"Ms. Nelson, that is not a proper objection. Overruled."

My attorney had prepared me for this, so I went on. "Yes, there was a confrontation between Larry Hogermiller and myself." I spoke in words that painted a sympathetic picture, just the way Sherri taught me. "I had discovered that Jeremy had a bruise on his back that day. When I asked Jeremy what happened, he told me that Larry . . . I mean, Mr. Hogermiller, had hit him with the TV remote."

"That's not true," Kathy yelled.

"Ms. Nelson, I thought I told you no outbursts. You'll have your turn."

I continued. "When I confronted my mother about the bruise, Mr. Hogermiller came at me. I defended myself by putting Mr. Hogermiller in a hold that a police officer here in

Austin once showed me. All I did was to stop him from attacking me."

Kathy huffed but kept her words to herself.

I told the judge about the day that Larry punched Jeremy in the face, how I went to my mother's apartment to get Jeremy, to rescue him, and how Larry tried to prevent me from leaving. "I kicked at Mr. Hogermiller and caught him in the knee. I wasn't trying to hurt him; I just wanted to get my brother out of there."

Kathy was about to come up out of her seat at that one. I finished my testimony by telling the judge about the year and a half since the night of the big fight, about how Kathy never once tried to get Jeremy back until she got busted for possessing meth and wanted to use him to garner sympathy in her criminal case. I had the letter to prove it.

When it was Kathy's turn to ask me questions, she opened with, "You're a lying little shit, aren't you?"

"Objection," Sherri said.

"Sustained."

"Admit it. You're nothing but a backstabbing, ungrateful lying little—"

"Ms. Nelson!" the judge hollered. "When I sustain an objection, it means that you can't ask that question. If you have another question to ask, do so. If you're just going to sit there and call your son names, then none of what you want to say will be permitted into the record. Do you understand?"

"Yes, Your Honor."

"You broke Larry's leg, didn't you?" she said.

"I was told that I tore his ACL."

"Same thing. He had to be on crutches for months. He lost his job."

"Is that why he started selling meth?"

"He wasn't selling. It was a possession charge."

"And because of that, the man you chose to be with—over your own son—is now in prison."

"You can be such a hurtful prick, you know that?" I could hear a tremor in her voice.

"Mr. Talbert! Ms. Nelson!" The judge's voice boomed across the room again. "I will not have this hearing devolve into a mud pit of name-calling. Ms. Nelson, you ask questions and, Mr. Talbert, you answer them. No extraneous arguing. Am I clear?"

Kathy lowered her head into her hands.

I felt stupid for how quickly I had become the snarky kid I had been in high school. I cleared the anger out of my head and awaited her next question.

She didn't look up at me when she asked it. "When did you stop loving me?" she said.

I wasn't prepared for that one. I struggled to find an answer. Finding none, I said, "I don't know."

CHAPTER 23

I pulled into the Caspen Inn and parked in front of room eight, telling Jeremy to follow me as I got out, but he remained in his seat, his hands on his lap, the fingers of his right hand rubbing the knuckles of his left. I went around to the passenger side, grabbed his bag from the backseat, and opened his door. He didn't move. I unbuckled his seat belt. He still didn't move.

"Jeremy, come on." I gave his biceps a light squeeze, and that was enough to convince him that I wouldn't be changing my mind.

As he stood up, I heard gravel crunching as a car pulled into the lot. I looked up to see Charlie's Lexus ease into the lot and park a few feet away from us. Charlie had his window open, a cigarette in his mouth, the sides of his lips arched up in this strange Machiavellian smile. He stepped out of his car, looked at Jeremy, and his smile grew bigger.

"Is this Jeremy?" he asked.

"What? How . . . ?"

"You brought your autistic brother to a shithole motel. Well, doesn't that beat all. Regular guardian-of-the-year stuff."

I couldn't talk. How did he know about Jeremy? About the guardianship?

"Why so surprised, Joe? You claim to be my kin, well that means that I'm going to take an interest in you—get to know you . . . and Jeremy." He gave a wink at Jeremy that went unnoticed by my brother.

"You leave Jeremy out of this."

"You'd be amazed what you can find out about a person if you know where to look," he said. "Court records, police reports, that kind of thing. Did you know that Larry Hogermiller and I went to high school together? Imagine my disappointment when I found out he was in prison. Oh, by the way, Larry asked me to pass his love on to your mother."

"Go fuck yourself," I said. My retort fell far short of what I would have liked, but my mind was reeling, and those were the only words that made it through the clutter.

"Such language. And in front of your brother."

Charlie took a step in and started to raise his hand to shake Jeremy's. I slid in between them, Charlie stopping inches from my face, his outstretched hand bounding off of my stomach. "You keep away from my brother," I said.

"Ah, and there it is. That famous Joe Talbert temper I've been hearing so much about. I'm surprised you were able to get guardianship over your brother, you being such a hothead. Your mother must be far more wretched than Larry remembered."

I put a hand on Jeremy's arm and led him to our room, unable to think of anything to say beyond pointless curse words.

"Where are you going?" Charlie said, holding his arms out to the side in a beckoning gesture. "I was just trying to be neighborly—get to know my kin." Then he laughed and made his way to his room.

I got Jeremy inside, closed the door, and huffed as pithy comebacks flooded my head, all too late. Then I noticed Jeremy standing by the door as still as a brick, his hands balled together and pressed against his stomach. I turned my attention to my brother, asking him which of the two beds he preferred, knowing full well that he wouldn't be able to sleep on the bed nearest to the exit. That would also put him on the bed closer to the bathroom. "I think you should sleep here," I said, patting the inside bed. "Look, it's right in front of the TV."

"Maybe..." He looked around the room, the muscles in his jaw flexing as he began to grind his teeth. "Maybe we should go home."

"Jeremy, I'm sorry, but you have to stay here with me. Besides, you've never been to a motel before. This'll be fun. Look." I walked to the bathroom. "We have a bathroom right here. I can put your toothbrush in this cup, and look at this." I showed him the drawers in the dresser beneath the TV. "You can put your clothes in here. Remember in *Guardians of the Galaxy*, when Quill and Rocket and Groot went on that adventure? This is like our own adventure."

The old television in the room didn't have an HDMI port, so I had to use my laptop to play one of Jeremy's movies. Once I had the movie queued up, I coaxed Jeremy to the foot of what would be his bed, and he sat down, one hand rubbing the knuckles on the other hand. Then he looked around the room as though searching for a door that might lead to a place where he could feel safe, a magic portal that would whisk him back to Lila and our apartment in St. Paul.

"Pretty cool, huh?"

Jeremy didn't answer.

I backed my way toward the door, doing my best to be invisible. Jeremy seemed settled. He had his movie, which would run for an hour plus. That would give me time to go through the first part of my plan. In order to get to Moody Lynch, I would need to find his parents, and to find his parents, I would start with my best source of information, Vicky Pyke.

"I'm going to go get some stuff, Jeremy," I said. "I'll be right back. Are you okay watching your movie for a little bit?"

Jeremy sat on the edge of the bed, his hands on his lap, his eyes fixed on the familiar characters moving across my laptop screen. He didn't answer, so I slipped out and quietly closed the door behind me, keeping my departure away from not only Jeremy but Charlie. I crept along the face of the motel until I turned a corner and was well out of view from Charlie's room. I gave one last look back, and then, satisfied that Jeremy was safe, headed to the Snipe's Nest.

The Snipe's Nest had a handful of people scattered about the place, none of them being Harley Redding, so I walked in and took a seat at the bar.

"Hey, stranger," Vicky said with a smile.

"Is it too early to get a bite to eat?"

"Cheeseburger basket?"

"Two. I have my brother staying with me for a day or two."

She turned to the opening between the bar and kitchen and yelled, "Marv, two cheeseburger baskets." Marv, an older man with a trace of white hair frosting the sides of his head, was watching monster trucks on a TV in the kitchen. He nodded to Vicky and turned to his grill.

"I was hoping you might stop by," she said to me.

"Oh, yeah? Why's that?"

"I wanted to tell you that I've been thinking a lot about what you said . . . you know, about me maybe going to college. Getting out of Buckley."

"Vicky, don't pay any attention to me. I can be a horse's ass sometimes."

"No, I wanted to tell you that you were right. Last night, I went to talk to my Uncle Don, my dad's brother, and he agrees with you. He said that I've done my duty, and if I decide to go to college, he'll see to it that Dad's taken care of. Can you believe it? And I never would have had the guts to talk to my uncle if you hadn't said what you said out there by the river."

I watched the light dance in Vicky's eyes as she told me her news. She reminded me of a giddy schoolgirl who's just been asked to the prom. Her excitement seemed infectious. But then she leaned into the bar, her eyes locked onto mine, and where the schoolgirl had been now stood a woman whose calm, steady gaze demanded my attention. She slid her hand across the bar and laid it on the back of my hand, and said "I'm still not sure if I can do this, but I want to thank you for . . . well, for making me believe that it's possible."

"You're welcome," I said, my words faltering just a bit before finding some footing.

She pulled back, and the giddy schoolgirl returned. "I also wanted to tell you that I know why Harley Redding wants to beat you up. My uncle Don knew the story. It's all about Harley's stupid car."

"His car?"

"Yeah. Harley had this Pontiac GTO. Needed a little body work, but basically it was a pretty nice car. He always talked about fixing it up and selling it for a small fortune. The problem was that Harley didn't know the first thing about fixing up cars. That's how he and Toke got together."

"Toke was a body man," I said.

"He was. And Harley used to go down to Dub's and bug Toke about fixing that car. Of course, Harley didn't have a dime to spare, so it was all a pipe dream. But then old man Hix died, and Toke and Jeannie were looking to inherit a buttload of money. Also, about that time, Harley fell into some legal entanglements."

"Let me guess, DUI," I said.

"No. He beat the shit out of a good old boy from St. James, some guy who got a little too mouthy with Harley and wasn't able to back it up the way you did. Harley needed money for a lawyer. He was desperate. And that's when the whole deal got cooked up."

"Deal?"

"Harley needed five grand for his lawyer, so he went to Toke to see if he could sell the car to him. Now, the way Harley puts it, Toke said that he wouldn't have that kind of scratch until the Hix estate got settled. And because Harley couldn't wait that long, they agreed that Toke would pay Harley five grand up front, and another fifteen once Toke got the farm. But when they did the title transfer, Toke convinced Harley to put down that he was selling the car for five grand so Toke could save a few bucks on taxes."

"I'm betting there was no documentation about the other fifteen grand," I said.

"Bingo. Not a single scrap of paper. As far as Harley's concerned, Toke stole the car."

"Why didn't Harley just take Toke to small-claims court?"

"He did. But it was Harley's word against Toke's. Toke told the judge that they set the price at five thousand because Harley was desperate and needed the five grand for his attorney, that last part being true. Harley tried to convince the judge that there was more to the deal, but all the documents showed that the price was five grand. The judge ruled against Harley. Toke got a twenty-thousand-dollar car for five grand."

"When did this happen?"

"The judge's ruling came down two weeks ago."

A guy, eating by himself up near the front of the bar, waved a hand to get Vicky's attention.

"Excuse me," she said. "I'm being summoned. Don't go away."

I watched as she smiled and chatted with the patron, and handed him his lunch bill. She had a great smile, the kind that could make a man forget the world outside of the Snipe's Nest.

When she came back, I said, "Vicky, I need a favor."

"Name it." There was that smile again.

"I want to interview Moody Lynch's parents."

"Why would you want to do that?"

I didn't tell her the real reason—that I was laying the groundwork to get him to turn himself in. Instead I said, "I'm a reporter, and I want to see if there's any way I can help him."

"Help him?"

"He's not doing himself any favors by staying out in the woods. If he's innocent, I can help clear his name. I've done it before."

"But his people . . . they don't talk to strangers."

"Why's that?"

"You ever hear of Posse Comitatus?"

"The white-supremacist group?"

"Well, around here, they're not so much white supremacists as they are haters of anything government. They don't believe that the law has any authority over them."

"Moody's family is Posse Comitatus?"

"That's the rumor. They live in the valley about ten minutes north of my dad's place. I can tell you how to find their house, but you should be careful."

"They won't shoot me or anything, will they?"

"They haven't shot anyone yet, but there's always a first time." She smiled when she said it, so I wasn't sure if she was joking or not.

I said, "If things look fishy, I'll haul ass out of there. Trust me."

She wrote an address on a napkin and handed it to me. About that same time, Marv slid my lunches through the window, sacked and ready to go. I added a couple drinks to the tab, paid my bill, and as I was leaving, Vicky said, "I mean it. You be careful. It's best to stay on the good side of the Lynches."

CHAPTER 24

Uncle Charlie's car was gone when I got back to the motel. Jeremy hadn't moved from his spot at the foot of the bed. His movie was two-thirds finished, and I could see his lips moving slightly as he ran through the lines in his head. The oddness of the motel room no longer seemed to press on him, and I gave him his cheeseburger and pop, which he ate without taking his eyes off the computer screen.

While I ate my lunch, I plotted my route to the Lynch place on my phone. Twenty minutes there and twenty back. I would need to find a longer movie for Jeremy to watch, maybe *Pirates of the Caribbean*, which ran two hours and twenty minutes. That would give me more than an hour to talk to the Lynch clan.

By the time Jeremy finished his lunch, *Guardians of the Galaxy* was running the closing credits, and I brought him a washcloth to wipe the food from his face. "This is a pretty nice room, isn't it?" I said. It was a lie, but Jeremy didn't know a good motel room from a bad one.

"When will we go home?" he asked.

"We're staying the night. That's your bed and this is mine. We're sleeping in the same room, just like when we were kids."

"Maybe we should go home."

"No, Jeremy. We can't go home right now. Lila needs to study for her test so we're going to stay here. You like it here, don't you?"

Jeremy scratched at the bandage on his wrist.

"How does your arm feel?"

"Maybe it hurts a little."

"You want an aspirin?"

"No."

Jeremy wasn't a fan of swallowing pills, so I bought a bottle of chewables on the way down. I handed him two. "You can chew these. They're good."

Jeremy took the aspirin, and I started his second DVD. When the movie started, he became still, sitting on the end of the bed in his rigid way. Charlie's car was still gone, but a sense of unease followed me around the room as I gave it a final look. Everything seemed to be in its proper place, yet something wasn't right, and I couldn't put my finger on it. I shook away those doubts and slipped out the door.

The Lynch house lay at the end of a long gravel road, with a turnaround butting up against their front yard. They had a chain-link fence lining their property with several no-trespassing signs posted around the perimeter. The fence had a gate but no lock. Not wanting to risk walking up to the house to ring a doorbell, I parked my car with the nose facing away from the property, leaving it running just in case, and I hit my horn three times. Then I took a seat on the trunk.

I could see curtains rustling in the front window. They moved, came to rest, and then moved again. I pulled out one of my business cards and waited.

A tall man came out of the house carrying a shotgun in one hand, the barrel pointing at the ground ahead of his feet. I gave serious thought to jumping in my car and taking off. I'd done some stupid stuff in my life, and I was starting to think that this might be another one. But there was something in the man's demeanor that kept me there. He walked with an easy gait, his face relaxed—just a guy out for a stroll with his shotgun. Besides, why come out of the house to kill me—he could have accomplished that from the window.

"What the hell you think you're doing, sitting out here making all that racket? Who are you?"

"Your sign says no trespassing," I said. "I would have come up and knocked, but that might be construed as a trespass."

"Well, making noise is trespass enough. I'll ask you again, who are you?"

The man stood at least six foot six, with black hair slicked back and a long beard that gave him the look of an old-time trapper. He stopped at the gate with his gun resting in the crook of his right arm.

"Are you Moody's dad?"

"Mister, I'm not going to ask you again, who are you?"

"I'm a reporter," I said. "I work for the Associated Press."

My introduction seemed to slap the man in the face. "Get the hell off my property," he said, his right hand now gripping the stock of his shotgun near the trigger. He kept the muzzle down, but it would take less than a second for that to change.

"I'm also the son of Toke Talbert," I said, hoping that his curiosity might kick in and get us past this dustup. It worked.

"Bullshit," the man said.

I held up my card and waved it. He flicked a finger to signal me to approach, and I handed him the card. "I'm not one hundred percent sure about Toke being my dad, but it's a good bet. My mom told me that she named me after my father. I never met the man. He abandoned us."

"Well, that sounds like Toke all right."

"I'm here to look into what happened."

"I got nothing to say to you, so you may as well hit the road."

"I think I can help Moody."

"Help Moody?" He had what seemed to be a permanently downturned mouth, a frown carved there by years of fighting against the world. But I caught his attention. I could tell by the way he rolled the ball of his tongue against the inside of his cheek as he considered my words. When he spoke again, he sounded more curious than angry. "How in the hell do you figure on doing that?"

"The sheriff thinks Moody killed Toke. They've been building a case that lands Moody dead in the middle of it all. The problem is that they don't have Moody's story to put a stop to that nonsense. I want to get Moody's version out there. If I could just talk to him—"

"Moody ain't here." The man squinted to look past me up the gravel road as if checking to see if I came with backup.

"I'm alone," I said. "I know about Moody's trouble with Deputy Calder. I understand why—"

"Nathan Calder's a no-good son of a bitch," the man said. "He's been after my boy ever since Moody was a kid. Ain't right that a man like that gets to carry a gun and go around arresting people." Mr. Lynch was angry again. He had moved his gun back up so that the butt rested in his armpit, thus freeing up his hands so that he could pound the index finger of one hand into the palm of the other as he fumed. "They're trying to pin this on Moody because Nathan has it in for my boy."

"There's more to it than that," I said, thinking about the text messages that Jeb told me about. "They have reason to believe that Moody was out at Toke's barn the night Toke was killed."

"Moody didn't kill your old man," he said. "I know that for a fact."

"How do you know that?"

"He told me, and Moody don't never lie to me. His word is all I need."

"Did he go out there to see Angel that night?"

"I'm not sayin' one way or the other."

"But they were dating?"

"I'm not saying they were, and I'm not saying they weren't." He rocked back on his heels slightly as if pleased with his stonewalling.

"Look, if I could talk to Moody, I might be able to help him."

"Don't be blowing smoke up my ass. If you're Toke's son, you ain't here to do Moody no favors."

"I'm here to get to the truth. You say Moody didn't kill Toke. Well, if that's the case, he has nothing to worry about. I'm not the law. I can't arrest him. I only want to talk to him. If he talks to me, I can tell Sheriff Kimball what he says. That's got to help, don't you think?"

"Toke Talbert was a low-down snake, and the world is better off with him dead. Everyone in the county knows that. Hell, even his own daughter would agree. She hated the man."

"Angel hated Toke?"

"With a passion. Toke was trying to break Angel and Moody up. Your old man told my son that if he didn't stop seeing Angel, he was going to kill Moody. Does the sheriff know about that?"

"Toke said that?"

"As God is my witness. He said that if he ever caught Moody on his property he'd beat him to death. He said that to my boy."

"Why did Toke want them broken up?"

Mr. Lynch's shoulders eased the way they do when a man forgets that he's supposed to be angry. Talking about Moody and

Angel brought out a softer side of this tough guy, and for the first time since he came out of his house, I had hope that my plan might work. "I don't know. Your old man was crazy in the head. He lived to piss people off. And when it came to Angel, it wasn't so much a matter of pissing her off as it was just plain meanness—especially after her mom died. It wasn't enough just to knock the girl to the ground—he had to grind his foot on her for good measure."

"You know that she's in a coma?"

Mr. Lynch dropped his eyes. "I heard that, and I'm sorry for it. She did Moody some good; she really did. I ain't never seen Moody care for someone like he cared for her. I always figured that boy was too much a free spirit. I raised him that way, I guess. But she brought out this whole other side of the boy. I think he brought out a better side of her as well."

"What do you mean?"

"You ever meet Angel?"

"I saw her in the hospital."

"Well, when you first meet her, she's like this scared little mouse. I thought she might be a mute or retarded, the way she never talked. But as time went on, and she got comfortable around us, I could see that under all that fear was a lit firecracker."

"That's interesting," I said. "The way everyone else talks about her—"

"Everyone else don't know her the way my Moody does. She's a lot smarter and tougher than she lets on."

"You think she had anything to do with Toke's death?"

Mr. Lynch gave me the hard glare of a man who had just realized that he had let his guard down, and that seemed to piss him off again. "Don't you be getting that idea in your head. That girl had a tough go of it, and she don't need talk like that floating around."

"She swallowed a bunch of pills that night," I said. "Why would she do that? Moody was supposed to be meeting her out at the farm. Toke ends up dead, and she attempts to commit suicide? You see why the sheriff thinks it's Moody?"

"No, I don't." He averted his gaze, looking at my shoulder rather than my face. "How does her taking those pills lead to my boy killing Toke?"

"Moody showed up. Toke saw him. They fought, and Moody killed Toke. It might have been an accident or self-defense, but it adds up. Maybe Angel saw the fight, or maybe she went out to the barn afterward and found Toke dead. She lost it and took the pills."

"Bullshit!"

"Could be bullshit, but it's a viable theory. If you want the sheriff to believe that Moody's innocent, they'll need to hear his story. If they don't, they'll keep hunting him, and in the mean-time, any evidence that might be out there that can help your boy will be disappearing. I know he's good at hiding, but one day they'll find him, and if they don't find him, he'll live the rest of his life on the run, a fugitive. Is that what you want for your son? All I'm asking is that you let him know that I want to talk to him—just talk, that's all. You have my card with my cell number. Tell him to call me."

The man looked at the card. I could see he was struggling with my logic. I decided to quit while I was ahead. "I'm staying in Buckley," I said. "If you know how to reach him, have him call me. It's the only way."

I stepped into my car, took a deep breath to relax, and then I drove away.

CHAPTER 25

I could have sworn that I saw Mr. Lynch lick his lips as he considered my proposition. A good sign, I thought. It was a simple plan, really. First, pique Dad's interest with the promise that my involvement could help get justice for his son. I may have overstated my clout on that point, but Moody was a fugitive from justice, wanted for murder; his options were somewhat limited. If I could convince Papa Lynch that my offer had value, he would convince Moody.

Now all that I had to do was sit back and wait for the call, and maybe work on my spiel to get Moody to surrender. I'd tell him that an innocent man doesn't run. If he didn't kill Toke, he should quit hiding and let the truth set him free. Those words sounded far loftier than what I really wanted to say, which was, "Stop dragging this thing out. Step into the light and let the chips fall where they may." Because deep down, I think that my crusade had less to do with seeking justice for Moody Lynch and more to do with clearing a path for what I wanted.

I got back to town, satisfied with how things played out with Moody's father and still well before Jeremy's movie should have finished. As I pulled into the motel parking lot, I gave myself an attaboy for my good timing. Then I saw the door to my motel room standing ajar. I parked and ran into the room. The movie was still playing on my computer, but Jeremy wasn't there. I ran to the bathroom. Empty. The room squeezed in around me. "Jeremy!" I yelled. No answer.

I raced outside, looking in every direction. Nothing. "Jeremy!" And then to myself, "Oh, fuck!"

I ran to the motel office. The door was open, but there was no clerk behind the desk. I looked for a bell to ring, and not seeing one, I yelled. "Hey! Hey, is there anyone here?"

Through a door behind the reception desk I could hear movement.

"Excuse me! I need help!"

More movement. Then the woman who had checked me in the first day came sauntering out of the office. "Yes?"

"Did you see my brother?"

"Your brother?"

"Yeah. Tall. Blond hair."

"I think I saw him in the parking lot about...oh, maybe an hour ago. He was talking to that guy from room nine."

"Charlie Talbert? He was talking to Charlie in the parking lot?"

"I don't know the guy's name, but he drives that red Lexus."

I darted out the door, my eyes scanning the landscape; Charlie's car nowhere in sight. I jumped into my car and fired it up. I should never have left him alone, not with Charlie in the area. I knew that when I did it. What the hell was I thinking?

I drove to the Sheriff's Office, my car skidding into a parking space in front. I was about to charge in and report my brother missing or maybe kidnapped when I saw the red Lexus, parked halfway down the block in front of a red brick building. I ran to that building, the words COUNTY OFFICES painted on the glass doors. Beyond the doors, I saw Charlie standing in the hallway, chatting with the older woman from the bar—the one doing Charlie's background study.

"Where is he?" I yelled as I marched down the hallway toward them. "Where's my brother?"

Charlie cocked his back, obviously trying to feign surprise. "How would I know where your brother is?"

"What'd you do with him?" I said, stopping face-to-face with my uncle.

"You lost your brother?" He said. "Your *autistic* brother?"

The woman stepped into the conversation. "Young man, what's going on? What's all this yelling about?"

"Where is he?" I kept my eyes on Charlie, ignoring the woman's questions.

Charlie turned to the woman but gestured at me. "Joe here is the guardian of an autistic brother—Jeremy, right?"

"You know damn well it's Jeremy."

"And you've misplaced him? Is that what I'm hearing?"

"Oh, my," the woman said, putting a hand to her mouth. "Have you called the sheriff?"

"The motel clerk saw you," I said pointing my finger at Charlie. "He saw you talking to Jeremy in the parking lot. Where'd he go? What did you tell him?"

"The clerk is mistaken," Charlie said calmly. "I haven't seen your brother since you introduced us this morning."

"He's autistic?" the woman said. "You need to report this right away. You need to tell the sheriff."

I hesitated, waiting for Charlie to come clean. He just shrugged. What was this man's game? Why would he risk harming my brother? As I turned to leave—to run out of the building, I swear I heard Charlie say, "That's no way for a guardian to treat his ward."

I raced into the Sheriff's Office and up to the receptionist behind the glass. "My brother's missing," I said through gasping breaths. "My name is Joe Talbert. I'm staying at the Caspen Inn with my brother, and he left. He's autistic. I can't find him."

The woman behind the glass picked up her phone and punched some buttons. She said some words that I couldn't hear. Then she looked at me and said, "I have dispatch on the line. What does your brother look like?"

"He's six feet tall, twenty-five years old, and he has blond hair. His name is Jeremy."

"What's he wearing?"

"He should be wearing blue jeans and a shirt...green, I think. Yeah, a green T-shirt. Wait, I have a picture." I pulled my phone out and started scrolling through my photos.

"When did you last see your brother?" the receptionist asked.

"This morning, around eleven. He was in room eight. I left for a little while, and when I came back he was gone."

I found a good picture, a close-up of Jeremy's face holding a present from last Christmas. Right then, Nathan Calder walked into the reception area, and the look of concern on his face almost made him look like another man altogether. Gone were the sharp eyes and ready scowl that had greeted me before. "Your brother's missing?"

"Yeah, this is him." I showed Calder the picture. "He's autistic."

He took my phone. "I'm going to get this into our computer system. We can send the picture out to the squads that way."

It occurred to me that Calder didn't ask me how to operate my phone or how best to send the picture out to his computer. I felt embarrassed that I automatically assumed that because of his large size, he might not be smart enough to handle modern technology. He disappeared through the door to the offices, and I paced, waiting for him to come back.

Three minutes later—minutes that filled my head with a

thousand terrible outcomes—Calder reappeared, handed me my phone, and guided me to the chairs in the reception area. When we sat down, he leaned forward, elbows on his knees, leaning my way slightly, the way a friend might do when times turn hard. "I emailed the picture out to all of our squads," he said. "Is there anything else you can tell me about your brother?"

"If you find him, he's not going to react like most people do."

"What do you mean?"

"He won't look at you. He'll look at the ground or turn away."

"Will he obey a command to stop?"

"I . . . I think so. He's never dealt with police before. He doesn't like to be around people in general, so he won't be in any store or restaurant. He'll be outside, most likely."

"We have everyone looking for him," Calder said. "Don't worry, we'll find him." The confidence in Calder's eyes made me want to believe him, and I remembered Jeb saying that there was no one better to have on your side when things got hairy than Nathan Calder. I liked this version of the deputy. "The best thing you can do is go back to the motel and wait there and let us know if he shows up. We'll handle the search."

Calder left, and with him gone, I suddenly felt helpless again. I got in my car, drove back to the motel, checked the empty room, and returned to my car. I couldn't just sit in the room and wait. I had to look for my brother.

I began my search by circling the block around the motel, moving at parade speed, peering into shadows and corners for any sign of Jeremy. When I'd finished the block, I expanded my search to the eight blocks that surrounded the motel. Still nothing. I was about to expand my search once more when I saw a small bridge crossing a good-sized creek, and beside the bridge, a gravel access sloped down to the water.

The scene made me think about how Jeremy loves creeks. Any

time we took Jeremy to a park with a creek, he would make his way to the water's edge, drawn there as though the ripples whispered to him. He never got so close that he might fall in, but he loved to sit in the grass and watch the water trickle by.

I pulled to the side of the road, stopping at the top of the access. "Jeremy!" I yelled as I ran down the slope. "Jeremy? Are you here?"

I could see no one, and the only sound I heard was the rush of the water, water deep enough to pull someone in and drown them if they were careless. I looked under the bridge. He wasn't there. I was about to head back up to my car when I saw shoe prints in the dirt, the tracks of a grown man heading down to the water's edge. I followed the trail to the edge of the creek, hoping to see the shoe prints turn around. They didn't.

"No, no, no." I muttered. The pattern in the dirt looked like tennis-shoe tread, and that's what he was wearing. Beyond that, I couldn't tell if it was him or not. "Jeremy!" I yelled again. "Jeremy!"

I pulled my phone out and dialed 911.

"Dispatch," a woman's voice said.

"This is Joe Talbert. I'm the one with the missing brother. Have you heard anything?"

"Mr. Talbert," she snapped. "I know you're worried, but this line is for emergencies only."

"Isn't this an emergency?" I said "Do you have more pressing tasks going on right now? I just want to know—"

"Hold on a second, Mr. Talbert."

The line went silent as though she might have hung up on me. I was about to end the call and call her back—on an emergency line—when she came back on.

"Mr. Talbert, I just got a call from one of our deputies. They found your brother. Deputy Lewis is requesting that you go to his location. He's on Highway Five, just east of town."

"Is Jeremy okay?"

"One second." The phone went silent again, then, "Yes, your brother is okay."

The relief hit me so hard it put tears in my eyes. "Just keep him calm," I said. "Tell Jeb I'll be right there."

I jumped in my car and flew to a spot just east of town where I found Jeb sitting on the hood of his squad car talking to Jeremy, who stood on the shoulder of the road looking down.

"Jeremy," I said as I climbed out of my car. "You had me worried sick." Jeremy looked up, and then back at the ground like he was a dog about to be scolded. I did my best to keep my emotions in check. "You can't just walk off like that. What if you got hit by a car?"

"I'm sorry, Joe," Jeremy said without looking up.

"Thanks for finding him, Jeb."

"Just doing my job. Besides, Jeremy and I were having a nice chat, weren't we?"

"I think we were," Jeremy said.

"I don't normally leave him alone," I said. "I was only gone for a little bit."

"Had an errand to run?" Jeb asked, using the same tone that Lila uses when she already knows the answer to her question.

"I should probably take him back to the motel." I led Jeremy to my car, and Jeb followed, leaning his hand against my open window after I got in.

"I hear that you made a trip out to see Homer Lynch today."

"Is that Moody's dad?"

"His wife called me; wanted to know if you were really a reporter for the Associated Press. I told them that you were."

I started the car, hoping that Jeb might step back. He didn't.

"Can I ask why you went out there?"

"I told you, I'm trying to make contact with Moody."

"That's really not a good idea, Joe."

"Did you know that Angel hated Toke?"

"Well, there's always been tension there."

"Homer Lynch told me that Angel hated Toke with a passion because Toke wanted to break Moody and Angel apart. Homer said Toke even threatened to kill Moody."

"I guess that doesn't surprise me," Jeb said.

"You never talked to Homer Lynch about that?"

"I get along with the missus, but Homer's not much of a fan of badges."

"That's my point," I said. "People sometimes say things to reporters that they wouldn't say to law enforcement."

"We just need you to get Moody to come in. That's all. I don't want you involving yourself beyond that. If he makes contact with you—call me. Okay?"

"Sure," I said.

Jeb nodded and gave me a small pat on the shoulder as if to seal our agreement. "Nice to meet you, Jeremy," he said, giving a wave to Jeremy in the passenger seat.

After Jeb left, I turned to Jeremy, who was sitting with his hands on his lap and his eyes cast down. "Jeremy, you really scared me. I couldn't find you."

He didn't respond.

"Where did you think you were going, anyway?"

The corners of his lips tugged downward as though he might cry, but Jeremy never cried. And then he said, "Maybe I was going home."

"That's a long way away, Jeremy. You can't walk to the apartment."

"Maybe I was going to Mom's house."

CHAPTER 26

I shouldn't have been hurt by Jeremy thinking that our mother's apartment was somehow still his home—but I was. He had merely responded honestly. He carried no allegiance to one side over the other, and maybe that's what bothered me. I wanted him to understand what I had done for him, what I had given up for him. But he still saw Austin as a place he could call home—and he was willing to walk there.

What would have put that idea into his head—that he could walk to Austin? Looking at a map, St. Paul, Buckley, and Austin would be three points of a triangle, St. Paul on the top, Austin to the south, and Buckley to the west, with roughly a two-hour drive from any one point to the other. Walking from Buckley to Austin was crazy, yet Jeremy had made that decision and was actually walking in the right direction. How would he have known which way to go? That drew to my mind the clerk telling me that she saw Jeremy in the parking lot talking to Charlie.

"Jeremy, do you remember that guy we met this morning when we got to the motel?"

Jeremy didn't answer.

"His name was Charlie. Do you remember him?"

"I think I do," he said.

That was a yes. "Did you talk to him after I left?"

Again no answer.

"Jeremy, it's important. Did you talk to him in the parking lot of the motel after I left?"

"Maybe he told me I should go home."

"He told you to go home? To Austin?"

"Maybe he just said I should go home."

"Did he tell you which way you needed to go?"

Jeremy began rubbing his knuckles, a sign that I was pushing too hard. So I dropped it for now.

Charlie's car was nowhere to be seen when we got back to the motel. I didn't know what I would have done if I had run into my uncle Charlie. My instinct would have been to grab him by the collar and shake him until he admitted that he sent my autistic brother walking down that highway. But he would never admit that. He was building a case to become Angel's guardian. Putting Jeremy's life in jeopardy would kill his case.

And that's when it hit me. He was working not only to prop himself up, but also to make me look bad. I had lost my brother— my ward. He made a point of saying that when I confronted him in front of the social worker. That's why he smiled when I got into that bar fight with Harley. He sees me as a threat, a rival for Angel's guardianship. He was beating me in a game that I didn't even know I was playing.

Jeremy again refused to get out of the car on his own at the motel. He didn't resist so much as just sat there until I opened the door to usher him to our room. As he climbed out of the car, his foot kicked some trash onto the parking lot: an empty water bottle, a wadded-up McDonald's bag, and that letter from my mother. I picked up the trash and carried it into the room with me. Jeremy took a seat on the edge of his bed and began reading *Dumbo* again.

I dropped the water bottle and sack into the trash. I was about to drop my mother's crumpled letter in as well, but paused. I peeled the edges of the envelope back and turned it around in my hand, studying the half-cursive, half-print style of penmanship that I recognized as my mother's. I examined those pen strokes, looking for the sharp angles and flairs that I often saw when she wrote in anger. I didn't see any of that.

I slipped a finger under the flap of the envelope and held it there. This was exactly what I swore I would never do. No communication. No contact—ever. I needed to remember why I had made that pledge and why I had kept it all these years. I let my mind drift back to the last day that I saw my mother, that day at the guardianship hearing when all hell broke loose.

My mother held it together for most of the hearing. There were a few moments when I half expected her to come unglued, rush the witness stand, and start strangling me, but she remained in her seat. Toward the end of my testimony, I could see her twitching and rubbing the skin on her neck, and I knew that her unraveling was about to begin.

After we had presented our case, the judge gave my mother the opportunity to testify. The sight of Kathy raising her hand and swearing that meaningless oath almost made me chuckle. She settled into the witness chair and scratched at some invisible bug on her forearm.

The judge spoke first. "Now, Ms. Nelson, because you're here without the assistance of an attorney, there's no one to ask you questions. You can just tell me what you think I need to know."

"Yes, Your Honor." Kathy unfolded a piece of paper upon which she had apparently jotted down some notes for her testimony. The corners of the paper trembled as she tried to read the words. Finally, she pressed the paper against the rail of the witness stand to steady it and began to recount her life as Jeremy's loving and devoted mother, a tale that held only the occasional hint of truth. She had re-created every event of my testimony to suit her delusion that she had been the glue that held our family together. She even went so far as to present herself as heroic. Where I had testified that she ignored Jeremy, she told the judge that she was giving him the freedom to work on his independence. The fight I had with Larry was a kidnapping that she couldn't stop. Scene after scene had been embellished, or flat-out changed, with me as the bad guy.

"And that's not all," she said, playing up her street-urchin sincerity. "Joe has a temper. He once smashed a glass picture on Jeremy's head, cutting him bad."

I whispered to Sherri, "That was an accident. I was ten years old, and the picture fell off its nail in the wall. I didn't hit him with it." Sherri held her hand up to shush me.

"He's always been mean to Jeremy. I've seen Joe hit Jeremy . . . so many times."

"That's not true," I whispered again.

"When they were in high school, Joe used to push Jeremy around. Once he threw a can of pop at Jeremy, hitting him in the eye."

My brow popped up in confusion. What was she talking about?

"I had to take him to the hospital. I told them that Jeremy had hit his eye on a window sill."

Then I remembered. Jeremy *had* hit his eye on a window sill. She was making stuff up out of whole cloth. She knew damn well that Jeremy fell. I wasn't even in the house at the time, but I remember the trip to the ER—there would be records.

"And one time, I caught Joe trying to smother his brother with a pillow. Joe was mad at something Jeremy had done. I heard some commotion and went to check. Joe had Jeremy on the floor and was smothering him with a pillow."

"That's a lie," I blurted out. "That never happened."

"Mr. Talbert!"

"I'm sorry, Your Honor," Sherri said, grabbing ahold of my forearm. "It won't happen again." She looked at me is if she wanted to punch me. I nodded my understanding.

"Your Honor," Kathy continued, "I can't tell you how scared I am for Jeremy's safety. I know Joe comes across as a calm person, but I have the medical records. Jeremy's eye, Larry's leg. I've seen it, Your Honor. Joe is…. he's …" She was struggling for the word she would use to sum up her case. She looked at her piece of paper to find it. "He's volatile."

I leaned over to Sherri and said, "And yet, nothing has happened to Jeremy since he came to live with me."

"I know that I'm not perfect," my mother said, scratching the side of her neck. "But I'm clean now. I'm in treatment. I'm getting my life back together. All I'm asking for is a second chance. Let me prove that I can be the mother I used to be. Let me keep my son."

The judge looked at his watch and then at Sherri. "It's already five minutes into the noon hour. Is your cross-examination going to be long?"

"Most likely," she said.

"Then let's adjourn for lunch and pick it up at, say, one thirty?"

"Yes, Your Honor."

"Ms. Nelson, we're going to break for lunch, and after lunch, we'll start with your cross-examination. So be back here by twenty after."

She nodded, her cheeks turning white when she heard the

words *cross-examination*. The critters under her skin had to be buzzing at the thought of getting grilled by a real attorney. She stayed in the witness chair for a few minutes, as though she needed to catch her breath. Her monster was awake.

When I first learned that my mother had been using methamphetamine, I researched the hell out of it. I wanted to know what signs I had missed: sores on her face, the gaunt cheeks, fidgeting, picking and scratching, the inability to sit still. I also researched how a meth addict could cheat the system and continue using even while on probation. I was amazed at the level of creativity and effort that they would put into cheating a drug test. I didn't know which method Kathy would use, but having lived with my barfly mother as long as I had, and knowing that she would always consider herself smarter than any probation agent, I had no doubt that she would try to find a way to feed the monster that seethed inside of her.

She walked past me as she left the courtroom, her hands tucked into her stomach, the fingers of her right hand scratching the back of her left. She didn't look at me. I waited a couple beats before following her, pausing at the door of the courtroom to watch. She went to the row of small lockers where people had to stow their possessions before going to court, and there she pulled out her purse, tucking it up under her armpit as though it held a winning lottery ticket. She looked over her shoulder at the courtroom, but I ducked back before she could see me.

Kathy left the courthouse and walked—because she still didn't have a license—down to the end of the block. Then, instead of turning in the direction that would take her to her apartment or toward any food establishment, she turned the opposite way, looking over her shoulder again. She was up to something, and I had a hunch I knew what. I followed at a safe distance, being careful to hide behind cars and trees whenever she glanced around. I followed her until she came to a row of buildings that had been abandoned due to a fire. I hid behind a parked car as she looked over her shoulder one last time and then slipped behind the buildings.

I knew where she was going. One of the buildings damaged in the fire had been a dive bar call Bingo's, a particular favorite of Kathy's. Behind the bar was a patch of gravel big enough for a handful of parking spots. That patch was surrounded on three sides by windowless walls of other buildings. That locale offered seclusion in the middle of town.

Bingo's had been boarded up after the fire, but someone had pried the plywood off of the front door, and I easily slipped in, pulling out my phone and queuing its video camera. I crept back to where the kitchen had been and found a window that had not been boarded up because it had metal bars across it. I turned on my camera and slid my hand between the bars.

From there, I watched as my mother squatted on the ground between two dumpsters, something precious cupped in her hand. Then she lifted a small glass pipe to her lips and lit a flame. My mother was smoking meth. One hit—two—then she stood up, packed her pipe back into her purse, and left.

I waited in the kitchen of Bingo's until I was certain that Kathy was well out of sight. Then I made my way to a café I hadn't been to since high school, where I ordered a fish sandwich, a root beer, and a piece of cherry pie to eat for lunch while I repeatedly watched the footage of my mother smoking meth.

Later, when I showed Sherri the footage, she started laughing. "This seals it," she said. "Your mother just swore under oath that she was clean. She lied to the judge—and they hate it when that happens." Then Sherri turned to me and, in a serious tone, said, "You understand, this will likely get Kathy sent to prison?"

I hadn't thought that far ahead.

"If I show this to the judge," she said, "they'll search her purse. They'll find the pipe, or they'll make her give a urine test. Either way, it'll be a probation violation—her second one. With that in mind, do you still want me to use it?"

I started having doubts, but then I remembered how my mother lied about my hurting Jeremy. She told the judge that I abused my brother. She was playing dirty. She'd set the rules for this fight; she couldn't hold it against me if I fought back. I didn't make her smoke that meth. I didn't put her on probation. This wasn't my doing. I had to save Jeremy from her. I had no choice.

"Yes," I said. "I want to use it."

When the hearing resumed, Kathy went back on the stand.

"Ms. Nelson," Sherri began, "one of the last things you said before we broke for lunch was that you are clean and sober now."

"Yes," Kathy said.

"Is that true?"

"It's true, as God is my witness."

"And all of those allegations you made against your son, Joe, those are equally as true?"

"They are."

"So you haven't smoked any methamphetamine or any other illegal substance since your last arrest?"

Kathy narrowed her eyes at me, undoubtedly seeing a trap coming but unable to stop herself. "I have not," she said.

My attorney then played the footage from my phone, explaining to the judge that I had followed my mother over the lunch break. The judge's face froze in shock as he watched my mother get high.

After that, things got crazy. The judge ordered the bailiff to seize my mother and had a city cop confiscate her purse from the locker outside. They kept Kathy in a holding cell attached to the courtroom while law enforcement got a search warrant, signed by a different judge. More cops showed up, and the judge disappeared back into his chambers with them.

When the judge returned, the bailiff brought Kathy back into the courtroom in handcuffs, her eyes red and smudged from crying, her skin brittle with rage. As they escorted her up to the bench, she kept her stare locked on me, her hatred burning bright behind the tears.

"Ms. Nelson," the judge said, pulling her attention away from me. "I have been informed that a pipe was found in your purse, and that pipe tested positive on a preliminary test for the presence of methamphetamine. We are currently in the middle of a guardianship hearing, and you have the right to take the stand and continue with that hearing if you so choose, but I strongly advise that you do not. Anything you say can be used against you down the road. And as it stands, you are looking at charges for possession of a controlled substance as well as perjury. You should think carefully before you decide whether or not to give up your right to remain silent."

Kathy didn't take the stand, but she didn't remain silent either. She turned to me and yelled, "You piece of garbage! You goddamn worthless—" She lunged at me, but the bailiff and a cop held her back. "You'd better hope they put me in prison, because if they don't—"

The judge stood behind his bench. "Ms. Nelson! Do not—"

"I'll fucking kill you."

"Bailiff, get her out of here."

The bailiff and the officer pulled her backward through the door. The whole way, my mother continued to curse me.

When the courtroom fell quiet again, the judge took a breath and looked at his court reporter to see that she was still making a record of the hearing. Then he looked at Sherri and said, "Do you have any more evidence to present, Ms. Knuth?"

"I . . . um . . . no, I guess I'll rest my case."

The judge nodded. "I'll take the matter of the guardianship of J.W.N. under advisement. In the meantime, I'll issue a temporary order granting the guardianship request of the petitioner, Joseph Talbert. I'll have a permanent order out in due course. We are adjourned." Then, with the record closed, the judge took another deep breath, puffed his cheeks as he exhaled. "Wow," he whispered half to himself. Then he stood and left the bench.

Alone in the courtroom, Sherri leaned over to me and said, "Well, that went well."

CHAPTER 27

I sat on my bed in that crappy motel room, a finger edged up under the flap of the envelope, a thin piece of tape, placed there by Lila, the only impediment to my reading Kathy's letter—well that tape plus an avalanche of bad memories gathered over a lifetime of knowing my mother. I looked at Jeremy, who was quietly reading his book. *Dumbo*. I thought of Jeremy's words from that morning, wondering if his mother was dead. I remembered Lila holding the letter and telling me that I needed to read it. I struggled to push those thoughts aside, but in the end, I opened the envelope and read the letter.

Dear Joe, Jeremy, and Lila,

I am addressing this letter to you all, but my greatest hope is that you, Joe, will read this. I have many long roads to walk, but the road to you remains my longest and most difficult.

   As I write this, my head is flooded with the memory of the last time I saw you. I was being pulled out of a courtroom by two men with badges. I can't remember all the things I said to you, but I remember that I couldn't think of words strong enough to say at that moment. It's terrible to think that a mother can hate a son, but that day I hated you. As you know I was high on meth at the time. I don't say that as an excuse. There is no excuse. I only say it to let you know that everything you believed about me was true.

After they arrested me that day, I thought my life was over. I knew when they pulled me from the courtroom that I lost Jeremy. All I could think was that I was going to go to prison, and you were the reason why. I couldn't see that I had put myself there. I had committed every act that they accused me of, and still I could only see my downfall as being your fault. Somehow, I was able to see everything that went wrong in my life as being your fault.

I was sure that they were going to throw me in prison. The judge at my last probation violation hearing said that she was giving me one last chance, and if I blew it, she would have no choice. And so, what did I do? I blew it. I got high in the middle of Jeremy's guardianship hearing. I didn't think I could function if I didn't have a hit. I thought I could get away with it. But you knew me too well. I am ashamed to say this next part, but I have to be honest. When you showed that video to the judge, I wished that I had never given birth to you. I saw your act as the greatest of betrayals. I know now that I was wrong.

It may be hard to believe, may be impossible to believe, but you saved my life that day.

After they arrested me, they charged me with my second controlled substance crime. I had thoughts of killing myself. I thought that if I committed suicide, I might make you feel guilty. I tried to picture your face when you learned that I had died because of your betrayal. In truth, though, I could never really convince myself that my death would make you feel bad at all. I have done terrible things to you and your brother, and I have no reason to expect that you would feel anything for me.

When they brought me back to court, they offered me a way to stay out of prison. It was a program called Drug Court. They said that it would take at least eighteen months to complete and more likely a couple of years. I would have to go to court once a week and do what they told me to do. I didn't know much about it, but as long as I didn't have to go to prison, I didn't care. I figured I could fake my way through anything. I was wrong.

Early on, they made me go see a psychologist. I resisted, but deep down I knew that I was messed up. At first, things didn't go well. I hated everything about my psychologist. But then I got tired of fighting, and I started talking. She was nice, and she didn't judge me. I told her things I've never told anyone, things I've never told you. It felt good to talk about it. She said that I was suffering from posttraumatic stress disorder and bipolar. That explains why, my whole life, I felt like I was walking around with a thousand short fuses in my head.

I've made some big changes in my life. I got my driver's license now, and a job. I am in recovery, and I have been sober for four years. That hit of meth that you saw me do was the last time I did anything. I haven't touched a drop of alcohol either.

I know you are probably reading this and saying to yourself, what's her angle? But there is no angle. I am out of Drug Court now, and I go to meetings every week. I've been working the twelve-step program and doing good. The one step that I've been dreading is the one I take now. I must reach out to those who I have harmed and offer to make amends. I want to make amends with you, yet I know that I do not deserve your forgiveness.

So that is why I am writing to you today. I want to tell you and Lila and Jeremy how truly sorry I am for what I did. I was a terrible mother and a terrible person for so many years. I do not expect to hear back from you, and if you don't respond, I'll understand, but I need you to know that I am sorry.

I guess that's all I have to say. I will not contact you again. If you ever decide that you have it in your heart to forgive me, I'll be here with open arms.

Your mother, Kathy

I folded the pages together again, my head thumping as the words in the letter pushed against my memory. I couldn't remember my mother ever speaking to me with such clarity. It almost read like someone else was telling her what to write. I thought about that for a moment. I guess that was a possibility.

I read the letter again and felt the same confusion. I can't deny that I wanted to believe her. What son wouldn't want that person in the letter for a mother? But I had Jeremy to consider. I couldn't expose him to this new Kathy if the old Kathy still lurked in the corner. I had to know that the letter was genuine. I looked at the return address on the envelope and saw that she was still living in our old apartment. After everything that had happened in the intervening years, she was in the same place with the same landlord—Mr. Bremer.

I still knew Mr. Bremer's number, and I typed it into my phone, pausing my thumb over the Send button for a second before hitting it and making the call.

CHAPTER 28

I hadn't been back to Austin since the guardianship hearing, and frankly, I hadn't planned on stepping foot in that town ever again. But as afternoon bled into evening, I found myself sitting at a café in downtown Austin, watching Jeremy eat pancakes, and waiting for Terry Bremer to show up. I called him from Buckley to ask one simple question: had my mother really changed? His answer: "We should talk."

I don't think Jeremy realized that we were in Austin, even when our mother's old landlord entered the café and walked over to our table. Bremer wore what looked to be the same flannel shirt he wore the last time I saw him so many years ago. But then again, I'd known Terry Bremer for most of my life, and I couldn't recall ever seeing him in anything other than a long-sleeved flannel shirt, even in the middle of summer.

"Hi, Mr. Bremer," I said, reaching out my hand.

"I think you can start calling me Terry," he answered, giving me a firm handshake. I could feel thick calluses on his palm, and it brought me back to the days when I worked for him as a teenager. My hands must have felt like sponges in his grip now—the hands of a thinker not a doer, as he used to say.

He slid into the booth opposite Jeremy and me. "Hi, Jeremy," he said.

"Hi, Mr. Bremer," Jeremy said, not showing a hint of surprise.

I opened my laptop and started a movie for Jeremy to watch so that Bremer and I could talk. With earbuds in his ears, Jeremy became insulated from our conversation. Then I laid Kathy's letter on the table.

"Mom sent this to me...back in December. I didn't read it until today." I pointed at the return address. "Is Mom still living at her old apartment?"

"She is."

"Then you probably know what she's been up to over the past few years?"

"I do," he said with a nod of his head. "I've been keeping a close eye on her. You should probably know that I kicked her out of that apartment at one time. I try to be understanding, even when renters do a little jail time. She missed a lot of rent and I overlooked it. But I kicked her out when she got that second possession charge—the one that came out of that guardianship hearing."

"You heard about that?" I said.

"I heard her side of it. I think I have a pretty good idea of what happened. The bottom line was that I had to evict her." Bremer held his hands up in surrender. "I had no choice. I had to bring the unlawful detainer action. I put her stuff in a storage unit. Your mother was in a bad way, and I agreed not to toss her stuff if she managed to stay out of prison. But if she went to prison, well, I can't pay to store her property for years."

"And yet she managed to wiggle her way back into the apartment?"

"That's not exactly how it went, Joe. When I told her that I put her stuff in storage, she told me to just burn it. She thought she was going to prison and nothing mattered." Bremer looked at Jeremy, who was paying attention to his movie. "Joe, what happened at that hearing tore her up inside. She always came across as tough and sometimes just flat-out mean, but after that hearing, she was a whipped dog."

"She brought it all on herself," I said, my words sounding defensive, even to me.

"There's no doubt about that," he said. "What happened to your mother wasn't your doing. In fact, I want to tell you how proud I am of you. I saw your mother heading for that cliff, but there's nothing you can do if a person doesn't want the help. That's just how it is. But you took your brother on. That had to be tough, and I respect you for it."

I shrugged my shoulders.

"Sometimes, Joe, it takes the world crashing in around you to realize that you're not in control. Some addicts can't see any way out until they hit that rock bottom. When I went to see your mother in jail that day, I think she found her rock bottom."

Bremer reached up to his neck and lifted a silver chain up through his collar, a gold medallion hanging on the end of it. He unhooked the chain and handed it to me. The medallion, about the size of a half-dollar, had a triangle in the center with XXV stamped in the middle. Around the edge of the medallion was the inscription To Thine Own Self Be True Along the three sides of the triangle were the words Unity, Service, Recovery.

"I hit rock bottom over twenty-five years ago," he said. "It cost me my family, my job, everything."

"I didn't know," I said.

"Not many people do. But I wanted you to understand that I'm talking to you as someone who's been where you mother was."

"Where she *was?*"

"Well, maybe that was a poor choice of words. Addiction is a struggle. Most people think that the only thing you have to do to stop being an addict is to stop drinking, or stop using. That's not the case. If you stop drinking, you may be sober, but you're just one bad day away from going back to the gutter. Recovery is a lifestyle. You have to change how you see the world and how you see yourself. That's what your mom's trying to do right now."

"So, she could go back to being a meth head at any moment? You see the problem, don't you . . . Terry?" It felt strange addressing him by his first name. "I can't let her . . ." I nodded toward Jeremy. "I can't open that door again. Not unless I'm sure."

"Joe, I could pick up a bottle of beer tomorrow, and I'd be back in the hole that I spent twenty-five years climbing out of. No one can give you a guarantee."

"But I'm responsible for him." I again nodded at Jeremy. "I can't just forget everything and trust her. It doesn't work that way."

"I understand," he said. "It takes time. It took me some time to trust her again. I didn't just let her walk back into that apartment. In fact, I rented it to another family for two years. When your mom got out of jail, the court put her into a halfway house, then a sober house. They helped her get a job, and she's really good at it."

"What does she do?"

"She works for me." Bremer smiled. "She's my bookkeeper."

"Bookkeeper? Like . . . she handles money?"

"She does. She collects rent, pays the bills. She does it all."

"You trust her with cash?"

"Joe, when I hit my rock bottom, I was fired for stealing tools from my employer. I have a felony conviction for theft, so I know what it's like trying to find a job when the world has you branded a certain way. I saw that your mother was trying. I gave her a chance, and she's come a long way."

"That's why you let her back into her old apartment?"

"Not completely." Terry had his fingers laced together on the table, and he looked me in the eye as he spoke, glancing away occasionally when he needed to draw upon a memory. "She worked for me, so she knew that the apartment had become vacant. When she asked me to let her move back in, I hesitated."

"So you don't fully trust her yet?"

"It wasn't that. Not really. Going back to your old haunts can be a bad idea. Those places have ghosts—memories. Why take the risk? I didn't think it was a good idea for her to move back into her old apartment, and I said so. But she told me that she needed to do it. She needed to face her past. Either she would be strong enough or she wouldn't. Her ghosts are you boys. She can't run from that by changing apartments. She had to face it head-on."

"And... how did it go?"

"She's been there a year and I've never seen her stronger."

I tried to picture my mother as a strong person and couldn't.

"Joe, I can't tell you what to do. You have to make the decision on your own. But I gave your mother another chance, and I don't regret it."

"You don't have an autistic brother to worry about though."

"True enough," he said. "But if you want to see for yourself, Kathy's going to be at an AA meeting tonight in the basement of Grace Lutheran. Starts at seven thirty. As it happens, I'm the scheduled speaker this evening. It's an open meeting, so you're welcome to join."

"She'll be there?"

"Come see for yourself."

Jeremy pulled his earbuds out and spoke for the first time

since Bremer arrived. "I think I have to go to the bathroom," he said.

"Sure," I said, sliding out of the booth. I walked Jeremy most of the way to the men's room and stood by to make sure he went through the correct door. Then I returned to the booth where Bremer was standing.

"I know it's hard to make a leap this big," he said. "There's been a lot of history. Just keep in mind that people can change. I did."

I nodded, not wanting to argue. Bremer held out his hand, and I shook it.

"It's good to see you again," he said. "And I meant what I said: I'm proud of you. I really am. If you decide to leave well enough alone, I'll certainly understand. And this little meeting of ours..." He waved his finger above the booth where we'd been sitting. "Your mother will never know about it unless you tell her."

"I appreciate that," I said.

Bremer gave me a tight-lipped smile, patted my shoulder, and walked away.

CHAPTER 29

I drove to a park on the north side of Austin to ponder the minefield—the many minefields—before me. Was I crazy for even considering going to the meeting? I'd fought so hard to get that woman out of our lives. And I had done it—I had won. Lila, Jeremy, and I were a family, just the three of us. I knew that I should just hit the road and make the two-hour trip back to Buckley, but every time I committed to leave Austin, I would hear Lila's voice telling me that there's no such thing as a lost cause.

Lila had read Kathy's letter; she had talked to Kathy on the phone, and she believed that my mother had changed. Bremer believed it too. If they were wrong, I would wield one hell of an I-told-you-so. But in all honesty, I didn't want to be right about this. I didn't want my mother to be the mess I remembered. It seemed to me that the only way to put this tug-of-war to rest would be to go to that AA meeting.

At seven thirty I rolled up Sixth Avenue and parked across the street from Grace Lutheran Church, far enough away to be inconspicuous, but close enough that I could watch people drift in from the parking lot. I didn't see Kathy, but I saw Terry Bremer.

As he approached the church doors, he stopped and turned, scanning the assortment of parked cars until he spotted me in the distance. Then he smiled, nodded, and headed inside. A few more stragglers made their way in before the parking lot fell quiet.

I couldn't leave Jeremy alone in the car, but taking him with me carried an enormous risk. How would he react if he saw his mother? I would need to find a place where we could eavesdrop and not be seen. And Jeremy would need to obey me without arguing or fighting. This undertaking had calamity written all over it, yet for better or worse, I had to go in.

I turned to Jeremy. "Remember how sometimes in the movies people go into churches, and they have to be very quiet?"

He nodded.

"You see that church over there?" I pointed.

He nodded again.

"We're going to go in there for just a little bit, and I need you to be very quiet. Can you do that?"

"Maybe I can."

"I mean no talking at all. You understand?"

"Maybe, I'll be very quiet for you, Joe."

"Great, and stay by my side, okay?"

He didn't answer.

My watch read 7:38 as we made our way to the church. The meeting would be started already. With everyone in their seats, they might not notice a couple guys slipping in through the back. We stepped inside the entrance, and light, spilling from a doorway to my left, caught my attention. I could hear voices coming through that door, and I motioned for Jeremy to follow me. The doorway led to a set of stairs and a basement. From the top step, I could hear a woman—not Kathy—making announcements about an upcoming sober camping trip.

The stairs were open on the sides, except for the wooden spindles and handrails, and if we stayed on the top step we'd be out of view of the people below. I put my finger to my lips to tell Jeremy to keep quiet, and we sat down. From there we could hear the meeting as if we were in the same room.

As Jeremy took his seat beside me, my phone dinged a single chime. A text message. I forgot to put my phone on silent. Gritting my teeth, I pulled my phone out, silenced the ringer, and looked at the number. I didn't recognize the caller.

"Tonight's speaker," the woman below said, "is someone we all know. He's kind of the rock of this group."

I read the text on my phone: *R U the reporter?*

I typed back: *Yes. Who is this?*

As I waited for the reply, I turned my attention again to the speaker. "So without further ado, I would like to introduce Terry B." The smattering of claps suggested that there were around twenty people in the basement of the church.

I looked at my phone again. *This is Moody. You want to talk?*

I nearly dropped my phone. I quickly typed: *Yes. Call me.* Then I switched my phone to vibrate, stood up, and motioned for Jeremy to follow me outside so I could take the call. Moody Lynch, the fugitive, was about to contact me. I wasn't prepared. My head wasn't in the right place, but I'd be damned if I was going to miss this opportunity. I motioned again, but Jeremy didn't move.

My phone buzzed. *Not over the phone. In person. Tomorrow. 1:00. I'll text you where to go.* Then, a few seconds later, another text: *NO COPS!*

From below, I could hear Terry Bremer's voice. "Thank you. My name is Terry, and I'm an alcoholic."

"Hi, Terry."

I sat back down beside Jeremy. Moody wants to meet in person. That wasn't the plan. This was supposed to be a simple conversation over the phone. I typed my reply: *Bad idea. Why would I meet with someone accused of murder. Call me.*

Terry Bremer had one of those deep, soothing voices, the kind that should belong to an aging country singer. He said, "I know I'm supposed to be talking to you tonight, but I have a favor to ask everyone here—and one person in particular. I've heard Kathy N. tell her story before, but there are some new folks here who I think would be truly inspired by listening to her. So, if she'd be willing, I would love to have her take my place at the lectern. Would that be okay, Kathy?"

There was a hushed mumbling, and then I heard my mother speak. "I haven't prepared anything. I'm not sure."

I looked at Jeremy's face, trying to gauge his reaction to hearing his mother's voice for the first time in years. At first he looked confused, as if trying to place it. Then his eyes came to rest on some blemish on the wall ahead of us, his expression reminiscent of someone straining to hear a dying whisper.

Bremer said, "Kathy, I would be honored if you would tell your story in my place. Please?"

"I guess I could," she said.

My phone buzzed again, and I looked at the message. *I didn't kill anyone. If you're Angel's brother, then you need to hear what I have to say. I love her and won't harm you. Just no cops.*

I didn't want to argue with Moody at that moment. Kathy was about to speak, and what she had to say mattered to me more than the logistics of my meeting with Moody Lynch. I sent a quick answer back to Moody—*okay*—telling myself that I could always change my mind later, after I had time to give it some thought.

From below, my mother's words, sad and quiet, climbed the stairs to where Jeremy and I sat. "Hi, everyone, I'm Kathy, and I'm an alcoholic and a meth addict."

Those words sent an unexpected chill through me, her cold admission putting into words the source of much of my own pain. But I shook off my reaction. They were just words, the dogma of Alcoholics Anonymous. I had no doubt that Kathy could chant a pretty convincing liturgy if she needed to. One thing I knew for certain about my mother was that she could fake it with the best of them. I gathered my skepticism back up around my shoulders and waited.

"I . . . I didn't plan to speak tonight," she said. "I usually have time to get my head right, so please bear with me if I stumble a bit." She paused, and I could hear her taking deep breaths. Then she began with, "I used to be the mother of two beautiful boys, Joe and Jeremy."

When Jeremy heard Kathy say his name, he began to stand up. I tugged at the sleeve of his shirt to pull him back to the step. He sat on the very edge and began rubbing his right thumb against the knuckles of his left hand, his eyes again locked on the wall ahead. This was a bad idea.

"And because I chose my addiction over them, I haven't seen either of them, or spoken to them, in a long time."

I fully expected my mother to whitewash our shared history, those parts of her life that I had experienced and could refute. I readied myself for a tale of how she'd been wronged by her defiant and selfish son, and how the system had it in for her. I waited for the excuses and the half-truths—and, quite frankly, the lies. She didn't know that Jeremy and I were hiding on the steps. She could paint our past with any color she chose.

But Kathy didn't whitewash her story. She spoke slowly and honestly about the shipwreck that had been our lives. Sometimes she would pause to choke back her emotions as she talked about her drinking and leaving us boys alone. I could hear rawness in her words as she told those gathered that she had come to see her children as a burden. "I thought of my sons as stones around my neck," she said. "It's a terrible thing to admit, but I believed that if I didn't have them in my life, I'd be happier."

Her words began to falter and lose their footing, so she paused again. When she was able to continue, she said, "And then it all came to a head one night when I watched a man hit my autistic son, Jeremy. It was a man that I was dating at the time. We had been doing meth and we were drinking—and when he hit Jeremy, I did nothing."

Her sobs cut into her words, and she stopped again to take another deep breath. "He punched my son in the face with his fist, and all I could do was make excuses for why it was okay." She pushed ahead, her voice rising in pitch as her emotions peaked. "I was his mother. I was supposed to protect him. I should have done something. I should have called the police. But all I could think was that I didn't want to be alone."

Kathy fought to hold it together, taking another pause in her story. Jeremy had stopped rubbing his hand, his eyes now cast down to the bottom of the stairs, his face pinched like he was trying to piece together a puzzle that had no picture.

After Kathy regained her composure, she said, "That night, my son Joe came and took his brother away for good. You'd think something like that would be enough to turn your life around, but for me, it wasn't." An edge of anger began to grow in Kathy's voice. "I got arrested for possessing methamphetamine—and that wasn't enough. My son sued me for guardianship of his brother and won—and that wasn't enough. I still thought I'd get through probation and go back to using. I knew that I could beat the system. None of those things were going to change me because the harder the world pushed at me, the harder I was going to push back."

Mom's angry tone fell away. "But then one day I was walking

home from an appointment with my psychologist, and I stopped at a park to rest. There, I saw these two boys playing, and one of the boys, the younger brother, had Down syndrome. It struck me how caring and protective the older brother was. I became mesmerized by them. And when it came time to leave, the older brother picked up his younger brother's coat and helped him put it on.

"When he did that, a memory came to me, something I had forgotten a long time ago. Joey had to be maybe eight, and Jeremy six. I was taking them to my father's house so he could watch them while I went out drinking. I remember that I was in a rush, and I was yelling at the boys to hurry up.

"We walked out of the house, and I was holding both their hands, but Joey pulled free and ran back into the house. It was cold that day, and I yelled at Joey, I mean I really laid into him, for making me wait in the chill. When Joey came back out, he carried...he carried Jeremy's winter coat." My mother's voice shook with emotion as she struggled to keep going. "I...had dragged Jeremy out into the cold without his coat. Joe brought it out and helped Jeremy put it on.

"That day in the park, when that memory came back to me, I started to cry. I ran home, my eyes so full of tears that I could barely see. I ran to my bedroom and sat on the floor in the corner—and I cried and cried and cried. It was as if all the mistakes I'd made came flooding back to me. I saw what I had done and what I had missed out on for all those years. I couldn't stop crying, because for the first time in my life I was able to see who I really was—and it hurt."

Jeremy leaned forward, like he wanted to stand up. I think he was waiting to see if I would pull him back. I didn't.

"I lost my boys," my mother said, her words breaking under the weight of our history. "I loved alcohol more than I loved them. I loved meth more. I had everything I needed to be happy. They were right in front of me the whole time. All I had to do was open my eyes and see them."

I stood and walked with Jeremy down the stairs.

"My addiction robbed me of—" Kathy stopped mid-sentence, her mouth frozen open. She stared at us as if she were unable to understand what she was seeing. She brought her fingers to her mouth, a muffled wail escaping her lips. Her knees buckled beneath her, and Terry rushed forward to help her to the floor.

Others in the room turned around to see what had caused their speaker to collapse. Many of them had already been crying, moved by Kathy's story. When they saw us, they quickly put two and two together, and pretty soon, it seemed like no one in the room had a dry eye—except for Jeremy.

CHAPTER 30

Jeremy and I, materializing in the back of the AA meeting the way we did, brought the whole proceeding to a screeching halt. Jeremy walked up to Kathy and said hello as though he'd just seen her yesterday. Mom then gave Jeremy a light hug, keeping it short because Jeremy doesn't like hugs. I stayed in the back of the room and waited as Bremer led Kathy and Jeremy out.

We headed up the stairs and out of the church, none of us having any idea what to do next. Once outside, the evening became thick with unspoken conversations as we stood next to one another making awkward small talk. Finally, it was Bremer who suggested that Jeremy and I accompany our mother back to her apartment.

Walking into my old home, the apartment where I last shared a meal with my mother and my brother so many years ago, made my knees a little shaky—like that feeling you get as adrenaline starts to leave the fibers of your muscles. It looked the same, yet it looked different. Gone were the dishes stacked high in the sink, the clothing hanging over the backs of chairs, the subtle aroma of decay born of a want of vacuuming. Kathy now owned a couch devoid of drink stains, and all around were items that seemed out of place: fragile China figurines, porcelain vases, glass bowls of potpourri—things that would never have survived in our old world.

Mom looked different too. She had cut her hair short, the flowing locks of her youth replaced by a simple bob that gave her face a soft frame. In that one simple act, it was as if she had signaled to the world that she was done seeking attention, and instead wanted to be taken seriously.

Mom turned on the television for Jeremy, and put an old movie into her DVD player—*The Lion King*. "I bet you haven't watched this in a while," she said to him.

Jeremy pulled his chin into his chest as he considered her question and then said, "Maybe it has been a long time." He sat on the couch to watch the movie, his back straight and his hands on his knees.

Kathy nodded toward the kitchen table. I followed her there, and we sat and stared at each other for an uncomfortable few moments. I wanted to say something nice, but the only thing that came to mind was to compliment her on cleaning up her act, and that sounded more like an insult when I practiced it in my head. I'm sure she was having a similar struggle. Finally, it was Kathy who spoke.

"I guess you could tell by my reaction that I wasn't expecting you tonight."

"You can thank Terry Bremer for that. I think he knew that we were listening in the back. That's why he wanted you to tell your story."

"I'm glad he did it."

"I didn't know you were such a good speaker," I said.

"I didn't either. It's just something you do when you go through recovery, I guess. You want to tell others how you screwed up, and maybe they can learn from your mistakes."

I wanted to be comforting and tell her that she wasn't that bad of a mother, but we both would have known that to be a lie. As I watched this stranger across the table from me, I felt a need to be careful in my words; I didn't want to say something that might cause her to unravel and revert back to the Kathy of my youth.

"How is Lila?" Kathy asked.

"She's great," I said. I didn't see any need to go into the difficulties pressing down on Lila and me at the moment.

"She's a sweet girl. She called me a while back. Did you know that?"

"Yes," I said, doing little to hide my displeasure.

"I hope you're not mad at her about that."

I shook my head.

"She said she's studying to be a lawyer. I didn't know that she wanted to be a lawyer—or if I did know it, I don't remember. I don't remember a lot of what I should. It's strange how your mind really does heal once you get off everything. They used to tell me that kind of thing in treatment. They said that it took time, but I never gave it time. It probably took two years for the fog to fully lift."

"Well, you're looking...healthy."

"Thanks. I feel healthy. I'm in therapy now."

Bremer told me about that, but I acted like I didn't know.

"They have me on lithium."

"Lithium? That's...isn't that, like a major medication?"

"It is. I've been living with bipolar for most of my life, and there's the PTSD stemming from my mom's death."

I knew that Grandma Nelson died when Mom was still in high school, but in my youth, that tragedy—a car accident—never seemed to carry any weight. My grandmother's death and her absence from our lives seemed to be little more than ammunition my mother used to show what an ungrateful wretch I was—how I had it so much better than she did because I *had* a mother.

"There's a lot about her death that I never told anyone, not even my father. I thought I left it behind, but that's the thing I'm learning in therapy—stuff like that doesn't go away."

"Can you talk about it now?" I asked as gently as I could.

Kathy looked at the table between us, her eyes locked on a memory far away, her fingers folding together like someone about to enter into a prayer. Then she said, "I was a senior in high school, on the volleyball team, and we were playing regionals. Mom didn't really like coming to my games. I think if she had her way, she would have stayed at home so she could watch TV and drink wine." My mother looked at me with a wry smile. "I'm afraid this apple didn't fall very far from that tree."

I didn't let myself respond in any way.

"I threw a fit that day," Kathy said. "I screamed at her and told her that if she didn't come watch me play, she could just give up on being my mom, because I was going to give up on being her daughter. We said a lot of terrible things to each other that day. Your grandpa usually refereed our arguments, kept us from going too far, but he wasn't there that time."

Kathy got up, pulled some tissues from a box in the kitchen, and returned to the table, touching a tissue to the corners of her eyes.

"My mother came to the tournament, but not before drinking enough wine to get her through the evening. I was standing outside the gym, warming up, practicing my bumps and sets with some other girls, when we heard this terrible screeching sound and a crash."

She paused to take a few breaths to calm herself.

"I saw the smoke and ran toward it. When I got there, one

of the cars was already on fire. That's when I saw my mother, slumped over in the driver's seat of the burning car. I screamed and ran toward her door, but before I could get there, the car erupted in flames."

Lost in her story, my mother stopped dabbing at the tears that now flowed down her cheeks. "I watched my mother die—burn to death. I know she was unconscious, and all I could do was pray that she didn't feel the flames. Her autopsy showed that she was drunk when she blew the stop sign. Thank God the other woman lived."

Kathy's hands remained folded together, limp, inches away from my hand. I slowly reached out and laid my fingers on hers. I think this surprised her because she gave a short inhale, and then smiled through her tears.

"I never told my father about the argument we had that day. I didn't want him to know that it was my fault Mom drove drunk. Her death was my fault."

"That's not true, though," I said. "You understand that, don't you?"

My mother wrapped her hands around mine and gave a squeeze. "I know," she said. "But that's how I saw it for all these years." She gave a slight chuckle to relieve the tension. "You have no idea how messed up I was."

I smiled. "I have some idea."

She turned serious again. "I want to thank you for what you did."

"What I did?"

She gave a nod toward Jeremy. "You saved Jeremy's life. That day you took him out of here, I . . . well, I think deep down I was glad. I knew that things were getting out of hand with Larry. It was only a matter of time before Larry would take the abuse to another level. I knew that."

"I was just acting on emotion. I didn't mean to mess his knee up," I said, although I really didn't believe that.

"Good riddance to him," Kathy said. "Except, I always thought this was a temporary thing—you taking Jeremy. I thought I'd get myself together, and we'd go back to how it was. But then you sued me for guardianship."

I braced for the impact.

"If you hadn't done that, I don't know what might have happened to Jeremy."

My shoulders relaxed.

"He needed someone to take care of him, and I couldn't even take care of myself. I'm so proud of you, Joe, and I can't tell you how happy I am right now. I never thought I'd see you and Jeremy again. Can you stay for a while, or are you going back to the Twin Cities tonight?"

"Actually, Jeremy and I are staying in Buckley."

"Buckley?"

"Joe Talbert Senior died there on Tuesday night. Did you know he was living in Buckley?"

She pulled her hands back from mine. "Joe's dead? I didn't know. How did you . . . I mean, have you been in contact with him?"

"I found out through a press release. He was . . . well, someone killed him."

Kathy picked up her tissues and wadded them together in her palm, her eyes lost in a kind of melancholy haze. "It doesn't surprise me that he died that way," she said. "He wasn't a very nice man."

"Was he really my father?"

"What do you mean?"

I considered telling her about the money but quickly decided to keep that information to myself. Things were complicated enough already. "I mean, is there a possibility that he's not my biological father?"

She didn't answer right away, and I could see in her eyes that my question struck a nerve. "He's your father." She sounded less than sure.

"Is there any chance he's not?"

"Joe, I wasn't in a very good place at that point of my life. That's no excuse. I...I did a lot of foolish things. I found my worth in the eyes of the men I was with." Her cheeks flushed pink as she fumbled with her explanation. "It's a hard thing to say...especially to your own son, but...there were a number of men in my life back then. It's hard to know a hundred percent, but I'm sure that Joe was your father."

"But not a hundred percent sure."

"Joe, please don't—"

"Did you know his brother, Charlie?"

Kathy grimaced, as if the name alone was enough to put a bitter taste in her mouth. "Charlie Talbert is a vile human being. I'm doing my best to see the good in people, now that I'm in recovery, but that man...."

"I heard that Joe and Charlie didn't get along."

"Joe hated Charlie."

"How come?"

Mom gave me a look, as if to say, *Don't make me go down that rabbit hole.* Then she wiped her nose on a tissue, licked her lips, and nodded.

"People always thought that it was because Charlie was everything Joe wasn't: smart, successful, polished. Back in high school, Charlie was one of those boys who seemed to come out on top, no matter what. They were both bad boys, but Charlie was the one you dated so you could brag to your girl-friends about it. Joe...well, Joe was the guy you settled for."

I could see a wave of regret building up in my mother's eyes.

"I found all this out when I was dating Joe, but Charlie had a secret, something that his family kept hidden from everyone. Their mother used to babysit for extra cash, kind of an illegal day care, and Joe and Charlie used to help. One day, Joe walked in on Charlie molesting one of the children, a little girl named Poppi Sanchez. She lived on the same street as me growing up. Charlie was a teenager, and Poppi was only six or seven at that time."

"Holy crap," I whispered.

"Yeah. Joe freaked out and told his mother, but nothing happened. His parents swept the whole thing under the rug. Charlie went on living his charmed life. No consequences. And he never seemed to regret what he did to Poppi."

Then Mom took on a questioning expression, leaning in and asking, "Do they think Charlie killed Joe? That wouldn't surprise me."

"They don't think so; turns out, the people who wanted Joe Talbert dead make up a pretty long list. Everybody thought he was an asshole—their words, not mine."

"I suppose he was that, and more."

"And yet you named me after him."

I could hear the accusation in my voice. Between the two of us, I was the one slipping into old patterns. But Kathy didn't react the way she would have in the past. She took a slow breath, in and out. Then she did it again and said, "Joe, I have caused a great deal of harm in my life to many people, not the least of which is you and your brother. I have a lot on my plate, and I'm dealing with it as best I can—one day at a time, as we say. Can we have this . . . discussion later? I just want to enjoy being with you and Jeremy tonight."

I felt bad about trying to get that jab in. "I'm sorry. You're right."

"Do you have to go back to Buckley tonight?"

"Well . . ."

"I still have your old bunk bed."

"I don't know—"

"I'm sorry," she said. "I shouldn't have . . . ."

I hadn't thought this through. How did I not see her request coming? I looked around the apartment at the traces of this new life my mother had been forging. Nothing I saw hinted that the old Kathy might be lurking behind the quiet smile of this new woman. But I had been proven wrong before. I wanted to be outside of my mother's influence as I considered this new wrinkle.

"I need to run an errand," I said. That was a lie. "Can you watch Jeremy for a little bit?"

My mother beamed at that and didn't have to answer.

I left Kathy's apartment and drove through Austin, curling around old and familiar places, drawing from them the memories of why I shouldn't leave Jeremy with my mother. But the woman in that apartment bore little resemblance to the woman who cursed my birth after the guardianship hearing. My mother had changed. Bremer saw it. Lila saw it. And if I were being honest, I saw it too.

I had already crossed one line by letting Jeremy see his mother. Would crossing another one be all that bad? And if I could leave Jeremy with Kathy, it would help me in all kinds of ways. Where would Jeremy stay if I decided to meet with Moody Lynch? I couldn't leave him in the motel again. If she could keep it together for a couple days, I might have things worked out. And if she fell apart—well, I'd just have to cross that bridge if it happened.

Before going back to Kathy's, I stopped at a store and bought Jeremy enough clothes to last him a few days—and a green toothbrush. When I got back in my car, I called Lila—my call going straight to voice mail.

"Hi, Lila. You're not going to believe this, but I'm in Austin of all places. I wanted to let you know that...you were right about my mother. It's a long story, but Jeremy and I are spending the night at her apartment. And then I'm going back to Buckley in the morning. It'll be strange not having him with either one of us for a night. I can't remember a time when it was you and me without him being there. I'm sorry, I'm rambling. I just wanted to say that you were right to keep the letter, and I'm really sorry that I made such a case of it. I'm sorry about a lot of things. I hope the studying's going well, and...I really miss you."

CHAPTER 31

The next morning, I got started for Buckley a little later than I had hoped. Kathy made a breakfast of pancakes and bacon and eggs—actual food. Jeremy and I grew up on a menu of fast and easy—anything microwavable or box ready. Sure, we had the occasional home-cooked meal, but I could only remember a handful, and even then, the quality of the cooking was questionable. I think what surprised me most that morning was the real maple syrup. The rest of the meal could be faked, but to have real maple syrup in the cupboard, ready to go, meant that Kathy probably made pancakes on a regular basis, and not just to impress us.

In my last text with Moody Lynch, I had agreed to meet him face-to-face, telling myself that I could always back out of it. Now, I had two hours of drive time to decide. I'd been down that path once before—going to meet with someone who might be a murderer—and I just about lost my life over it. My experience and my good sense were both telling me not to go.

But there was something in his text that tipped the scale in his favor. His last text read in part: *If you're Angel's brother, then you need to hear what I have to say.* Those didn't seem to be the words of a man setting a trap. Why would he think that I needed to hear what he had to say if he planned on killing me? He had no quarrel with me. It sounded like he genuinely wanted to talk, nothing more. I struggled with my decision as I headed back to Buckley.

Around midmorning, I stopped in a town half an hour east of Buckley and bought a couple ham sandwiches, one for me and one to give to Moody as a show of goodwill. And just like that, I had made my decision. Because I had promised Jeb that I would call him if Moody contacted me, I dialed his number as soon as I got back on the road.

"Jeb here."

"Hi, Jeb. It's Joe Talbert."

"Hey, Joe."

"I got a text from Moody Lynch yesterday. He wants to meet."

"Meet? As in face-to-face?"

"Yes."

Pause—"I don't think that's wise."

"I know, but I've given it some thought, and I'm going to meet with him. I'm only calling you because I told you I would."

"Where are you meeting?"

"You're kidding, right?"

"Joe, tell me where you're meeting, and I'll bring him in peacefully. He won't be hurt, I promise."

"If he sees a cop, he'll be gone, you know that. Besides, I don't know where we're meeting. All I know is that the meeting will be at one o'clock today. I just wanted you to know that in case . . ."

"In case anything goes wrong?"

"Nothing's going to go wrong."

"If you believed that, you wouldn't be calling."

"I'm calling because I told you I'd call. Besides, I wanted to see if I can offer Moody anything to bring him in. I suppose immunity is out of the question?"

"Completely."

"He doesn't trust you locals. If I could get him to agree, could he turn himself in to, maybe, the state patrol?"

"Joe, he could do that now if he wanted to. Tell him that we only want to talk."

"You won't arrest him?"

"You know I can't promise that."

"Well, I guess I'll just have to hear him out and let you know what he says."

"We can rig you up with a wire so you could—"

"I'm not going to wear a wire. I'm not working for you."

There was a pause on the other end as Jeb, I assume, tried to come up with some way to insert himself in my plan. He must have come up empty because he said, "I can't condone what you're doing."

"I'm not asking you to."

"Would you at least check in here as soon as you're done? I'd really appreciate it."

"Sure, Jeb."

My phone beeped in my ear, and I looked and saw that there was a text message waiting. "I got to go," I said, and killed my call to Jeb.

I pulled onto a field approach to read the text: two strings of numbers and nothing more. The text came from Moody, but it made no sense. Then it hit me. They were GPS coordinates. I had never tried it before, but I typed the GPS coordinates into the navigation app on my phone, and to my surprise it gave me directions to a spot about twenty miles north of Buckley.

The drive took me around the outskirts of town, which was good, because I didn't want Jeb or Nathan spotting me and tailing me. As I neared the dot on the map, fields gave way to patches of woods, so I knew that I was close to the river again.

I drove down a mildly sloping gravel road and could see the

river ahead of me, the road turning to run parallel to the bank. After about two hundred yards, my navigation system announced that I had arrived at my destination. I stopped the car and got out. The only structure in sight was a barn about a hundred yards down the road, half hidden in a patch of overgrown scrub. He could be in the barn, or he could be hiding in the trees down closer to the river. If it were me, I'd be in the barn with the woods behind me in case I had to make a quick exit.

I was about to get back into my car when my phone rang. In the sun, I couldn't see the number, so I answered. "Hello?"

Nothing. Not even breathing.

"Hello?" I said again.

I thought maybe the connection had died on me. I killed the call. I waited for a minute in case they called back, but my phone remained silent. I looked around again, this time listening as hard as I could, straining to hear the sound of someone who might be crawling through the cornfield or the rustling leaves in the woods, but I heard nothing. I grabbed the sandwiches out of the car and started walking to the barn.

I hate old barns. The Minnesota countryside is littered with them, and each one could send a jolt of panic through me stronger than anything a scary movie could do. I had nearly died outside of an old barn once. I had nearly lost Lila there. Now I stood at the entrance of yet another one, a bag of sandwiches in my hand and my heart pumping harder than it should have been. It's strange how the structure itself could instill more fear in me than the possibility of meeting a murderer inside. I summoned my resolve, took a deep breath, and walked in.

Sunlight cut through the gaps in the boards, painting stripes on the ground in front of me. Dust clung to the walls and floated through the air, twinkling in the thin rays of light. If old had a smell, that barn had captured it. Nothing hung on the walls, although I could see wooden pegs and tenpenny nails sticking out where stuff used to hang. At the other end of the barn, a ladder climbed up through an opening leading to the hayloft.

"Moody?" I called out.

No answer.

"Moody?" I said again, listening for any sound and hearing nothing. Maybe he was down by the river.

I turned to leave and heard, "Stay put." The low, slow delivery stopped me in my tracks. "Did you come alone?"

His call came from up in the hayloft. I turned around and saw no one. "I came alone. Are you Moody Lynch?"

Boards creaked somewhere in the back of the loft, and a tall, thin figure rose to his feet. He stood in the shadows for a second, then stepped forward to where a pillar of light fell through a hole in the roof. His right arm hung heavy at his side, and as he walked to the edge of the hayloft, I could see the gun.

"Oh, hell no," I said. "It doesn't work that way."

"Doesn't work what way?"

"No guns. I didn't bring one. I came here in good faith. You put that thing down or I'm out of here." In my head I was calculating my retreat. Five, maybe six paces to the door at a dead run. Could he hit me in that time? He'd have a pretty good chance. As long as it took more than one bullet to stop me, I'd make it out. Keep running. Get to the car. Get to the highway.

"You don't make the rules here," he said.

"You want to get your story out? Then you put that gun down. Otherwise, I'm leaving." I took a step back to see if he would raise the gun. He didn't. I took another step.

"Wait," he said. "Fine. No guns." He leaned over and dropped the weapon to the deck of the hayloft with a thud. "Just wait there. I'll be right down."

I let out the breath I'd been holding.

Chapter 32

Moody Lynch was a string bean of a kid, a good six inches taller than me, but he couldn't have weighed more than a buck sixty. He wore a patch of bruises along the left side of his face and a thin scab on his bottom lip. The bruising and his hard eyes gave him age, but his thin beard, a sprinkling of whiskers that poked out, scruffy like the hair on a pig's back, worked against that age. Behind the wear-and-tear of it, he had a kind face, although it might have looked a little bit kinder had he bothered to close his slack jaw.

"Sandwich?" I said, tossing him the bag.

"Thanks. You're Joe, right?"

"Joe Talbert . . . Junior, technically."

He opened the bag and pulled a sandwich out. "Are you wired, Joe?"

"I'm not working for the cops," I said. "I came here on my own."

"You mind opening your shirt and showing me?"

He took a huge bite out of his sandwich, and I thought him oddly casual, eating my food while he had me strip to prove I wasn't wired. I opened my shirt and turned in a circle to prove my sincerity. "But this conversation is on the record, Moody. You understand that, don't you? Anything you say is fair game for me to report."

"Yeah, I get that. Are you really Angel's brother?"

"I don't know for sure," I said, buttoning my shirt back up. "I'm leaning toward yes. Were you out at Toke's place that night?"

"Toke's place. It's hard to think of it as Toke's place. That no-good bastard didn't deserve it."

"But you were there. You sent a text to Angel saying you were meeting her."

He looked confused for a second, and then said, "Aw hell! I forgot about that."

"Why did you go to the farm?"

"Angel needed me."

"But Toke threatened to kill you if he ever found you out there."

"You ever been in love, Joe?"

"I suppose."

"Then you know that some things are worth the risk. They are worth anything. That's how I feel about Angel. I met her when I was in town one day getting some parts from Dub's. She was there bringing something to Toke, or getting something from him, I don't remember. When I saw her I couldn't help what I felt. You ever met Angel?"

"I went to the hospital to visit her a couple days ago."

"How is she?" Moody's eyes lit up. "Is she going to be okay?"

"They don't know. She's in a coma."

"My mom heard that, but we didn't know for sure."

"Do you know what happened to her that night?"

"No. I mean, I know something happened, but I'm not sure what."

"What do you mean?"

"She'd been acting really strange those last couple days. It was like she had a secret that she couldn't tell me. I asked her about it. I said, 'What's gotten into you lately?' All she would say was she couldn't talk about it. Not yet at least. I think that's why she wanted me to come over that night."

"Did she say that?"

"No. But I talked to her earlier, and she was really nervous. She said she was on her way to the Sheriff's Office to talk to Jeb Lewis about something, that she would call me later."

"Did she call you?"

"That's when I got the text. Said she was freaking out and she needed me to come over. We were going to meet in the horse barn. That's where we always met. She would sneak out after Toke fell asleep."

"What time did you go over there?"

"Just ahead of midnight. I parked my truck at the boat launch a mile away and took the path up through the woods."

"The boat launch under the bridge?"

"Yup. There's an old horse trail that follows the edge of the field and brings you up behind the barn. I normally sneak in through the back door, but the light was on. The light's never on in that barn. I thought Toke might have left it on by acci-dent, so I waited outside for a while—"

Moody stopped talking and straightened up, like a deer hearing the break of a twig. We both stood perfectly still, listening to the nothingness around us. He looked at me out of the corner of his eye. "Are you sure you weren't followed?"

"I'm sure," I said. "The highway has a long, straight section a few miles back. If anyone was within five miles of me, I would have seen them."

"I was watching the sky as you pulled up. There weren't any airplanes either."

It never dawned on me to look up at the sky. I probably wouldn't make it as a fugitive.

"Anyway, I opened the barn door real slow like and peeked in. I saw something on the ground near the front door. I didn't know what it was, so I eased in and closed the door. I was listening to hear if Toke was around, and that's when I heard her moan."

"Heard who moan?"

"Angel."

"Angel?"

"Yeah. She was the thing I saw on the ground. I mean, I didn't know that at first. I just heard the moan."

"How was she—describe her to me."

"She was wearing her normal clothes and everything, but she was just lying there moaning. I thought maybe she fell or something. I bent down to look at her, you know, see if she hit her head, but I didn't see any marks. I tried to wake her. I had her in my arms, and I was shaking her, and she wouldn't wake up. That's when I heard Toke. I don't know where he came from. I turned around and—"

Moody jerked his head up again. "Did you hear that?" he asked.

"No, I didn't hear anything." Again we stood in silence. The midday sun beat down on the roof and wall of the barn, heating the air inside, turning it thick and stagnant around us. Sweat trickled in thin rivulets down my face. I strained to listen but heard nothing. "What happened when Toke saw you?"

"I told him something's wrong with Angel. And instead of doing anything about it he took to hitting me. He was pissed and screaming. He had a coil of rope and was hitting me in the face with it. He was yelling that he was going to kill me. He was saying that he told me to never set foot on his property, and he was going to beat me to death."

"Did he see Angel there?"

"He had to. I don't know how he could miss her. I fell back against the wall, and he threw the rope down and started hitting me with his fists. He kept hitting me. Then . . . then I remember, my hand knocked against something hard hanging on the wall. It was a gear or a flywheel or something. I just remember grabbing it and swinging it. I hit Toke in the head."

Moody tossed the uneaten half of his sandwich into the bag and dropped it to the ground. "I didn't mean to hit him that hard. He was trying to kill me. I just hit him the once, that's all. He fell back and was lying on his stomach, but he was breathing."

"What happened next?"

"I didn't know what to do. I dug around in Toke's pocket and found his cell phone. I dialed nine-one-one and put the phone beside him. I figured they'd come help Angel and him both."

"You left them there?"

"No. I sat beside Angel until I heard a car coming."

"Did you carry her to the house?"

"Carry her to the house?" Moody looked at me like I had stumped him with my question. "Why would I do that? They might not find her. I sat by her side until they came."

"Until who came?"

"I didn't see who it was. I heard the sound of a vehicle coming up the highway. There was no siren. When I saw the headlights on the treetops, I took off."

"Your fingerprints will be on that gear. They know it's the murder weapon."

"I'm not stupid," he said. "When I was waiting for help to arrive, I wiped off the phone and that gear with an oil rag."

"Why'd you run? It was self-defense."

Moody gave me a half-smile. "I'm a Lynch," was all he said.

A snap of a twig made us both freeze to listen. I looked at him, and he started to shake his head no when both the front and back door of the barn exploded open.

"GET ON THE GROUND! ON THE GROUND! NOW!" I could see Nathan charging through the back door and Jeb and Sheriff Kimball at the front. There were four other law officers in their company, all wearing black Kevlar vests and helmets. "I SAID GET ON THE FUCKING GROUND! NOW!" Nathan shouted.

Moody looked up at the hayloft where his gun lay—because of me. I went to my knees in the hope that he would follow. He hesitated, then went down on his knees, his hands in the air. I went belly down in the dirt and watched him do the same. Nathan ran up and put his knee on Moody's back.

"I'm not talking," Moody said, grunting. "I want a lawyer."

Nathan cranked a pair of handcuffs around Moody's wrists, his knee now pressing Moody's face into the ground, the dirt sticking to the boy's sweat, his eyes on fire with rage—staring at me.

CHAPTER 33

H ow'd you find me?" I asked Jeb from my seat in the back of his squad car, my hands cuffed behind my back. I thought about asking where he was taking me, but I already knew.

"Your cell phone," Jeb said. "At one o'clock you got a call, remember?"

I remembered. I had just stepped out of the car. "There was no one there," I said.

"That was our dispatcher calling you. When you called nine-one-one yesterday, because your brother was lost, you created a link between your phone and the dispatcher. Once that connection is made, dispatch can call back and we can locate your phone. It's a handy piece of technology. You wouldn't believe how many times we get assault calls that get cut off. The system is designed so we can call back, use GPS to locate the scene if we need to."

"It was a dirty trick," I said.

"Moody's wanted for murder. I couldn't let you go through with your scheme. Had to protect you, Joe."

"So why am I in handcuffs? What did I do?"

"Sheriff Kimball wants to talk to you, kind of a debriefing."

"You have Moody," I said. "You can debrief him."

"You heard him yelling that he wants a lawyer, didn't you?"

"Maybe I want a lawyer too. Am I under arrest?"

Jeb paused to think that one over, and something churned in my stomach. "That's still up in the air."

We arrived at the Sheriff's Office, and Jeb escorted me in—still in handcuffs—and put me in a room with thick steel doors on either end—a visiting room for lawyers and inmates, I assumed. The table was bolted to the floor, and the plastic chairs were non-lethal. They left me alone for almost an hour before anyone came in to "debrief" me. I assumed the delay was to let me stew and maybe scare me, but all it did was make me mad.

When they finally came in, Nathan Calder led the way, sitting across from me and placing a digital recorder in the middle of the table.

"You mind taking these handcuff off me," I said. "They're starting to chafe."

"You have bigger problems than a little irritation on your wrists," Nathan said.

Sheriff Kimball also sat down at the table, and Jeb hung back by the door, his arms folded across his chest with a look on his face that let me know we were not friends at the moment. I could see that Nathan was going to be the bad cop, but as I looked around the room, I didn't see a good cop.

"What did Moody Lynch say to you in that barn?" Nathan asked.

"You should go ask him," I said.

"I'm asking you," Nathan said. When I didn't answer, he added, "You ever hear of aiding an offender?"

I'd heard of it but chose to play dumb. As a reporter I some-times walked a fine line between getting information and obstructing an investigation. I had taken great pains to know the legal limits and was pretty sure I hadn't crossed any lines. "Aiding an offender? What's that?"

Nathan smiled. "If someone obstructs an investigation by helping someone who committed a crime, that person is guilty of a felony."

"Well, it's a good thing that I didn't aid an offender," I said.

"Oh, you aided Moody—we know that well enough. The question is, do you want to get your ass out of the sling?"

"And exactly how does my having a conversation with Moody Lynch rise to the level of aiding him?"

"You brought him food."

On the inside I screamed, "Fuck!" On the outside, I was doing everything I could do to keep my face in check. I brought Moody a sandwich. I gave food to a fugitive. I thought back to my memory of the statute. Can giving a fugitive a sandwich constitute aiding? I think it can.

At that moment I fully intended to tell them everything they wanted to know. I mean, why keep it a secret? I made it clear to Moody that I was there to get his story out, and he had given me facts that contradicted the official version. I could help his cause. So what if it looked like I was doing it to save my own skin.

I opened my mouth to speak when a new thought flashed by, one that painted a thin smile on my face. They were bluffing. No one had come to take my fingerprints. I thought back to the sandwich bag, plastic with loops in the top for a handle. The clerk handed the bag to me using the handle. Did I ever hold it by the side? Did I leave a fingerprint on it? I don't think so. They never asked me for a fingerprint sample; that meant that they didn't find useable prints on the bag. I paid with cash and didn't keep the receipt. With Moody not talking, they had no way to prove I gave Moody the food. It was a bluff.

"What food?" I asked.

"Don't treat us like we're stupid," Calder said. "We know you brought him those sandwiches."

I feigned indignation. "You have me handcuffed here for an hour because you think I brought Moody Lynch a sandwich?" Now it was my turn to bluff. "I'm going to have one hell of a story to write about this. I didn't come to Buckley in search of an article, but you just gave me one."

The worry showed on Kimball's face, but Calder kept his composure. "Are you denying that you took sandwiches to Moody?"

"I'm saying you're making shit up. Am I under arrest for something? If so, lock me up. If not, take these handcuffs off me."

Kimball exchanged a look with Jeb, and then nodded. Jeb came around the table, digging his key out, and undid the cuffs.

"You didn't need to threaten me," I said, rubbing the rings on my wrists. "Moody knew I was going to tell you what he told me. But now I'm not so sure." I made a point of displaying my injury.

Jeb, who was standing by the door again, said, "Joe, this is a murder investigation. We need to know what Moody said."

"I'll tell you," I said, "but only if you let me see Toke's autopsy report."

"Out of the question," Calder said. "We don't share those kinds of facts. You're still a possible suspect in all this."

"That's bullshit and you know it," I said. "You want what I got? Then I get to look at the autopsy report."

"Why?" Jeb asked.

"That's my business," I answered. "Do we have a deal?"

Kimball nodded toward the door, and the three of them left. I sighed my relief in short breaths so that the surveillance camera didn't pick up on my doubt. After ten minutes, they came back in, Kimball carrying the report. He dropped it on the table in front of me. "This is off the record," he said. "Agreed?"

"Agreed," I said.

I paged through the report, pausing for a minute on the autopsy photos. I'd seen pictures like that before, so I was prepared, but this was my father—possibly. For some reason that made it different. The crime-scene pictures showed him lying on his stomach against the barn wall where Vicky had shown me the blood. His eyes were open and staring into the dirt. The curve of his skull had been interrupted where the bone had been caved in. Next to his head lay a metal gear about the size of a bread plate, and next to that, the oil rag that Moody had used to wipe off his fingerprints.

I turned to the next page and found a report that explained the cause of death. The medical examiner cataloged three separate locations on the skull where Toke had been bludgeoned with a heavy object. The wounds were consistent with the gear found at the scene, and the gear contained visible hair, skin, and bone fragments, making it the likely murder weapon.

I closed the file.

"First," I said, "Moody gave a version of events that is inconsistent with your theory of the case."

Kimball leaned in as if I had piqued his interest.

"Moody admits he went to Toke's barn. He went there because Angel sent him a text that she was freaking out. But after that, everything is different. My understanding is that Angel was found in the house." I looked at Jeb, who had given me that piece of information. "But Moody said that she was in the barn when he got there. He also said that she was acting groggy, consistent with an overdose. If he's right, the overdose happened before the murder."

"If you believe Moody Lynch," Calder said with a measure of contempt.

I threw a cold look at Nathan. "You wanted to know what Moody said. Well, I'm telling you what he said. What you do with that is up to you."

"Let him talk," Kimball interjected.

"Moody said he was trying to give aid to Angel when Toke came up behind him and started beating him with a coil of rope—you saw the bruises on his face, right? Moody said he hit Toke with the gear in self-defense, but he only hit him one time."

"He admitted he hit Toke with a gear?" Jeb asked.

"The gear was on the wall," I said. "When Toke was hitting him, Moody fell against the wall, grabbed the gear, and hit Toke."

"Did Moody actually say that he only hit Toke once, or is that what you interpreted?" Nathan asked.

"We were in the middle of that conversation when you guys came rushing in, but he said he hit Toke once, and Toke fell to the ground."

"I suppose he didn't want to admit that he crushed Toke's skull in," Calder said.

"It was Moody who called nine-one-one," I said. "Toke was unconscious, but he was breathing, at least according to Moody."

"According to Moody," Calder repeated.

"Moody used Toke's phone to call nine-one-one. He didn't say anything to the dispatcher; he just dialed the number and waited. You tell me—did the nine-one-one call come in like that?" I pretended as if Jeb hadn't already told me those details. "If it happened that way, it corroborates Moody's story. How would he know that there was a silent nine-one-one call unless he made it?"

"That doesn't mean he didn't kill Toke," Nathan said. "He called nine-one-one because of Angel, that's all."

"But what was Angel doing in the barn, and how did she get back into the house?"

"Moody took her to the house before we arrived," Jeb said.

"Moody said he stayed in the barn until he saw headlights coming. Why would he lie about that? Why not just say he took her into the house to wait."

"Because she was never in the barn, you moron," Calder said. "Moody went to the barn to kill Toke. He killed Toke and left. That's all there is to it."

"Then he wouldn't have known about the overdose, would he, you moron?"

Nathan started to stand up, the heat of his contempt burning holes in his britches.

Kimball put a hand on the deputy's arm. "Nathan, let me handle this. Maybe you should step outside?"

Calder gave Kimball a double take, and then looked at me with a scowl.

After he left, Kimball said, "Is there anything else you can tell us? Anything else that Moody said that might be relevant?"

"No. Like I said, we were just getting going when you guys came in, but Sheriff, for what it's worth . . . I believe him."

"That's fine," Kimball said, dismissing my opinion. He shut the recorder off and took it with him when he got up to leave.

"I'm free to go?" I asked.

"You are," Kimball said. Then he walked out, leaving Jeb and me alone.

"I'll need a ride to go get my car," I said to Jeb.

He rolled his eyes. "I'm not a taxi service."

"No, but you did arrest me for no good reason. And that's why I'm here and my car's out in the middle of nowhere. Come on, give me a ride."

"Fine," he said with another roll of his eyes.

This time he let me ride in the front seat with no shackles. The ride was quiet for the most part. He asked me a lot of the same questions that Calder had asked me already, and I gave the same answers. It wasn't until he had parked behind my car, and I was about to get out, that he brought up a new topic. "Before you go," he said, "there's something you should know."

"Yeah, what's that?"

"Back when you gave that DNA sample, we expedited it. Sheriff Kimball thought you might actually be a suspect."

"And?"

"The results came back this morning."

"And?" I said again, with a little more irritation in my voice.

"And what?"

I gave him a stop-messing-with-me look.

"Okay. Fine. It turns out that...you are definitely Toke Talbert's son."

Chapter 34

I was a millionaire! Well, I was about to become one.

It amazed me how the thought of getting free money like that could change a man's perspective. It was as if the wet cement I'd been trudging through suddenly hardened beneath my feet, and I could sprint in any direction I chose; I could feel the contours of a world that had always existed beyond my reach. Ideas pinged and ricocheted in my head so fast that I had to pull my car over and let my thoughts clear. I gripped my steering wheel and tightened just about every muscle in my body, pulling the energy and excitement all up into my chest and squeezing it there until a shrill screech escaped through my clenched teeth. Then I took a few deep breaths and tried to calm down.

One thing at a time, I thought. I need to get a handle on what this means. What are the mechanics of probate? How does one start such a process? I decided that it would be wise to pay another visit to Bob Mullen. Maybe I could get some of the paperwork going while I was still in town.

I drove to Bob's house, the beautiful Victorian across from his office, and rang the bell. I could see a ceiling fan churning inside and hear a hint of music seeping through an open window, so I assumed that he was home. I rang it a second time and was about to ring a third when he called to me, standing on a sidewalk that ran around the side of the house.

"Mr. Mullen, do you have a second?"

"I suppose I do."

"The DNA test came back," I blurted out. "I'm Toke's biological son."

His eyes lit up, but for only a second. Then his face took on the look of a chess player thinking past his next move. He stroked his beard and let his mouth curve down in thought. "I'm glad you stopped by," he said. "I have something I'd like to talk about. Come this way."

We followed the walkway, which took us to his backyard, an impressive space dotted with maple trees and pine. In the middle of it all, a paver-stone patio surrounded a fire pit and held some Adirondack chairs. A woman sat in one of the chairs, working a crossword puzzle. She had long silver hair, and I recognized her from the picture in Bob's office as his wife. Bob gestured for me to sit in one of the chairs.

"You brought company," the woman said.

"Sarah, this is Joe Talbert Junior. Joe, this is my wife, Sarah."

Sarah gave me a warm smile and said, "It's very nice to meet you, Joe. Would you like some tea?"

I was about to say no when Bob said, "Some tea would be lovely. I'll get it."

"Don't be silly," she said. "I'm perfectly capable of carrying a little tea." It took Sarah some effort to rise to her feet, and Bob lent her an arm. Once up, she seemed steady. She gave Bob a pat on his hand and departed for the house.

After she'd gone, he took a seat in the chair next to me. I had come there with a thousand questions that I wanted to throw at

Bob, questions that all led to the same final point—how do I get my money? But Bob had something heavy on his mind, something more serious than my game-show winnings, so I waited for him to start.

He leaned forward to rest his elbows on his knees. "Joe, I want to tell you some things, but before I do, I need to know that you will never reveal what I have to say. I need your word on that."

His solemn tone sobered me right up. I leaned forward to mirror his posture and to better hear his whispery voice. "I promise to keep this conversation a secret," I said.

He nodded. "As you know, I worked for the State Department for several years. In that time, I made a lot of friends and personal connections—people who know how to get information, if you know what I mean."

I nodded my understanding.

"Well, after you told me about Charlie Talbert's partner getting killed in a fire, I had a good friend of mine look into it. Turns out, there was an investigation, but no charges ever came from it. They found evidence of an accelerant, so they knew that it was arson. But the question had been: who set the fire? It started in the upstairs office, and they found Charlie's partner dead at the bottom of the stairs with a crack in his skull. Kind of looked like the partner dowsed the place with gas and fell down the steps after striking the match."

"What about Charlie?"

"He had an alibi. Not a good one, but good enough that it muddied things up."

"You don't believe him?"

"It's not my call. But my friend spoke with the investigator on that case, and *they* don't believe him. The office had a sprinkler system, and they found traces of epoxy on one of sprinkler heads. Sprinkler heads are heat activated. They have solder that melts when the temperature gets hot enough. The right kind of glue might keep the solder from melting, slow things down, or maybe even stop the sprinkler from working altogether. That epoxy would have taken some time to dry, and the partner had just gotten back from a trip the afternoon of the fire. Also, the partner had no smoke damage in his lungs or esophagus. That means he died before the smoke got to him."

"Charlie killed him?"

"That's the thing. None of this proves that Charlie was involved. The partner could have put epoxy on the sprinkler head days before. And they don't know how long the man lay at the bottom of those steps before he died. It could have been a minute or two, in which case he could have set the fire, or he could have lain there for twenty minutes while Charlie sloshed gasoline around the place. In the end, though, Charlie never got charged, and he was the sole beneficiary of the insurance policy. One point five million."

"Can you use this to stop Charlie from becoming Angel's guardian?"

"Not a word of it. It's technically still an open investigation. What I just told you is confidential information. It will never find its way into any background study on Charlie. On paper, he looks like a white knight riding in to save the day. I spoke to Mariam Baker, who's doing his background study, and she's completely gaga over the prospect of Charlie becoming Angel's guardian. He's got the judge on his side too. Hell, the whole town is falling in love with this guy. I've never seen such a concerted effort to fast-track the appointment of a guardian."

"Charlie's a conniving prick," I said.

Bob smiled at that one. "Not only that, but he has everyone convinced that you are a violent, irresponsible gold digger. The word at the courthouse is that you're only here to cash in on the Hix money. Miriam is telling everyone that she saw you beat up Harley Redding down at the Snipe's Nest and that you lost your own autistic brother."

"That son of a bitch," I said. "He's been undercutting me this whole time."

"The man knows how to work the system," Bob said.

"But he won't hurt Angel—if he becomes her guardian. I mean, he can only get at her money if she lives, right?"

Bob leaned back in his chair, crossing one knee over the other. "Charlie's smart. If he becomes her guardian, he'll have control over her interests until she turns eighteen. But there's a good chance that Angel will have cognitive issues when she comes out of her coma—*if* she comes out of her coma. In either case, Charlie could have control of her inheritance for life. But I don't think that's good enough for Charlie."

"What do you mean?"

"On Friday, Charlie's lawyer filed adoption papers. Charlie's going to adopt Angel."

"He can't do that, can he?"

"I think he can. Angel's fourteen. At fourteen, the child doesn't need to consent to the adoption, and with her being in a coma, that part is settled. The only consent they would need would be that of the guardian—and Charlie's going to be the guardian. I suppose the court could put the brakes on if the judge had any concerns, but Charlie's got them all hoodwinked."

"But how is being her adoptive father any different than being her guardian? Either way, he'll siphon her money away."

Bob looked at me with the seriousness of a hangman and said, "As her adoptive father, he inherits all of her assets if she dies."

"You . . . you think that he might kill her?"

"He'll make it look like an accident or natural causes, but yes, I think Charlie would kill Angel to get at her money. Charlie puts on a big show, but my source tells me that he's a huge gambler and is in debt up to his neck. His whole life's an act. He needs that money, and if he killed his partner to get a big payday, why not a girl he's never met before?"

"Can you stop him?" My words sounded weak and impotent, even to me.

"No. But I think *you* can." Bob paused, waiting for me to catch up, but I didn't see it. "Joe, you have to become Angel's guardian."

"Me? I already have a ward. I couldn't—"

"If you became Angel's guardian, the court would need your consent for the adoption."

"I don't even know her."

"But we'd have to get your petition to the court as soon as possible. Charlie's got a big head start. It's the only way."

"You don't know what you're asking."

"I know I'm asking a lot, especially of a young man like yourself, but Angel needs you."

"I've been taking care of my brother, Jeremy, for nearly six years now. It's hard; you have no idea. Sometimes I get so frustrated, I can't breathe. I feel like I've been taking care of my brother my whole life, living for him, sacrificing for him. Now you want me to take on another one?"

"I understand," he said. "I really do."

"I don't think you do." I stood and paced to the opposite side of the fire pit, fighting the urge to run that pulled at my legs. "You've lived all over the world. You've had an exciting life. You've done what you wanted to do. I've never even been on a plane." I turned my back to Bob so that he wouldn't see my frustration tightening along the muscles of my jaw. "You're asking too much of me."

Bob waited for my ranting to die away. Then he said, "Can I

tell you a story?" It was a rhetorical question because he launched into his story without pausing for my input.

"I understand your desire to see the world. Hell, I grew up here in Buckley. But sometimes the world looks prettier from a distance."

I turned to face Bob, who had his gaze set on a patch of pines in the distance, a melancholy smile curling up on his cheeks as he gathered his thoughts.

"Sarah and I dated all through high school. I think I fell in love with her before we even shared our first kiss. But like you, I had that wanderlust, and I couldn't bear the thought of staying here in Buckley, or in Minnesota for that matter. It was hard, but after graduation, I broke up with Sarah and set off to see the world.

"And I did see some amazing places, cities and countries that most people only dream about. But every time I woke up in a new bed—every time I gazed out of my window at some view that I had dreamt of as a child—I felt...well, empty. It didn't matter how blue the waters or how white the snow, there was always something missing. I began to realize that I was terribly unhappy. Lonely.

"One day, I was sitting on a balcony overlooking the Alps, trying to remember if I had ever been happy in my life, and I thought of Sarah. That's what brought me back here to Buckley. Sarah was a widow by then, and I had never married. I guess life has a funny way of working out sometimes. I don't know how to explain it, Joe, except to say that sometimes home isn't a place, it's a person, and my home had always been right here, with Sarah."

Bob pulled his gaze away from the pine trees and looked at me. "You're a young man, though. You'll have to figure these things out for yourself. Hell, back in the day if some old fart had tried to tell me that the great *out there* wasn't all it was cracked up to be, I would have told him to mind his own damned business. You know the stakes. All I can ask is that you think about it before you say no."

Sarah came out of the house carrying a tea tray.

"But you have those great experiences," I said. "That has to count for something."

Bob glanced at his wife, and his disquiet seemed to melt away. "At the end of the day, Joe, only one thing counts. Everything else is just shiny baubles and empty noise."

CHAPTER 35

I left Bob's house more confused than when I'd arrived. Back at the motel, I sat on my bed and contemplated the enormity of what he was asking of me, calculations of selfishness and regret and virtue all fighting to be heard. I knew what was right, but also knew what I wanted, and those two ends remained miles apart.

I pulled my phone out and considered calling Lila. Would this too be a selfish act? I wanted her opinion, but more than that, I needed her calming influence. She would know what to do, but it seemed unfair to spring this on her so close to her bar exam. As I stared at the phone, going back and forth, I noticed that I had missed a call from Allison Cress. That was all I needed—one more angry cat to toss in the gunnysack. I called her back.

"Hi, Allison, what's up?"

"Hi, Joe. I need to talk to you about something. You got a second?" I could tell by Allison's tone that the news was not going to be good.

"Sure," I said.

"I wanted to let you know that we wrote a follow-up story to your article on Senator Dobbins."

"A follow-up?"

"Yes, Joe. We're running a story to explain how we know about Dobbins assaulting his wife. We're going to identify the source."

"But . . . you can't do that. I gave my word."

"I'm sorry, Joe. This is coming from higher up. I wrote the story myself. It'll go online Wednesday."

"You'll destroy her family. Penny trusted me. You can't give her up. I won't allow it."

"Joe," she said sharply, but then in a softer voice continued, "Joe, you can't stop the story. The decision's been made. I'm just calling to give you the heads-up."

"They made the decision without even talking to me?"

"It's not your call."

"Well, it's my call whether I'll work for an organization that would do something like this."

"Joe, don't."

"Allison, if you run that story, I'll have no choice but to quit."

The words came easier to me than I would have thought, and I wondered whether I would have said them at all if I didn't have the promise of three million dollars in my back pocket. Maybe I wasn't meant to be a reporter. Maybe my calling would be to gather needy half-brothers and sisters to my home and take care of them. Perhaps Allison's call was what I needed to make up my mind about Angel.

"I hate to hear you say that, Joe, but I understand. If I were in your shoes, I'd probably do the same thing. You're a good reporter, and I'd hate to lose you."

"You've been a good boss," I said. And with that, we said our goodbyes.

I looked around my empty motel room and felt the urge to be anyplace but there. Buckley may not have had a nightlife, but it had fresh air and sidewalks aplenty. And if that didn't do the trick, there was always the Snipe's Nest, which appealed to that small part of me that felt like basking in my imminent prosperity.

As I made my way toward Main Street, I could hear the sounds of laughter and loud talking coming from a nearby park, where a group of men stood gabbing and drinking beer. I thought I could see the tail of Uncle Charlie's car parked in the line of vehicles down there. I turned and walked in the opposite direction. Half a block later, I found myself at the door to the Snipe's Nest. I peeked in before entering, just to make sure that Harley Redding wasn't inside. The bar was fairly empty of customers, which wasn't surprising given that it was still well ahead of suppertime.

Vicky was leaning against the bar, studying some papers in front of her.

"Is the kitchen open?" I asked.

"Has to be," Vicky said. "We can't sell beer on Sunday unless we also sell food. What'll you have?"

"Can I get a cheeseburger basket and fries?"

As she relayed my order to Marv, I glanced at the papers she'd been looking at and saw that it was an application to Minnesota State University in Mankato. "You're applying to college?" I asked, unable to keep a big smile from stretching across my face.

"Yes, I'm applying," she said, with an impish grin. "That doesn't mean that I'll get in or get enough financial aid to make it happen, but yes . . . I'm applying."

"Well, that is outstanding."

"I have a long way to go before this happens—if it happens— so don't get too excited." She slid the application off the bar and picked up a clean glass. "Beer?"

"Sure—no, wait. You know what? I'm in the mood for something special tonight. I haven't had a Jack and Coke in forever. How about one of those?"

"You got it." She scooped ice into a glass and started pouring the whiskey, letting it flow until it was more of a double. "What's the occasion?"

"Well, I guess I'm celebrating."

"And what are you celebrating?"

"I'm Toke Talbert's son," I said. "The DNA test came back today."

"Well, hot damn and pass the gravy. I think that deserves a drink on the house." She slid my Jack and Coke to me. Then she grabbed a bottle of vodka and started pouring a drink for herself. We clinked glasses and took a drink. The whiskey went down like butterscotch.

"So whatcha gonna do with all that . . . you know . . ."

"Inheritance?" I finished her question for her. I took another pull from my drink as I gave her question some thought. "I don't know. What would you do?"

"I'd get the hell out of Buckley, that's for sure. I mean, with that kind of scratch, you could go anywhere."

"Where would you go, if you could go anywhere?" I asked

"Where wouldn't I go? I'd love to see Europe. Did you know there's castles in Germany where you can rent a room like it's a hotel?"

"I did not know that," I said.

My whiskey-Coke tasted good. I finished it off and put my glass down so she could pour me another—which she did.

"Could you imagine making love in a castle that's hundreds of years old?" Her eyes lit up as she spoke. "Lying naked in a room where some king put it to his queen?"

"Or to his chambermaid."

"There you go." She held her glass up, and we clinked them again.

"With my luck, I'd book the room that used to be the privy."

"The privy?"

"The bathroom."

"Aw, come on. What would be cooler than doing it in a castle?"

"How about on a beach?" I said.

"You've obviously never had sex on a beach."

"I've never even been to a beach, not one with an ocean attached to it."

"You've never seen the ocean?"

"Never."

"Oh, Joe, you have some living to do."

"Well, that's the plan now that I'm about to have the means."

"Then, here's to Toke Talbert." She raised her glass a third time, and I raised mine.

"To the founder of the feast," I said, channeling a little Charles Dickens.

This time, instead of a quick clink, Vicky moved her glass slowly in until the rim of her tumbler touched mine, holding it there before raising it to her lips.

At that moment, the front door to the Snipe's Nest opened.

"Well, look at this shit," Harley Redding hollered, his words stumbling over a drunken tongue. Uncle Charlie stood next to Harley with a big grin slapped on his face. They walked toward us, Harley holding the edge of the bar to keep his balance. Charlie didn't seem to have the same issue.

I turned in my seat and was about to stand to meet them when Charlie nudged the younger man into a booth a few feet shy of my position. Harley fell into the booth and laughed.

Charlie called out to Vicky, "A beer and a shot for me and my new friend here."

"I ain't giving that drunk skunk nothing," she said.

Harley's head wobbled on his neck as he leaned out of the

booth. "Who you gotta . . . fuck around here . . . to get a goddamn drink?" Then he burst into laughter and pointed at Vicky. "That's right." He laughed so hard he could barely get the words out. "I gotta fuck you."

Vicky turned to the kitchen, where Marv was working on my dinner, and whispered something to him—apprising him of the situation would be my guess. Out of the corner of my eye, I saw Charlie stand and make his way toward the bar. I didn't turn.

"Could I get a couple shots of whiskey?" he asked politely.

To that, Vicky raised an eyebrow and said, "I'm not serving Harley. He's too drunk already."

"They're not for him; they're for me—both of 'em."

Vicky kept her eyes trained on Charlie as she lifted a bottle and began to pour.

The liquor in my blood warmed my chest and loosened my joints. The man leaning on the bar next to me was my uncle—no doubt about it anymore—and I felt compelled to tell him the good news.

"Hey, Charlie, guess what?" I said as I turned in my seat. "Vicky and me, we were just celebrating. You know why?"

"I'm sure I don't care."

"Come on—is that any way to talk to your nephew?"

"Still holding on to that fantasy, are you?" he said.

"That's the thing," I said, dropping my pretense that this would be a friendly conversation. "It's not a fantasy. The DNA test came back. It's official. Toke was my dad, which also means that you're my uncle and Angel's my sister."

His fake smile skidded away.

"And to be honest, I'm not sure that I like the idea of you being her guardian."

His eyes narrowed on me. "You stay out of my business," he

said. "You're an irresponsible hothead. You just stay the hell away from that girl."

The time had come to show my hard side. "You know, Charlie, the other day, you said that you can find out some amazing things about a person if you know where to look. Turns out, you had a point."

"Don't try bluffing me, kid. You're out of your league."

I looked him dead in the eye and said, "Poppi Sanchez would beg to differ."

He tried to hold his poker face, but the heat of his blood broke through the fake tan on his cheeks. A glimmer of recognition flashed behind his eyes before he said, "Never heard of her." The he grabbed his two whiskeys, spilling some as he turned to rejoin Harley.

Marv slid my burger basket through the window, calling out to Vicky as he did. I peeked over my shoulder to see Charlie leaning across his table, whispering something to Harley, who was drinking one of the whiskey shots. Then Harley looked at me, his eyes darting back and forth between me and Vicky.

"Here you go," Vicky said, placing my meal in front of me.

I had just reached down the bar to grab some ketchup when I heard a groan in the floorboards behind me. But it was the sudden change of Vicky's expression that told me something was wrong. I turned in time to see Harley Redding bobbing his way toward me with his right arm cocked back and his teeth gritted in anger. Before I could say a word, he swung at my face.

With my reflexes slowed by the whiskey, I didn't have time to block his punch, and his knuckles plowed into the side of my skull, sending a jolt down my spine. A flash of white exploded in my eyes, and then everything went black for a second. The power of his punch had knocked me off my bar stool, and I stumbled back, flailing at anything to keep me from falling to the floor. I caught the edge of one of the booths and grabbed the tabletop. The room tilted as I fought stay on my feet.

Harley stumbled back twenty feet and leaned against the bar, clutching his right hand to his chest. I did my best to blink away the blur in my vision as I pulled myself back up to standing. We were both wounded, but I had recovered well enough to take the offensive, and I charged at Harley.

That's when Charlie jumped out of the booth. He grabbed me by the elbows, pinning my arms behind my back.

"Stop it," Vicky yelled. "I'm calling the cops."

"Fuck you, slut," Harley growled as he stumbled toward me.

I tried to break free of Charlie, but the man had a firm grip on my arms.

Harley let his wounded right hand fall limp to his side and used his left hand to give me a solid punch to my rib cage, knocking the wind out of me.

"Harley! No!" Vicky yelled.

He drew back and delivered a second punch to that exact same spot, and the right side of my body exploded in pain. I picked up my leg and kicked, but Harley stepped back and my foot swung through dead air. I kept it cocked waiting for Harley to come at me again.

Then Charlie let go of one of my elbows, freeing up his arm to wrap it around my neck. He jerked my head hard to the left, like he was trying to pop it off my shoulders. I turned my body to follow. Then he gave my neck a sharp yank to the right. I pushed against a table with my foot, knocking Charlie off balance. He fell to the floor, and I went down on top of him, his arm still around my throat, strangling me.

I reached back and punched Charlie in the side of the head

with my free hand, and that's when I saw Nathan Calder come bursting through the door. Charlie let me loose, and I rolled off of him, gasping for air and coughing.

Harley tried to run past me, to escape out the back door, but I kicked his knee as he jumped over me, his legs folding together, sending him crashing to the floor on top of Charlie. Nathan was on him before he could get back to his feet.

Nathan put Harley in an arm bar, pressing his face down on the floor. "Damn it, Harley, stop struggling or I'll have to Tase you."

"He started it," Harley yelled. "I was defending myself."

"That's right," Charlie chimed in. "It was self-defense." He pointed at me. "This guy came at Harley. I was trying to break it up when you got here."

"You weren't trying to break up nothing," Vicky yelled. "You were in on it. I saw you."

"That not true, Deputy," Charlie said, a look of utter indignation on his face. "I was breaking it up, I swear."

"Don't you believe him, Nathan," Vicky said. She was out from behind the bar now, standing a few feet back from the scuffle. "Harley attacked Joe. And this one . . . " She pointed at Charlie. "He jumped in and tried to twist Joe's head off."

"What're you doing, Nathan?" Harley yelled, but his words were barely intelligible through his slur. "I'm the victim here."

Nathan ratcheted handcuffs around Harley's wrists and stood him up. I'd managed to scoot out of the way to give Deputy Calder room to make his arrests. Charlie was on his feet, brushing dirt off of his nicely pressed khakis.

"Marv, did you see what happened?" Nathan asked.

"I'm right here," I said. "I can tell you what happened."

"What about it Marv?"

Marv was out of the kitchen now and leaning over the bar.

"Vicky told me that Harley was up to no good, but when the shit hit the fan, I was in the kitchen calling you guys."

Charlie thumped his finger into his chest. "I was trying to break it up. That's all I got to say."

"That's bullshit," I said from my place on the floor.

"I'm taking Harley to jail," Nathan said. "You," he said, pointing at Charlie, "should probably get on out of here."

"Aren't you going to arrest him?" I said. "He was in on it."

"I'll get a statement from you all later," Nathan said.

"I'll be at the Caspen Inn," I said. "Room eight." Then, more to myself, I added, "I think I need to lie down."

Nathan led Harley out the front door as Charlie slipped out the back.

"Are you okay?" Vicky leaned down and put her hand on my shoulder.

Breathing hurt like hell, but I said, "All things considered, I'm great."

"Can you stand up?"

"Sure." I started to lift myself up, but a bolt of pain exploded in my chest, and I sat back down on the floor. "I think he bruised my rib."

"Put your arm around my neck," she said, roping my left arm across her shoulders. "Marv? A hand please?"

Marv ambled out from behind the bar and hooked his wrist under my right armpit. Together, they lifted me off the floor. Good god it hurt. "Yup," I said. "He definitely bruised my rib."

They loosened their hold on me, and the room went blurry. I tipped back into the seat of the booth behind me as the lights in my head dimmed.

"Hold on there," Marv said, grabbing my arm to keep me upright. "You may have a concussion. Can you see my finger?"

I looked and could see that he held two fingers up in a peace sign, but they were blurry. I tried to blink the blur away, but his fingers remained fuzzy. "Two fingers," I said. "But everything's a little out of focus."

Vicky said, "We should probably get an EMT down here to take a look at you."

"I'm all right. I just need to rest for a while." I stood up with the help of both Marv and Vicky. My knees didn't seem to lock as tightly as I would have liked, but I didn't fall. "I'll just go back to the motel. I'll be okay."

Marv said, "Vicky, you'd better help him back. Don't want him passing out on the street."

"I think I can make it," I said.

"That's what they all say," Marv replied. "Right before they drop. I used to be a football coach. Let her walk you back."

Vicky wrapped her fingers around my elbow and led me out the front door of the Snipe's Nest, the evening sunlight adding to the throbbing in my head. As my eyes adjusted, I could see Charlie sitting in his car in front of the bar, his eyes on me, burning with rage.

CHAPTER 36

After walking a block, my ribs still throbbed with pain, but my legs had regained some strength. I felt a little strange letting Vicky help me back to the motel, but then I would have missed a turn had she not been there to steer me. "See," she said. "Marv was right to send me along."

I unlocked the door and said, "I can take it from here."

"Nonsense," she said. "I'll stay until Nathan stops by to take your statement. I don't want you passing out." She led me into the room, kicked the door closed with her foot, and sat me on the edge of the bed. "I had a bruised rib once. Even the smallest move can hurt like a bitch." She started stacking all the pillows from both beds together against my headboard. "I'm really sorry about what Harley did," she said.

"That wasn't your fault."

"I'm not so sure." She crawled onto the bed behind me and started fluffing the pillows, arranging them so that I could recline. "Harley and me dated back in high school, and I think he still has a thing for me. He can be a little crazy that way."

"Charlie put him up to it; at least that'd be my guess."

"I doubt Harley Redding needed all that much encouragement. He can be a troublemaker. Plus, you're Toke's kid, and that thing with the GTO probably still burns him up."

"Do you think Harley had anything to do with Toke's death?"

Vicky paused at that question, kneeling on the bed beside me, her hands squeezing her thighs as she contemplated that idea. "Harley? A killer?"

"You saw the way he came at me tonight."

"Harley loses his temper, but I can't see him killing anyone."

"Not even someone who swindled him out of his favorite car?"

"He did love that car," she said. "But killing Toke over that? I can't see it." She rolled off the bed and came around to my side. "We're going to ease you back. It's gonna hurt." She wrapped her arms around my shoulders. "Try not to use your chest muscles. Just let me do the work."

I relaxed into her as much as I could, but the pain shot up my right side anyway. I stiffened, and she held me tighter, settling me into the pillows, her long hair falling against my cheek. I could feel the strength of her hands on my back and the softness of her chest against mine. The smell of her perfume distracted me from the pain.

I settled into the pillows, and she moved with me, the tension releasing from my chest with a final exhale. But she remained in that embrace, one arm around my shoulder, the other holding my head, her cheek pressed against my cheek. Then she gently slid her lips to mine and kissed me.

And I let her.

A thousand shards ricocheted through my brain in that instant, half of them feeble rationales for why this was okay. I was hurt. This was compassion, nothing more. She was kissing me; I wasn't kissing her. I'd been drinking. I might have a concussion, so I wasn't thinking straight. It was only a kiss.

But those were all lies, and I knew it.

Her lips were soft and tasted of cinnamon gum. Her finger pressed against the back of my head, pulling me into her. The kiss was warm and gentle and lasted for only a few seconds before it was interrupted by a knock at the door.

She pulled back an inch, her hair still tickling my face, an expression of disappointment in her eyes. "Nathan," she whispered.

I didn't say a word. I wouldn't have known what to say if I tried. Deep down, I was happy for Nathan's intrusion. He put an end to something that I couldn't—or at least didn't. I felt a hundred ways of wrong at that moment.

Vicky gave me a coy smile and got up to answer the door. "Nathan, you have a terrible sense of..."

When she didn't finish her sentence, I looked at the door, expecting to see Nathan Calder. Instead, I saw Lila, standing in the opened doorway, a look of confusion on her face. She went back and forth between Vicky and me, and her confusion fell away. In its place was hurt, profound and raw. Her eyes filled with tears as she turned and ran. I tried to get up, forgetting my bruised rib for a second, but the pain knocked me back down onto the pillows. I held still until I was able to breathe again. Then I rolled onto my side and off the bed, hobbling to the door in time to see her drive away.

CHAPTER 37

I called Lila's phone twice on my drive back to St. Paul. She didn't answer, and honestly, I didn't expect her to.

I had two and a half hours behind the wheel to think about the coming conversation. The fog from Harley's punch had cleared from my head, and if I breathed in shallow breaths, and leaned slightly to my right, I could keep the pain in my ribs from shouting. With that under control, I turned my attention to what I would say to Lila.

She hadn't seen the kiss, I knew that. When Vicky opened the door, I was lying on the bed, and both Vicky and I were fully clothed. Lila would never know about the kiss unless I told her. "It's not what you think," I would tell her. "Nothing happened." But something did happen, and I knew it. I knew the taste of Vicky's lips and the feel of her breasts pressing against my chest as she pulled me deeper into that kiss. I knew the struggle of my words: yes and no, twisting up in my throat, with neither finding voice. I knew that telling Lila the truth would wound her in a way that could never be undone.

I knew all these things, but I also knew that I would not lie to Lila.

I paused in the hallway outside of our apartment. Should I knock? It was my apartment too, after all. Yet I had violated something sacred, and entering without permission seemed suddenly wrong. I took a middle path. I knocked and opened the door at the same time, peeking my head in to see that she wasn't in the living room.

"Lila?"

No answer.

Stepping into the dark apartment, I closed the door behind me and walked a few feet until I could see light cutting a line beneath the bedroom door. "Lila?" I called again, louder this time so that my entry into the bedroom would not startle her.

I listened at the door, and then knocked lightly. She didn't answer. I opened it to find her sitting on the bed tucked up into a ball, her back against the headboard, her arms folded across her knees, and her face buried in her arms. I walked in slowly, the way one does when trying to not frighten a wild animal.

"Who is she?" Lila didn't lift her head when she asked.

"She's nobody." As soon as the words left my lips I regretted saying them. All my practice on the drive up went out the window.

"Don't lie!" Lila lifted her head and looked at me, her eyes red from crying. "She was in your room. She's not nobody."

"You're right," I said. "I'm sorry." I sat on the edge of the bed, being careful to keep some space between us. "Her name is Vicky. She's a bartender down there. I . . . I got into a fight with one of the local boys tonight. Vicky walked me home."

"And that's all she did?" Lila searched my eyes for the lie she was expecting.

"No," I said. "That's not all."

Lila's breath caught on something, and she paused to take in my words. The corners of her lips tugged downward, but she swallowed and pressed on. "Did you...screw her?"

"No," I said.

"Did you kiss her?"

I tried to answer with words, but the most I could do was nod.

"What else?"

"Nothing—I mean, she gave me a ride on her motorcycle one night, out to see the Hix farm. We talked. And tonight, after the fight, she walked me home and..." I shrugged.

"I stopped you?"

"We just kissed the once."

"Do you really think that makes it better?" Lila's hurt was turning to anger. I braced for more, but she pulled back. Her eyes had filled with tears again. I can't remember ever seeing Lila cry before, and to see it now carved a hole in my chest.

"How could you do that to me? I...I don't understand."

"I'm sorry," I whispered. "It just..."

"Don't you dare say 'it just happened.' Nothing like this just happens. Don't disrespect me like that."

"No, that's not...I don't know what I meant."

"I don't get it." Tears flowed down her face now as she spoke. "All I needed from you was for you to be a good man. That's all I ever asked. You don't have to be superman to make me happy. All you had to do was be a decent guy, and you couldn't do that. Did I ask too much? I honestly don't understand. Help me get it. Why do you need another woman?"

"I don't need another woman. I don't want anyone else. I love you, Lila. I don't know what happened. She and I were talking at the bar. We were kind of celebrating because the DNA results came back, and I'm definitely Toke's son. Lila, we're going to have a bunch of money in a few months."

"You think I care about money?" Lila spit her words out with disgust, as if that notion repulsed her more than the kiss. "How could you think that of me? Who are you?"

"No, that's not what I meant. It's just that things have been stressful around here. If we had money—"

"So this is what I can expect when the going gets a little tough?"

"No."

"I trusted you. I actually came down to Buckley because I felt bad. I wanted to spend one night with you before I sit for the bar exam. I was feeling bad about all the stuff you've been going through. I wanted you to know that I was there for you. I wanted to surprise you...and I find you with another woman."

I almost blurted out that all we did was kiss, but I stopped myself. She was right. This wasn't about a kiss. It didn't matter if it was a kiss or if it was more. Lila trusted me. She loved me and looked at me in a way that made me feel like I was the center of the world. I wondered now if she would ever look at me that way again.

"I think you should go," she said.

"Go? But..." I had nothing to say that didn't sound trite and woefully lacking.

"If you want to stay here at the apartment, I'll go, but I don't want to see you for a while. I don't want to hear from you, so don't call me."

"Lila, I'm sorry. I don't want this."

"Please," she said, burying her face in her hands. "Don't make this harder than it is. I need to be alone. I have to get my mind back on passing the bar before I can think about us. Just go, please."

I walked to the door to our bedroom and stopped. I wanted to turn and fight for us. I didn't want to leave. But this was her call; I had no right to deny her request. Besides, I was pretty sure that if I forced the issue right now, it would end things between us. She needed me gone. Sometimes, retreat is the best course if it leaves open a chance to return, even if that chance is a slim one.

So I left.

PART 2

CHAPTER 38

I'm lying on the hood of my car, my back reclined against my windshield, my knees bent, my fingers laced together on my stomach. It's a beautiful night, weather-wise. The lateness of the hour and the easy breeze coming from the north is enough to keep the mosquitos at bay, and for now, the throb of pain in my ribs is quiet. In the calm, the ghosts of the day resurrect themselves and move against the backdrop of the starry night. There are so many regrets circling around me, but the thing that haunts me the most is the echo of Lila's voice saying that all she ever asked of me was to be a decent man—and I couldn't even do that.

When I left the apartment an hour and a half ago, I was a man adrift. I knew where I was going, yet I pretended that it was not my choice, as though I was being pulled here by a force outside of my own will, drawn to a place I once swore I would never again abide--Austin, Minnesota.

I don't think I can ever go back to Buckley. It's unfair, I know, but I want to blame the town for my downfall. I try to blame Vicky too—sheer cowardice on my part. I tell myself that I have to stay far away from her, even though it was I who failed to mention Lila's name in any of our conversations. I saw Vicky's flirtations. I knew the smell of her perfume and the lacy out-line of her bra long before she leaned down to kiss me. So how could it be her fault? I'm starting to think that I have always been an awful person, and the town of Buckley merely shone a light on it.

The drive to Austin had gone by in a whirl of noise and nau-sea, and as I got closer to town, I realized that I wasn't ready to confess to my mother that her golden boy was a fraud, that I had been kicked out of my apartment because of my epic failure as a human being. I couldn't face that. And then I re-membered a little trail where I used to take girls back when I was in high school, a long field approach surrounded by trees where we could make out undisturbed. I drove there and parked between two enormous cottonwoods, their thick leaves stirring the air above me. The field approach is as I remember it, dark, secluded—a good place to spend the night.

Now, as I lay on the hood of my car, I feel more alone than I have ever felt before. I have my car and the clothes on my back, and that is all. I have no home. I am moored to nothing. The chirps and trills of the night critters fill the air around me, seem-ingly undisturbed by my presence. To drown them out, and to avoid dwelling on my sins, I think back to the first moment when I knew that I loved Lila. I always expected such a moment to come with confetti and music, but for me it came in candlelight.

We hadn't yet moved in together, and the three of us had planned an evening of watching television and eating popcorn. It was April, and a spring storm came through, knocking out the power. With no TV, a bored Jeremy went to bed early, so Lila and I snuggled up on the couch and talked.

Our conversation that night touched on nothing profound. She told me about her favorite Christmas—she got a puppy named Annie. She told me about a day when she was eight years old, and was plucked from the audience and put on stage at a Shania Twain concert. She told me about visiting her aunt at work, a paralegal at a law firm, and how that lit the fire that would send her to law school.

For my part, I confessed to her how I often felt like a fraud. I was never the kind of guy who was meant to make a living without dirt under my fingernails. I told her how I felt like I didn't belong in school, and that I was sure someone would figure it out and send me back to Austin.

That's when she rolled onto my chest, her beautiful face brimming with sincerity. She told me that I was wrong, that I wasn't a fake. She called me amazing and ingenious, and as I listened to her, I began to believe it. I honestly never thought that I would become a journalist until that night when I saw it in her eyes. And I loved her for that.

She fell asleep before I did, and I remember looking at her soft face and thinking that I would never want for anything more from life than to be with her.

I shift my position on the hood of my car, and the pain in my chest flares to remind me of where I am and what I've done. I want the memory of Lila back. I want it all back. I remain on my hood for hours, staring up at the stars and remembering, until sleep finally comes to ease the pain.

CHAPTER 39

I wake up the next morning still reclined on my windshield, my clothes damp with sweat and dew, my mind pulled from sleep by the call of a mourning dove. I move, and the pain in my rib cage comes alive. I feel like a rusted hinge as I make my way off the hood of my car and into the driver's seat. I check my phone, knowing that she would not have called me or sent a text. And I am right.

I drive ten minutes to Kathy's place, pausing before knocking on her door. I've never knocked on this door before. This had been my home for more years than not, but it's not my home any longer. Right as my knuckles tap wood, I hear my mother's voice coming from inside.

"I can't believe it. Jeremy, what am I going to do with you?"

Not waiting for an invitation, I open the door and step into the apartment, but I don't find what I had expected. No argument. No backslide on Kathy's recovery. Instead, I see my mother and my brother playing cards. Kathy smiles at me, and Jeremy looks my way but then goes back to the game, his eyes studying his cards.

"How's it going?" I ask.

"Terrible," Mom says with a melodramatic flare. "Jeremy keeps beating me at Go Fish. He's real card shark. He's won every game so far."

She's letting him win—another small change in our mother. I remember when she used to say that letting a child win a game doesn't teach them anything. "It's a hard world out there," she would say. "The sooner you understand that the better." It's such a small thing to let Jeremy win at a game, but it is so much at odds with the mother I've known my whole life that I can barely reconcile what I'm seeing.

"I made muffins," she says, pointing to a plate on the counter covered with a towel. "I didn't make coffee. I don't drink it any-more, but I have some if you want to make it."

"You don't drink coffee?"

"That stuff can be addictive." She shrugs and gives me a smile. "In for a penny, in for a pound."

I grab two muffins, pour a glass of milk, and take a seat at the table. "How'd you like staying here?" I ask Jeremy. I suspect that Kathy knows that my question isn't just making small talk. I want a report on our mother's parenting skills as well as Jeremy's com-fort level, at least to the extent that he can make such a report.

"Maybe I like my bed," he says.

That tells me all I need to know.

Mom asks, "Are you taking Jeremy home today?" In her voice I could sense a hint of sadness.

"No," I say. "Not yet." I am not ready to tell my mother that I've been thrown out of my apartment. "In fact, I was wonder-ing if Jeremy could stay here another day or two." I calculate in my head. The bar exam starts tomorrow. It's a two-day test. After that, I'll find out where things stand between Lila and me. My chest starts to hurt just thinking about it.

"I'd love that," Mom says.

"Jeremy, would that be okay with you?" I ask.

"Yes. Um...do you have any eights?" he asks Kathy.

"Well, doggone it, you got me again." Kathy pulls an eight from her hand and gives it to Jeremy, who lays down a pair. Kathy gives an exaggerated sigh, and Jeremy laughs. As Jeremy is contemplating his next request, Kathy asks me, "Are you going back to Buckley then?"

"I'm not sure," I say. "I might go up to Mankato."

"What's in Mankato?"

"Oh, I didn't tell you—I have a sister."

Kathy looks perplexed at that statement.

"Toke married a woman in Buckley named Jeannie Hix. They had a daughter. Her name is Angel. So...that makes her my half-sister."

Kathy is shaking her head no as she processes the information. I feel bad for blurting it out the way I did. I didn't stop to remember how Toke treated her when she got pregnant.

"No, he can't. That's not possible." Kathy looks at me with an expression of utter confusion.

"I've met her," I say.

"Jeremy, can we take a break from cards for a little bit?"

Jeremy nods his head. "Maybe I can go watch TV."

"Would you, honey? I want to talk to Joe for a second."

After Jeremy leaves the table, Kathy goes to her bedroom and returns with a box. I'd seen that box in her closet going back to my earliest memories, but I never looked inside because it had a lock on it. Kathy opens it by prying the latch sideways with a butter knife. She digs through it, pulling out a few pictures and handing them to me before going back to her search. I recognize my mother in one of the pictures, young and attractive, sitting on a lawn chair with a man who I now know is my father. They are holding up Budweiser cans as if toasting the person taking the picture. In another snapshot, he's standing with one arm draped across her shoulders, and she's got both of her arms wrapped around his waist.

"Your father wasn't always a jerk to me. As you can see, there was a time when I'd say we were happy. But after I got pregnant, he became spiteful and cruel."

"I found the police report from when he hit you in the stomach," I say.

Kathy pauses as that memory washes over her, and I can see her embarrassment in the way she presses her lips together and drops her gaze. "I guess you could say that was the night we broke up. I sometimes saw him around town after you were born. I actually thought that he might change his mind about you if he saw you."

"That's why you gave me his name?"

She nods. "I'm sorry about that. It was a stupid thing to do. If anything, it backfired. It made him crazy mad. And then, one night when you were only a few months old, I got a letter from Joe. He was furious because the county was going after him for child support. They were going to garnish his wages. He wrote some very hateful things in that letter. One of the things he said was that the child support thing made him so mad that he went and got a vasectomy. He said that he did it so...so that no damn bitch could ever try to trap him into marriage again."

Mom pauses to take a breath, and I can see a slight tremble in her fingers. "That was Joe's goodbye letter. He said he was leaving Minnesota. I never heard from him again."

"Jesus, what a...jerk."

"Yeah. So you see, Joe can't have a daughter."

"Well, even if he was telling the truth about the vasectomy, those things can be undone, can't they?"

"Probably. But Joe hated the very thought of children. Here..." Kathy digs through the box again and pulls out another letter, handing it to me.

"What's this?" I ask.

"Joe wrote that when he was in jail after they arrested him for punching me. If you want it, you can have it. It's the closest you'll ever have to your father saying goodbye. But there's nothing nice about this letter. You don't have to read it if you don't want to."

I unfold the letter, scratchy, cursive text on white paper.

Kathy,

You are such a bitch. Did you really think it would work? Did you really think I would stay with you? Well the joke's on you. I'm not having anything to do with any kid. You will have to make due with the bed you made. And don't think I'm going to pay you any child support neither. You try that shit and I'll quit my job and be gone. You'll never find me. You ain't getting a dime from me. I'll live in the woods and eat berries before I pay you anything. I guess you're little game didn't have the out come you wanted. Go to hell and take the kid with you.

Fuck you.
Joe

I finish reading the letter and look up to see my mother staring at the table between us. I try to say something to lighten the mood. "He writes like a fifth-grader," I say. "It's a good thing he left."

That makes my mother smile.

CHAPTER 40

If Mom is right about Toke's vasectomy, then Kimball's investigation is being steered by a blind man. This could be nothing, but then again, it could be huge.

Despite my trepidation about returning to Buckley, I want to deliver this news to Sheriff Kimball personally. I want to watch his face as it sinks in, see if it hits him the way it hit me. If there had been a vasectomy, they can prove it with a second autopsy. Angel can only be Toke's daughter if Toke had the procedure reversed, and from everything that I'd learned about my father, he doesn't seem like a man who would be willing to go to that length to be a father. But then again, who knows what he might have done to get his hands on the Hix estate.

As I pull into town, another thought strikes me, and I take a turn that leads me to Bob Mullen's office. When I enter, I find Bob sharply focused on something on his computer. I knock on the wall to get his attention, and he looks up at me, lines of worry tracing across his forehead.

"They charged Moody Lynch with murder," he says.

"They what? How?"

"Second-degree murder." Bob waves me into his inner office.

"That's impossible. They don't have enough to charge him, do they?"

"They do, and you're the key witness."

Bob hands me a document—a criminal complaint—and I begin reading about how they believe that Moody Lynch killed Toke Talbert. They state: *Moody Lynch informed a witness, Joe Talbert Junior, that he (Defendant) had an encounter with Joe (Toke) Talbert Senior during which the defendant struck the senior Mr. Talbert in the head with a metal gear.*

"They left out where I said it was self-defense. Toke attacked Moody with a rope and beat the crap out of him. Where's that part? And Toke was alive when Moody left. Hell, Moody was the one who called the cops."

"Is it true that he hit Toke with a gear?"

"He said he grabbed it off the wall when Toke was hitting him. He wasn't trying to kill Toke."

"Your statement is evidence," Bob says. "They can spin it any way they want to—just like I'll be spinning it the opposite way."

"You're representing Moody?"

"His family just left. I'll be his attorney."

"I don't believe Moody killed Toke."

"That's admirable, Joe, but belief isn't evidence."

"You can get the evidence," I say. "You're his attorney, so you can get all the reports and tapes and stuff, right?"

"Yes, I'll get all that in time."

"How much time?"

"What? Oh, I guess they'll hand most of the discovery to me at the first appearance tomorrow. Why?"

"Can you get it today?"

"What are you driving at?"

"I have information that might help clear Moody. Can you get the discovery today?"

"If I have a good reason." Bob points at a chair, and I sit down. "You want to tell me what you're talking about?"

"I know something that the sheriff doesn't. I just came from my mother's house in Austin. We were talking about Toke, and I mentioned that I have a half-sister and..." I stop before I get too far ahead of myself and collect my thoughts, asking the question that I came there to ask. "Mr. Mullen, is it possible that Jeannie Talbert had an affair?"

Bob pulls back as if some foul scent just brushed his nose. "Affair?"

"She worked here. You were close to her."

"Jeannie was like a daughter to me, which is just one reason in a long list of reasons why this conversation is highly inappropriate."

"Before he left Austin, Toke told my mother that he had a vasectomy. He was rubbing my mother's nose in it."

"Those things can be reversed," Bob says.

"He treated Angel like he resented her."

Bob raises his eyebrows at that one. "Like a child he knows isn't his own."

"Exactly. If Jeannie had an affair, that would explain a lot. She worked for you. You had to see something."

Bob tugs at his beard, either concentrating on a memory or deciding whether to tell me what he knows—I can't tell which. Then he leans forward, his elbows on the desk, his hands clasped together, his face sad. "I think there might have been someone," he says. "She never told me, and I never asked, but...now that I think about it, I guess it might have been around the time she got pregnant. Toke was hitting the sauce pretty hard, I remember that. She would come to work with bags under her eyes. Her concentration was off. She'd only been working for me for a little while, so I didn't pry, although I wish I had. She seemed quite sad for a long time.

But then she made this swing, a complete one-eighty, happy and cheerful. I'd even catch her singing songs at her desk. She had a pretty voice. I just figured that she'd resolved whatever had been bothering her."

"She was having an affair?"

"It's possible. There was this one night that Toke showed up at my home looking for Jeannie. I got the impression that he thought she was still at the office. I hemmed and hawed until he let the cat out of the bag. He said that Jeannie told him that she was working late, but the office was already closed for the day. I kept my response simple and evasive, telling him that she had been working a lot lately. I told him that I had gone home early because of a headache, and that I didn't know when Jeannie left. That wasn't true. Jeannie left early that day."

"Did Toke figure it out?"

"I don't know. Like I said, I didn't pry. When Jeannie came in the next morning, I told Jeannie about Toke's visit. She didn't react one way or another to that news, but after that, Jeannie went back to being the old Jeannie, the one who didn't sing at her desk."

"She ended her affair."

"That'd be a reasonable conclusion."

"Do you have any idea who the affair was with?"

"No. But I might be able to figure it out. I have a program on my phones to record the number for all outgoing calls, even local ones. I use it to bill clients accurately. I never throw those records away, in case anyone wants to dispute my bill. I'm kind of a pack rat that way."

Bob stands and walks to a small door just outside of his office, disappearing down a staircase into the basement. I wait, listening to the clock on the wall tick away the minutes—twelve of them in all—before he returns. In his hand he carries a yellow folder, and he is reading from the pages of that folder as he sits down.

"These are calls made from Jeannie's phone nine months before Angel was born." He studies the page, and I watch as a glimmer of recognition grows on his face. "There's one number here—she was talking to this person multiple times a day and for twenty and thirty minutes at a shot. I had no idea."

"Who is it?"

"I don't recognize the number, but we can call it and find out."

"Use star–six–seven so they can't see who's calling."

"Good idea." Bob hits the speaker button on his desk phone and dials. We look at each other as it rings once, twice, then— *click*.

"Jeb Lewis here."

Bob hangs up.

CHAPTER 41

After we put together a plan, Bob and I leave his office together, heading toward the courthouse square. I break away as we pass the Sheriff's Office, and Bob continues on, limping his way up the granite steps of the courthouse to see the county attorney. His part of our plan is to sit in that office until they give him the evidence in Moody's case.

I walk into the Sheriff's Office and ask to see Kimball. At first the receptionist tells me that he's too busy to see me.

"Tell Sheriff Kimball that I have new evidence that he needs to know about. Tell him that I have proof that his investigation is tainted. He needs to see me."

She rolls her eyes, picks up the phone, and speaks a few words, her irritated expression never softening. A minute later, Sheriff Kimball appears at the door.

"This had better be good. I'm busy."

"Is there someplace we can talk in private?"

Kimball looks disgusted and shakes his head, but leads me to the conference room. "Now what's this all about?" he says.

I look at the camera in the corner of the ceiling. "Is Jeb listening?"

"No, Jeb's out on a call, so you'll have to talk to me."

"You're the one I want to talk to. I think you arrested the wrong man."

"Oh, for Christ's sake."

"Just hear me out," I say. "I know you and Nathan don't want to believe a word that Moody Lynch says."

"Is that what this is about?" Kimball stands up and starts for the door. "You're wasting my time."

"No, that's not what this is about." I raise my hands in a stay-put gesture. "I have new information, and it explains some of the problems in Moody's statement."

Kimball crosses him arms and stands by the door. "Fine, let's hear it."

"Moody said that when he got to the barn, he found Angel on the ground—groggy, like she'd already taken the pills. But Jeb said that he found her in the house. That doesn't make sense. So naturally, you assume that Moody was lying about seeing Angel there."

"Of course he was lying. She was unconscious when Jeb found her in her bed."

"But what if Jeb is the one who is lying?"

Kimball's demeanor drops from irritated to threatening. "Boy, you had better tread lightly."

"What if Jeb Lewis had an affair with Jeannie Talbert?"

That little bomb does less to chip away at Kimball's anger than I expect, but I can see fissures beginning to form. He narrows his stare and walks to the table to sit. "I'm not big on town gossip, son. If you have something, you'd better be sure of it."

"Toke Talbert had a vasectomy," I say. "After my mother got pregnant with me, Toke went ape-shit and had a vasectomy. He did it so that no woman could ever try to trap him again."

"You have proof of this?"

"I have my mother's word, but it should be easy enough to verify. I assume you still have Toke's body on ice somewhere. If he couldn't sire another child, then Angel isn't his daughter."

"How, exactly, do you make the leap from that to Jeb having an affair with Jeannie?"

"They were high-school sweethearts. You knew about that, right?"

"High school was a long time ago."

"Jeannie used to work for Bob Mullen. Bob keeps track of calls made from his office. He said that in the months just before Jeannie got pregnant, there were a ton of calls made to one particular number—Jeb's number."

"That doesn't prove anything."

"No, Sheriff, it doesn't prove anything, but if it's true, that means that one of the investigators in Toke's murder had a motive himself to kill Toke."

Kimball swallows hard, and I watch his eyes move back and forth, as though connecting dots in his mind. Then he picks up the phone and hits three numbers. "Shirley? Is Jeb still out on that domestic?" Pause. "Is Nathan in the office?" Pause. "Have Nathan join me in the interview room, and tell him to bring the Talbert case with him, please."

Kimball rubs the stubble on his chin and lets out a heavy sigh as we wait. The door opens, and Deputy Calder walks in carrying a box, putting it on a chair beside Kimball. Kimball pulls a folder from the box and starts thumbing through it. "Nathan, I have a question to ask you, and I need the absolute truth. I know you and Jeb are close, but this is important."

Calder eases into a chair next to Kimball.

"Nathan, do you know anything about Jeb having an affair with Jeannie Talbert?"

Calder turns a dark shade of pink when he hears the question.

He looks at me, and then back at Kimball, his jaw slackened, his eyes probably trying to read our faces, hoping to find some hint of explanation. "I'm not sure."

Kimball looks up from the file. "What do you mean, you're not sure?" Kimball says. "Either you know something or you don't."

"It was a long time ago. I remember there was a span of a few months when Jeb was asking me to cover for him. You know, pick up a call here and there and not ask questions. I don't know how to explain it exactly—it just seemed strange. I thought . . . maybe, you know? But I never knew for sure."

Kimball shakes his head. "Well, shit." He pulls a second file folder from the box, and I can see that it is the autopsy report. He starts flipping through it.

"What's this all about?" Nathan asks.

"Little Toke here thinks he has proof that Jeb and Jeannie were having an affair."

"So what?" Nathan asks. "What's that got to do with the price of tea?"

Kimball ignores Calder and continues reading the report. "This strange activity you noticed, would that have been around the time just before Jeannie got pregnant?"

Nathan straightens up. "I don't remember. It was a long time ago. Like I said—"

Kimball holds up a finger to stop Nathan, his attention aimed at the file in his hand. Kimball goes back to the previous file, which I can now see had Angel's name on the lip. He picks up the phone and pushes three buttons again. "Shirley, could you dig up Jeannie Talbert's suicide file and bring it here?"

"What is it, Sheriff?" Nathan asks.

"Probably nothing, but we may have a problem. You see, Little Toke also—"

"Don't call me that," I say. "My name is Joe." My tone yanks Kimball's attention away from his reading, but only for a moment. Then he shrugs and returns to his thought.

"Joe has reason to believe that Toke had a vasectomy." Kimball waits for Nathan to see the link. "Toke might not be Angel's father."

"You think Jeb might be...," Nathan says.

I ask Nathan, "How many times has Jeb gone to Mankato to visit Angel?"

"That's none of your business."

"How many?" Kimball repeats.

Nathan looks humble when he answers. "About every other day."

"Does his wife know that?" Kimball asks.

"He told me to keep it between us."

The receptionist walks in, hands a file to Kimball, and leaves.

I say, "Does that sound like the actions of a concerned deputy or a concerned father?"

"Aw, Jesus Christ," Kimball blurts out. He has a look on his face like a man who just caught his son shooting heroin. He throws Jeannie's suicide file onto the table.

"What is it?" Nathan asks.

"Toke Talbert's blood type is O negative. Jeannie was B." He looks at Nathan. "According to Angel's medical report, she's AB."

Nathan doesn't respond.

"Damn it, Nathan, they lectured about this at the blood seminar we went to last year. Weren't you paying attention?"

Nathan shrugs his confusion.

"An O and a B cannot give birth to anything with an A in it." Kimball looks defeated as he speaks. "Toke can't be Angel's father. It's medically impossible."

"And you think that Jeb...," Nathan starts.

Kimball props his elbows on the table and raises his hands to massage his temples. "Let's look at this and assume two things: first that Moody is telling the truth, and second, that Jeb knows or at least suspects that he is Angel's father. Jeb arrives at the barn and sees Angel, unconscious, lying next to Toke. Question one: is Toke dead or alive at this point?"

Nathan says, "I say he's already dead."

"If that's so, then Jeb could have easily drawn the conclusion that a girl, who just might be his daughter, committed murder and then attempted suicide. To protect her, he carries her into the house to throw us off her trail."

I say, "But according to Moody, he only hit Toke one time, and Toke was alive when the first car arrived. The autopsy report says that Toke got hit three times. Who struck the second and third blows?"

Kimball looks up, his face almost gray as he contemplates this worst-case scenario. "Jeb doesn't want Toke to wake up and implicate Angel, so . . . he has to silence Toke."

"That's crazy," Calder says. "Do you hear yourself, Sheriff? This is Jeb we're talking about. Damn it, you know Jeb. You know he'd never kill anyone. Not in a million years."

"I'm not saying Jeb killed Toke," Kimball says. "I'm just saying that if any of this is even close to true, we're in deep shit. A man who could be a suspect is hip-deep in the investigation. We need to bring him in and question him."

"Are you the right guys for that job?" I ask.

"What are you implying?" Calder says.

"I'm not implying anything. I'm telling you outright. You need to call the BCA down here. You're too close to this."

"We can handle it," Kimball says. "We'll bring him in and get his version. If it looks like you might be right about this, then we're off the case. But we'll be the ones having the conversation with Jeb. In the meantime, this goes nowhere." Kimball points his finger at me. "This is confidential stuff. We don't want it leaking it out, am I clear?"

I nod my agreement, despite my doubts.

CHAPTER 42

I walk back to Bob's office and sit on the hood of my car to await his return. My ribs still hurt, but the four ibuprofens I took earlier have knocked the pain down to a dull throb. The excitement that coursed through my veins when I told Kimball about the affair is replaced with a vague melancholy. It might be residue from Lila's words, or maybe I'm sad to think that Jeb is somehow involved with Toke's death. I like Jeb, and a part of me is hoping that somewhere buried in that file Bob is getting, we'd find the proof that I'm wrong.

Behind me, in the distance, I hear the rev of a motorcycle engine, and I don't have to turn around to know that it's Vicky. I'm sitting with my elbows resting on my knees, my chest curved to ease the pressure on my ribs. I cast a very small shadow as the sun climbs toward noon, and I hold that pose as she rides by, hoping that I might go unnoticed. It doesn't work.

Vicky turns her Triumph around, rides back, and parks on the street beside me, killing her engine. "Hi, stranger."

"Hi." I feel like I should be cold to her, but my situation wasn't her fault.

"So, how bad was it?" she asks.

"Pretty bad," I say.

"She break up with you?"

"I'm not sure."

"Not sure?"

"We're...taking some time off, I guess." I look at Vicky. Her cheeks are rosy from the wind, and she is sporting a half-smile, something that gives her face a hopeful appearance.

"Does that mean that I could...you know...stop by later?"

I hang my head back down and look at the pavement. "That's not a good idea."

"I see."

"I really love my girlfriend," I say. "I guess I should have made that clear."

"You could have started by telling me that you had a girlfriend at all." There is no spite in her voice. It almost sounds as if she's apologizing, and that makes me feel even worse.

"I'm sorry," I say.

"Yeah...me too." It is a wistful statement, one that sounds very much like a final goodbye. She starts her motorcycle, U-turns, and rides away.

I try to immerse myself back into thoughts of Jeb and Toke, but all I get are flashes of Lila, sitting on our bed, telling me to leave. The bar exam starts tomorrow morning. When it's done, there will be a reckoning, and that thought scares me.

I expect Bob to be back by now, but the minutes trudge by with the sluggish gait of a wounded soldier. An hour passes, and I'm about to walk to the courthouse to check on him when Bob turns the corner with an accordion folder in his hands, waving me to follow him into his office. He looks winded from his walk.

"I was getting worried," I say.

"I stopped by the Sheriff's Office to see how they were taking the news about Jeb."

"And?"

"They're throwing a conniption over there. I could hear Kimball yelling to beat all hell. Then they walked by with Jeb in handcuffs, taking him to jail."

"Jeb confessed?"

"Kimball told me that Jeb admitted to taking Angel into the house. That's as far as it got. Jeb must have figured out that he was in a heap of trouble because he invoked his right to remain silent."

"But they arrested him for Toke's murder?"

"Not yet. They have him for interfering with a murder scene. It's not a felony, but they can hold him overnight while they try to figure out what happened."

"Moody was telling the truth."

"Kimball's recommending that Moody be released. The complaint they have is wrong and they know it." Bob put the Lynch file down on Jeannie's desk. "I'm going back over to the jail. I want to tell Moody the good news."

"Would you mind if I took a look through the file?" I ask.

Bob considers this for a few seconds and says, "Sure. Just do me a favor and don't snoop around the office while I'm gone."

"Wouldn't dream of it," I say.

Bob is about to leave when he stops and slowly turns to face me, the thoughts in his head pinching his forehead into deep creases. "You know what this means, don't you?"

"What *what* means?"

"If Jeb is Angel's father . . . you see how that changes things."

"Sure, it gives Jeb a motive to kill Toke, if that's what you're getting at."

"No. That's not what I'm getting at. Jeannie's estate has been fully probated. Everything has been signed and sealed. That estate now belongs to Toke, and Toke alone."

I don't see where he's going with this.

"If Toke is not Angel's father, then by the laws of intestacy she can't inherit. The estate is Toke's, and every bit of it goes to his sole heir. The one person who can prove that he is Toke's biological son." Bob points his finger at me.

"That's not . . . I had no idea."

"Angel gets nothing."

"But she's Jeannie's daughter."

"I suppose Angel's guardian could bring a petition to reopen the case, split the inheritance between Angel and Toke, but right now she has no guardian."

"That's what should happen," I say.

"You say that now, but I've been doing this a long time. It's easy to sound noble when the money is theoretical. It's a different matter when the money becomes real. You'll start thinking that six million sounds a whole lot better than three million. I've seen it happen."

Twenty-four hours ago, I'd have been certain that Bob was wrong about me. After last night, though, I'm not sure of anything. "I won't change my mind," I say, but even as I say the words, I see myself standing where Vicky took me to show me the fields. I shake that image away and say again, "I won't change my mind—I promise."

Bob says, "No offense, Joe, but I'll believe that when I see it." With those parting words, he heads out the door.

CHAPTER 43

Bob's office is quiet after he leaves. I spread the Moody Lynch file out on Jeannie's desk. The accordion folder holds four sets of papers clamped together with big, black binding clips. There's also a large manila envelope with the word *Recordings* written on it. I open the envelope and let the CDs slide onto the desk. At the top of the heap is Nathan's squad video. I figure that would be a good place to start.

It takes me a minute to fire up Jeannie's computer, and another two or three to launch the squad video. When it opens, the computer screen divides into five boxes, a big box on the left and four smaller boxes stacked on the right. The bigger box is obviously the forward-facing squad camera. One of the smaller squares is a camera pointing into the backseat of the squad car. After some study, I figure out that the other three are views of the sides and rear of the car.

At the start of the video, Nathan's squad is speeding down a country highway, thin reflections of the emergency lights bouncing off the car's hood. I hear dispatch inform Nathan that 2804 is near the scene and is responding off duty. I look through some reports to confirm that 2804 is Jeb's badge number. Nathan replies, "Ten-four," his voice as calm as a man reading a newspaper.

I watch for fifteen minutes before I see something I recognize—the bridge where Vicky's mother died. I know now that Nathan is almost at the scene. He slows as he gets to the farm, and I lean forward to examine every second of footage carefully.

Through the front windshield, the world rotates as Nathan pulls into the courtyard and parks facing the house, a dim glow falling from one of the windows on the second floor. To the right of the squad car is the horse barn, its door open, light spilling out into the courtyard. The squad camera facing left shows Jeb's personal vehicle, the one he drove on our trip to Mankato.

Nathan gets out of his squad and walks to the barn, enters, and bends down over a black lump lying just inside the door. Then he stands up, walks to the door of the barn, and keys his shoulder microphone. "Um, dispatch, we have a ten...um...a ten...Aw, hell, Marlene, we have a homicide here. Better send an ambulance and the coroner. Wake Sheriff Kimball up too."

Dispatch responded. "Ten-four. Be advised that 2804 called. He is in the house with a medical."

"Ten-four." Nathan starts running toward the house but stops to look at the highway. Something caught his attention. I click on the rearview camera, and out of the back of Nathan's squad, I see Vicky sitting on her motorcycle. I can hear her muffled voice as she yells something to Nathan. Nathan hollers back, "It's police business, go on up to your house and stay put."

Vicky pulls her motorcycle into her driveway, and I watch the red brake lights reflect off the white pole barn as she goes to park it.

Nathan jogs to the house, disappearing inside.

Nothing happens for a few seconds, but then Ray Pyke's porch light comes on. Vicky and her father step out and walk down to a split-rail fence that separates their lawn from the highway. There they take up a position to watch the action.

A few minutes later, Nathan walks out of the house, heading for the barn. As he approaches the black lump again, I realize that the lump is Toke. I can only see his legs because of the angle of the squad to the barn door. For the next fifteen minutes, I watch the flash of emergency lights reflect off the house and the barn and the trees, waiting for something to happen. Vicky and her dad are like statues in the strobe of those lights, their images appearing and disappearing as the red bulb pulses on top of the squad car.

Then, the cavalry arrives. First, Sheriff Kimball pulls in, followed closely by an ambulance. Nathan directs the EMTs to the house. They enter, and a minute later one returns to the ambulance to grab a gurney. When they wheel Angel out of the house, Jeb is at her side, holding her hand. They load Angel into the back of the ambulance and leave, with Jeb following in his Explorer.

Things slow down after that, with more squads showing up and more cops milling around the courtyard with flashlights, probably looking for trace evidence. About forty minutes into the footage, a car pulls in, and a woman gets out and walks into the barn. I assume that this is the coroner, there to certify the death of Toke Talbert. Then a second ambulance arrives, the one that will haul Toke Talbert off the property in a body bag.

I watch as that ambulance leaves the courtyard, its lights off, no emergency. It rolls past Vicky and Ray who are still leaning up against the split-rail fence, and I wonder if Ray might not be silently happy to see Toke zipped in that body bag. But then again, did he even know what was in the bag?

That thought is but a fleeting curiosity, and is about to leave my head forever, when it digs in and demands my attention. I pause the CD. Something's not right here. Something terribly important is missing.

I start the footage from the beginning and watch again, this time focusing on the rear camera. I see Vicky pull up on her motorcycle, talk to Nathan, and then go park her bike in the shed. I slow the footage down, moving it forward frame by frame. When I do that, I glimpse her silhouette walking from the pole barn to her house. I can only see it in a couple of the frames, when the cast of red light from Nathan's strobe flashes that way. Then she and her father walk down to the fence and stand there for the rest of the video.

As I'm watching it the second time, I think about the trip she and I took to the Hix Farm on my first day in town—the day Vicky showed me the bloodstain on the barn wall. What did she say? She said that Toke was up against the wall, *lying on his stomach*. But in the video, Vicky is across the road with her father the whole time. It's not possible for her to see Toke's body from there.

How did she know he was on his stomach? I had seen the autopsy photos—she hadn't. She knew that his head had been bashed in. She knew where he fell and how he had lain. Yet, she never left her fence until after Toke was hauled away.

There had to be an explanation. Maybe someone had told her what the scene looked like—Jeb, another cop maybe? Or maybe her father killed Toke, and he told her how Toke had fallen. That made some sense. He hated Toke Talbert. Blamed Toke for the death of his wife. Toke had just executed the option contract that would take the final section of Ray's farm away.

I back the footage to the beginning for a third run. This time I focus on the side and rear cameras when Nathan drives up to the farm. As Nathan passes Ray's house and starts to pull into the courtyard, I pause the CD and begin clicking forward one frame at a time.

Nathan pulls into the courtyard. Parks. The other camera angles pull at my attention, but I keep my eyes locked on that rearview. Click. Click. Click. I'm watching Ray's house for any movement at all. Click. Click.

Then I see it—something so hidden that I wouldn't have spotted it unless I was looking for it. I enlarge the picture, zeroing in on a small patch of space beside Ray's house. The truth was there the whole time, hidden in the darkness, but caught in a single flash of a red light.

I drop my head and mutter, "Son of a bitch."

CHAPTER 44

With the sun slouching just above the western horizon, I find myself pulling into the courtyard of the Hix farm, on a quest to view in the daylight what I had seen in the darkness of Nathan's squad video. I cross the road and stand where Vicky and Ray stood as they watched the happenings on the night that Toke died. I am right—there is no way that Vicky could have seen Toke inside the barn from her position at the fence.

I turn and face Ray's house. There's a tree line to my left, and the house is dead ahead of me. But between the house and the trees lies a small patch of lawn about forty feet wide, where Nathan's camera caught the image of someone running toward the little house. I'm leaning against the fence calibrating the picture in my mind, when Vicky steps out of the house. I expect her to walk down and join me, but instead she sits on her porch steps. "I'm kind of surprised to see you," she calls out.

"I thought I'd take another look at the farm."

I walk up to the house, scanning the windows for any sign of Ray. When I am within a few feet, I stop. "Besides, I wanted to talk to you."

"You came all this way to see little ol' me?" She scoots over, making room for me to sit beside her on the porch steps. I hesitate, but then I sit.

"Did you hear that they arrested Jeb Lewis?" I asked.

"They did what?"

"This morning."

"Why?"

"What I hear is that they charged him with altering the crime scene, but they are holding him because they think he might have killed Toke."

"Why would Jeb kill Toke?"

"You haven't heard?"

"No. Heard what?"

"Jeb might be Angel's biological father."

Vicky's jaw drops open, but she remains mute.

"It's true. Jeb and Jeannie had an affair. Kimball thinks it's the key to what happened to Toke."

"That doesn't make sense. I can't see Jeb killing anyone."

"If he's willing to break the law, why stop with altering the crime scene?"

"There's a world of difference between altering a crime scene and killing a man," she says. "I mean, sure, if Angel's his kid then maybe I could see him moving her, but killing Toke in the process? That's a bridge too far. Now that Charlie character's a whole different story. I could see him . . . ."

She stops talking because I've dropped my head, and I'm shaking it slowly back and forth.

"What?" she asks.

"Vicky, I know what you did." I don't say it as an accusation but as a confession, my voice barely rising above a whisper.

"What are you talking about?"

"I know that it was you who killed Toke."

"Are you insane? I didn't kill Toke. Why would I do a fool thing like that?"

"For starters, he killed your mom."

"Good god. That was a decade ago. You think that I would wait this long to—"

"He was going to execute the contract and take away the last section of your dad's farm."

Vicky looks at me with surprise and quickly turns her focus to the ground in front of her.

"Yeah, I know about that," I say.

"I didn't kill him," she says. "I wasn't even here when he was killed."

"Then how did you know that Jeb carried Angel to the house?"

"What?"

"You just said that you could understand Jeb moving Angel if she were his kid. How did you know that Jeb moved Angel?"

"You just told me he did."

"No, I told you that Jeb altered the scene. I didn't say how. You were the one to say that Jeb moved Angel." I keep my words calm, explanations not accusations. "You couldn't have known that if you hadn't been here to see it."

"I must have heard it somewhere." She shrugs her shoulders up around her neck. "You know how gossip gets around this town."

"Gossip?" I say. "No one knew about Jeb moving Angel. The sheriff only learned about it when they arrested Jeb a few hours ago. You didn't even know Jeb was in custody, so your source of information isn't gossip."

"What are you getting at?" She looks at me again, and I can see a hint of fear in her eyes.

"And how did you know that Toke was lying dead on his stomach?"

"Lying on his stomach?"

"When you took me to the barn that first day, you said that Toke was lying on his stomach up against the wall."

"I saw it when..." She stops herself. "Why are you doing this?"

"Because I know the truth."

"You don't know anything. Nathan saw me come home after Toke was already dead. It's probably on his squad camera. I couldn't have killed Toke."

"It's on the video, that's true. Bob Mullen had a copy in his office, and I watched it today."

"So you saw me come home." Cracks in her voice tell me that she's afraid. I don't want to scare her too much. I want her to keep talking, so I pretend that this next part is hard for me to say.

"I saw you stop and say something to Nathan Calder. You were on your Triumph."

"You see? I couldn't have...."

She's looking at me now with eyes that implore me to believe her. I feel sorry for her, and I no longer have to pretend that I am sad to be telling her what I know. I say, "When Nathan first pulled in—long before you stopped your bike in the middle of the highway to set up your alibi—I saw you."

Vicky swallows hard, and her eyes grow with either fear or understanding.

"You ran from those trees over there." I point to the wind-break. "To the shed where you park your bike. A few seconds later, I saw the reflection of your brake lights against the wall of the shed as you rolled your motorcycle down the trail behind your house."

"I don't believe you."

I pull a piece of paper from my back pocket. It's folded so she can't see the picture inside. I hold it between my index and middle finger, and lightly tap it against the evening breeze, letting Vicky's curiosity grow until that paper becomes the center of her world. Then I unfold the photo and hand it to her. The picture of her running across her lawn is grainy and out of focus, but it was the best I could do with the single frame of squad video. Her reaction—a sharp inhale—tells me that she won't try denying that it's her.

She curls her shoulders down and puts her face in her hands, the picture of her guilt falling to the porch steps. "You don't understand," she says.

"It's okay," I say, although my words are a lie. Vicky is crying, and I put an arm around her shoulders. She's talking to me and I don't want that to stop, so I play along. "If ever a man on earth deserved what he got, it was Toke."

"He called me a bitch," she says between her sobs. "I went to the barn to help him. He was barely moving—like he was trying to wake up or something. I bent down to help him, and when he saw me, he called me a bitch. I don't know what happened. I got so mad. He killed my mom, and he was calling me a bitch? I couldn't stop myself. I saw that gear lying there and . . . ."

Behind us, some floorboards creak, and I look over my shoulder to see Ray Pyke standing in the doorway, his hair mussed like he'd just gotten up from a nap. He looks at me and then at Vicky, who is crying in my arms—his face twists up in anger.

"What's he doing here?" Ray yells.

Startled, Vicky jumps to her feet and backs away from the porch. She's wiping tears from her cheek with the back of her hand as she says, "Dad, he knows."

"Shut your mouth!" Ray shouts. He's saying the words to Vicky, but he's pointing his finger at me. "Don't you say another word to this bastard. He ain't your friend."

"Daddy, he's—"

"I said shut up!" Ray charges down the steps and grabs me by the shirt, pulling my face into his. I can smell the whiskey and chewing tobacco on his breath. A father's rage burns in his eyes. I expect him to throw me into the wall, but instead, he rips my shirt open. Both he and Vicky are struck dumb when they see the microphone taped to my chest.

CHAPTER 45

The evening air fills with the distant sound of police sirens. Ray throws me to the ground. "Get going," he hollers as he turns to run into the house. I'm not sure if he's talking to me or to Vicky. I don't think she knows either because she doesn't move. He yells again. "Go to where I took you camping when you were a kid. I'll get you help. Now go!"

Vicky runs to the pole barn where the Tiger is parked. Ray walks out of the house with a shotgun in his hand, but he doesn't aim it at me; in fact, he walks right past me as if I'm not even there, taking up a position in the middle of his yard.

The closest squad car, Nathan's, had been parked behind some trees about a quarter mile away, close enough to monitor the wire. The rest of the troops had been waiting down at the bridge. Nathan is leading the charge, but as he nears the driveway, Ray raises the shotgun and fires, causing Nathan to drive into a ditch. The other three squad cars park on the shoulder behind Calder, creating a defensive wall.

Ray keeps the gun aimed at the deputies as Vicky backs her bike out of the shed. Ray is talking to himself, and I hear him say, "No daughter of mine's going to prison for killing Toke

Talbert—I'll goddamn guarantee you that. I should have killed the prick years ago."

Vicky looks back at her father one last time, fires the Triumph to life, and tears down the trail behind the house.

After Vicky is safely away, Ray lets the gun settle into the crux of his arm, the butt resting in his armpit. He pulls a pack of cigarettes out of his shirt pocket, lifts one to his lips, and lights it. He takes a long drag, and then raises the shotgun back up. "Come on, you cowards!" he yells. He fires again, with no noticeable damage to any of the vehicles.

"Damn it, Ray, put down the gun." I recognize Sheriff Kimball's voice calling out from behind one of the vehicles.

"Go to hell," Ray shouts back.

The sound of the motorcycle fades into the distance. Ray's impromptu plan is working. His daughter is escaping.

"Put the gun down before this gets out of hand," Kimball yells. "We don't want anyone getting hurt."

"Bring it on, you sons of bitches," Ray yells, and when he does, he holds his arms out to the side, opening his chest up to be a target. He is standing about twenty-five feet away from me with his gun in his left hand, the muzzle pointing toward the sky, his finger nowhere near the trigger.

I scramble to my feet and charge the big man, hoping that Nathan and the others are watching. I run as fast as I can, my shoulders down. Ray hears me when I'm about eight feet away and tries to ready his shotgun, but I hit him in the back with all the force I can muster. Pain explodes through my neck, and my bruised rib comes alive with a whole new level of hurt. We tumble forward.

I land on top of Ray's back, his arms outstretched in front of him, the gun still clenched tightly in his hand. I roll forward and grab the shotgun, trying to wrestle it away. I start to twist it around to break his grip, but he grabs the stock with his free hand and tries to jerk it back. The gun is facing the sky, so I jam my thumb onto the trigger and the gun explodes, the butt slamming into the ground, the pellets shooting harmlessly skyward. He can't shoot it now without ratcheting another shell. All I have to do is hang on and not let him chamber another round.

He's on his knees and I'm still on my backside, kicking my feet into him and pulling at the gun with everything I have. Pain lights up my chest, and I feel like I'm being bludgeoned with a board full of spikes. Ray has strong fingers and hands, but he's worn out and breathes in chunks. Spittle bubbles from the side of his lip, white and frothy against his dark-red cheeks.

I pull on the gun, expecting him to yank back and make this a tug-of-war, but instead Ray lunges at me, the stock of the gun landing across my throat, his heavy body pinning me to the ground. I can't breathe. I claw at the back of his hands, but he keeps pressing. The light around his face is fading, shrinking, and I'm pretty sure I'm about to pass out.

That's when something slams into Ray from the side. I don't know what it is at first, but then I see Nathan Calder, clamped onto Ray's back, the two men rolling down the slope of the lawn. I can breathe again, and I gulp at the warm summer air. Tiny dots of light squirm in my vision as my blood pressure settles, and in my hand I am still holding the shotgun.

Two other deputies pile on top of Ray, each one grabbing an arm and prying them behind his back. Nathan has scooted out from under the big man and is reaching for a pair of handcuffs.

"Quit squirming, Ray, or I'll have to Tase you," Nathan yells.

"Fuck you, Nathan." Ray twists back and forth, unable to shake free of the three peace officers. Nathan clicks the handcuffs around one wrist, then the other.

"Where's Vicky?" Sheriff Kimball asks as he lumbers up the driveway, a latecomer to the party.

"She took off on her motorcycle," I say, pointing past the house.

Kimball looks in the direction of the pole barn, grits his teeth, and curses under his breath. Then he turns to the two deputies whose names I don't know, and says, "Get in your squads. Tank, you head east, and John, you go west. Keep an ear out for that bike of hers."

"You ain't never gonna find her," Ray growls between gasps of air.

"Shut up, Ray," Nathan says, taking a knee beside him like a hunter posing next to his trophy. "No one's asking you."

Kimball walks over, and together, he and Nathan lift Ray to his feet. "I'll take Ray in," Kimball says. "You go help with the search."

Nathan and Kimball each take an arm and walk Ray Pyke to Kimball's car, while I remain sitting in the yard alone. I guess I expect a thank-you or something, but they completely ignore me.

After Sheriff Kimball drives away, Nathan stays behind, inspecting his car for damage from the shotgun blasts. I peel off the tape that held the wire and battery pack to my body and walk down to hand the transmitter to Calder. "I told you she'd confess," I say. "You heard her, right?"

He tosses the gear into his squad car but doesn't answer. He's mad, and I think it's because it was my idea to wear the wire; I'm the one who cracked the case. I'm the one who saw the female cutting across Ray's lawn and the glow of the Triumph's taillight against the shed. I'm the one who figured out that Vicky had been to the barn before Nathan got there. And when I showed Kimball and Calder what I'd found, Nathan couldn't wait to criticize it.

"It's too blurry," he said. "And even if that's her, that doesn't mean she killed Toke. I guarantee you that a good defense lawyer will come up with a reasonable explanation as to why she's running through that gap."

"Let me wear a wire," I said. "I can get her to talk. I know I can."

Nathan had been flatly against it, but I convinced Kimball. I would go in first, get her talking, try to get her tangled up before they charged in and arrested her. If she later invoked her right to remain silent, they'd have my conversation to take to court. It was a simple plan. "What could go wrong?" I had said. Now I knew what could go wrong.

"You got her confession on tape, didn't you?" I say again.

"You should go," Nathan says.

"Why are you such a dick?" I say. "What'd I ever do to you?"

Nathan stops inspecting his car and turns to look at me with dead eyes. "I had to call Jeb Lewis's wife today and tell her that we were arresting him. I had to tell her about Jeb's affair with Jeannie. She went to pieces. You have any idea what that's like? Delivering that kind of news? Jeb has two girls. His life's in shambles right now, and all because of you."

Nathan looks at the road between us, shaking his head like he has more to say but is holding it back. "Go home," he says. "You've done enough damage."

CHAPTER 46

I don't go home because I have no home to go to. I spend the rest of the evening alone at the Caspen Inn, Nathan Calder's words echoing off the walls around me. I had exposed Jeb's affair, broke up his family, and got him arrested—all for nothing.

Vicky Pyke, my father's murderer, was now on the run. I should have hated Vicky for what she did, but I couldn't seem to muster that emotion. She had killed a man who wanted me to die in my mother's womb. He was a first-rate asshole—ask anyone. And now, because of some bizarre chain of events, I am on my way to becoming a millionaire. If Toke hadn't wormed his way into the Hix line of succession, and if Vicky Pyke hadn't murdered the son of a bitch, none of this would be happening. Conflicting emotions keep me awake deep into the night as I search for a calming thought to settle me down.

I pull up the memory of Jeremy playing cards with our mother this morning, Kathy letting my brother win. I had seen my mother happy at various times in my life, but not like what I saw today. This wasn't the careless glee that accompanied the opening of a new bottle of vodka, or the passing delight tied to a new pair of jeans. What I saw this morning

305

was deep-down happiness, something new. I suspect that Jeremy saw it as well.

Then I turned my thoughts to Angel. If Toke wasn't Angel's father, then Charlie has no claim to her, and just knowing that she'll be safe from Charlie lulls me deeper toward sleep. How I want to be there to see the look on Charlie's face when he learns that he isn't Angel's uncle—that his guardianship petition will fail.

But I don't fall asleep until I conjure up a daydream of me walking into Bob Mullen's office to sign papers to split Jeannie's estate equally between Toke and Angel, the way it would have been if the world had known about Jeb being Angel's father. I'll inherit from Toke, and Angel will inherit from Jeannie. I can get by just fine on three million. The dream makes me smile because Mullen doesn't believe that I'll go through with it, but I will. I spin that scene over and over in my head, taking comfort in how it slows my pulse. Before I know it, sleep comes for me.

Somewhere in the dark hours of morning, I wake from a dream. I don't remember the details of the dream, but I recall something about sliding down a hill toward a churning river. I remember the river because at first it smells of mud and rot, but the odor turns into the smell of gasoline. It becomes overpowering, and I wake up—but the smell of gasoline is still with me.

Before I can make sense of it, my motel room erupts into flames, the *whumph* of the ignited fuel hitting me like a cudgel, throwing me off my bed. The room lights up as fire licks its way toward the ceiling. I'm on the floor between my bed and the wall, staring at a curtain of fire that's blocking my path to the door and the window. The heat is unbearable.

I have to get through the flames. I pick up the mattress off of my bed and throw it onto the burning carpet between me and the door. Then I grab my jeans and shoes and charge through the flames, jumping onto the mattress using one of my pant legs as an oven mitt to try to open the door.

The handle turns, but when I pull it, the knob jerks out of my hand and the door springs back shut. I yank again and feel that the door is caught on something. Then, through the small gap in the door, I see that someone has tied a small chain to the door handle, looping it around a bar across the door frame outside.

The heat is lashing at my skin as I fall back. Thick, black smoke is filling the room, burning my eyes. I can't breathe.

I retreat into the bathroom, shut the door, and turn on the faucets in the sink and tub, closing the drains. I soak a towel and shove it under the door and then slip into my shoes and jeans, all the while contemplating my failed attempt to get out of my room. Someone barred the door shut. Someone is trying to kill me. I shake that thought away; I need to focus on getting out. Think.

The window? I'd never be able to wrestle the air conditioner out of the way with that whole wall on fire. And who's to say my attacker hasn't thought of that exit as well. I'd burn to death before I'd be able to get out.

And why isn't the sprinkler going off? I stand on the edge of the tub and grab the sprinkler head. There's something wrong with it. Someone has packed it in epoxy. "Goddamn him!" I yell.

I look at the mirror as the smoke seeps in, creating a veil that blurs my reflection. I could lie down in a tub full of water, but smoke inhalation would kill me even if I managed to survive the flames. My throat burns. My image in the mirror is getting hazier. Then an idea hits me. My escape is through the mirror. Beyond the mirror, and the wall behind it, is another bathroom and another motel room—one that's not on fire.

I jump to my feet and lift the lid off the toilet tank, smashing it onto the tile floor. It breaks into a dozen pieces, one of which is shaped like a large slice of pizza. I pick up that wedge, close my eyes, and slam it into the mirror, ignoring the pain in my ribs. The glass shatters into a thousand shards that rain down onto the vanity.

I wrap a towel around my hand to keep my tool from cutting me, and drive the point of the porcelain into the drywall. It makes a smaller dent than I had hoped. I change my angle and start whacking away, cutting an ever deepening groove in the wall with each chop. My chest is screaming in pain, but I keep chopping, white gypsum spraying and ricocheting against my arms as I strike again and again.

As the cut expands, I see that there are two layers of drywall—a firewall. I chop harder. The flames have reached the bathroom door, and thin, yellow fingers are lapping through the crack. My eyes water from the smoke.

I chop harder and feel my blade break through to the insulation. I put the tool down and slide my fingers into the cut, pulling until some nails pop. It's giving way. I grit my teeth and pull again and a seam splits. One more pull and a chunk of drywall about the size of a clipboard falls off.

Flames are licking through the top of the door, the heat pricking at the skin on my left side. I can smell the odor of my own burned arm hair. I grip another section of wall and pull, ripping away another plate-sized section. This creates an opening big enough for me to wiggle through.

I tear the insulation out of the wall and give the drywall on the other side a hefty kick. It doesn't budge. I kick again. Same result.

The sink in front of me is full of water, and I use my hands to slosh water at the flames. It does no good. I dunk a towel in the water and drape it over my head and shoulders. The smoke is so thick that I can't see. I feel across the vanity until my hands fall on my porcelain tool.

I close my eyes and stab the wedge at the wall, hitting it five times in quick succession. I hear the sound of glass breaking as the mirror on the other side of the wall splinters. I drop the tool and raise my foot again and kick. The wall pops out a little bit. I kick again, and this time nails give way. My third kick sends my foot through the wall.

I can't see. I've been holding my breath, and my lungs are about to explode. I put my face to the hole and suck in fresh air. I'm dizzy, but I can't wait for that to pass. I hold my breath again, close my eyes, and tear at the drywall with all I have until a big section breaks free.

The door beside me is on fire. I jump onto my side on the vanity and stick my head through the hole. My shoulders get caught because the hole is too small. My arms need to go through first. I back out and slip my arms though, then my head. My hands grab for anything solid as I pull my torso through. The glass from the mirror slices into my skin as I crawl out of hell. When my legs slide through, I fall to the floor. A billow of smoke follows me through the hole, blooming and spreading on the ceiling of this new bathroom.

I take a moment to cough and wheeze and catch my breath. But now that I am safe, my fear turns to rage. My only thought is to find the shovel-faced son of a bitch who tried to kill me and put an end to his miserable existence.

Chapter 47

I charge out of room number eighteen, startling Mitch, the night manager, who is knocking on doors to get the last few guests out of bed. When he sees me, his face lights up.

"You're alive. Christ, how . . . ?"

"Did you see anyone outside my room tonight?"

"I was sleeping when the alarm went off. Did you break through the—"

"Anyone lurking around earlier?"

"The guy from room nine was sitting in his car when I took out the trash around midnight."

Charlie.

I run around the backside of the motel, where the glow from the fire creates shadows that dance against trees. I hug the edge of the property until I circle to the parking lot in front of my burning room. A handful of guests have gathered well back from the flames. Among them, I see Jeb Lewis, barefoot, wearing jeans and a T-shirt.

In the distance I can hear the approach of the volunteer fire department cutting through town. I scan the crowd for Charlie but don't see him. Then, as the firetrucks pull into the motel, their headlights sweep across the empty lot next door, and I catch a glimpse of the unmistakable outline of Charlie's Lexus. And there's Uncle Charlie leaning against the front bumper, his arms folded across his chest.

I ignore my bruised rib and take off on a dead run, charging past the cluster of guests in the parking lot. I hear Jeb shout my name, but I don't slow down. I don't take my eyes off Charlie.

It's dark, but early shades of morning gray are filtering in from the east. In that penumbra, I can see that Charlie is looking at me, but he must not recognize me because he doesn't move. Maybe he can't believe his eyes, his thick brain refusing to accept the possibility that I am still alive given the inferno spiking up through the roof where my motel room had been.

When he finally realizes that it's me charging toward him, it's too late. He takes off running, old legs paddling as fast as they can. But Charlie doesn't stand a chance.

He makes it to the mouth of an alley, but I tackle him before he can fully turn the corner. We go down together, me on his back, riding him like a sled. When the slide stops, he gets into a pushup position, trying to rise up off the ground, and I drive my fist into his back, landing it right between his shoulder blades. I hear his breath leave. I punch again, and my knuckles rattle loose, my wrist folding in. Pain shoots up my arm, and I pull my hand into my chest.

Charlie makes a second attempt to get up, and I throw my shoulder into him, sending him back to the gravel. He's yelling something, but I don't listen. The only thing I hear as I grab the back of his head and shove his face into the ground, is the voice in my head screaming, *Kill this man*.

I don't hear the footsteps approaching from behind me, but

suddenly, two arms wrap around my shoulders and yank me off Charlie. I twist and land an elbow on someone's jaw. Breaking loose, I jump back on top of Charlie, hitting him in the back again. I want to crush his spine. I want to destroy his lungs.

Again, the man's arms lock around my chest and pull me up. This time, I hear Jeb Lewis holler, "Joe, get off him." He throws me to the side, and I fall to the ground. When I look up, I see Jeb with his hands stretched out in a *calm-the-hell-down* position, standing between me and Charlie.

"He tried to kill me," I say, scrambling back to my feet. Jeb's a big man, but I am determined. I take a step toward him.

"What are you talking about?" Jeb asks.

"That's my room on fire," I say, pointing to the blaze. He barred my door. He locked me in and set my room on fire."

Charlie rolls onto his side, coughing and spitting up what might be blood. When he talks, he sounds like he's swallowed glass. "You saw him attack me." Charlie's talking to Jeb and pointing at me. "He tried to kill me. You saw it."

"Shut up, you psychopath!" I charge at Charlie again, but Jeb grabs me around my waist and pulls me back. I manage to land a kick to Charlie's ribs before I'm out of reach.

"He set your room on fire?" Jeb asks.

"Yes."

"Why?"

"Because of the Hix farm. He wants to get guardianship of Angel, so he can get his hands on her money. He thinks I'm in his way. The dumbass doesn't know that he's not even related to Angel."

"She's my niece," Charlie says. "I have every right be her guardian if I want."

"She's not your niece, you fucking moron," I yell. "Toke wasn't her father. She's nothing to you."

That caught Charlie off guard. He's sitting on his butt in the middle of the alley, and all he can do is look at me with the raised brow of a confused chimp. He glances at Jeb and then back at me. "You're full of shit," he says. "Toke's her daddy. I know that for a fact."

"No," Jeb says. He turns to face Charlie, as if to give his next words extra heft. "Toke wasn't her father. I'm her father. Angel's *my* daughter." Jeb's words carry a deep sadness in them.

"You're lying."

"No," Jeb says. "I'm not."

"So trying to burn me alive was all for nothing," I say.

"I didn't do any such thing," Charlie says as he climbs onto one knee.

"Just stay put," Jeb says. "Don't move."

"To hell with you. I don't have to listen to this bull." He starts to stand up, and Jeb is on him, twisting Charlie's arm behind his back and escorting him back to the ground.

"What the hell you doing?" Charlie yells.

"You smell like gasoline," Jeb says. "Why is that?"

"Because he used it to set my room on fire," I say.

Jeb pulls a cell phone from his pocket and dials 911. "Yeah, it's Jeb Lewis. Did Nathan get called for the fire?" He pauses as the dispatcher says something, and then replies, "I'm in the alley behind Billing's Hardware. Could you send him over here?" Another pause. "I know, but I have a situation—call it a citizen's arrest. I need someone with a badge to take over."

CHAPTER 48

You got no reason to arrest me," Charlie says. He's grunting his words because Jeb has the man's arm twisted in the air and a knee in Charlie's back.

"Arson," I say. "Attempted murder. Take your pick. Before the fire erupted, I could smell gas. Somehow he poured gas into my room, maybe under the door or maybe he punched a hole through my window when I was gone."

"That's bullshit," Charlie mutters.

"When I tried to get out, my door was barred shut. He chained some kind of rod across the jamb. I saw it. I know it was him."

"You don't know diddly-squat," Charlie says.

"And the glue." I mime the way my finger groped at the sprinkler in the bathroom. "The sprinkler head had dried glue on it."

"You'd better let me up," Charlie says. "This is police brutality."

"I'm not a cop," Jeb says, giving Charlie's wrist a tweak. "This is just plain-old citizen's brutality." Jeb begins to inspect Charlie's fingers in the light of the streetlamp. "Well, looky here," Jeb says. "I do believe you have some kind of residue on your fingers. Is that glue?"

I bend down to see—and there it is: a smudge of dried epoxy on the tips of his index finger and his thumb.

A squad car slides into the alley and stops with its headlights trained on the three of us. Deputy Calder gets out, and Jeb tells Nathan to bring some evidence bags. When Nathan gets to where Jeb is holding Charlie to the ground, Jeb says, "Nathan, I need you to place this guy under arrest."

"What for?" Nathan asks.

"I'm pretty sure he started the fire at the motel. Give me your knife."

Calder pulls a folding knife from its sheath and hands it to Jeb, whereupon Jeb uses the blade to peel a tiny chip of the glue off the tip of Charlie's finger. "Put this in an evidence bag. You'll also want to bag his hands and preserve his clothing. I can smell gasoline on them."

"Why would he set the motel on fire?" Nathan asks.

"He was trying to kill me," I say.

Calder looks at Jeb, and Jeb nods. "We . . . I mean you, have enough to hold him on suspicion of arson at the very least. Joe thinks that the sprinklers in his room had glue on them to stop them from working. That fits the m.o. of another case in Charlie's past."

Nathan leans down and gives a sniff. "Yeah, that's gas all right."

"This is bullshit!" Charlie is twisting and cursing as Nathan locks the man's wrists into the cuffs. "This ain't right. I was attacked!"

Nathan and Jeb lift Charlie to his feet, and Calder takes him to the squad car.

"I was assaulted! I'm the victim here!" Charlie is yelling those words as Calder tucks him into the backseat of the squad. When the door slams shut, Charlie's voice dies away.

There's an awkward silence in the alley after Nathan leaves. In the glow of the streetlight, I see that I'm bleeding from a dozen or so small cuts to my torso, some with tiny glass shards still embedded in them, but nothing too serious. The hair on my left forearm is gone, and I smell like burned protein. I run a hand over my scalp, and it feels like all my hair is still there.

"Want to borrow a shirt?" Jeb asks. "I'm pretty sure my room got spared." He starts back toward the burning motel.

"Your room?"

"I'm staying at the Caspen. My wife . . . well, let's just say that things are a little complicated at home."

As Jeb and I walk beside each other, he doesn't act like he's angry with me, and I wonder if he knows that I was the one who brought his affair to light.

"I'm sorry," I say.

"Why's that?"

"I'm the one who set the hounds on you."

He stops walking. "You . . . did what?"

"It's my fault you got in trouble. I learned that Toke had gotten a vasectomy after my mom got pregnant. That started me thinking, and . . . well, then one thing led to another. I'm the one who figured out that you had an affair with Jeannie."

We stop at the edge of the motel parking lot. Jeb keeps his gaze on the fire and says, "This isn't your doing, Joe. I brought this on myself. I'm the one who screwed things up."

"Did you know Angel was your daughter?"

"No. I mean, I suspected that I might be her father. I even asked Jeannie about it once. She denied it, but still, deep down, maybe I knew."

"Is that why you took Angel into the house that night?"

Jeb doesn't answer right away. We watch as two firefighters climb onto the motel roof and move to within twenty feet of the blaze, the brilliant yellow flames leaping skyward into a halo of smoke. Three others on the ground shoot a stream of water through what used to be the door to my room, and it sends up a burst of steam to mix with the smoke.

"I wasn't thinking," Jeb says, finally. "I saw her lying on the ground; I really thought she hit Toke with that gear. I could hear Nathan's siren, and I just reacted. I figured I'd come up with a story to explain it all before the dust settled. I screwed up, and for that, I'll pay the price."

"How bad is the price?"

"I've been suspended. And who knows about my marriage."

"I'm sorry," I say again. "You were a good cop."

Jeb shakes his head. "I altered a crime scene. That's the opposite of being a good cop. That's about the biggest sin a cop can commit. Now I have to take my lumps."

We watch as the firefighters on the roof get their hose going, this second front having an immediate taming effect on the fire.

Then Jeb says, "I've carried the secret of that affair around for fifteen years. It's been killing me. Now it's out there. I had an affair. I'm Angel's father. There's a new normal, and we'll just have to deal with it."

"Is that how your wife will see it?"

Jeb shrugs. "I suspect she'll come around someday. She's a good woman. She's hurting right now, but I think she'll come around. She'll have to—for Angel's sake."

"How is Angel doing?"

"I got a call from the doctor last night. She's showing new signs of lucidity. I'm heading up to Mankato in a little bit—after I get cleaned up and things calm down here. Want to come?"

"She's not my sister," I say, as if that is a perfectly good answer. Then, "I probably shouldn't."

"I understand."

"She's going to need you," I say. "Probably more than any girl has ever needed a father."

To that, Jeb just nods.

The night is fading into the pink glow of dawn, and the volunteer firefighters are gaining the upper hand on the blaze, more smoke now than flame. They're calling out their progress as they choke off the spread of the fire. My room is gone. The rooms next to mine are partially damaged, but most of the motel has been spared. When it seems appropriate, Jeb walks to his room, far away from the damage, and comes back with shoes on his feet and a spare shirt in his hand. He tosses the shirt to me.

As I'm putting it on, one of the firetrucks moves, and I see my car, parked nose-in next to the remains of my room. The front of my car is a charred mess. Both tires are burned off, and I have to assume that everything under the hood followed suit: belts, hoses, wires, anything plastic or rubber. I no longer have a car.

Chapter 49

After they reduce the fire to smoldering coals, and after they tow my car down to Dub's Repair, I remain sitting on one of those concrete parking stops, watching the firefighters mill around. I have no car. I have no place to stay. My wallet and my phone were both in my jean's pockets, so I should count myself lucky—but I don't. What I want, more than anything, is to go back to my apartment in St. Paul, and back to Lila. But I can't do that.

The sun is already warm, and it's not even eight o'clock. I haven't moved from the parking lot because I have nowhere to go. I feel hungry and gross and untethered. There's not much I can do about those last two, but I can grab a bite to eat—and that's what gets me off of my butt.

I'm not going to go to the Snipe's Nest—not that it would be open this early—but I'm pretty sure that Marv would spit in my food, given my role in setting the law after Vicky. I wonder if he even knows yet that she's on the run.

As I walk through town, I spot a small café that I had noticed my first day in town and go in, taking the last available booth. The place is filled with old men wearing worn caps with logos like Pioneer, John Deere, and Peterbilt emblazoned on them. They're talking about crops and weather, but mostly they're talking about the fire, and a great many eyes follow me as I take my seat.

The waitress, a plump gal with strawberry cheeks, brings me my eggs and bacon with a smile, and keeps my coffee filled. Lila should be starting the first day of the bar exam about now. I wonder if she's thinking about me. I hope that she isn't. I've been too much of a distraction already.

While I eat my breakfast, I put together a list of what I need to do that day. It includes things like find a new car, file an insurance claim on the old car, and figure out lodgings for the night. I still have one more night away from home before I can go back to St. Paul, and I don't think the Caspen Inn will be open for business anymore. I'm sure that my mother would let me stay at her place, if I could figure out a way to get there.

I ask the waitress if there is a car dealership in Buckley, and she tells me that the closest thing they have is Dub's Repair, down the street. "He has a handful of used cars that he fixes up."

As I sit in the café, doing the math on how I might pay for a car, it occurs to me that I'm half-owner of a large farm just outside of town—or at least I will be. That gets me to wondering if there might be some old truck tied to the estate that I could borrow until things get settled. With that hazy thought in mind, I pay my check and strike out for Bob Mullen's office.

I arrive to find the door unlocked, so I let myself in. Bob is at his desk reading some papers. When he sees me, he walks out to the reception room to greet me.

"I hear you've had quite the morning," he says.

"You heard about the fire?"

"Things get around pretty fast here in Buckley. I also know about what happened out at Ray Pyke's place yesterday."

"Yeah, I guess I made a mess of things."

"How do you figure?"

"Vicky got away," I say.

"Not for long. They picked her up early this morning."

"They did? Where?"

"Ray called his brother Don from the jail. Those calls are all recorded, and they heard Ray tell his brother to take camping supplies and food down to Vicky, who was hiding out on some sandbar in South Dakota. Wasn't hard to figure it out."

"Did they bring her back?"

"She's in jail in Yankton. She has to go through extradition."

I don't know why it made me sad to think of Vicky in jail, but it did. "Are you going to represent her?"

"No," he says. "Ray's sister called me up this morning. I'll be representing him on that standoff yesterday. I've been calling around to find an attorney for Vicky. I suspect Ray's going to sell everything he has to help Vicky out."

The phone rings, and Bob excuses himself to go answer it, closing his office door behind him.

I sit in the chair behind Jeannie's desk to wait. The papers from the Moody Lynch case lay strewn where I had left them, so I decide to be helpful and put the file back together. As I'm sliding papers into the accordion folder, I see a page that stands out as being different than the others. On the top of the page are the words, *I'm sorry*. I pull the paper out and read it. It is a single page of writing, and at the bottom is the name Jeannie Hix Talbert— typed, not signed. It's Jeannie's suicide note.

I read it.

I'm sorry. I can't do this anymore. I can't fight the sadness. I have lived my life believing that my Bapoo hated me and that I hated him too. Now I know I was wrong. My life has become a never ending nightmare and I can't stand the person I have become. I have been sad for so long now and it is more than I can handle. My world is black. I am a terrible person for what I did and I don't deserve to live. Angel I know that this will hurt and I know that I am being selfish but this is the only out come left for me. I see no other way out. Please forgive me. Toke I ask for your forgiveness too although I know you will find a way to make due without me. I'm sorry to leave you both this way. I love you Angel. Good bye.

Jeannie Hix Talbert

The letter sinks to my lap as the words and phrases on the page move around in my head, aligning like the internal workings of a combination lock. I can't believe what is happening. New facts begin to fall into order, making sense of one final loose end. From the next room over, I hear Bob's voice rise the way voices do when ending a call. He'll be coming out soon. I don't know what I'm going to do with the secret I've discovered. I need time to think. I take the suicide note and run away.

There's more to Toke's death, and no one knows it but me. I walk against the breeze, blind to where I'm going. When I look up, I find that I am near a park bench. I wobble over to it and sit down. In my hand I hold the proof—a suicide note from a woman I've never met. If I throw the piece of paper away, I'll leave Buckley heir to the vast farmlands of Arvin Hix. All I have to do is drop this note into the nearest trash can, and I'm golden.

I think about Jeremy. If I had money like that, I could do so much for him. I could set up a trust fund. He would never have to work. He would never want for anything. I could help other autistic kids too. I could start a foundation. I would do that if I were a millionaire. I would be a good man that way—I swear.

A good man. Those three words ricochet back at me and strike me dumb. Weren't those the words that Lila used as she held out her broken heart for me to see? I'm lying to myself again, trying to rationalize what I know to be wrong. Lila would be ashamed of me if she were here and knew what I was thinking. I hear her voice, soft and sad and all alone in my head: *All you had to do was be a decent guy . . . and you couldn't do that.*

Every muscle in my body seems to slump forward, and I rest my elbows on my knees. I know what I must do. "It's not my money," I say to no one. "Nothing I do will ever change that. I'm the only one who can make this right."

I stand, ready to walk to the Sheriff's Office, when it occurs to me that if I'm right about the note—which I know I am—the final turn of that combination lock clicking in my head will be found at Dub's Repair. It's the key to what Toke did the night he died. I fold the note, put it in my pocket, and make my way to Dub's.

Chapter 50

"Y ou mind telling me what's so goddamned important that you can't tell me over the phone," Kimball says as he and Bob Mullen walk into the body shop.

"I'm a bit curious myself," Bob says.

"And why here?" Kimball waves a hand at the walls of the body shop.

"Bob," I say, ignoring the sheriff. "Did you ever read Jeannie's suicide note?"

He looks surprised at the question. "I never had a copy . . . so, no."

I say, "I found a copy in Moody's file."

Kimball, as if needing to explain it, says, "We found it under Angel's pillow. Thought it might be relevant to the investigation."

To Kimball, I say, "You also kept a copy of the note in Jeannie's suicide file, because you thought there might be more to her death than a simple suicide."

"We had some concerns, yeah."

"In fact, you suspected that Toke might have had a hand in Jeannie's death."

"Toke had an alibi." Kimball pauses to look around the body shop. "He was working down here that night."

I pull the suicide note out of my pocket and hand it to Bob. "This is her note. Give it a read and tell me what you think."

"You stole her note from the file?" Kimball barks, though Bob is already reading the note, his eyes narrow.

"This isn't right," Bob says.

"What's not right?" Kimball asks.

"This letter. Jeannie was my legal assistant. She was proficient with grammar."

"So?" Kimball says.

"There are errors in this note. She writes *make due*, spelling it d-u-e instead of d-o. And *goodbye* is one word, not two, and so is *outcome*."

"You may not know this," Kimball says, "but Jeannie was under the influence of her anxiety medication when she committed suicide. She took enough pills that night that the drugs would have done the job if the noose hadn't. We didn't release that to the public."

"Even knocked out on meds, I can't see Jeannie writing this note. There are no commas in the whole thing. I used to call Jeannie my comma Nazi because it drove her crazy when I'd skip a comma."

"And look how she spelled Bapu," I say.

Bob reads: "B-A-P-O-O." He looks up at me, his mouth open, trying to speak words that his mind can't find.

"What?" Kimball asks.

I turn to Kimball. "Jeannie had a nickname for her father. She called him Bapu—B-A-P-U. It's a term of fatherly endearment in Hindi. She would never misspell that, no matter how many meds she was on." I pause to let Kimball catch up. Then I say, "Yesterday, my mom showed me a letter that Toke wrote after he was arrested for assaulting her." I pull Toke's letter from my back pocket, where it had been since leaving Mom's house, and hand it to Bob; Sheriff Kimball leans in to read it as well.

I continue talking as they read. "He made two of those same mistakes. He misspelled both *make do* and *outcome,* spelling them the same way they appear in the suicide note.

"Toke wrote Jeannie's suicide note," Bob whispers.

"What about his alibi?" Kimball says. "None of this matters because he had an alibi."

"Follow me," I say, leading them into the guts of the body shop. Greg Dubinski is waiting for us and shakes hands with Bob and Sheriff Kimball as we walk in. Then I continue laying out the case. "Toke knows that he's going to be suspected of killing Jeannie: he knows that he's going to need an alibi."

"He was here working on his GTO," Kimball says. "We have surveillance footage to back that up."

"Toke knew about the surveillance cameras," I say. "He knew they point at the parking lot and at the office. He knew that he'd be seen coming in and leaving. But when he's working on the car—there's no camera on that. All he has to do is slip out that window." I point at a row of windows lining the back wall of the shop. He slips out, stages Jeannie's suicide, and slips back in, letting Angel find her mother hanging in the barn."

"That's a nice theory," Kimball says. "And I'm willing to bet that it's true, but we need proof."

"We're getting there," I say. "But there's another aspect that we need to cover. We now know that Toke wasn't Angel's father: Toke knew it too. That fact changes everything." I can see the wheels turning in Sheriff Kimball's head, but they're not spinning fast enough for my taste, so I come at it from another angle. "Start from the end and work backward. The night that Toke died—what if he was planning to kill Angel?"

Bob looks aghast. "Why would he do that? He already had the inheritance."

"But Jeb found Jeannie's suicide note under Angel's pillow, alongside a photograph of Jeannie, Angel, and Hix," I say. "On the back of that picture Jeannie wrote: My Bapu, my baby, and me. Bapu—B-A-P-U. Angel had her mom's suicide note with Bapu misspelled. That's the night she texted Moody, saying that she was freaking out. What if she put it together? What if she understood that her father had killed her mother?"

"Toke must have caught wind that Angel was on to him," Bob says. "Maybe Angel confronted him, or maybe he found what she had under her pillow."

"That still doesn't get us past the alibi when Jeannie died," Kimball says. "On the surveillance tape we saw shadows moving around in here," Kimball says.

"His brother Charlie?" Bob asks.

"Believe it or not," Kimball says. "We looked into that. Charlie had an airtight alibi that night too."

"Besides," I say. "Toke and Charlie hated each other. It doesn't make sense that Toke would trust Charlie on something this risky. Charlie could blackmail him. No, Toke did this all by himself. Actually, it was pretty simple."

I turn to Dub. "Go ahead," I say.

Dub clears his throat and says, "Toke has this GTO over here, the one he bought from Harley Redding." Dub points to a car in the farthest bay, a sleek black muscle car with gray patches of Bondo covering parts of its side. "A little while ago he asked me if he could use that bay to work on the car. He was willing to pay me, now that he had money. Well, one morning, I come in here and...well, come look."

Dub leads the three of us to the GTO. Behind the rear bumper lay a hand lamp and an oscillating fan with a balloon attached to it by a piece of thread. "This ain't the same balloon I found here the morning after Toke got killed, but Joe here asked me to set it up the way I found it, so . . . there it is."

I turn on the fan, and it begins to move back and forth, stirring the balloon, making it dance in front of the light in a random pattern. We all look at the wall by the office door to see the shadow of the balloon on the wall, simulating a man passing in and out of the light.

"Is that what the surveillance cameras picked up on the night of Jeannie's death?" I ask.

"That dog," Kimball whispers. "Did Toke say he was coming in to work on his car the night he died?"

"He didn't have to," Dub says. "He had a key, and I was up in Glencoe that night for my mom's birthday. I found the balloon and the fan and stuff that next morning. I kicked it to the side and didn't think much about it other than it was kind of weird to have the balloon here. But Toke could be a weird guy sometimes."

I say, "I had Dub pull the surveillance footage from the night that Toke died."

"I got it all cued up," Dub says. "In case you want to see it, but yeah, Toke came in here that night."

"Does the footage show him leaving?" Kimball asks.

"No. It shows him coming in, and then there were those shadows on the wall like we just done. I never saw him leave."

Kimball rubs the scruff on his chin. "Well, I'll be damned. He tried to set up the same alibi."

"That's why he started beating Moody with a coil of rope," I say. "He was going use the rope to make Angel's death look like a copycat suicide. Moody interrupted Toke's plan. Then Vicky finished him off. He never made it back here to clean up the balloon or walk out on camera."

Bob says, "Angel's overdose wasn't an overdose at all. Toke drugged her to get her out to the barn. He was going to hang her the same way he did Jeannie."

"Moody saved her life," Kimball says in a quiet voice.

"What about Vicky?" I ask. "Will this affect her case?"

Bob says, "Unfortunately, what Vicky did is still murder. True, the man she killed was a monster, but under the law, that doesn't matter."

"That may be so," Kimball says, "but I doubt the folks in this county will have much of a stomach for punishing her once they hear about this. Hell, they'll probably want to give her a medal."

Mullen nods his agreement. "I'm sure there'll be a damned good plea offer made. The county attorney's up for election next year—I doubt he'll be out for blood on this one."

Then Bob turns to me and, with a serious look on his face, says, "Joe . . . you understand what this means for you. Don't you?"

I nod. "The slayer statute," I say.

"The slayer statute?" Kimball asks.

Bob says, "A man can't benefit from killing someone. He can't inherit if he murders the person he's inheriting from. It's called the slayer statute. When Hix died, the farm passed to Jeannie. When Jeannie died, the whole estate went to Toke. After yesterday, and the revelation that Angel isn't Toke's daughter, Joe here is the sole heir to the Hix estate."

"Okay," Kimball says. "I'm with you so far."

Bob continues, "But Toke can't inherit the estate from Jeannie if he killed Jeannie. That transfer will become null and void because of what Joe just uncovered here."

Kimball gives me a puzzled look and then a sad smile. "So, by figuring all this out, Joe just cut himself off from inheriting the Hix estate."

"Exactly," Bob says.

"And you knew this when you called us down here?" Kimball asks.

"I knew it," I say. "But it's not my money. I don't want it. I've made it this far without Toke Talbert giving me a goddamned thing. I don't see a need to change that now."

"Well, that's not entirely true," Bob says.

I'm confused, and I'm sure my face shows it. I had worked through the falling dominos at least a dozen times, and every time, the last domino to fall was my inheritance. "What am I missing?" I say.

Toke Talbert did have one possession that doesn't belong to the Hix estate—one piece of property that's in his name and his name only.

I shake my head, still lost.

Bob nods at the GTO. "I understand you might be in need of a car?"

CHAPTER 51

The next morning, I wake up on the top bunk of a bed that had been Jeremy's and mine since before I had a memory, the same bed I had lain in when I swore that I would never lift a finger to find my father. I could hear Mom already moving around the kitchen. Apparently, without alcohol, drugs, and depression to sedate her, she's a morning person. I find her at the table reading a book. She's a reader now as well. She offers to make me something to eat, but I beg off.

"Cup of coffee at least?"

"Sure," I say, and sit at the table while she pours water into her coffeemaker.

"Are you going back to Buckley?"

"No, I have to go to St. Paul. Lila will be finishing up with the bar exam this afternoon."

"You should buy her some flowers or something."

"Yeah, I probably should."

"You know, Joe, you're lucky to have someone in your life like that. Never take that for granted."

"Actually . . ." I scratch at a tiny stain on the table; I can't make

331

eye contact or I won't be able to finish my sentence. "Lila and I are . . . I'm not really sure where things stand with us."

"I'm sorry to hear that, Joe."

"My fault, not hers. I messed it up."

Mom nods as if she understands, even though I don't go into the details. Then she says, "Joe, I know a thing or two about messing stuff up. What you see here . . . ." She gives a short twirl of her finger to indicate the apartment around us. "This is me at my best. I get up every day and pray that I don't mess it up again."

Her hands fidget as she speaks, one hand rubbing the other as if trying to warm the stiffness from her joints. "Do you remember that picture that used to hang over there?" She points to a blank wall in the living room. "The one where you're holding Jeremy, when he was a baby?"

At the guardianship hearing, she accused me of smashing it over Jeremy's head. I don't say that, of course.

"I have it in my room now. I see it every morning when I wake up. I put it there to remind me of what I lost when I became an addict. Whenever I feel like I can't do it anymore, I look at that picture and remember what I did to you and your brother. I used to pray that one day I'd have you both back; I knew that it would only happen if I stayed in recovery."

"I'm proud of you," I say. "More than you can imagine."

She smiles at that. "You have no idea how happy I am to hear you say that." Her eyes start to glisten. She reaches out her hand and puts it on my wrist. "And to have Jeremy here, asleep in his bed, I'm about as happy as a mother could be."

"Speaking of Jeremy," I say. "Do you think you could keep him for another day or so?"

"Nothing would make me happier."

"I'm not sure how things are going to go with Lila."

"If you love Lila, don't give up. Forgiveness isn't easy, and it doesn't happen overnight. I mean, look at me. It's taken me thirty years and a lot of therapy to forgive myself for what happened to my mother. And there's a lot I'm still working on. It takes time—sometimes maybe even years—but don't give up."

I take a moment to admire my mother, something that I had never done before. She seems so calm in her new skin; it's easy to forget about the havoc that used to inhabit that body. What she says gives me solace, and I'm ashamed that it surprises me to find wisdom laced in her words. I tuck her sentiment away in a place that has been empty for a long time.

Mom gets up to pour my coffee, and my phone buzzes in my pocket. For a second, I think that it might be Lila, but then I remember that she should be sitting for the second day of the bar exam, and they don't allows phones in the room.

I pull my phone out and look. It's from Allison at the AP office:

Any chance you could stop by today?

I am reminded that today is the day that the follow-up article on Senator Dobbins is going to post—the day that I'm quitting my job. I suppose there's a procedure we have to go through. She probably wants me to get my stuff out of there before they change the pass code on the door. I type back:

I'll stop by this afternoon.

Then I go to the website to read the article, but they haven't posted it yet. I think about Penny, my source, and her fear that she might lose her family over this, the desperation in her voice as she made me promise to keep her secret. I failed her too.

CHAPTER 52

I arrive in the Twin Cities still wearing the clothing I wore when I escaped the motel fire—and Jeb's shirt. I think about going to the apartment to get some new clothes, but I would be disrespecting Lila's wishes. Instead I spend part of my morning shopping at a thrift store for something to wear that doesn't smell like smoke. I spend another few hours sitting in the grass at Minnehaha Falls, under an ever-graying sky, pondering where to start my search for a new job. I eat my lunch, a convenience-store granola bar and banana, in my car—my GTO. After stalling for as long as I can, I drive downtown to meet with Allison.

The other reporters in the room look up as I pass by on my way to Allison's office; Gus is the only one to smile. Allison's door is open, but I knock anyway.

When she sees me, she says, "You look like hell."

I'm bent over slightly because of my bruised rib, and I have a few cuts on my face and neck from crawling through that mirror. "I *feel* like hell," I say. She motions for me to take a seat, and I do.

"You haven't posted the story yet," I say.

"The story's not going out." Allison smiles as she gives me this good news. "Senator Dobbins dropped his lawsuit."

Of all the directions that our conversation might turn, I didn't expect that one. "Why?"

"It took some talking, but I managed to convince the folks in Legal that your story was true. If that was the case, then the lawsuit they brought hinged on the senator's confidence that we would rather retract the story than name the source. We called his bluff."

"So the follow-up story—?"

"I wrote it yesterday," Allison says, serious now. "We really were planning on publishing it today, but we wanted to give the senator and his wife an opportunity for comment. We sent them the story, telling them that we were forced to do the follow-up because of the lawsuit. We gave them a day to respond, promising to include any comment they wanted us to include. I suspect that his wife was the one who pulled the plug. Regardless, they dropped their suit this morning."

"What about Penny?" I ask. "Did you show her the article?"

"No," Allison says, lowering her voice a little. "I was supposed to, but I didn't. I kept imagining that poor woman confessing the affair to her husband to get ahead of the article. I didn't want that to happen unless I was one hundred percent sure that the story would post—and I was never one hundred percent sure of that."

"You bluffed the senator?" I say.

She smiles again. "I guess I did."

I glance through the glass wall that separates Allison's office from the worker bees and see my empty workstation.

"I'm sorry I put you in that bind," I say.

"You were doing your job, Joe. I approved the story because it was important. We had a state senator beating his wife to the point of unconsciousness—and he was going to get away with it. I'm really proud that you were willing to lay it on the line to get that story out. You did the right thing, Joe. No matter how it might have turned out, you should never regret that."

"So where does that leave us?"

"It leaves us where we were before all this crap happened. You said you would quit if I published the story. I didn't publish it—so the way I see it, you have a job whenever you're ready to come back."

A sense of relief washes over me. I have a job again—or still. I thank Allison repeatedly and tell her that I'll start back to work in the morning. She really is a good boss.

My rendezvous with Lila is fast approaching, and I'm nervous as hell. She's in Brooklyn Center, a suburb of Minneapolis, sitting at a table at the Earle Brown Heritage Center, filling in little ovals with her number-two pencil. Eight hours of multiple-choice questions. I know that the afternoon session ends at four thirty, but I want to be there early. I want her to see me as she walks out. I'll know by looking in her eyes whether my sin is forgivable.

The parking lot is full, but I find a space in the farthest back row. The sky has grown appropriately gloomy, with a ceiling of gray clouds gathering above me to bear witness to my fate. A few raindrops tap my head and shoulders as I stand outside of the entrance, holding a black-eyed Susan I stole from Minnehaha Park. It's a little after four, and the first bleary-eyed lawyer wannabes are beginning to wander out. That trickle grows until they are coming out two abreast. At four thirty, the test is called, and the bodies pour out in a flood. Near the end of the surge I see Lila, and my breath catches in my chest. It's like I'm seeing her for the first time, the dust of my own complacency now wiped clean.

She doesn't see me at first. She's talking to some guy walking beside her. He's tall and handsome, and she's smiling up at him, the way she used to smile at me. I know it's only my imagination, but that doesn't mean it hurts any less. She sees me, and her smile falls away. The guy looks confused for a second before he too sees me. Then he says something to Lila and walks away.

Lila remains in the doorway, a stone in a stream as the last few people part and flow around her. I wait for a smile, but it doesn't come. We stare at each other as time freezes around us. Then she shakes her head, looks down at the sidewalk, and walks away.

I'm gutted. Nothing inside of me. I want to follow her, chase her. I want to convince her that she's wrong, but how can I? I did this.

I walk back toward my car but pass it by and keep walking until I get to a small knoll at the edge of the property, a strip of grass lined with pine trees and a white fence. I let the black-eyed Susan fall to the ground before I sit in the grass and bury my face in my arms. I close my eyes and see six years of memories playing out in my mind. Even in the worst of times, life with Lila was good. I should be crying, but that seems too self-serving. She's doing what she needs to do to protect herself. I understand that.

Soon, the sound of cars leaving the parking lot dies away, and I'm pretty sure that I am alone. That's when I hear a sound of something on the grass near me. I look up and see Lila sitting against the fence just beyond my reach. I don't know how long she's been there, but she's watching me in silence.

"You really hurt me, Joe," she says. "I don't think you know how much."

The words *I'm sorry* seem inadequate, but I say them anyway.

"Why?" she asks. "That's what I want to know. Why did you do it? I don't understand."

I look back at the ground so that I can keep my composure.

"I've been asking myself that question. I've been beating myself up trying to understand it. But everything I come up with is weak and pitiful. The truth is there is no excuse for what I did."

"I'm not enough for you?" Her question spills out like it had been on the tip of her tongue for days.

"Enough for me?" I look hard into her eyes. What I'm about to say is the most honest thing I've ever told her, and I need her to believe me. "Lila, you are the love of my life. If you walk away from me, you will still be the love of my life. It may be too late. I may have screwed this up beyond repair, but know that I will love you until the day I die. No matter what happens next, I just need you to know that."

Lila looks at the grass beyond her feet as my words evaporate into nothing. The quiet between us grows until I can't take it anymore, and I try to fill the void. "How'd the test go?"

"I'll have to wait and see, I guess."

Again, we return to an uncomfortable silence. I struggle to find something to say, finally coming up with, "Jeremy's with Mom. She's doing really well."

"I know," Lila says. "We talked."

"You talked...to Kathy? When?"

"I called her last night. I wanted to see how Jeremy was doing. You know what she said?"

I shake my head no.

"She thinks I should give you another chance. Apparently, she doesn't believe that a person can be a lost cause."

I look at Lila, hoping to see a smile, but she continues to stare at the grass. "What about you?" I ask. "Do you think I'm a lost cause?"

She hesitates before answering, and then says, "I don't believe in lost causes, remember?" She smiles a fragile smile, and it means everything to me.

"I'm not a millionaire," I say, thinking that I needed her to know that for some reason.

"I never thought you were."

"And I don't have a sister. I did for a while, but not really."

Lila gives me an expression of confusion. "Was the man who died...was he your father?"

"He was, and I think the whole world should be thankful that he's gone. It's a long story. Oh, and my car got burned up."

"Your car got—" She looks around the parking lot. "Then how'd you get here?"

I point at the GTO, parked all alone about thirty feet away from us, calico patches of body putty running down its side. "That's part of the long story."

Now she smiles a genuine smile—in spite of herself, I think. She picks up the black-eyed Susan lying near her feet and twirls it gently in her fingers. "Maybe we should go home and you can tell me this story of yours," she says.

"Home." I whisper the word to myself, and it makes me think of something that Bob Mullen said. *Sometimes home isn't a place, it's a person.* I take a slow breath in and smell the crisp scent of grass and pine—and hope.

THE END

ACKNOWLEDGMENTS

I would like to thank Robert Spande, Amy Forliti, Tim Volz, Margaret Korberoski, Tami Peterson, and Ronda Rolfes Dever for their insights and expertise; I hope I got the details correct.

I would also like to thank my first readers, my wife, Joely, and my good friend Nancy Rosin, for their help and support.

Thank you Amy Cloughley, my agent, for your continued steady hand.

And a special thank you goes out to Joshua Kendall, Maggie Southard, Shannon Hennessey, Pamela Brown, Michael Noon, Shannon Langone, and the rest of my new team at Mulholland Books. I'm honored to be working with you.

About the Author

Allen Eskens is the *USA Today* bestselling author of *The Life We Bury, The Guise of Another, The Heavens May Fall,* and *The Deep Dark Descending.* He is the recipient of the Barry Award, the Rosebud Award, and the Silver Falchion Award, and has been a finalist for the Edgar Award, the Thriller Award, the Anthony Award, and the Minnesota Book Award. His debut novel, *The Life We Bury,* has been published in sixteen languages.

Eskens lives with his wife, Joely, in out-state Minnesota, where he has been a practicing criminal defense attorney for twenty-five years.

Backad TK